"One must row with the oars one has."
- English Proverb

"Measure twice, cut once."
- The Carpenters Rule

"One doesn't become an adult until
one's parents are deceased."
- John F. Kennedy Jr.

THE
SURVIVING
SIBLINGS

GLENN
GALLAGHER

WORD ASSOCIATION PUBLISHERS
www.wordassociation.com
1.800.827.7903

ISBN: 978-1-63385-050-7

Library of Congress Control Number: 2015901153

Designed and published by

Word Association Publishers

205 Fifth Avenue

Tarentum, Pennsylvania 15084

www.wordassociation.com

1.800.827.7903

ACKNOWLEDGEMENTS

I would like to thank God for my ability to write. I thank Tom and Francine Costello of Word Association Publishers for accepting my manuscript. Francine and Emily Hardie did a superb job of editing my tale and April Urso for the cover design and the interior layout. I thank Jo Brown from Wise Library at West Virginia University for printing my story from the cd and for letting me use his thumb drive. I thank Dr. John Ernest for letting me use his laptop computer and Rebecca Ernest for her support. I thank Cheryl Paul of the Morgantown Public Library for submitting my manuscript to Word Association by way of thumb drive. Her help is most appreciated.

Fr. John Peck of St. John's Catholic Church gave me more insight about the priesthood. Debbie Parnell of the Morgantown Post Office gave me information as to how to apply and be employed at this government agency and the duties that many new employees have. I'd like to thank Dave Ramsey, radio host and author.

Michael Beto at Brookes Tower on the Evansdale campus of WVU gave me insight as to how a student becomes a resident at these dorms. I would also like to thank these people for their contributions: Susan Hilling; Office of Admissions and Records at WVU, Dee Meyers, parishioner at St. John's church, Rob

Klein, teacher of ESL, and the late Paul Candella. My professors, Gail Adams, T. S. Cook, and Dr. Ellesa High at WVU, Sylvestor Stallone and Kirk Douglas for their inspirational quotations, Paul and Dixie Martinelli, Vicki Christopher, Judith Helen and Victor Janisch. John Grisham for his tip on writing on the Charlie Rose Show. Stephen King for his book, "On Writing." Carrie Oestreicher, Dona Blum, and Debi Burdette for their kindness, Maureen Gallagher and Reid Goff for their caring. 'Mr. English" at Ruby Memorial Hospital, Laboratory Corporation of America, (Lab Corp) who helped me 'at the last minute.' My 7th grade typing teacher, Brother Thomas Henning at LeMans Academy. And I would especially like to thank Michael Welshans for letting me recover at his place after my surgery. While there, I proof-read and co-edited my manuscript. Thank you, Mike—a friend in need is a friend indeed!

I would also like to thank the people I may have forgotten. Any mistakes within are mine alone.

DEDICATION

To Miss Beth Ann Bliler, one of my English teachers at Rich South High School who inspired my love of thoughtful quotes. She would write one on the blackboard every morning. Copying it was optional—but I always chose to do so.

CHAPTER **ONE**

Rich South High School; Richton Park, Illinois. Friday, September 1, 1978. 7:45am:

Sixteen year old Randy Taylor walks quickly to the smoking area. There, he finds his friend and cross-country teammate Douglas Elgin. Randy opens his chemistry textbook, as Douglas takes a drag from his cigarette.

"There you are Dougie. Hey man! I've got a question for ya concerning chapter one."

Douglas stares at his friend.

"Look Randy. There's Sara Kingston. Man, is she a bitch!"

Randy's *wheels* begin turning. He holds up a forefinger to his friend. "Ya know Dougie. I betcha five dollars, I can kiss her on the lips!"

Douglas opens his mouth and whispers, "No way." **After focusing on his friend he** says, "Randy, you're serious and you're on!"

The two shake hands. Randy Taylor walks towards Sara Kingston. When he's very near, he bends over slightly and begins to moan while rubbing his eye. Randy has hit a nerve with the girl. She's concerned as she leaves her girlfriend and walks to Randy.

"What's wrong?" she asks.

"There's something in my eye," Randy says.

"Let me see," Sara says. Randy squints as Sara looks. When their faces are very near, Randy plants a huge smooch on Sara's lips. He laughs as she realizes she's been had.

"You son-of-a-bitch!" She chases him—everyone laughs. Randy hears an unfamiliar voice. "Run Randy! Run like hell!" He darts inside as Sara fumbles for the door. Randy makes it to his chemistry class and sits at his desk, still laughing. First period will begin in under a minute. Randy looks to his right at Jami Ledoux while trying to contain himself.

"I forgot my five bucks!" then laughs harder as he slaps his desk three times. Jami, not knowing what he's talking about, laughs with him anyway.

"I'm bad. I'm so bad." Randy says. Several other students are also laughing, though not as hard as Randy.

Forty minutes later, students are finishing their first project. They're talking but not loudly. The teacher, Mrs. Logan makes an announcement.

"May I have your attention please?" she asks.

"Next week, I will be absent for a while due to my maternity leave. I want you *all* to behave yourselves. When I come back, I want to hear nothing but good reports. Now, you'll probably have different substitutes—yes Randy." A slight grin comes across Randy's face, "How do you spell douche-bag?" The boys hoot and the girls giggle as Mrs. Logan puts her fists on her hips and glares at Randy.

"Mr. Taylor, this is not a spelling class."

"I know it's a little off the subject, Mrs. Logan. But I…Oh, there goes my friend, Chris!" Randy runs to the window, opens it and calls to Chris. Taking something out of his pocket, he yells, "Chris, here's your ten bucks. Thanks friend."

Randy closes the window and returns to his seat as everyone stares at him.

"I owed him ten bucks. I'll be good, check me out, my head's down."

Mrs. Logan looks up as if in prayer.

The following Monday, when the chemistry class is half over, Mister Arnold, the substitute teacher addresses the class.

"Students, turning sixteen happens only once in a lifetime. It is a special milestone. And among us is someone who's turning that special age. I'd like to congratulate Randy Taylor!" Mr. Arnold claps and the whole class joins in with surprising enthusiasm. Randy, who actually turned sixteen the previous June, stands and takes a bow. One of his friends unveils a cake, another opens a package of hotdogs and proceeds to cook them over a Benson burner. Some one opens bottles of soda (that have seem to have magically appeared), and two others tape a large 'Happy Birthday' banner to a wall. A portable record player appears along with 45's. (small vinyl black discs with a song on each side; forty-five revolutions per minute) As the needle touches the record, Ted Nugent begins playing. Someone whips out a small cooler filled with ice cream, along with disposable spoons and bowls. Randy is handing out party hats and whistle blowers then pauses to make an announcement.

"Let's hear it for our favorite substitute, Mister Arnold!" The class cheers then Randy says, "This is the best birthday I've ever had!"

The chemistry class is on the first floor, in a corner of the high school. As Randy's luck would have it, the classroom next door is vacant due to a water problem so there's no one close enough to hear the goings on in the chemistry room.

Tuesday through Thursday, the class has different substitutes and the birthday parties are repeated without any problems. Each day, Randy makes his speech. "Let's hear it for our favorite substitute…" On Friday, with his party hat on, Randy stands at the front of the class with each arm around one girl. His speech this day is different.

"Ya know class, I feel great! Because out of everyone in this whole school, you have chosen me, Randy Taylor, to honor with a birthday celebration. I feel loved and so special. Now let's hear it for our favorite substitute Miss Olsen!" Everyone applauds as Miss Olsen takes a bow and begins to cough.

"Must've been too many bongs," Randy remarks as he puts his arms back around the girls and gives each of them a kiss on the cheek.

"Now, you've probably have heard this before, but this is the best birthday I've ever had!"

"Aw Randy, you've said that before," a friend says.

"And another thing before I forget," Randy says, just as the door opens, and principal Steven McGraw steps in.

"Mister Taylor, I need to see you in my office," the principal says in a strong voice. Randy looks at his classmates and says, "I should've invited him!!" The class roars with laughter. Randy walks confidently out into the hallway. On the way upstairs Randy asks, "So how'ya doin' *Quick Draw* uh, I mean Mister McGraw?"

The principal gives him a stern look. "Fine Mister Taylor. I can see you're having a nice day."

"Oh I am sir. God is good. He's so good to me, I wanna shed tears of joy!" The two enter the elegant office as the principal closes the door.

"Sit down Mister Taylor. The principal sits in his large black leather chair and places his elbows on the desk and his fingertips together. He stares at Randy for a moment.

"Mister Taylor—you've been a little naughty. Now, can you tell me why a student with a 3.8 grade point average would pull a stunt like this?"

"Yeah, number one, I had to let off a little steam and number two, Mrs. Logan gave me the idea." The principal's eyebrows tighten.

"I don't understand," McGraw says.

"Well last week, Mrs. Logan told us that we'd probably have different substitutes and the idea popped in my mind."

"Mister Taylor, you could've let off steam in other ways. Why don't you try out for the football team?"

"I run cross-country."

"Well Mister Taylor. There's an old saying, 'No good deed goes unpunished'. Are you familiar with the Bible?" McGraw asks.

"A little," Randy replies.

"The number seven appears frequently in the 'Good Book'. I've chosen this number as your punishment. For seven weeks after school, you'll be spending time in detention in room number two-thirty one."

"Oh sir, don't do this to me," Randy says.

"Mister Taylor, you've done this to yourself, but don't worry— you'll be in the loving care of one Mrs. Harrison." Randy places his hands to his temples.

"Good God, not her! Mister McGraw, can I change your mind? Does your grass need cut?"

The principal shakes his head no.

"Does your car need washed? Does your house need painted? Does your dog need walked?" Randy's questions come out like bullets from a machine gun. The principal is adamant, as he looks upward.

"Mister Taylor, I'm beginning to see ten weeks."

"Okay Mister McGraw, I'm outta here. I'm gone. Where's the door?"

Lakewood Estates, in southern Cook County, was established in the early 1970's. Most of the houses are split level with three bedrooms and a two car garage. The road leading to this subdivision is called Sauk Trail. Rich South High School is on this road— walking distance to Lakewood Estates. This school was built in the middle of a cornfield in 1972.

The families who live in Lakewood Estates are middle to upper middle class. Randy walks to his house on Royal Drive after a short cross-country practice. He had overlooked the fact that his practice sessions would be affected by his prank.

The head of the household is Donald, who is a professor at Prairie State College in Chicago Heights. Tammy, the mother, is a receptionist at Hennington, Barker & Stone—a law firm on Cicero Avenue. Brian is fifteen and is a sophomore at Rich South. The youngest child, Amy, is four and attends Kinder Care just six houses down the street. (Between Rich South and the Taylor household).

Randy is greeted by his mother upon entering the house. She hugs her first born.

"How was school Randy?"

"Fine mom. Basically the same day, just different assignments." Donald walks up from the family room. He also hugs his son.

"I've got a question Randy. Why didn't you pick up Amy after school?" Randy motions his head to the right, as his father walks over. In a soft voice Randy says, "I've got detention for the next seven weeks." A puzzled look comes over Donald's face.

"What did you do?" he asks.

"Well, last week my chemistry teacher, Mrs.Logan began her maternity leave. We had different substitutes each day and I threw myself five birthday parties."

Donald tightens his lips then softly says, "Jesus, Mary and Joseph. Bend down son." Randy obeys as Donald gets him in a playful headlock. He takes his knuckles and rubs his son's head vigorously.

"Is this what you need boy?" Donald asks.

"No Dad. I don't need a rubby-dubby!" Donald releases his son as Randy places his hand on his head, trying to contain his laughter.

"Ow, that hurt!" he says.

"I'm not gonna punish ya. I wish I would've thought of that when I was your age." Amy emerges from the kitchen with Tammy.

"I want rubby-dubby, Daddy," she says. Donald picks her up and rubs her head, though not as hard.

"I can never punish her this way—she likes it!" Donald says as the child giggles.

Brian walks in the house and is greeted by his family. After taking off his coat, boots and scarf, Tammy asks her son a question.

"Brian, why are you always the last one home?"

"Simple Mom, I do most of my homework in the library after school." Tammy places her hand on her forehead.

"You alright Mom?" Randy asks.

"Sure honey. Just a little headache. Would you mind helping me finish dinner?"

"No problem mom. I'd love to."

In the past, when Randy picked up his sister at Kinder Care, she wouldn't let her brother hold her hand. Randy is terrified that she'll run in the street, so he uses psychology on her.

"Amy, if you don't hold my hand, I won't pick you up anymore, and you'll have to take a nap," Randy says. The child reluctantly holds his hand, only to release it near the curved driveway.

Halfway through the meal, the phone rings. Tammy answers it and discovers it's Donald's boss. She covers the mouth piece.

"Do you want to talk to him?" she asks.

"I better. It's probably important. I'll take it upstairs." Donald gets up.

"I wish the phone were never invented," Donald says as he walks upstairs.

Randy has just finished his dinner and and stretches his arms. To his left he notices Brian drinking his milk. On a whim, Randy says, "Drink up mate," as he taps the bottom of Brian's glass. Milk spills all over his brother's face. Randy leaves the table in a hurry with Brian in hot pursuit. Randy laughs as he purposely traps himself in a corner of the foyer.

"Randy, that wasn't nice. Tell Brian you're sorry," Tammy says.

"Brian, you're sorry." Brian punches his brother's arm saying, "Don't ever do that again." Randy laughs even more. Donald walks downstairs from his bedroom.

"What's the problem boys?" he asks.

"Randy spilled milk on my face," Brian says. Randy makes a face at Brian and as Brian lunges at him, Donald steps between the boys and breaks up a would-be fight.

In this period of his life, Randy has entered a teasing phase, aimed more at his brother than his sister. The teasing comes on the spur of the moment. While doing dishes one evening, Randy filled a large plastic cup with water, crept up behind Brian as he sat on the floor in the family room alone watching TV and dumped the water down his brother's back.

"Oh Brian, I'm so sorry. How could I be so clumsy?" As Brian begins to stand, Randy begins laughing as he traps himself in a corner while Brian punches his arm.

When Donald is finished with his supper he looks at his children.

"Why don't you kids go downstairs for a while. I have to talk with her mother."

"What about the dishes, Dad?" Brian asks.

"You can do them shortly. I just need ten minutes."

"Yes sir," Brian says. The kids walk down to the family room. "Do you wanna go for a ride, sister?" Randy asks.

Amy smiles and nods although she doesn't know what ride her brother is talking about. Randy holds up his left hand.

"Amy, keep your feet where they are and lean toward my hand." The child connects her torso with her brother's hand, as Randy gets hold of her crotch. He lifts the child over his head. Randy speaks in an announcer's voice.

"This boy is so strong! Who can fully believe how strong he actually is?" Tammy senses trouble as she walks in the foyer and looks in the family room.

"Randy, put her down! What's wrong with you?"

"Oh Mom, we're just having a little fun," Randy replies. He carefully sets his sister on the carpet. Ten minutes later, Randy walks upstairs to the kitchen and begins preparing the dishwater.

"I thought it was Brian's turn to do the dishes," Donald asks.

"No Dad, it's mine," Randy replies as Tammy walks upstairs to the bathroom.

"Well son, before you do the dishes, would you mind getting me a beer?" A sly grin spreads across Randy's face.

"No Dad, I don't mind," as he heads downstairs to the utility room. Opening the refrigerator, Randy takes out a Budweiser and opens it. Randy takes several gulps eliminating half of the can. He walks upstairs to the kitchen and gives the can to his father. Donald immediately notices the weight difference.

"What's this?" he asks.

"I had to taste it to make sure it was okay."

"Don't give me that bullshit. So besides your little prank, how was school today?"

"Well, I wasn't planning on detention but it's going fairly well. Geometry and biology are giving me a little trouble though."

"Keep your nose to the grindstone son, you'll do alright."

"Dad, I've narrowed down my college choices," Randy says.

"You have?! That's great! What are they Randy?" Donald asks.

"Penn State, Dartmouth College, or Indiana State University," Randy says.

"They're all good schools. I'm sure you will be satisfied with the one you pick," Donald says. Amy comes into the kitchen.

"Daddy, read me a story," she says.

"It's time for your bath," Donald says as Tammy walks downstairs.

"I don't want a bath!"

"Amy, Mommy's bought you a rubber ducky!" Donald opens his eyes wide and stands with his hands on his hips.

"I'm gonna play with that rubber ducky!" he says. The child smiles as she shakes her head.

"My rubber ducky, Daddy!" Randy, alone in the kitchen, finishes the dishes then walks downstairs to the half bath. Using Donald's electric razor, he shaves. Black whiskers have formed on his upper lip and chin. Randy showers, then walks upstairs to his bedroom. Brian is getting into his pajamas.

"You done with the desk little brother?" Randy asks.

"Ah-uh," he says.

"You always amaze me how you do your homework so fast." Randy works on his assignments until 11:45. Moments after his head hits the pillow, he's fast asleep.

The image is blurred. And yet, the viewer can make out a woman wearing a red dress, yelling at the top of her lungs. The veins in her neck stick out. She turns. Her back is toward someone who's holding a knife. This person is walking slowly, like a lioness stalking her prey. When the person gets near, the knife is raised.

Randy sits up in his bed with a slight gasp. He's perspiring. He turns, finding Brian still asleep. The aroma of bacon fills his nostrils. Getting out of bed, Randy puts his slippers on, walks to the bathroom, and closes the door. The sound of the toilet flushing, precedes the sound of running water. Randy emerges from the bathroom and walks downstairs. His mother, is at the stove turning bacon. Donald is reading the paper, and Amy is eating her cereal. Randy kisses her cheek.

"Morning mom," he says.

"Good morning Randy. My goodness, you're sweating."

"Just a bad dream," Randy says.

"Do you want to talk about it?" Tammy asks.

"No I don't,"

"My son—is getting to be a typical man."

"You seemed low on energy last night. You feel okay Mom?" Randy asks.

"Yes I am. Although these headaches are like aftershocks of an earthquake. Randy, go upstairs and wake up Brian."

"Okay mom," he replies. Randy heads upstairs and tries to wake his brother by shaking his shoulder. Randy detects a slight grin.

"C'mon Brian, get up." Brian groans then rolls over. Randy again shakes his shoulder. No response.

"Alright little brother. Last resort comin' up." Randy un-tucks the sheet and blankets at the end of Brian's twin bed and tosses them to his headboard. The younger brother is exposed. Brian is irritated.

"Cut it out you jerk!"

"Do you want me to floss your teeth with my fist? Get out of bed when I first shake ya, and then I won't remove your blankets. You know I woke you the first time Brian. That's why you're smiling."

Brian laughs.

Randy is first out of the house; then Brian. Donald drives Amy to Kindercare. On this cold morning in December, the temperature stings Randy's cheeks, but inside he feels warm. Christmas break begins in four days. Randy will get more hours at Lakewood Bowl, where he works part-time as a porter. (Lakewood Bowling alley is in Lakewood Plaza; pretty much between his house and Rich South High School). The extra money will go toward presents as well as savings.

Randy's thankful the wind isn't blowing. Many times, he has to walk backwards on Sauk Trail. *It's either looking stupid, or being unable to breath. Man, that wind can be ruthless at times,* he thinks. Randy turns his head left. This direction is north. The sun is shining and the sky is a cloudless blue. Randy can make out the Sears Tower in the Loop. Chicago's famous Loop and towering skyscrapers are some thirty miles away. Whenever Randy sees this spectacular sight, he always has a great day.

Upon entering Rich South, Randy's glasses immediately fog up. He pulls them down to the end of his nose so he can see. Unsnapping his letter jacket, he takes his left hand and feels his interior pocket. His menthol cigarettes and a lighter are there, His friend Barbara Tennant, whose locker is next to Randy's, sewed it in his jacket right after cross-country season had ended. Randy walks quickly to his locker, places his blue cloth briefcase inside, then leaves for the smoking area. Douglas is there.

"Morning Randy. Here's your five bucks. Sorry I gotta go. I forgot my damn report at home."

"See ya Dougie, and thanks." He lights up a cigarette and thinks. Randy is considering skipping his senior year of cross-country. He's an above average runner, but recently his knees have been hurting. (Arthritis runs in the Taylor family.) *I can use my cross-country time to get my grade point average up. I'm so close to 4.0!* Randy's thoughts are interrupted when he overhears another student say. "You can make plans, but don't plan the outcome." The nine words remain in Randy's mind for several seconds. He takes one more drag as he looks at his watch. It's nearly time for his first class.

Donald and Tammy Taylor arrive home within an hour of each other. Randy has finished his detention and has resumed his duty of picking up Amy at Kindercare. Brian is usually the last member of the family to come in for the day. Tammy tells her friends, "Brian was late being born, and he's been late ever since." Randy starts dinner until his mother comes home and takes over. Donald is on the phone talking with his boss. Brian is watching television. Tammy turns the gas on low, as the spaghetti sauce simmers. She walks to the bathroom and takes three aspirins for her headache.

In the family room downstairs, Randy is on his hands and knees with Amy riding on his back.

"Here comes the daddy gorilla walking through the jungle with baby on his back. He stops to pick up a plant and puts it in his mouth and chews. *Ptuee!* Daddy gorilla spits the plant out. That's nasty. Daddy gorilla doesn't like that plant." Amy moves her heels against her brother's ribs.

"C'mon on Randy, get going," she says.

"Oh—baby's getting impatient. Daddy gorilla begins to move again. He'll eat better plants when baby's asleep." Tammy opens the bathroom door.

"Are you two having fun?" she asks.

"We're playing daddy gorilla, Mommy," Amy says.

"Well, supper's almost ready. You kids wash your hands before yuz come to the kitchen." Tammy walks upstairs. When she enters the kitchen, Donald hangs up the phone.

"Tam honey, I have to go back to the office. I forgot my papers," Donald says.

"Can't you get them after supper?" Tammy asks.

"They're closing the second floor for carpet shampooing over Christmas break. I won't be gone long." The couple embraces. Donald whispers in his wife's ear.

"Later on, I'll put my tongue where it was last night." Tammy playfully hits his arm.

"You bad boy, you!" she says.

"You say that with a smile,"

"How do you know I'm smiling?" Tammy asks.

"Because I know you." The embrace is broken, as Tammy looks at her husband.

"Get your papers and hurry back."

At the dinner table in the kitchen, Tammy says grace. "Dear Lord, we thank you for this meal, and all of the blessings You bestow on us everyday—Amen." The bowls of each side orders are passed to the right. Tammy stands to serve spaghetti, as Randy prepares his sister's plate. Amy sits on a thick padded cushion so she can sit higher at the table.

"Don't like yucky beets," the child says.

"Well honey," Tammy says. "You can eat beets or turnips. Take your pick." Reluctantly, Amy takes her fork and pokes a small sliced beet. She places the beet in her mouth and begins chewing. She makes a terrible face. Randy laughs, then says,

"If I can only get that face on film!"

"Mommy, Randy's laughing at me."

"Little sister, you're *making* me laugh!"

"Alright you two. Let's just eat. There are children in other countries that would love to have those beets." As the minutes go by, Tammy notices her other son taking thirds on turnips. He can't get enough of them.

"Brian, save some for your father."

"Yes ma'am," he replies.

The snow gives the night a certain glow and as the peach cobbler is nearly finished, the family hears the garage door opening.

"Daddy's home!" exclaims Amy. The four year old gets off of her chair, as the cushion falls to the floor. Donald pulls his '78 yellow Ford station wagon in the two-car garage.

"Hi Daddy!" Amy says.

"I missed my sweet pumpkin," Donald says as he gives her a kiss.

"Read me story daddy," Amy says.

"After your bath, Honey." Donald carries her to the kitchen, gives Tammy a kiss, and sits down at the table.

"I'm gonna go and play with my dollhouse," Amy says, as she slides off Donald's lap and runs downstairs to the family room.

"She's a hummingbird on speed," Donald says. Tammy places a plate of food onto the table for Donald.

"I wished I hadn't forgotten those papers," Donald says.

"Why's that?" Tammy asks.

"'Cause I have to grade them tonight."

"Are you serious?" Tammy asks, her voice rising in anger.

"Look Tam, my assistant is sick, the semester is nearly over and we've got Christmas shopping to do this week-end. You know Lincoln Mall is going to be packed." "We never have time for anything," Tammy says.

"Hon, we'll have time. I've got nearly three weeks off."

"Well I don't!" Tammy says indignantly.

"Let's not argue, Dear. I'll make time for ya. You know I always do."

"What do you want for Christmas, Donald?"

"A hug and a kiss." Tammy playfully pokes her husband in the rib.

"I ask for so little," he says.

In the family room, Amy is sitting on the sofa watching television. She's sucking her left thumb and twirling her hair with her right forefinger. It's playtime again as the phone rings and Randy gets on his hands and knees and begins moving toward his sister in his 'daddy gorilla' stance.

"I wanna suck your thumby," Randy says. A little smile forms on Amy's face.

"I wanna suck your thumby," Randy says again as he moves closer. When he's face-to-face with his sister, Amy takes her four fingers and grabs Randy's nose while still sucking her thumb. Randy stretches his arms in back of him and begins acting silly. Moving his mouth in exaggerated motions, he speaks fast.

"Ow, ow, ow! I changed my mind! I changed my mind!" Amy laughs softly, with her thumb still in her mouth. She releases her brother's nose. Donald emerges from the kitchen.

"Randy, I'm on the phone. What's your problem?" he asks.

"Sorry dad. Just playing with Amy." "Amy, time for your bath," Tammy says.

"Don't want no bath."

"Come on honey, you can take one with mommy." The child gets off the sofa and runs upstairs.

Upon entering the kitchen, Randy discovers Brian is preparing the dishwater. WLS is on the radio, the volume on low. Donald is in the dining room, getting ready to grade papers. (Randy knows that his brother is slow at this chore, maybe because he likes to listen to the radio.)

"Let me know when the dish rack is full," Randy says.

"Okay." Randy walks upstairs and sits at the desk in the corner of the bedroom. The next day is Thursday, December 21st. The day after will be the start of Christmas vacation. Randy takes out his calculator from the desk drawer and focuses on his algebra assignment. Thirty minutes later, he hears his name. Randy gets up and walks to the doorway and sees Brian at the foot of the stairs. His younger brother motions to him. Randy walks downstairs shaking his head.

"What's the name of this song?" Brian asks. Randy listens, "Hot Child in the City," he says. Randy notices the dish rack is full. He takes a clean towel from a drawer near the sink and begins drying. Tammy and Amy emerge from the bathroom. Tammy in her nightie and purple robe and Amy in her pink pajamas. Mother and daughter walk to the dining room.

"Daddy, time for my story!" Amy says.

"Okay Pumpkin. Let's go down to the family room." Father and daughter leave as the mother enters the kitchen.

"Thank you boys for doing the dishes," Tammy says.

"You don't have to thank us, Mom, we live here too," Randy says. Brian wipes the table as Randy decides to play a joke. He sneaks a number of clean plates and glasses back in the wash sink. Randy tries hard not to smile. Brian resumes his post.

"Man, we sure have a lot of dishes tonight—huh Randy?"

"We sure do."

The next day dawns clear but cold. In the smoking area, ten minutes before first period, Randy talks with his friend Scott Benning. (Dougie is home with the flu.) Scott lights his cigarette, then says,

"My girlfriend's pregnant Randy. Do you know what that means?"

"No I don't."

"It means, 'goodbye college!' I knew I should've worn that damn condom," a frustrated Scott says.

"Hold on, friend," Randy says. "You have options. You love cars, right?" Scott nods.

"And you love working on them—agree?" Scott continues nodding.

"Well, recently I saw a 'Help Wanted' sign in front of Bill's Auto Repair on Kedzie Avenue. Why don't you go and apply?" Randy asks.

"That's a good idea Randy! Do you have the phone number?" Scott asks.

"No I don't, but I'm sure they're in the Yellow pages." Randy looks at his watch.

"Scott, I gotta go man."

"Thanks for the information Randy, I'll call during lunch period. You're a life-saver." Both students crush their butts, and depart.

In the hallways of Rich South High School, boys hold their books in the right or left hand, with their texts resting against their leg, just below the hip. Girls hold their books against their bosoms. At his locker, Randy gets his books and folder for his first period class—chemistry. He's wearing blue jeans, a long sleeve thin white turtle-neck, and a short sleeve shirt over it. Barbi, a class-mate walks up to him.

"Hi Randy," Barbi says.

"Hi Barbi, how ya doin?" (Barbi likes Randy more than he likes her).

"Oh—alright I guess. I broke up with my boyfriend."

"Gene Smith?" Randy asks.

"Huh-uh."

"I thought yuz were a hot item."

"We were, until I found out what a creep he is," Barbi says then pauses.

"Randy, do you wanna go out with me?" Randy glances at her while looking for his protractor.

"Well Barbi I'd love to, but with school, work and college in just over a year," the bell rings.

"Oh shit, I'm late for class," Randy says as Barbi looks down. He feels compassion for her.

"Okay, let's go to a movie. Have you seen 'Grease'?"

"Five times, but I'd love to see it with you!" Barbi says passionately. Randy scribbles his number on her notebook.

"Give me a call after Christmas. I gotta go." Randy slams his door, then makes haste. Barbi smiles then slowly walks to the girls locker room.

An hour later, Randy emerges from his chemistry class as students fill the hallway. Randy's next class is physical education. To get to the gymnasium, Randy walks through the east cafetorium. An acquaintance waves at him.

"There's Randy Taylor," Mick Wilson says. "He sure has his shit together."

"Randy Taylor?" his girlfriend, Cheryl replies. "I think he's one of the biggest jerks at Rich South." Mick resumes eating.

In the gym, Randy witnesses something unusual. While waiting for the P.E. instructor, Coach Webster, his classmate Ronnie Riggins does something funny. Taking a lone volley ball pole, that's attached to a large, metal half-dome with two black wheels on one side, Ronnie pole vaults over a volley ball net. He bows as everyone applauds. Coach Webster walks in carrying a clipboard.

During the day, Randy sees Brian but only at a distance. The freshman locker section is across the west cafetorium from the junior locker section. The sophomore lockers are a hop-skip-and-jump from the freshman section, with the senior section halfway around the circumference of the former two.

At the end of Randy's last class, he turns his American History test over. *If I didn't get a hundred, I'm damn close,* he says to himself. Five minutes later, Randy's at his locker putting on his scarf and letter jacket. Even though it's only three in the afternoon, snow clouds are blocking out the sun, bringing a darkness that makes it seem later than it is.

On the way to the glass double doors, Randy runs into his cross-country coach; Perry Bonham.

"Have a great Christmas break Randy," Bonham says.

"You too coach," Randy replies.

"Next year will be the year-uh Randy?"

"Waddya mean coach?" Taylor asks.

"For you to break seventeen minutes!" Bonham says.

"I'll give it my best," Randy replies. Coach Bonham gives him a thumbs-up sign.

CHAPTER **TWO**

As soon as he steps outside, Randy pulls down his wool hat as he makes his way, against the wind, to Sauk Trail. The wind takes his breath away, forcing him to put his gloved hand over his face. The snow feels like needles stinging his cheeks. Randy curses himself for not taking his extra scarf. *It sure is keeping my albums warm in my drawer,* he thinks. Upon reaching Sauk Trail, Randy turns and walks backwards for part of the way. Twenty yards from the Lakewood Estates entrance he turns around. Kinder Care is in plain sight. Randy walks faster.

Entering the preschool building, Randy's glasses begin to fog up. Children are taking their naps. One child gets up and runs to him.

"Randy, guess what I did today?" Amy exclaims. Randy kneels and places a finger to his lips. He whispers.

"Amy, your friends are trying to sleep."

"Guess what I did today?" Amy whispers.

"What?" Randy asks.

"I made a finger painting."

Mrs. Manning the owner, hands it to Amy who hands it to her brother.

"My, that's beautiful!" Randy whispers.

"It's upside down," Amy replies with her whisper. Randy turns it right-side up.

"Oh, how could I've been so silly," Randy says as he carefully places the small painting in his geometry book, then helps his sister get dressed. Boots, coat, gloves, scarf and hood.

"Have a nice Christmas," the owner whispers.

"You too, Mrs. Manning," Randy and Amy whisper in unison. Exiting into the frigid cold, Randy's glasses are clear within seconds. Amy begins to run.

"No, no sister. Come back here," Randy says in a semi-authoritive voice. Amy turns around to find her brother's right arm extended. She holds his hand.

"You know the rule."

The next morning, Randy's frying sausage patties and Tammy is making scrambled eggs. Donald's reading *The Star*, Richton Park's newspaper. Brian and Amy are eyeing a box of donuts on top of the refrigerator as Tammy places her right hand on her forehead.

"You alright mom?" Randy asks.

"Yes honey. Just a little headache." When the food is ready, it's placed on a large oval plate. Eggs on one side, sausages on the other. Donald folds his paper, and sets it under his chair.

"Alright everyone, let's fold our hands," Donald says. The family complies and bows their heads. The man of the house prays.

"God is great, God is good. Let us thank Him for this food. By His hands we all are fed, give us Lord our daily bread. Amen." The family begins eating.

"Mommy, you forgot the donuts," Amy says.

"Yes I did," the mother replies. Tammy stands, as a pain ignites in her head. She pauses, then retrieves the box from on top of the refrigerator. She places them on the table and opens the lid.

"Only one Amy," she says. The child points to a chocolate one.

"What do you say?" Tammy asks.

"Please?" Amy asks. The mother hands her favorite.

"Sank you, Mommy."

"You're welcome, Honey. My, your manners are so gracious!" Tammy says. Amy chews with her mouth closed then swallows.

"When I grow up, I want to be Queen of England."

"Why's that?" Tammy asks.

"I want to live in a big castle."

"May we live in your castle?" Donald asks. Amy nods.

"What would I do?" Donald asks.

"Drive my horses," Amy replies, as the father laughs.

"What would I do?" Randy asks.

"Clean out stalls," the child says.

"I don't wanna do that, I wanna drive your limo."

"Okay," the child says.

"What would I do?" Brian asks.

"Plant flowers," Amy says. Brian opens his mouth in bewilderment.

"I don't want to do that, I wanna go shopping," Brian says. The child shakes her head. "Girls go shopping!"

"Alright kids, less talking more eating," Tammy says. The sound of utensils against plates seems magnified. Minutes later, Tammy looks at her sons.

"You're both welcomed to join us at the ice skating rink," she says. In unison they reply, "I don't like ice skating." The teenagers look at each other as Tammy shakes her head.

"You two are so alike, yuz oughta be twins!"

When breakfast is over, Randy and Brian do the dishes, as Donald, Tammy and Amy brush their teeth. Tammy gets Amy bundled for the cold and Donald helps Tammy with her coat, then puts his own on. Outside, the sky consists of purple and grayish waves of clouds with a thin sliver of sunlight separating each hue Randy finishes drying the dishes, as Brian wipes off the table.

"Randy, it's December 22nd. We're on Christmas vacation, isn't that cool!"

"Yeah, you'll like it more when you're a junior." Randy walks downstairs to shave then returns to his room to fill out college applications.

Brian finding nothing good on TV, decides to taunt his brother.

"Hey Randy! I have a great idea. Why don't you stick it up your ass." Randy smiles as he continues work on his applications. Then in a quick voice, Brian says, 'Stickitupyourass!'" Chuckling, Randy stands, "I'm gonna fuck you up!" Brian charges downstairs as the phone begins to ring. He picks it up in the kitchen.

"Hello," he asks.

"Is Randy there?" a girl asks.

"Yeah, here he is," Brian hands the phone over.

"Hello?" Randy asks.

"Hi Randy. This is Barbi!"

"Oh, hi Barbi. How ya doin'?" Randy asks as Brian gets his jacket on. He mouths that he's going to Lakewood Bowl.

"I'm doing fine now that we're on Christmas break. Do you wanna see 'Grease' this afternoon?" she asks.

"Well Barbi, I'll ask my dad for the car, but he's not here right now."

"When will he be back?" Barbi asks.

"He oughta be back by two. He took my mother and my sister ice skating."

"Oh, I'd love to go ice skating!" Barbi exclaims. *You had to open your big mouth didn't you?* Randy thinks.

"Barbi, maybe some other day. Let me have your number, and I'll call you after my dad gets home." She obliges.

Moments later, Randy continues filling out his college applications. After the fourth one is finished, he sets his pen down and leans back in his chair. Misjudging, he nearly falls off. Recovering himself, Randy gently rocks on the back legs. The house is quiet—too quiet. Randy realizes that it's not often that he's the only one home. Placing his hands at the end of the arms of the chair, he closes his eyes. Slowly, his thoughts leave him. His muscles relax and his breathing slows. Three words enter his mind—*silence is golden.* He can't remember who originally said it but to Randy it doesn't matter. The slow rocking has a hypnotizing affect on him. As time goes by, Randy's head lowers. When his chin nearly touches his chest, his rest is broken by the sound of the garage door opener. Randy sets his chair down and looks at his clock on the wall. It reads 3:15pm. He thought he had relaxed for mere minutes. Walking downstairs, Randy stands at the front door until he sees Tammy and Amy emerge from the garage. "Hi Mom, hi Amy. Did yuz have a nice time at the rink?"

"We sure did!" Amy replies in her high voice. "You should skate with us!"

"Some day, little sister," Randy says. Tammy takes off Amy's coat and then her own.

"Are you kids hungry?" she asks. Amy jumps up and down.

"Me! I'm hungry, I'm hungry!" the child says. Tammy bends down.

"How 'bout some toasted cheese and tomato soup?" Tammy asks. Both Amy and Randy respond positively. "Where's Brian?" Tammy asks.

"At Lakewood Bowl shooting pool," Randy says. Tammy walks to the kitchen as her daughter follows her. Donald walks in "Hi son, where's Brian?" Donald asks.

"At Lakewood Bowl. Dad, may I talk to you for a minute?"

"Sure."

"Dad, may I use the car today?" "What for?"

"This girl wants me to take her to a movie."

"Oh—a hot date?" Donald asks.

"Well, it's a date," Randy replies.

"What time will you be back?" Donald asks.

"She may want to get something to eat after the movie, I'd say around nine o'clock?"

Donald takes out his keys and removes his Ford ones.

"Sure Randy, just make sure you put gas in it."

"Thanks Dad." Randy replies. Donald takes out a 'Jackson'. He hands it to his son.

"Dad, I have money."

"You're a good kid. Beside, I was sixteen once. Now take the sumbitch!" "Just a word of caution," then lowers his voice. "You knock her up—you marry her."

"Dad, it's not gonna be that type of night," Randy says.

"Still son, you've got to be careful," Donald says as he stands up to go to the bathroom. Randy picks up the white rotary phone and dials Barbi's number. Five minutes later, all are at the kitchen table, minus Brian, the middle sibling. After Donald says grace, Tammy looks at her husband.

"Honey, do you think I should call Lakewood Bowl and tell Brian to come home for lunch?"

"Naw Tam. He's on Christmas break. The boy needs a little freedom. Besides—I'm sure he's having a good time."

After lunch, Randy does the dishes, as his parents and little sister settle down in the family room to watch the afternoon movie. When the last dish is dried, the dishtowel is hung on its rack over the sink. Randy walks to the bathroom downstairs and checks his face. His complexion has only traces of stubble. Opening the mirror, Randy takes out a bottle of cologne and splashes some on the sides of his neck.

"I'll see yuz later."

"Love you," Tammy says.

"High-test," Donald replies. Amy takes her little hand, places it over her mouth and releases it with a smacking sound. Randy laughs and does the same.

The yellow LTD wagon is larger than a tiger, but purrs like a kitten. Randy places the metal transmission lever in reverse. Randy backs up as far as he's able, then turns the wheel as far to the left as he can, as the Ford moves slowly. He repeats this process. *I wish mom would park on the left side of the garage ,* Randy thinks. Three years earlier in 1975, when the Taylors moved in, Randy loved the curved driveway. Now as a driver, he loathes it. He turns the wheel to the left as far as it'll go. The front bumper nearly touches the black metal design pole that supports the porch-like overhang. Another switch to reverse, and Randy backs out effortlessly onto Royal Drive. He drives the large vehicle to a stop sign. Randy looks in the rearview mirror. Even though no one's behind him, he turns his left turn signal on. The green triangular arrow blinks loudly. Randy makes this turn as the vehicle rides like a cloud. He stops then turns right onto Sauk Trail. Randy's experiencing the same exhilaration as he did when he first learned to ride his bike. He notices the tank is half full. Randy turns on the AM/FM stereo radio and switches the station from WMAQ country to WLS; American Top 40. The vehicle smoothly accelerates to forty-five miles per hour.

"This cruise-control is boss, even though I don't know how to use it," Randy says out loud as he glances at the thin rectangular buttons on the steering wheel. Randy grips the thin brown sphere automatically at 'ten o'clock' and 'two o'clock'. He drives to a gas station on Route 30/Lincoln Highway and tops off the tank with high-test. Even as a boy Randy learned that a gas tank half-filled or less will cause the gas lines to freeze in the bitter Illinois winters. The total bill for the top off is $14.85. After paying, Randy takes a squeege from its container and washes the windshield with blue fluid. Randy drives to Barbi's house in nearby Matteson. He picks her up and takes her to one of three interconnecting theaters near Lincoln mall. 'Grease' will be showing in fifteen minutes. The cost of each ticket at a matinee price is $2.50.

While in the dark theater, Barbi moves closer to Randy. Barbi is beautiful, but Randy simply isn't falling for her. Even though Randy is tall, handsome with movie star looks, it takes him a while to warm up to a girl, let alone fall for her. His hormones haven't completely kicked in. The two watch 'Grease' as Randy unconsciously taps his foot quietly to most of the songs. Ever since Olivia Newton John's tune "If You Love Me' hit the airwaves four years earlier, Randy has developed a little crush on her. When the film is over, he stands up.

"No Randy, I have to see the credits," Barbi says. *I've done my patriotic duty. I just hope she doesn't want to get something to eat,* Randy thinks. When the words, 'Soundtrack on albums, eight-tracks and cassettes' appears, Barbi speaks.

"Randy, I'm hungry. Let's go get something to eat."

Randy lets out a long slow sigh. The two decide on Sambo's restaurant on Rt. 30/Lincoln Highway. This trip takes all of five minutes.

Once inside, a waitress seats them at their booth. After ordering, they talk about the movie, school, their families and goals in life.

"I want to be a registered nurse."

"Why's that?" Randy asks.

"I enjoy helping people," she replies. "What do you wanna be Randy?"

"Either a professor like my dad or a researcher. Either way, it's important that I get into college," Randy replies, as he begins to notice that horizontal stripes on females, enhances their bust lines. When the meals arrive, Randy bows his head and prays.

"Lord, we thank you for this food that we're about to eat. Amen."

"Do you say grace at every meal?" Barbi asks.

"Try to," Randy replies. "Bites later," Barbi says something that startles Randy.

"You look like a young Rock Hudson, Randy."

"Really? No one has ever said that to me before."

When the meal is finished, Randy stifles a burp.

"Excuse me," he says.

"You're such a gentleman," Barbi says as she places her hand on top of his. Randy pulls his hand away then asks, "Do you uh—do you want any dessert?"

"No thank you. We better get going," Barbi states. The two stand then Randy helps her with her coat. She picks up her purse and places the strap over her shoulder. Randy leaves a tip, pays for the bill, then they depart. "Randy, before you take me home, I want to show you something." *Aw man! Now what?* He thinks.

"Okay," He replies. After warming the engine for a minute, Randy drives south on Cicero Avenue. Ahead, the red lights blink for an oncoming train. Randy steps on the gas and beats the descending gate just in time. The clock on the instrument panel reads 8:05pm.

"Make a right onto Sauk Trail," Barbi says.

"We're going to my house?"

"Not quite," she replies. The LTD wagon makes a smooth turn at the intersection, towards Rich South High.

"Now turn right at the first road," Randy slows, placing his right turn signal on. The road is familiar as it leads to a parking lot at the back of the high school, near the baseball diamond. Barbi instructs Randy to park at the end of the parking lot. He complies. As he places the transmission in park, he kills the engine.

"Check this out Barbi. Everything looks peaceful, but with all this snow, it looks like dawn," he says.

"Yeah," Barbi replies as she removes an item from her purse. "But for some reason, the parking lot lights are out," she says.

"Randy, my dad got a new job in Orland Park. I may be attending Carl Sandburgh High next year."

"Oh—you're leaving Rich South," he says more to himself.

"I may never see you again," Barbi says slowly.

"Well, Orland Park isn't too far away. We can get together for another movie," Randy replies. Barbi looks at him affectionately.

"I've always liked you Randy. And since we're moving soon, I want you to do something."

"What's that?" he asks.

"Hold out your hand." Randy obeys as he feels a small metallic/plastic object in his palm. Examining it closer, he discovers it's a single packaged condom. Thoughts of his friend Scott and his girl flood his mind.

"Oh Lord have mercy, Barbi, I like you but I'm not in love with you." The girl hangs her head.

"Will you hold me?' she asks quietly.

"Yes, I'll hold you," Randy whispers. The teenagers embrace in the frigid winter night.

Five minutes later, headlights appear in the distance. They get brighter as the interior of the Ford becomes illuminated.

"Who the hell's that?" Randy asks. Their embrace is broken. A Richton Park police officer gets out and walks to the driver's side, between the two doors. Randy rolls down his window.

"Yes officer," he says.

"License and registration," the officer says. Randy takes out his driver's license from his wallet and hands it to him. Opening the glove compartment, he begins to search. He straightens his torso.

"This is my dad's car," Randy says. "I don't know where he keeps the registration card."

"That's alright," the officer says as he hands him back his license.

"What are you two doing out here?" the officer asks.

"We're discussing our English class," Randy replies.

"Do you expect me to believe that?" the officer asks.

"No, I don't."

"You two love birds get otta here," the officer says as he motions with his thumb.

"Yes sir," Randy says as he places his seatbelt on. Barbi buckles up also. Randy starts the engine then slowly pulls out. The all-weather tires grip the snow-covered parking lot with ease. Randy drives to Matteson. Pulling up to Barbi's house, she gives him a hug and kiss.

"Thank you for the date Randy. You're a real nice guy. Have a great Christmas and I'll see ya next semester."

"See ya Barbi. Don't feel bad because I resisted—okay?" She nods.

Christmas Eve day dawns gray and cold. After breakfast, Donald warms up the station wagon and the family gets inside and heads south to Kankakee, where Donald's parents live. Randy loves both sets of his grandparents, but a trip to Kankakee is always extra special to him. Looking between his parents, with his head slightly low, Randy can see swirls of snow gliding gently on the highway in front of the Ford. It reminds him of white snakes.

"You're squishing me!" Amy complains, in her high voice.

"Sorry sister," Randy says as he returns to his position near the window.

"Did you remember the presents?" Tammy asks her husband.

"Yes dear."

"Did you remember the fruit punch?" she asks.

"No I didn't." Donald replies. "I'll get some at the grocery store when we get off the highway."

"Are they open Christmas Eve?"

"Should be."

"Mommy I'm cold," Amy says. Donald turns up the heat. Brian sits behind Tammy gazing out the window and enjoying a song by Don Williams on WMAQ. Amy has climbed up on Randy's lap.

"Randy gonna give you a kissy." He smooches Amy's cheek as she sucks her thumb and brushes her left cheek with her left hand.

"Randy gonna give you another kissy." The smooch is repeated and Amy continues the game of brushing it from her cheek. Amy makes monkey sounds in protest. After several more kisses, the child removes her thumb and exhales air, smacking her lips together rapidly. Randy laughs as Tammy turns around.

"All right son!" she says.

"Just having fun, Mom," he replies. Fifty minutes later, Donald pulls up to his parents' house near the Roper factory. Randy helps carry the presents as Brian carries the bottles of fruit punch. Once inside, the aroma of pork roast fills Randy's nostrils. "Hi Grandma!" he says.

"Merry Christmas Eve, Randell. My, you're getting big!" Greetings and hugs are exchanged then coats and jackets are piled onto the bench near the door.

"I love your tree, Esther," Tammy says.

"Thank you honey. I wanted something different, so I chose the white branches and the blue ornaments, Grandma Taylor says. "And what I really like about it was that everything was on sale!" Grandma Taylor picks up Amy and showers her with kisses.

"How's my little turnip?" she asks.

"I'm happy to see you, Grandma!" Amy says. Ten minutes later, everyone is seated in the dining room, as the patriarch says grace.

"Dear Lord, we thank you for this food, we thank you for this wonderful family and for the blessings you bestow on us each day. Amen." The Christmas Eve feast consists of a lovely roast, scalloped potatoes, rice pilaf, beets, salad, garlic bread and red wine. Amy is served a little glass of grape juice.

In the Taylor family, Christmas Eve day is spent in Kankakee every other year. This year, 1978, Christmas day will be spent at Tammy's parents, the Plant's house in Marionette Park in the northern south suburbs of Chicago.

When the meal is over, plates are cleared then Grandma Taylor serves pecan pie, vanilla ice cream and coffee to the grownups. Fumbling in the pockets of her smock she says, "I can't find my cigarettes."

"My turn Grandma!" Brian says. Esther Taylor pulls two dollars from her pocket book and tells her grandson to go to Checker gas station nearby. Brian knows the rest—he can keep the change.

When Brian arrives back, his siblings are opening their gifts. He gives his grandmother her cigarettes and she, in turn, gives him his presents. Opening them, he discovers a new robe, two flannel shirts, a book of classical poetry and a long playing record album—Boston's "Don't Look Back."

"Thank you, Grandma, but how'd you know I wanted this album?"

"Your father told me."

"Thanks, Dad." Donald gives him a thumbs-up. After the gifts and thank you's Randy, Brian, their father and grandfather sit in the living room to watch college bowl games on television while Tammy, Amy and Esther Taylor prepare homemade chocolate chip cookies. When all of the ingredients are placed in the large bowl, Grandma Taylor helps Amy mix them with a wooden spoon. Tammy turns away, placing her fingertips on her temples. Her headaches are becoming stronger and more frequent.

It's growing dark as Randy helps his dad carry presents to the station wagon, while Brian takes charge of the plate of chocolate chip cookies and sneaks one from under tin foil covering. Phil and Esther Taylor wave goodbye as the LTD wagon backs out of the driveway.

Christmas Day, 1978. Church is attended at Flossmoor Community Church in Homewood. After the service, the family is off to Marrionette Park where Tammy's parents live in a simple two bedroom, one story house with a one-car garage.

After Christmas greetings and catching up on the latest news, it's time for the holiday feast. There is roasted chicken, with stuffing, mashed potatoes and gravy, buttered corn, cole slaw and white wine for the adults. Apple pie, vanilla ice cream and coffee are served for dessert.

The next day, Tuesday December 26th, finds Randy back at work as a porter at Lakewood Bowl. Thirteen months earlier, while walking back from school, Randy decided to stop and apply as a 'pin chaser'. A pin chaser works behind the machines and takes care of any mechanical problems that occur. Joe, the tall old assistant manager told Randy that to be a pin chaser, one has to go to a mechanics school. Disappointed, he thanked Joe and turned to go. Joe beckoned him back and asked him if he'd liked to be a porter instead. Two positions were opened. Randy didn't know what a porter was. Joe told him that porters clean the score tables after each league is finished bowling. They also bring empty bottles and glasses to the bar, clean the restrooms, take out the trash and keep the pool room in order. Randy filled out the application and was hired four days later. He was excited because that meant that he could walk to work. (The distance from home to the bowling alley is a mere five minutes).

Randy punches his time card, puts on his thin cranberry porter's jacket, straightens his tie and greets Joe.

"Hi'ya doin' Randy! Didja have a nice Christmas?"

"Yes I did. How was yours Joe?"

"Mine was wonderful," he says as he removes a cigarette from its black container.

"Randy, you're the perfect example of the all-American boy."

"Thank you Joe."

"We're having open bowling all day. You don't mind cleaning the parking lot do ya?" Joe asks.

"No sir." Randy enters the storage room between the bar and the entrance and picks up a large off white bucket by its handle. Setting it outside the office he retrieves his scarf and jacket then goes outside. The only car in the parking lot is a 1973 Oldsmobile which is Joe's. Randy begins picking up beer cans, candy wrappers, and white McDonald bags. At the corner of the parking lot, Randy spots a pack of cigarettes that are unopened. Picking it up, he unwraps it, takes a cigarette out and lights it. He then places the pack in his inner jacket pocket. Seven parking spaces later, a small flat green square catches his eye. Bending down, he picks up a twenty-dollar bill that was folded in half. Randy sets the bucket down and takes out his wallet.

"No Joe, I don't mind cleaning the parking lot at all," Randy says to himself. He places the 'Jackson' in his billfold, puts the wallet in his front pocket and resumes his duty.

Fifteen minutes later, he's inside. Taking the lids off of many gray plastic garbage bins, Randy empties the contents of the bucket. The next procedure doesn't bother him—cleaning out the bucket Joe emerges from the 'control center' wiping his forehead.

"Ya know Randy, President Carter's raising the minimum wage to two-ninety an hour on January first dontcha?" Joe asks.

"That's cool Joe."-

"I'll tell you what's even cooler. We need you to work Friday nights 'cause Willie's quitting."

"Really?" Randy asks.

"Yeah, but I won't miss the lazy-good-for-nothing-bastard. You put him to shame."

"Well, it's time for my candy bar," Joe says.

"Do you want a cup of coffee too?" Randy asks.

"Sure. Black with no sugar," Randy walks to the snack bar and prepares the coffee machine. Steve Germaine, the pin chaser, walks by on his way to the restroom and bids him a good morning. Randy exchanges the greeting.

While the coffee is brewing, Randy walks to the well-lighted storage room and begins cleaning the white bucket with Soft Scrub. The aroma of the thick white cleaner is sweet. Randy cleans it so well, one would be tempted to eat out of it. After washing his hands, he pours Joe a cup of coffee and gives it to him.

The next order of business is cleaning the glass doors and windows. Randy gets the paper towels and glass cleaner from the storage room and begins to clean. Five minutes later, two couples arrive and Randy opens the door for them.

An hour later at 12:30pm, ten lanes are open out of thirty-two. Randy is wiping down the orange counters near the scoring areas when he hears, "Porter to the counter" on the intercom. He quickly walks to the 'control center".

"You hungry Randy?" Joe asks.

"Yes!"

"I'm gonna order some corn beef sandwiches from Cal's." Randy takes out his wallet.

"That's alright, son. I only have this job to keep me busy. I'll get one for Steve too." Joe turns, picks up the rotary phone and dials as Randy thanks him.

CHAPTER THREE

1979 arrives in the 'Land of Lincoln' with eleven inches of snow. Randy and Brian shovel the driveway. When the chore is completed, Randy takes a shower and sits down to plan his courses for the spring semester. Among them are calculus I, algebra II, English III (Popular Literature) and biology. Brian plans his classes; weight training, Home economics, Foods II, Art I, physical education and Jewelry I. Always seeking approval, the middle sibling walks downstairs to the family room where Donald and Tammy are watching a movie. (Amy's taking a nap in her bedroom).

"Dad, do you wanna see my new schedule?" Brian asks. Donald has an unlit cigarette in his mouth and a lighter in his left hand. He holds out his right hand as Brian hands him his schedule. Tammy sits nearby knitting a hat for Amy, while glancing at the movie. Moments later, Donald begins to shake his head. He looks at his son.

"Brian, these are all bullshit courses. Oh, and by the way, I don't see basket weaving on here." Brian hoots with laughter.

"Brian, your sister is sleeping," Tammy says.

"Sorry Mom," he replies. Donald hands his schedule back.

"Go upstairs and make some changes. You need courses that'll help you after you graduate."

School resumes on January 8th. Routines are established. As the days fly by, Randy's confidence grows. He scores 100% on all of his quizzes. He senses he has gotten out of the 'starting gate' early. Also during this month, Randy shaves more frequently. His beard is coming in thicker. At first he would only shave his upper lip. Now his chin, and part of his cheeks are added in the process.

While typing at Hennington, Barker & Stone, Tammy Taylor places her hand on her forehead. She gets up, takes her purse and walks to the ladies room. Opening her handbag, she takes out a bottle of aspirin and downs three of them with a paper cup of water. Her headaches have worsened. Tammy thinks it's the pressures of work and raising a family. Since she had Randy, she's made it a point to spend two weekends a year alone at her parent's house. The weekend retreats are a welcome change-of-pace from her hectic life. Tammy emerges from the restroom. She places her purse down at the side of her desk. On the large calendar on her desk, she makes a note on Saturday, January 20th.

That evening, Randy finishes his homework early. He too likes a break from his routine. Turning the desk light off, he turns towards his brother.

"All done Brian, you can use the desk now."

"That's ok I like reading in bed." Randy walks downstairs to the family room.

"Dad, I'm gonna shoot pool at Lakewood Bowl. Is that okay?"

"Are you finished with your homework?" Donald asks.

"Yes sir," Randy replies.

"Be home at ten o'clock and not a minute later," Donald says.

"Thanks dad. I appreciate it." Randy bolts upstairs to the foyer. He retrieves his scarf and Rich South jacket. Looking up towards the foyer floor Tammy calls, "Love you, Randy."

"Love you too, Mom."

The front door is opened then gently closed. Randy walks to Lakewood Bowl in the bitter cold.

The wooden triangle is lifted carefully. The pool cue is chalked as the shooter takes his stance. The cue ball hits the others with a loud *crack!* The solid green six, and an orange stripe ten fall into opposite pockets. Deciding to play *sloppy* pool, Randy shoots at random. Out of the corner of his eye, he sees a large figure. After sinking the yellow one ball, Randy notices his friend from English class.

"Hey big Al!"

"Hi Randy. What's happening?"

"Just thought I'd shoot a little pool. I was lucky to finish my homework early tonight."

"Do you wanna play nine-ball?" Al asks.

"How do you play nine-ball?" Randy asks.

"Let me show ya," Al says as he removes his jean jacket. "Randy, the nine ball is always in the middle and the one ball is always in the front. Balls ten through fifteen remain in the pockets. It doesn't matter where the other balls are. The object of the game is to shoot the balls in order. Now break 'em," Al says. Randy chalks his pool cue, takes his stand with his left leg straight then hits the cue ball following through with the cue stick. The white one hits the others with the same *crack!* Two balls fall into two different pockets.

"You've won the game,' Al says.

"How's that?" Randy asks.

"You got the nine ball in on a brake," Al replies as he racks the balls again. The wooden triangle is slowly removed, as Randy chalks up his cue. He brakes the balls and the nine slowly makes its way to the corner. At the edge of the pocket, it seems to stop, when it falls in.

"Randy, you lucky bastard! The first two times you play 'Nine ball', you get the yellow stripe in on a brake!" Al racks the balls once more, but this time, the yellow striped one doesn't go in on the brake. The boys play until 9:50. Upon leaving, Randy purchases a pack of gum at the snack shop stand to cover his breath.

The morning of Saturday, January 20th, 1979 dawns sunny with a heat wave—43 degrees. Tammy Taylor packs her over night bag, hugs and kisses her family then gets ready to leave.

"Mommy can I go with you?" Amy asks.

"No honey, mommy has to go to a meeting. I'll see you tomorrow night." The child begins to whimper. Donald quickly changes the subject.

"Amy, do you want to go ice skating?" he asks. The child's eyebrows raise, as she begins to clap.

"Yes, I want to!" she replies.

"I'll get your coat," Donald says. He kisses his wife then opens the front door for her. Randy's at work nearby and Brian's upstairs at his desk, hitting the books. Algebra isn't his favorite subject.

Tammy gets in the LTD wagon, buckles up and thirty-five minutes later, she's in her parents house in Marrionette Park enjoying the wonderful smells coming from her mother's kitchen.

"I know stuffed pork chops and applesauce are your favorite," her mom says. "And I have a surprise for dessert." The three sit down at noon for the main meal of the day. After grace, Tammy says.

"Years ago when I began taking these breaks, I felt a little guilty. Now, I realize how much I've needed them."

"Tammy honey, we all need a break from our routine. It's actually good for us," Linda Plant says.

Along with the stuffed pork chops and applesauce are glazed carrots, mashed potatoes, spinach salad and red wine. Tammy takes a sip from her wine glass, when the pain in her head ignites. She places her hands on her temples.

"Are you okay honey?" Linda asks.

"Oh Mother, I'll be alright. Do you have any aspirin?"

"Sure honey."

"I'll take three mother," Tammy says.

"Do you want me to take you to the doctor, little girl?" Alex asks.

"No thank you father, I'll be alright."

After the meal is finished, Tammy helps her mother clear the table. Linda pours the coffee then tells Tammy to close her eyes.

"Okay Tammy," Linda says.

She opens them and sees her favorite dessert—German chocolate cake.

"Oh mother, thank you so much! I haven't had this in ages." After a bite, Linda asks,

"How is it?"

"Delicious Mother," Tammy replies. She chews slowly, savoring the sweet taste, then swallows.

"I feel I died and went to heaven." The remainder of the dessert is relished in silence.

After the table is cleared and the dishes are finished, Tammy and her mother sit down to watch the afternoon movie—"Lassie."

The evening meal is light—soup and sandwiches. Later, Tammy takes a bath. She slips into her warmest nightgown and robe and goes back to the living room to work on the scarf and hat she's knitting for Amy. Half an hour later, she puts her hand on her forehead.

"Mother, I think I'll go to bed now. A good night's sleep will help this headache."

"Oh, I'm sure it will. Goodnight honey," Linda says.

"Goodnight father."

"Sleep well little girl."

Tammy walks into her old bedroom and closes the door most of the way.

It's not quite midnight when Linda gets up to relieve herself. On her way back to bed, she hears an unusual sound coming from her daughter's bedroom. She walks to the door and slowly opens it.

"Tammy, are you okay?" Linda asks. There is no response, just uneven breathing and a slight raspy sound.

"Tammy, what's wrong?" Linda tries to wake her daughter, but to no avail. Beginning to panic, Linda rushes to wake her husband.

"Something's wrong with Tammy. She won't wake up!" Alex runs to Tammy's bedroom. He also tries to wake her, but doesn't succeed. He phones for an ambulance as his wife holds Tammy hand and strokes her forehead.

Donald Taylor is sleeping soundly when the phone rings. Lazily, he rolls on his right side and holds the phone to his left ear.

"Hello."

"Don, this is Linda. We're at Saint Francis Hospital in Blue Island." Donald is fully awakened thinking something has happened to his father-in-law.

"Tammy is on a ventilator and is hooked up to an IV bag."

"What happened?"

"I heard Tammy breathing irregularly and couldn't wake her," Linda says as her voice cracks.

"I'm on my way!" Donald hangs up, turns on the lamp and quickly gets dressed. His sons' bedroom door is half open. Donald quietly walks in without turning on the light. Brian is snoring slightly. Sitting on the edge of the bed he gently shakes Randy's shoulder.

"Randy—Randy wake up."

"Randy, listen to me. Are you awake?"

"Yeah, what's the matter?"

"Your mother's in the hospital in Blue Island. I'm going up there right now."

"What happened?" Randy asks.

"Her breathing is irregular and," Donald pauses to be certain he doesn't frighten the boy too much, "Grandma couldn't get Mom to wake up. Now get Amy up no later than eight-thirty. When she asks where I am, tell her I had to go see Mommy and nothing else. Tell Brian what I told you, but tell him not to tell Amy. I don't have all of the details, and I don't want her to get scared. Is that understood?"

"Yes sir," Randy whispers.

"You're the man of the house now."

Donald walks to his daughter's room. He quietly kisses her on the cheek. Donald leaves his house quietly, never noticing the biting cold.

Randy lies in bed for ten minutes. Unable to sleep, he gets up and walks downstairs to the family room. A small crucifix hangs on the wall near the corner. Randy prays.

"Dear Jesus, make my mother well. Please help her get over this; whatever she has."

Randy will not be going back to sleep this night.

Donald arrives to Saint Francis Hospital. As he's greeted by his in-laws, a doctor walks into the waiting room and approaches them.

"Mr. and Mrs. Plant, I'm Doctor Sherry Olsen." "I'm Tammy's husband," Donald says, stepping forward and extending his hand.

"I'm sorry to meet you under these circumstances. Let's all go over here so that we can talk."

"After looking at the results of her preliminary tests, it seems that Tammy may have a brain tumor."

"How can this be? She wasn't sick. Is there a way you can shrink the tumor—or can you operate?" Alex asks, hardly able to remain seated.

"They'll be doing more tests. I'm sure there will be a conversation about treatment after the neurological team has had a chance to study the test results. We have to learn more about what we're dealing with."

"That's why she was having those headaches." Tammy's mother says through tears.

"Did she ever awaken? What did Tammy say to you?" Donald asks.

"Tammy is in a coma," the doctor explains.

Tammy's mother begins to sob.

"Yes, that's why we had to put a breathing tube in."

Tammy's father puts his arm around his wife. "This is unbelievable!"

"May we see her?" Donald asks.

"Of course," the doctor replies.

The three follow her to a dimly-lit room where Tammy is hooked up to machines and tubes. Donald pulls up a chair, takes hold of his wife's hand and holds it to his cheek. Tammy's parents stand beside him—all three in tears.

At six o'clock, Randy decides to make a pot of coffee. As the pot brews, he walks upstairs to find Brian getting dressed.

"I have something to tell you little brother," Randy says.

"What's that?"

"Mom's in the hospital," Randy says in a soft tone.

"What happened?" he asks. Randy motions his hands downward, indicating to Brian to keep his voice low.

"Grandma found Mom's breathing to be off in the middle of the night. And when Grandma tried to wake her—she couldn't. Now you mustn't say anything to Amy. I will talk to her—understand?" Brian nods.

Randy gets dressed and has a quick smoke outside, while Brian is in the bathroom downstairs. Once back in the house, Randy goes upstairs to wake his sister.

"C'mon Amy. It's time to get up. What do you want for breakfast, oatmeal or French toast?"

"French toast. Where's Daddy?"

"Daddy had to go see Mommy. Now, go potty, and I'll help you get dressed." The child slowly walks to the bathroom and shuts the door. Randy takes her clothes from the drawer and sets them on her bed. When she comes back, Randy helps his sister get dressed.

It's 9:00 and a nurse walks into Tammy's room. "Doctor Olsen has asked me to tell you that Mrs. Taylor isn't scheduled for any more testing until later in the afternoon. You might want to go and get some breakfast or even go home for a while to rest. We'll be monitoring her closely and of course we'll call you if there is any change.

"Thank you," Donald answers. "I'll be staying but I think you two should go home to rest a little and have something to eat," he tell is in-laws.

"No, Donald we're not leaving…"

"Now dear," Alex interrupts his wife. "Donald is right. Let's go home, have a bite to eat, rest a little and we'll be back here by the time they're finished with those tests."

"Please," Donald says, "Tammy wouldn't want to know you're not taking care of yourselves. In fact, I'm going to run down to the cafeteria to get some coffee, check in with the boys and then I'll just sit here with Tammy and rest a little myself."

When Randy is finished speaking with his father, he hangs up the phone. Then he quickly picks it back up and dials their neighbor's number. He briefly explains that his mom was visiting her parents and that something of an emergency has come up and asks if they can watch Amy at their house. The neighbor is happy to help and after hanging up, Randy tells his sister that he's taking her to Stephi's to play.

"Why?" the child asks.

"Because Brian and I are going to a meeting."

"What meeting, Randy?" asks Brian.

"Just follow me, Brian." Once Amy is dropped off, Randy and Brian take the short walk to Lakewood Bowl.

Joe is ready for them. "Randy, the lounge is open. You boys want a pop?"

"I'll get it Joe. Thank you kindly," Randy responds. He retrieves two colas from the cooler and sets them down on the bar. Brian immediately opens one. Randy walks around to the other side and joins his brother.

"I have a feeling this isn't going to be good," Brian says.

"We have to keep the faith little brother. We don't know all of the details yet. Almost an hour later, Donald walks in the lounge. He embraces his sons then says,

"Boys, let's sit at a table." The three walk to one that is lit the best. They all sit.

"Sons, I'm not going to sugar coat this."

"Your mother has an inoperable brain tumor."

"What does that mean?" Brian asks.

"That means," "that her tumor is too large for the doctors to operate." Donald pauses and says that next ten words slowly.

"Boys, your mother is probably not going to make it." Brian begins to cry softly. Randy places his arm around him.

Donald tells his sons that shortly after the Plant's left the hospital, Doctor Olsen came into Tammy's room and told Donald that they were not going to wait until afternoon as planned but were going to take their mother down for tests immediately. The boys look grave as their dad explains that when Doctor Olsen came to see him in the waiting room after the tests were completed, he knew immediately that the situation was grave.

"Doctor Olsen wasn't exactly certain but she doesn't think Mom has more than three months." Both boys are sobbing now.

"I had to come to tell you right away. I know how much this hurts. I didn't want to leave your mom but they're taking good care of her and I really needed to see you kids."

"Oh Dad," Randy says, "What about Amy? She'll be lost without Mom."

"Now boys, we can't tell Amy. She's too young and she won't understand."

"She's gonna want to know where Mom is," Randy.

"All you can say to her is that she needs a rest. You realize that Mom is in a coma and she may never come out of it. But this is much too much for Amy to grasp and we have to be strong for her. Randy, you'll have to take over at home. I'll be at the hospital every day so you'll be picking Amy up from school and then you're gonna have to get dinner started. And Brian— when I'm not at the house, you do what Randy tells you. You have to pitch in and help. No questions asked. Is that understood?"

"Yes sir," Brian replies softly as he wipes his eye with his right wrist. Joe walks into the lounge.

"Donald, can I get you a beer?"

"Sure Joe."

"I'll get it Joe," Randy says, as he gets up, and retrieves a brown bottle. Randy uses the immobile bottle opener without spilling a drop, much to his surprise. He walks back to the table and gives his father his beer.

"Can we see Mom?" he asks.

"Of course," Donald replies, "But not tonight. I called Grandma and Grandpa after I talked with Doctor Olsen and they'll be going to the hospital to be with Mom. But I made them promise they wouldn't stay too late. They agreed that the four of us should be together tonight." Twenty minutes later, Donald finishes his beer.

"Well, let's go pick up Amy." "Take care Joe. Thanks for letting us use your lounge," Donald calls.

"No problem, Don."

"Randy," Joe whispers motioning the boy toward him. Joe extends his right hand. Randy shakes it and is puzzled—until he senses a small item. Randy opens his hand and finds a folded fifty dollar bill.

"A little bonus for ya," Joe whispers.

"Aw thank you so much. I really appreciate it!" Randy replies. He puts the 'Grant' in his front pocket and runs outside.

When the Taylors get home, Donald quickly walks across the street. Ringing the doorbell, Stephi answers it.

"Hello Mister Taylor. Come on in. I'll get Amy." Moments later, the child runs from the living room as the father picks her up. Donald gives her a kiss, as Amy gives him a huge hug.

"Do you want to go out for pizza?" Donald asks.

"Pizza! Pizza! I want pizza!" the child exclaims.

"I think that's a 'yes'." Stephi says. Donald sets his daughter down, takes out his wallet, and gives Stephi a 'Hamilton'.

"Thank you Stephi. Sorry for the short notice," Donald states.

"No problem. Any time," Stephi says. "Is everything alright?" she asks.

"We're working on it," Donald says as he bundles up his daughter.

"Bye Stephi, wuv you," Amy says.

"I wuv you too my precious angel," Stephi replies.

As Donald holds Amy's hand crossing the street, Amy asks;

"Where's Mommy?"

"Mommy's a little tired. She needs to rest," Donald replies.

Another routine is established, minus Tammy. After Randy leaves his last class, he walks to his locker and retrieves his texts to study for the evening. Two girls walk up to him; a blonde and a brunette. He doesn't know them.

"Pardon me, are you Randy Taylor?" the brunette asks.

"Yes I am," he replies.

"Have you seen Brian?" the blonde asks.

"Everyday," Randy says.

"We need to talk to him."

"Well, the sophomore lockers are on the other side of the cafeteria. He's probably there now," Randy says.

"Thank you," the brunette replies. The girls hurry off.

"My little brother is getting to be a little stud," Randy says to himself. He leaves quickly for Kindercare.

When they arrive at the house, Randy removes Amy's coat, scarf and boots "Now Amy, I have to make dinner. You be a good girl and watch television." Randy places a cartoon videocassette in the Sony Betamax recorder. Bugs Bunny comes on.

"I'm thirsty," Amy says. Randy walks upstairs to the kitchen, fills a cup of water and walks back downstairs.

"Here's your sippy cup, sister."

"Sank you," she says. Randy chuckles and replies, "You're welcome." He goes back into the kitchen and fills a large pot of water, three quarters full. He places it on the stove, and turns on the gas. Vegetable oil is added. Randy washes his hands. Taking out a cutting board, he chops some lettuce, places it in a colandar and rinses it with cold water. He washes and slices tomatoes, peels two cucumbers cuts them and places them in the bowl. Randy opens the cupboard and looks at the cans of tuna. *I can't remember how many mom uses.* Randy decides on four. Taking the folded washcloth from the spigot, he rinses it under hot water then wipes off the tops of the cans, just as his mother taught him to do. Randy takes out a can opener and begins to open a can. *Do I drain the water or don't I? I'll drain two of them.* Opening the other cans, he spoons out the meat into another bowl. He covers it. Randy retrieves a medium pot and fills it with cold water. He places it on the stove, making sure the handle is turned inwards on account of Amy.

With water boiling in the larger pot, Randy adds the egg noodles as Brian walks in the front door.

"Well, there's 'Sammy Stud'!"

"Hi Randy. Whatya cookin'?" Brian asks as he hangs up his coat and takes off his boots.

"Tuna casserole. I hope it turns out okay. Did you talk to your little sweeties?"

"Aw Randy. I'm not interested in those chicks," Brian says.

"I don't know, Brian," that blonde is awfully cute."

"I like Gloria Conners." Brian says.

"Who's she?" Randy asks.

"She's in my Pre-Algebra class. She's a freshman, but she's so shy. I can barely get her to talk."

"Ask her to a movie then," Randy says.

"I don't have my driver's license," Brian replies.

"I'll drive ya," Randy says. Brian pauses.

"You will?" he asks.

"Sure, Dad'll let me use the car."

"Let me think about it," Brian replies.

"Well, while you're thinking about it little brother, get outta the kitchen I need to concentrate." The noisy garage door begins to lift. Amy is in the foyer in seconds.

"Daddy's home! she exclaims.

Donald picks her up. "How's my little sweet pea?"

"I missed you honey." Donald gives her a kiss, then sets her down. Taking off his coat, he places it on a hanger.

"How's my boys?" he asks.

"Fine dad," they reply in unison. Donald hugs them, then walks in the kitchen. He retrieves a beer from the fridge.

Half an hour later, the family is sitting at the dinner table holding hands. Donald prays. "Lord, we thank you for this meal that Randy has cooked. We thank you for the blessings you bestow on us, and we thank you most graciously for my wife and their mother. Amen." Shortly into the meal, Donald compliments his son.

"This tuna casserole is good Randy. I'm proud of you."

"It's not Mom's cooking, but it'll stay down," Randy replies. After several swallows he warns them that the biscuits are burnt on the bottom.

"Well, just eat the top," Donald says. Sitting on a pillow that's on her chair, Amy whines.

"I don't like these!"

"Cucumbers? That's the best part of the salad!" Randy says.

"Honey, just eat two pieces."

"No, Daddy!"

"Okay, eat four pieces."

"No!" Amy says sternly and with a scowl.

"Well, I'll just eat your dessert then," Donald says. A neutral look comes over her.

"Two pieces, Daddy?" she asks in her high voice.

"Two pieces," the father replies. The child picks out the smallest ones and places them in her mouth.

"What's for dessert son?" Donald asks.

"I think there's some butter cookies in the cupboard," Randy says. After a swig of his beer, Donald looks at his other son.

"Brian, since Randy did the cooking, you do the dishes—fair enough?"

"Yes sir," Brian replies.

"Cucumbers gone. I want cookies!" Amy says.

"Please?" Donald asks.

"Please Daddy." Amy asks. Donald gets up, opens the long narrow cupboard and retrieves a package of cookies.

"She ate all of them," Brian says.

"All of what?" Donald asks.

"All of her cucumbers."

"She did?" Donald asks. "Let me give her a big kiss." Donald smooches his daughter.

"She cleaned her plate too," Randy replied.

When the meal is finished, Brian clears the table, Donald draws Amy's bathwater and Randy hits the books. Sitting at the desk, he thinks, *I've got a strong B in geometry— better to focus on this English literature reading assignment.*

Two hours later, it's break time. Randy stands up from his desk chair and opens the door. Donald has just walked up the stairs with his daughter.

"Night Randy," Amy says.

"Goodnight little sister. Let me give you a kiss." He pecks his sister on her cheek, then walks downstairs into the kitchen. Pouring a glass of milk, and taking a couple of cookies from the package, Randy eats a little snack. At six-foot two inches and a hundred and eighty pounds, Randy's on the tail end of his growth spurt. His appetite remains ferocious. Donald walks downstairs after putting Amy to bed. When Randy is finished, he walks downstairs where Donald is sitting in his lazy-boy reading the newspaper. Randy sits on the sofa near him.

"What time are we gonna go to Saint Francis on Saturday?" He asks.

"First thing in the morning. One of my student's will babysit Amy. Stephi has to work."

"There's no way mom's gonna get better?" Randy asks.

"I'm praying for a miracle," his father says.

"Me too," Randy replies.

"School going well for you?" Donald asks.

"Yes sir. My three-point-five is consistent. I'm now taking a little break from studying," Randy says.

"Son, you're gonna go far in life. I admire your discipline."

"Dad, you're a professor. It took a lot of discipline to get where you are."

"Randy," Donald says with a smile, "You didn't know me when I was your age." The two chuckle.

"Uh-dad, I have to talk to you about somethin'," Randy pauses. "I've been smokin' for the past three months. You mind if I light up?" Randy asks. Donald frowns as he pauses. He was his son's age when he began to smoke.

"Only in the utility room. When the weather breaks, you smoke outside. The next thing I'll hear is you've started drinking."

"I did that four months ago." Randy replies. The teenager stands to walk upstairs, but then has an after thought.

"Dad, may I use your electric razor?"

"You've been using it for a while—why ask now?" says Donald.

"Better late than never?" Randy asks. The father chuckles again then says,

"Sure son, you can use it, but you buy Williams 'Lectric Shave. It doesn't cost much. Beard's comin' in huh?" Donald asks.

"Only my upper lip and chin," Randy says.

"Wait a while." Donald says.

"Thanks dad." Randy walks to his bedroom and retrieves his pack from his jacket. He makes a pit-stop in the kitchen and retrieves an old cup that'll serve as his ashtray. In the utility room, Randy lights a cigarette. Even though he has his father's permission—he feels awkward. Then he walks to his bedroom to finish his studies. When he's finished, Randy walks back to the family room. "The doctors have told me your mother is still in a coma, and her tumor isn't getting any bigger. That's one small ray of light at the end of the tunnel." "Maybe that's all we need," replies Randy.

CHAPTER **FOUR**

Karen Olmstead, arrives at eight o'clock sharp —Saturday morning. Karen takes off her coat after Donald introduces her to his children.

"I'll hang it up for you," Donald says.

"I want to go," Amy says.

"Amy, we have to go to a big-boy meeting. We'll be back this afternoon. Karen will read and play games with you. You'll be a good girl for her won't ya?" Donald asks. The child nods.

"Okay, give Daddy a kiss." The child complies. Once in the car, the three head north on Cicero Avenue. Randy sits in the front in silence. He's closer to his father, but he loves his mother dearly. He can't imagine life without her. Randy thinks of the practical jokes he played on her. A rubber snake in her slipper, an empty wine bottle and rubber vomit on the kitchen floor next to a 'drunk' Randy. Watered down liquor in the glass bottle. Randy nearly busted out laughing when Sharon, his mother's friend from work said, "Gee Tammy, this liquor tastes kinda mild." Randy's thoughts are interrupted .

"Are you alright son?" Donald asks.

"Yeah Dad, just thinkin'." Randy replies.

"I'm proud of you boys holding up and staying strong," Donald says. Fifty minutes later, Donald pulls into the parking lot of Saint Francis Hospital in Blue Island. Brian is a little apprehensive. Randy feels sad, yet hopeful that his mother will pull out of this. The three step out of the warm station wagon into the bitter cold. Clouds are thickening. It will snow again soon.

"We're here to see Tammy Taylor."

"Mrs. Taylor has been moved to the third floor in I.C.U. She's in room number three, twenty-nine."

"Thank you miss," Donald says. They take the elevator. Randy has never liked hospitals. Especially the odor—rubbing alcohol. When the elevator door opens, another receptionist desk appears. Donald informs her that he and his sons are here to see his wife and their mother. She points, since she's chewing on her sandwich. Donald thanks her then walks to his wife's room.

The first thing Randy notices is the room is fairly dark and cool. Tammy is hooked up to several machines. An IV bag, hanging from a metal pole is near her pillow. Each son holds one of her hands. Randy feels her hand is very warm. This gives him hope that she'll get better. Tammy appears younger in the dim light. No one speaks at first. After a few minutes Randy whispers, "Please get well mom. We love you so much." Then Brian says, "I never knew how much work you did, but now I know. Mom, I'm sorry I took you for granted." Four minutes later, another silence is broken.

"Boys," Donald whispers. "I need to be alone with your mother. Wait in the hallway." Each son kisses the opposite cheek, then they quietly leave. In the hallway, they find both sets of grandparents. Hugs and kisses are exchanged. Each set of grandparents take turns visiting Tammy. Everyone is somber.

February 14th, 1979 arrives all too soon.

"Wonderful breakfast son," Donald says. Randy takes a bow.

"Sank you," Amy says.

"You're welcome little sister." While walking to Rich South High, Randy is grateful that his father is taking Amy to Kindercare.

Even though he's behind schedule, Randy takes a quick detour to the boys restroom for a fast smoke. Afterward, when Randy goes to his locker, he discovers a valentine taped to it. Setting his bag down, Randy takes off the envelope and removes the card. It's from a secret admirer. At the bottom it's signed, *I'm a sophomore.*

"Well, that narrows it down," Randy says aloud. Taking off his jacket and retrieving his books, Randy walks quickly to his first class.

In the middle of third period, Randy is sitting in his English class, when there's a knock on the door. His teacher, Mrs. McPherson answers it. Outside of the door is the dean of students, Mr. Boyer. His eyes lock on Randy.

"Mister Taylor, get your books and come with me." Walking in the hallway, Randy thinks that Mister Boyer found out about his smoking in the boys room.

"I'm not in trouble am I?"

"No son, you're not." the dean replies. Around the corner are several benches and a couple of chairs.

"Wait here for a moment," Mr. Boyer says. The dean departs. Randy is puzzled. *What the hell is going on,* he thinks. Even though the feeling in the pit of the stomach tells him all he needs to know. Moments later, Mr. Boyer returns with Brian.

"Follow me, boys." The look on Brian's face tells Randy that they're fearing the same thing. When they arrive in front of the Principal's office, Randy sees his father. Once inside, Donald opens his arms.

"Boys, she's gone." Donald embraces his sons as all three weep.

Hearing the principal approach, Donald composes himself and says, "My boys will be out of school for several days."

"Take all the time you need Mr. Taylor. I'm so sorry for your loss, sons." Mr. McGraw places a hand on each student.

"Randy and Brian. You're among the best students here. Don't worry about missing school. May God give all of you strength during this difficult time."

"Thank you Mr. McGraw," Randy softly says. Donald looks at his sons.

"Boys, get your coats. Meet me at the car. I'm parked right out in front." Donald shakes the principals hand then departs. Once they're in the car, Donald speaks. "Boys your mother slipped into cardiac arrest. The doctors and nurses did everything they could."

"But Dad, they said three months!"

"Randy, that was just an estimate—a guess."

"The wrong, damn guess! How could there not be any warning?"

"Brian, there was a warning, it was all those headaches getting worse and worse and then Mom slipping into a coma and the terrible results of all those tests. We were all *hoping* for three months. Hell, we were all hoping for a miracle!"

"It's not right, Dad. We didn't get to say goodbye."

Randy is just staring silently out of the window. Finally, in what is almost a whisper, "Dad, what about Amy? What's she going to do without Mom?"

"She'll have us."

Donald drives the short distance to the day care center. As he parks, he tells his sons to remain inside. Moments later, he emerges with the little girl. Donald opens the passenger door, and places the child on Randy's lap.

"Hi Amy. Did you have a good day?"

"Yep," the child says. "I was swimmin'," as she holds up a piece of paper.

"No sister, it's too cold for swimming" Randy says. The child hands him her drawing.

"See," she says, holding the paper closer to his face.

"Oh, a picture of you swimming. Did you draw this?" Randy asks.

"Yep. See, that's me."

"That sure is pretty. I'm gonna put it on the refrigerator as soon as we get home!" Randy says.

When the family gets into the house, Amy runs to the kitchen. "Put it there, put it there, " she says pointing to the refrigerator door.

Randy complies and Amy claps her hands in approval. Donald holds out his hand.

"Come on honey. Let's go downstairs. Daddy wants to talk to you." The child takes his hand as the boys follow. Donald sits in his recliner and places the child sideways on his lap. Randy and Brian sit on the sofa. Donald clears his throat.

"Amy, you know Mommy hasn't been here for a while. She's been needing a rest. But she wasn't just tired, she was very sick. And today, God decided that since Mommy couldn't get better, he would take her to heaven where she'll be an angel watching over all of us. So now Mommy is with God," Donald says slowly.

"With God?" Amy asks.

"That's right honey, with God," Donald replies. A concerned look comes over her face.

"When's she coming back, Daddy?" Donald pauses and looks at his sons, and then to his daughter.

"Honey, Mommy isn't coming back." Donald says, his voice cracking. Amy begins to cry as Donald holds her and rocks her gently.

"Amy, Daddy's here and your brothers are here. And Mommy will always be looking down from heaven." Both of the boys are weeping as they watch their father and sister. After several minutes, the phone rings. Randy stands and picks it up. He covers the mouth piece.

"Dad, it's Grandma Plant."

"Tell her I'll call her back," Donald replies.

At DuPont Funeral Home in Matteson, people arrive shortly after the immediate family. The heavy scent of flowers dominates the room. To Randy, this doesn't represent the scent of flowers in nature. At her white casket, lined with pink satin, Randy breaks down again. Donald's hands rests on both of his son's shoulders. Randy composes himself, then wipes his eyes. Brian stands beside his brother and father, head bowed, weeping quietly, when a tall gray-haired man wearing black walks over.

"Mister Taylor, may I see you in my office?" he whispers.

Once inside, Mr. DuPont closes the door and instructs Donald to have a seat. The funeral director sits behind his desk.

"Mr. Taylor, with this terrible winter we've been having, the ground is frozen. We won't be able to bury your wife, until the weather breaks. We will keep her here until it does. We'll give you a call once Saint Anthony's cemetery notifies us. Will this be alright with you?"

"Yes Mister DuPont. That will be fine. I want to think that this is all a bad dream, and I'll wake up with her in my arms. We were going to celebrate our twentieth anniversary this week."

"I'm very sorry. I know how hard this must be for you and the children," the funeral director says.

"Thank you Mister DuPont for all you've done." The two men stand and shake hands. Out in the hallway, Donald removes his wedding band, and places it in his pocket.

After the second visitation , the funeral reception is held at Mr. Benny's restaurant on Cicero Avenue. Randy sips his coffee. With no appetite, he now picks at his food. He's remembering the first day of school, when he was entering third grade. Tammy had walked Randy to his bus stop. His friends were nearby.

"Give mommy a kiss," she said. Randy complied reluctantly but pushed her away when she tried to give him a hug.

"Oh Mom, the guys are lookin'." It was one of the last times that he had kissed her. Being the oldest child, Randy had learned at a young age that it's not cool to kiss your *mother.*

"You're going to eat your steak, aren't you, son?"

"Yeah, sure Dad." But the steak is left, hardly touched.

The next week-end, eight more inches of snow fall on Cook County. The Taylor routine is established once more. When the school and work week begins, Randy walks slowly to the boy's locker room after second period. His physical education class will start in eight minutes. On his way to the gym, people say hi to him. Crossing paths with Barbi, she kisses him on the cheek.

"I'm so sorry for you Randy. Are you doing ok?" she asks.

"Hanging in there," he replies weakly.

"I'll keep you and your family in my prayers," she says.

"Thank you Barbi. That's very kind of you." Barbi hugs him then leaves.

In the locker room, Randy slowly changes. As he sits on the bench, he thinks,

I don't feel like going to gym. I don't feel like going to my classes. I don't feel like studying. I don't wanna pick-up Amy. I don't feel like cooking. I don't feel like doing nothin'. But I have to move on—oh Mom, I love you and miss you so much.

Minutes later, Randy slowly leaves the locker room. Near the gym, he passes two girls. One of them blushes, as another places her hand over her mouth. *What the hell are they giggling about?* he thinks. Randy looks.

"Oh shit!" he says as he runs back to the locker room. Randy realizes he's in his underwear.

Several mornings later, Randy is frying bacon, and making blueberry pancakes. Donald is pouring himself a cup of coffee. He pours a little cream in, then takes the lid off the small bowl. It's empty.

"Randy, are we out of sugar?"

"Yes Dad, but I put some brown sugar in my coffee. It tastes pretty good. You should try it."

"Sure," Donald says. Taking the bag out from the cupboard, he opens it and places one teaspoon in his coffee. He stirs it and sips it.

"Yeah, it tastes good." Donald places another teaspoon in his cup. When the food is on the table, he seats Amy on a chair, cushioned by a thick pillow.

"I'm hungry," she says.

"Lord," Donald says. "We thank You for this food we're about to eat, and we thank You for all the blessings You bestow on us each day. Amen." Randy is about to ask why he didn't mention his mother, but holds his tongue.

"Randy, do you know what today is?" Donald asks.

"Friday," he replies.

"Do you know what that means?" Donald asks.

"No sir," Randy says.

"It means we're going out to dinner tonight."

"Where?" Randy asks.

"Jardine's, New/Old Place," Donald replies.

"Excellent! I don't have to cook!"

After sixth period, Randy walks to his locker and gets his books and his jacket. On his way home, he senses a change in the air. The temperature is rising slightly. Still, Randy will continue to wear his scarf well into April.

This spring semester of 1979 is a little different. On Fridays, Donald teaches only three classes at Prairie State College. He's been given a grant to write a textbook on business. Donald picks up Amy on his way home from work.

As Randy enters the house, he's greeted with a hug from his father, and a kiss from his sister. He takes off his jacket and boots.

"Randy, you haven't seen your brother have you?"

"No Dad, I haven't. Ironically, I hardly ever see him but he should be home soon."

"That boy would be late for his own funeral," Donald says more to himself. Randy decides to shave. He walks downstairs to the half-bath and takes out his father's electric razor. Randy splashes 'Lectric Shave on his face. He's always amazed that this pre-ritual is as sweet as after shave itself. As soon as Brian gets in, Donald hands Randy his keys.

"You're driving," he says.

"Aw, thanks dad." Randy replies. As soon as Randy gets in, he puts his seatbelt on. He glances at his father.

"You're not gonna buckle up?"

"No son, I've never liked them. Besides, I have a child on my lap."

"Put on WMAQ," Brian says. Donald turns his head partly.

"Son, the wheel isn't in front of you is it?"

"No sir," Brian replies. Randy turns on WLS. The station wagon backs slowly out. Randy pushes the 'genie' button on top of the visor as the garage door noisily closes. Leaving Lakewood Estates, he turns right onto Sauk Trail.

"I love your car dad," Randy says. "I want my first car to be an LTD."

"We'll see what we can work out," The Ford turns left onto Cicero Avenue north; towards Tinley Park.

In the warmth and dimness of Jardine's New/Old Place, the Taylor party of four are escorted to their table, near a 'sculpture in the round' fireplace. A buffet seat is added to a chair for Amy. She points. "Tent on plate," she says. Donald laughs.

"No honey, that's a folded napkin," he says. The child sees a small shallow metal bowl containing a yellowish soft ball.

"I want ice cream!" Amy says as she picks up her spoon. Randy's about to say something, when Donald places his finger to his mouth. Taking a spoonful, she places it in her mouth. Her happy face is now contorted. She spits it out. "Amy, that's butter!" Donald says. At a booth nearby, are four women. One of them is a strawberry blonde. She looks not at Amy—but at Donald. She sees no wedding band.

A young lady arrives at their table.

"Hello, my name is Kim. I'll be your waitress this evening. Here are your menus. May I get you anything to drink?" The blonde in the booth turns toward her friends but still glances at Donald. The Taylors order their drinks. Five minutes later, they order their dinners. Kim arrives momentarily with three salads and one bowl of potato soup—for Donald. Randy places a little sweet and sour dressing on his salad and begins to pick at it.

"What's wrong son?" Donald asks.

"It's different without mom." The father puts his hand on his son's shoulder and tenderly says, "It's different for all of us. Now eat your salad. Your mother would want you to."

Randy's appetite builds as he slowly eats. When his steak, sautéed mushrooms and garlic mashed potatoes arrive, it's shifted to a higher gear.

"How's your classes Brian?" Donald asks.

"Okay Dad, but I'm struggling in history."

"We'll talk about it when we get home."

CHAPTER FIVE

Donald Taylor has seen Iris Johnson, but only peripherally. Iris is new and is usually with a group of people. This time, she is holding books and folders against her bosom. On this bitter cold day in February, 1979, Donald walks into the faculty lounge to get a cup of coffee. Third period is his free period. Iris is at a vending machine. She is wearing black boots, with black slacks, an orange silk blouse and her strawberry blond hair is medium length. Her left arm is in a sling. Donald notices her figure.

"What happened to your arm?" he asks.

"I had an operation on my tendons," she replies. Iris pushes the rectangular plastic door with her right arm and picks up her candy bar with her right hand. She stands from bending over. Donald notices she's as tall as he is.

"Would you like some coffee?" Donald asks.

"That would be nice. Sure. Cream, no sugar." Donald prepares her beverage from the counter then hands it to her. He extends his hand.

"My name is Donald Taylor. Please to meet you." She gives him a firm handshake.

"I'm Iris Johnson. Nice to meet you Mister Taylor."

"Oh, call me Don." The two sit at a table facing each other.

"You're new here, aren't you?" Donald asks.

"Yes. A whole two months," she chuckles.

"How long have you been here Don?" she asks.

"Fifteen years."

"Well, that's just a little longer than me!" The two laugh.

The next Saturday evening Randy is at his desk working on his geometry assignment. Normally, he'd be out with friends, but his grade for this class is a C minus. He knows he has to get it higher. The bedroom door opens.

"Randy, Dad wants to see ya."

Randy walks into the bathroom where Donald is shaving.

"Son, do you have any plans for tonight?"

"I might go bowling with some friends later on," Randy says.

"Well, Brian is going to the movies with his buddies. You wouldn't mind babysitting—would you?"

"No, I guess I don't. You going to a meeting?" Randy asks.

"I've got a date," Donald mouths.

Randy's heart sinks to his stomach.

"Gee dad, isn't it kind of early?"

"I'll be the judge of that son, not you."

"Mom hasn't been gone that long."

"I said I'll be the judge of that!"

Randy has never seen this side of his father. Donald walks past him as Randy muffles a "yes sir."

"Daddy, read me story," Amy says.

"Honey, Randy will read to you. I have to go out for a while."

"Where?" she asks in her high voice.

"Daddy has to go to a meeting." Randy walks back to his desk with a scowl on his face. He tries to resume his studies, but to no avail. He walks downstairs where his father and his sister are in the kitchen.

"Fix your sister a small bowl of ice cream, would you?" Donald asks.

Like I don't have anything else to do! Randy thinks.

Donald walks downstairs and takes a quick shower.

The next day is Sunday. After church, Randy takes an hour nap, resumes his studies, then gets ready to go to Lakewood Bowl. *I'm glad I'm going to work tonight. It'll take my mind off of Dad's new girlfriend. Whoever she is, she'll never replace my mother. I'd puke for twenty-four hours if I could have her back.* Randy bundles up, takes two of his textbooks with him then leaves.

Sunday is open bowling which means you can bowl whether you're in a league or not. Out of thirty-two lanes, eight are being used. Randy punches in, puts on his thin cranberry porter's jacket and does some minor cleanup of several tables near the lanes. He walks to the 'control center' when he's finished.

"Joe, since we're kind of slow, would you mind if I study a little in the storage room?"

"Naw, your grades are important. If I need ya, I'll call ya."
"Thanks, I appreciate it." Randy takes his textbooks from the office, walks between the bar and entrance foyer and 'hits' them. Many of the people have arrived just before Randy. It'll be a while until they're finished. Ten minutes later he says, "I'm getting paid to do my homework!" Randy chuckles. He takes a cigarette out, lights it, then continues reading.

That night, Randy has trouble sleeping. He still feels his mother's presence. When sleep finally comes, it is short. His alarm goes off all too soon. Randy is groggy, but he forces himself out of bed. He has something to do.

After getting dressed, and putting his jacket on, Randy passes his father in the hallway.

"You aren't having breakfast son?"

"Naw, I've got my science project to finish." It's a lie. Randy leaves the warm house and walks quickly to Rich South High. Once he gets to the second floor of the school Randy walks towards the counselor's section. Opening the glass door, he finds the receptionist on the phone. She points towards the seats. Randy takes off his jacket and sits. A minute later, she hangs up.

"May I help you?" she asks.

"I'm here to see Mr. Jenkins."

"What's your name?"

"Randy Taylor." The receptionist picks up the phone and pushes a button.

"Mister Jenkins, a student by the name of Randy Taylor is here to see you. "He'll be with you shortly."

Moments later, a short, clean shaven man with balding brownish-gray hair and a grayish-blue suit appears. "Good morning Randy. Follow me." Walking down the hallway towards his office the counselor asks, "How are you doing?"

"I've been better," Randy replies. The two enter a small but cozy office. A lamp emits its soft glow on a small table. A small bubbling fountain spills over stones near the corner of the office. A counter is on the other side of his desk. It contains a cookie jar, a tiny refrigerator, and a coffee maker that has just finished brewing. The aroma fills the office. Two soft dark blue chairs are in front of his wooden desk.

"Close the door Randy. Take a seat. Would you like some coffee?"

"Sure Mister Jenkins."

"Cream and sugar?"

"Yes sir. That'd be fine," Randy says as he places his jacket on the other chair.

"How can I help you?" he asks.

"Well Mister Jenkins, other than talking to you about my schedules, this is the first time I've talked to you on a personnel basis." The counselor nods.

"You know I've recently lost my mother."

"I know, I'm very sorry Randy."

"Well, here's the problem. My dad is already seeing another woman. And my mother isn't even buried." Randy chokes. "I find this very hard."

"Randy, there is an old story about an eagle who loved flying, as I'm sure all eagles do. But this particular eagle *really* loved to fly. One day, this eagle loses a wing. He can walk, he can hop around—but he can't fly. He barely survives on what food he's able to capture. And then after a period of time, he miraculously grows another wing. Now the eagle can fly again." A puzzled expression appears on Randy's face. He takes a drink of his coffee.

"Are you saying, my dad is like an eagle who wants to fly again?"

"Exactly," the counselor replies.

"Randy, I've known your parents since their I.S.U. days and I'm certain that your father loves your mother dearly and nothing will change that."

"But why is this happening so fast?" Randy asks.

"I once knew a man who had been married for twenty-five years. After a brief illness, his wife dies. He was so broken hearted he vowed that he would never marry again. Just sixteen months later, he meets a young woman. They fall in love and the 'knot' is tied." After a pause, Jenkins says, " That young bride was my grandmother."

Randy takes another drink of his coffee then slowly says, "But this isn't even sixteen months later, my mom just died! Why couldn't he wait a little?"

"Randy, when someone loses their mate, they can be absolutely devastated and lost. This woman may be providing some sort of comfort that he desperately needs right now. I understand your feelings. Losing you mother is horrible, but to be a surviving spouse can sometimes make a person feel that they just can't deal with the emptyness."

"But why is this happening so fast?"

"Maybe you can't begin to understand the depth of your father's suffering. And even if this isn't the proper thing to do, it may be the only thing he can do to ease the pain right now. But here's what's important, Randy—the fact that your dad loves you and your brother and sister. Nothing will change that. Do you understand?"

"I don't know. I just don't know anything anymore. I have to get ready for first period. Thank you for your insight Mister Jenkins."

"Things will settle down for your family. Please believe that. If you ever want to talk again, I'll be here. You hang in there, now." The two shake hands.

The icicles on gutters begin melting. The huge piles of snow are getting smaller. Randy leaves for school minus his scarf and knit cap. On March 5th, 1979, Donald gets a call from Mr. DuPont the funeral director. The ground is thawed.

The next week-end Donald drives his sons to the funeral home. Both sets of grandparents are in attendance, along with several close friends and relatives. Among them are a Great Uncle, Timothy Brady who is chief of police for the suburb of Chicago Heights. Amy remains at home with Stephi.

Tammy's casket is closed. Her best friend Patricia Ryan gives the eulogy. Reverend Conners of Flossmoor Community Church leads the mourners in prayer.

"Dear Father in Heaven. We thank you for your servant, Tammy Lynn Taylor. May You keep her forever in Your embrace. " Many of the mourners wear black. The pallbearers are friends of Donald and Tammy's. When Reverend Conners is finished, the mourners file past the casket, paying their last respects. Randy and Brian kneel together, weeping softly. Later, Brian gets up but Randy remains. He whispers.

"I will always try to do what's right mom. I love you very much." He slowly stands, kisses the casket then walks outside with his head down. The father kneels.

Donald Taylor walks outside wiping his eyes with a handkerchief. The white casket is carried by the six pallbearers into a gray hearse with a black vinyl top. Donald and his sons are escorted to a black limousine. Mister DuPont opens the door for them. The funeral procession makes its way to Saint Anthony's cemetery in Chicago.

Monday morning is different. The previous evening, Donald had phoned his boss to inform him he wouldn't be in. He gets Amy up, washes her face and gets her dressed. In the kitchen, Randy is already dressed, and brewing coffee after a quick smoke in the utility room. Brian is slowly getting out of bed. Donald walks his daughter downstairs by the hand into the kitchen.

"Good morning Dad. Morning Amy," Randy says.

"Good morning son."

"Morning Randy," the child says. The oldest sibling picks up the youngest and gives her a kiss. He sets her down on her cushioned chair.

"What do you want me to cook dad?"

"How 'bout toast and cereal," Donald replies.

"Can't go wrong with that!" Randy places four slices of bread in the toaster. Taking out three boxes of cereal, he prepares Amy's Chocolate Toasties. Brian comes down and bids everyone a good morning. The family bows their heads as Donald says grace.

"Lord, we thank you for this food, and for the daily blessings You bestow on us. Amen." Randy looks at his father.

"Dad, why aren't you wearing a suit?"

"I'm taking the day off. I have some things I have to do." "Will you pick up Amy at three-thirty?" Randy asks.

"I will, I'll even start dinner, although I'll need your help son. You know I'm not much of a cook." Ten minutes later, Randy is excused. He puts his plate and glass in the sink and rinses them off.

The sun is shining. A warm spring breeze is blowing. Near Sauk Trail, Randy sees a puddle covered with thin ice. Thinking it's a quarter of an inch deep, he steps on it. His whole boot submerges. Randy removes it quickly.

"Damn!" he says out loud.

After Donald takes Amy to Kindercare, he arrives back to an empty house. Walking in his house, he makes his way to the master bedroom. Opening Tammy's closet, he views the many dresses. He lifts up a hanger that holds a light purple one and places it across his left shoulder.

"Oh Tammy, he says through his tears, I always hoped that I would go first. Darling, my love for you will remain with me forever."

Minutes later, Donald gets to work. He takes the dresses to his car. This procedure takes four trips. Next, he removes the shoeboxes. After these are loaded, he walks back to his bedroom. Looking in the empty closet, Donald goes back in time to when they first moved in.

"Gee Tam, I believe this is your largest closet ever!"

"Well Don, it'll get filled up soon. You know how I love dresses."

"So that's why I buy second hand suits!" Tammy pokes her husband in the ribs as he laughs.

Donald stares at the empty closet for several minutes more then slowly closes both doors. He walks downstairs, and places the metal latch to the right so the screen door can close. Locking his house, he closes the rear door of his vehicle, gets inside and starts the engine, oblivious to his seatbelt. Donald backs out slowly. He makes his way to Christian Help on Sauk Trail in nearby Park Forest.

In biology class, Randy sits calmly. His teacher, Mrs. Drysdale is handing back tests. He isn't anxious or nervous. He already knows what his grade is. Mrs. Drysdale announces a name when she hands back each test. She walks slowly.

"Mister Webster—Miss Cunningham—Miss Hastings—Mister Galloway—Mister Taylor. Mrs. Drysdale hands Randy his test while giving him a look that says, "You've done better than this." Randy looks at a red lettered grade. A large 'D plus' is at the top. Mrs. Drysdale continues. Miss Jones—Mister Rawlings—Mister Gonzales…"

At Christian Help, a man in his thirties helps Donald. After the wagon is unloaded, Sister Doris walks up to him.

"Thank you kind sir for your generous donation. May God bless you."

"Thank you sister. He already has." Donald gives the man a five dollar tip, then walks to his car. Donald, realizing he's hungry, drives to Cal's on Sauk Trail in Richton Park. The professor has never liked eating in any car. Parking his wagon, he gets out. Walking in, he orders a large coffee and a corn beef sandwich with coleslaw on the side. Taking his tray to a table, Donald thinks about the illness that he's never revealed to any one but his wife. Sometimes when his depression kicks in, he can't stand the sight of food. Other times, he is constantly hungry. Donald has chosen not to take any medication for these waves of extreme sadness, opting to use prayer instead. *Lord Jesus, thank you for my family and for my late wife. I miss her terribly and yet all the calls in life, You make. I still have my children, my job, my house I praise You everyday. And I know that the things in life that puzzle me are the answers that You already have. And by the way—I thank You for the food I'm about to eat. Amen.*

When he arrives back at his house, Donald picks up Tammy's jewelry box. His first thought is to bury it. Then Donald decides to put it in the crawl space, which is behind the closet downstairs in the family room. Walking in this room, he sets the golden box on his easy chair, and begins to remove items from the crawl space. A vacuum cleaner, clothes on hangers, several bowling balls … After the items are removed, Donald opens a small door.

To the left is a switch. He turns it on. A small light bulb in the center gives off a soft glow because it is covered with dust. Donald looks around. To him, this area of the house resembles a tomb. Donald leaves the closet carefully and stands up. Taking the jewelry box in his left hand he squats down and stretches to his left. Setting the box down gently, he says aloud, "It'll be out of the way. And I'll know where it is, if I ever need it." He backs out slowly and begins returning the items he had removed.

As the weeks turn into May, the excitement at Rich South High builds. The weather is warmer, the grass is greener, trees are flowering, and Randy is looking forward to becoming a senior. He finds himself babysitting Amy most Saturday nights.

Going over all of his tests one Thursday evening, Randy discovers his GPA has dipped from a 3 point 8 to a 2 point 5. *I've got to get it higher next year,* he says to himself.

At Nino's Pizza on Route 30/Lincoln Highway in Matteson the following evening, Donald wipes Amy's face. She fidgets.

"Honey, please be still for Daddy—okay?"

"Dad, I'm working late tomorrow night. Can Brian baby sit?" Randy asks.

"Sure," Donald replies.

"But I've got a date!" Brian says in protest.

"Cancel it," Donald replies as Brian scowls.

"Look son, Randy does all of the cooking, he picks up Amy after school, and he does most of the babysitting. Now, we all have to do our share—don't we?" he asks. "Yes sir," Brian says. He excuses himself to go to the bathroom. Randy cuts more of his lasagna.

"Dad, I've another question. After work tomorrow night, may I have a beer?" Randy asks, mouthing the last word. Donald pauses then replies softly,

"Just one. And don't drink in front of you know who," Donald moves his eyes towards Amy. "As a matter of fact, use my large coffee mug to hide it—okay?" Donald asks.

"No problem Dad," replies Randy. Brian comes back from the bathroom.

"I want ice cream," Amy says.

"Finish your lasagna and salad honey," Donald replies. Moments later, the father speaks. "I'm bringing my friend Iris over this week-end. I think you all will like her."

"Which night?" Brian asks.

"I haven't decided," Donald replies. Randy continues eating. His father's *girlfriend* is mentioned often. Now soon, Randy will meet her. He's less than enthused. His mother's love and presence remains with him.

This May Saturday in 1979 dawns sunny. Randy is dressed by eight. The rest of his family is asleep. The oldest sibling makes a pot of coffee, then walks into the utility room to have a cigarette. The stillness of the kitchen is unique to him. Randy has mixed feelings about this as he drinks his coffee. The quietness is soothing yet haunting because it lacks his mother.

Randy is working a double shift today because one of the porters is ill and he's looking forward to it because he can use the money. Randy rinses his dishes then quietly sets them in the sink. He wipes off the kitchen table, brushes his teeth, and leaves the house without his jacket.

After punching in, Randy bids Joe a good morning.

"Morning Randy." The assistant manager's voice is somber and slightly angry.

"What's wrong Joe?" Randy asks.

"I don't know why Mrs. Patterson doesn't fire that boy."

"Shaun?" Randy asks.

"Yeah him. Hell, he ain't sick. He's either getting into trouble or getting laid."

"Well, he's giving me his hours and that means a bigger paycheck," Randy says.

"You're a good man," Joe says.

"I do my best," Randy replies. The teenager puts his porter's jacket on, straightens his tie and begins work by cleaning the parking lot first. Slowly people arrive for open bowling. At twelve noon, Joe orders corn beef sandwiches from Cal's, as the skies darken. Twenty lanes out of thirty-two are being used.

That evening, Brian and Amy eat dinner of soup and sandwiches. In the bathroom Donald puts on aftershave and walks downstairs to the kitchen, wearing his brown sports coat.

"Don't go, Daddy. Don't go," Amy says. Donald squats down beside his youngest child.

"Daddy's only going to be gone for a couple of hours. Brian is gonna play games with you—okay? Now finish your soup and sandwich and Brian will give you ice cream." Donald gives Amy a hug and a kiss. The father stands and leaves. The child begins to whimper. Brian gets up from the table and retrieves a pint of raspberry ice cream from the freezer. He opens the lid.

"Look Amy. This ice cream hasn't been touched yet! Now finish your dinner and I'll give you a big spoon, and you can take all the ice cream you want—okay." A smile appears on her face. She finishes her dinner.

An hour later, Brian and Amy are playing a children's board game in the family room when they hear the front door open. Amy runs upstairs with Brian following.

"Randy," Amy calls.

"What happened?" Brian asks, looking at the soaking wet Randy.

"The electricity went out at Lakewood Bowl. I ran home. In this monsoon!" "I've gotta take a quick shower."

"I'm gonna call my girlfriend," Brian says.

"Well, you're not leaving until after I take a shower."

"I know, I'm not stupid."

Randy walks upstairs and gets a change of clothes from his drawers. "Read me story Randy," she says. He squats down.

"I will Amy, but first I have to take a shower and put on some dry cloths. Randy looks toward the kitchen, "Brian, get off the phone and watch your sister!" Brian holds up his middle finger, not realizing that Randy doesn't see him.

"Amy, go stand beside Brian until he gets off the phone—okay?" The child obeys. Fifteen minutes later, Randy comes out of the bathroom in dry clothes and combing his black hair.

"You going out with your honey, Brian?"

"Naw, she's out with her girlfriends."

"Let's play a game!" Amy says. Randy sits down on the floor next to Amy and Brian joins them.

"You can't make up the rules as you go along Brian!"

"I'm not! We're *supposed* to do it this way."

"Well, the rules say to do it that way!"

"Let *me* show you," Amy says.

"We'll do it your way, sister," Randy agrees. A deafening roar of thunder booms across the sky. Amy begins to cry. Randy stands and picks her up. He sits on Donald's easy chair and begins rocking gently—comforting his sister. The thunder in the distance, sounds like a deformed bowling ball rolling on a lane.

"It's okay Amy. That thunder is just a little noise," Randy says with care. Brian turns on the television to "Fantasy Island" with Ricardo Montalban. Ten minutes later, all three hear the garage door opener.

"Daddy's home!" Amy exclaims. She's upstairs in the foyer in a flash.

"Let's go meet Dad's new squeeze." Randy says, masking his sadness with sarcasm. Donald opens the front door with a tall blonde woman behind him. He picks up his daughter and gives her a kiss.

"How's my little sweet pea?"

"Iris, this is my youngest, Amy. My oldest son, Randy and middle son, Brian." The boys take turns shaking her hand.

"Please to meet you," each brother says.

"Likewise," Iris replies.

"Let's go downstairs," Donald says, as he sets Amy down.

In the family room, the three resume their board game. Iris sits on the sofa, as Donald takes off his sports coat. Randy looks at Iris.

"Would you like to play?" he asks.

"No thank you, I'll just watch."

"Iris, would you like a drink?" Donald asks.

"Scotch on the rocks, if you have it?."

"Sure thing. You kids want pop?" the father asks. Brian and Amy accept but Randy says, "Hey dad. I haven't had my beverage in your large coffee mug. Will you fix it for me if you be so kind?"

Donald looks at him as if he's crazy.

"You have broken legs?" the father asks. Randy stands and follows him to the utility room. Donald prepares two drinks, one for him, the other for Iris. He also prepares two colas. Randy retrieves the large coffee mug from the cabinet then gets a can of Old Style beer from the refrigerator. He opens it, tilts the mug and pours.

"I thought you were going to work late."

"The electricity went out on account of this storm."

"Who took you home?" the father asks.

"I ran. Dad, if Joe calls tomorrow, is it okay if I go to work?"

"Only if you finish your homework." "Give these to your brother and sister."

"Yes sir," Randy replies.

"Be careful not to spill, Amy," Randy says as he sets her cola on a coaster taken from the bottom of the cocktail table.

"Sank you," the child says. Randy walks back to the utility room and retrieves his 'coffee'. Iris sits on the sofa sipping her drink, wearing a polite smile. Randy senses it isn't genuine.

Half an hour later, Amy rubs her eyes. Iris yawns.

"Do you want me to take you home?" Donald asks.

"Yes, it's time," she replies.

"I'll put Amy to bed," Randy says.

"I'll be back in half an hour," Donald replies. The boys shake Iris's hand.

"It was nice meeting you," Brian says,

"Likewise," Iris replies.

As Randy tucks Amy in, she asks, "When's Daddy coming home?"

"He'll be home soon. Now you get to sleep—okay? Little children need a lot of sleep so they can grow." Brian is sitting on the sofa watching television. Randy sits in the easy chair.

"Here it is Randy. Here it is!" Brian passes gas and begins laughing. Randy shakes his head and says, "You sick bastard!" He stands and walks to the utility room where he lights a cigarette. Moments later, Brian turns the TV off and walks upstairs. Randy finishes his cigarette then crushes out the butt. He heads upstairs as well, making sure the porch light is on.

In their twin beds, the brothers talk.

"What do you think of Iris?" Brian asks.

"I don't know what I think. I can't even get the fact that Mom's gone into my head. How can he be with her? I hate all of this. There's something about this Iris I can't put my finger on."

CHAPTER SIX

On Randy's last day as a junior, a somber rain is falling. Ever the optimist, he thinks; *I only have half a day. And when my last class is over, I go to Lakewood Bowl to work full time!* He is making it a habit to save eighty percent of his paycheck for his first car.

At the end of the workweek, the Taylor family goes out to dinner, just as they did when Tammy was alive. On this particular Friday in July, while everyone is in the wagon, Donald says, "Kids, before we eat dinner, I'm going to pick-up Iris."
Randy is disappointed. He enjoys this family time together.

Donald pulls up to a small white house in Chicago Heights. "Amy, you'll have to sit in the back with the boys—okay?" When Iris gets into the car, Randy smells her strong perfume.

"Hello kids," she says as she buckles up.

"Hello Iris," Brian says.

"Hi Iwis," Amy says. Randy offers a subdued greeting. *She can't be much older than I am. What's she doing calling me a kid?* Randy thinks.

The LTD wagon makes its way to a Chinese restaurant, five minutes away. Each place has a paper placement that contains a Chinese calendar. Randy's sign is the tiger. Iris's sign is the monkey. Unknown to both, each sign should avoid each other.

After orders are taken, Donald looks around the table to be sure he has everyone's attention.

"Kids, I have an announcement to make." He places his arm around Iris.

"We're getting married!" Donald says as he glows with happiness.

Randy feels sick to his stomach.

"Con-congratulations," he says flatly.

"I don't know what to say," Brian says somberly.

"I have a new mommy?" Amy asks.

"That's right honey. Iris is going to be your new mommy," Donald says as the young woman smiles. Randy can't believe his father's timing. Donald is changing much too fast and Randy hates it.

"When are you…" Brian is unable to finish the sentence.

"We haven't set a date yet, but it'll probably be in August," Donald says. The entrees are served and Donald says grace. "Lord, we thank you for this food, we thank you for all of the blessings we receive everyday, and we thank you for Iris. Amen." Only Donald is smiling.

The next day, Randy resumes his running. Not only does he face his last year at Rich South High, he faces his last year on the cross-country team. He wants the upcoming season to be his best.

Randy keeps a record of the distance run plus the number of cigarettes smoked that day. *I've got to cut down on my smokes,* he thinks. Randy has a unique power to change any habit. Within days, Randy is down to one cigarette, although he smokes this one slowly.

Lying in bed, Brian sets his book down on his chest. Randy changes into his pajama bottoms and a clean t-shirt.

"What do you think of Dad getting remarried?" Brian asks.

"I sure as hell ain't gonna call her 'Mom'," Randy replies. He slips in between his sheets and gazes at a black and white 5X7 framed photo of Tammy on the nightstand between the twin beds.

Iris spends more time at the house. Amy likes her, Brian is politely quiet, but Randy keeps his distance. After coming home from running one afternoon, Randy finds Iris at the stove, Donald writing a letter of recommendation at the table, and his siblings playing a board game. Amy runs to him as he picks her up.

"How's my little sister doing?" he asks.

"Fine Randy. You're sweating!" Randy sets her down and gives his father a hug.

"How was your run?" Donald asks.

"Excellent. I'm up to five miles a day." Randy says. He looks at Iris, feeling a little sick that she's in his mother's domain.

"Cooking dinner uh?" he asks.

"It'll be ready in twenty minutes," Iris replies.

"That'll give me time to take a quick shower. What are we haven'?"

"Tuna casserole."

After his shower, Randy gets dressed and heads to the kitchen. Everyone is seated. An oval pot that's covered, is in the center of the table on two pot holders. Randy is seated next to Iris. Donald has begun a new tradition. Upon saying grace everyone holds hands. Randy holds Iris's right hand, but he feels uncomfortable. Heads are bowed.

"Lord, for what we are about to receive, we are truly thankful. Amen." Iris stands and removes the lid. Randy's jaw drops. His eyes stare at what looks like 'C' rations. He immediately knows what Iris did wrong.

"You forgot to make the chicken gravy," he says.

"I knew it didn't look right," Iris replies. Randy walks to the counter and fills a medium size pot with water and places it on the stove. He shows Iris where the packages of gravy powder are.

"Let's eat our salads while we wait for the water to boil," Donald says. Later, when the pot boils, Randy opens both packages and empties its contents. He takes out a large metal wisk from the drawer and hands it to Iris.

"Stir, until it all dissolves." He slightly lowers the gas flame.

Later that night, after Amy is put to bed, and Donald leaves to take Iris home, the brothers talk in their beds.

"I wonder why Iris wears those black shoes all of the time," Brian says.

"They're *announcing* shoes," Randy replies.

"Why do you call them that?" Brian asks.

"Because she's announcing her arrival. Goodnight little brother."

"Goodnight Randy." The lamp is turned off.

By mid-summer, Randy is up to eight miles a day and zero cigarettes. The craving is there, but it's controllable. Randy figures he won't be able to get a cross-country scholarship. In his mind, he's only average. And college will be unfamiliar territory.

Randy's hair is longer, and his tan is darker. At Lakewood Bowl, he talks to several girls but is too shy to ask them out. His intense focus on getting into college pushes most everything else to the side.

The wedding is set for the second weekend in August at Flossmoor Community Church in nearby Homewood. By the end of July, Randy weighs himself in the upstairs bathroom. He's lost ten pounds; 181 down from 191. His savings are growing for his first car and his first year of college. While shaving the next evening, Randy discovers his beard is coming in a lot thicker. As he turns off Donald's electric razor, an idea comes to him. He puts it away in the medicine cabinet, splashes after shave on his face, then walks upstairs. In the family room, Brian, Amy and Iris are playing a board game. At the dining room table, Donald is organizing his syllabus for the fall semester. Randy walks up to him.

"Pardon me Dad, may I talk to you?"

"Sure son. I need a little break anyway. What's up?" Donald asks as his son pulls out a chair and sits.

"I've been thinking. In another year, I'm going to college. Two of my choices are out of state and I'm gonna need a car. I was wondering, would you be interested in letting me buy the LeSabre from you? Donald rubs his chin as he pauses.

"You've been working a lot this summer. Have you saved any money?" Donald asks.

"Yes sir. Almost eight hundred dollars," Randy replies.

"Is that money going for your tuition?" Donald asks.

"Well—some of it is and some of it is going for a car," Randy replies.

Donald places his right ankle on his left knee. He clicks his pen.

"You know son, toward the end of his life, your great grandfather wasn't really taking very good care of that Buick. I tell you what Randy—I'll give it to you."

"Aw, thanks Dad!" He gives his father a hug.

"Before you get too excited son, remember that car needs some work. The timing belt's going bad, it needs a tune up, new tires and it's leaking a little oil. The money to fix these things will be coming out of your wallet. Next year, I can pay a small portion of your tuition, but you have to make up the difference. After you get the Buick fixed, save every dollar that you can."

"Yes sir. I will," Randy replies. Donald takes out his set of keys and removes two of them and hands them to Randy.

"Get duplicates at the hardware store just in case you lose them."

It's overcast on the day of the wedding. The air is cooler because of the cloud cover. Randy appreciates this because suits make him sweat. A small group waits inside Flossmoor Community Church. Among them are Donald's parents, Perry and Esther Taylor, Iris's Uncle Chris and cousin Sheila Johnson from Rockford and a few Taylor family friends.

Donald emerges from the rear of the church with his best man Frank Janis, a colleague from Praire State College.

Randy's holding Amy when she sees her father.

"Hi Daddy!" she calls as she waves her hand. Randy hushes her.

"Amy, you have to be quiet. We're in church." Moments later, an organist begins to play, "Here Comes the Bride" as her Uncle Chris walks Iris down the aisle. A loud clap of thunder startles everyone as Amy clings to Randy, drops of water pelt the roof. The uncle kisses Iris, then steps into a pew. The Reverend speaks; "Dearly Beloved. We are gathered here today to join this man and this woman. If anyone objects to the union of this marriage, say so now, or forever hold your peace." *I oughta stand up right now,* Randy thinks. The Reverend pauses then says, "In the beginning, God created Adam, but Adam was alone …"

The storm is so loud that Randy has trouble hearing the Reverend, but at the same time, is only paying half attention. *Isn't it bad luck for a bride to have rain on her wedding day?* Amy lays her head on her brother's shoulder. He rocks her gently.

"You may kiss the bride," the Reverend says. Randy looks away.

"I now present to you Mister and Missus Donald Taylor." Everyone but Randy politely applauds. Sheila Johnson has just turned her head and notices this. The newly weds walk down the aisle as the organist plays an upbeat tune.

When Randy reaches to Iris, he shakes her hand. "Good luck," he says flatly. Randy hugs Donald.

Donald and Iris take a short honeymoon in Wisconsin. Randy free of babysitting duties since Grandma and Grandpa Taylor are staying at the house, and cross-country practice begins the next day.

When Donald and Iris return from their honeymoon, the new lady of the house rearranges the counter in the kitchen She hangs new curtains, and a painting over the sofa in the living room. The artwork consists of a woman wearing a white dress. Her blouse runs up to her jaw line. Her chestnut hair is tied up in a bun. She sits near a waterfall, reading a letter. Red and yellow flowers are near her feet. A partial rainbow is in the sky. Randy doesn't think highly of the painting since he's not much into art in the first place. In fact Randy doesn't care for any of the changes Iris has made to the house.

Since his father's marriage to Iris, Randy Taylor is again leading the life of a normal teenager. He attends cross-country practice, he works at Lakewood Bowl, he works on his Buick LeSabre, he hangs out with his friends and buys record albums at Lincoln Mall. His burdened has been lifted. That's why he's caught off-guard when he comes home from practice one Thursday afternoon to find Iris and Donald putting suitcases in the car.

"Oh, Randy, I'm glad you're home. We need to talk with you."

"What's up, Dad?"

"Do you remember Iris' Uncle Chris from Rockford?"

"Sure, from the wedding."

"Well, Iris was just notified that he passed away last night."

Randy looks over at Iris who seems to have no expression at all. *Maybe it's just her way of handling grief*, he thinks.

"So son, we'll be heading for Rockford in a couple of hours. And since there is really no other family, Iris will be making all the arrangements. We were hoping that you could look after Amy and everything else here at home until we get back on Sunday. And of course, we'll be asking Brian to help as well."

"I'll have to rearrange some things but with Brian's help—and oh, Iris, you have my sympathy."

Iris only nods in response.

Randy is in his room doing is homework when he hears the phone ring. Twenty minutes later Donald and Iris walk upstairs and Iris goes directly into their bedroom and closes the door. Donald appears in the doorway to Randy's room.

"There's been a change of plans, son. It seems that Iris' uncle had requested that her cousin Sheila handle everything. He wanted no viewing or service and has apparently donated his body to some medical school—so that's that. We won't be going anywhere and you're free to do whatever you had planned."

The 1979-80 school year commences. On Wednesday's, Donald teaches only two classes. He walks quickly to his LTD wagon, gets in and, as usual, doesn't think to put his seatbelt on.

After lunch, Randy heads for the library. Seniors have their privileges. Instead of attending study hall in a classroom, seniors are allowed to go to the library/media center. Randy has always loved the library and is good friends with Mrs. Mitchell, the librarian.

Upon sitting at a cubicle, Randy feels queezy and tense. He shrugs it off as he concentrates on his American History assignment. Twenty-minutes later, he places his hand on his stomach as beads of sweat form on his forehead. He can no longer ignore this. *I've got a bug,* he thinks. Closing his textbook, Randy places his folder, notebook and texts in his briefcase. Getting up, he slowly heads for the boy's locker room. Once there, he discovers Coach Bohnam's office is locked. Taking a pen and a sheet of paper out, he writes a note explaining why he won't be at practice.

The teenager slips the sheet of paper under his door, then heads to the nurses office. There, Mrs. Walker takes his temperature.

"One hundred degrees Mister Taylor. You've got a little bug. My daughters have it but it passes quickly. I'd say by Friday you'll feel fine."

"I always feel fine on Friday Mrs. Walker," Randy says.

"Aauggh. A comedian in every crowd. I'm sending you home Randy. But I have to call your father first."

"He's at work Mrs. Walker." The head nurse pauses then says: "Go home Mister Taylor. Here's some aspirin before you go."

"Thank you Mrs. Walker," Randy says. When he walks outside, just mere steps from the nurse's office, the warm air soothes him. Since Randy is leaving early, the sun is in a higher position in the sky. To the teenager, it seems brighter. Since he's such a dedicated, loyal student, Randy feels like he's playing hooky, even though he isn't. He walks slowly home.

Upon nearing the split-level house, Randy sees Iris's 1972 Plymouth Duster in the driveway. He quickens his pace when he notices the Richton Park police cruiser.

Moments later, the teenager emerges from the house shaking his head and walking fast. Reaching Sauk Trail and heading towards Rich South High, Randy can see his brother walking towards him in the distance. Randy runs.

"Brian! Brian!" When the brothers meet, Randy collapses in his arms.'

"Randy what's wrong?"

"Dad, he, he…" but he's too overcome by tears to finish

"What—what did you say?"

"Dad's dead," Randy manages before collapsing in tears again.

"What happened? Randy, tell me what happened!

Randy takes a breath and tries to compose himself.

"A policewoman told me that when Dad left work, he pulled onto Halstead Street in Chicago Heights. A delivery truck crossed the center line, and hit him head-on." Randy runs a hand through his black hair. "Listen Brian, we've got to tell Amy before Iris does." Randy turns and runs towards Neil Armstrong

Elementary School. Brian runs too, but in the process, knocks his books against his right thigh, dropping them onto Sauk Trail. In his confusion and shock, Brian steps out onto the two-lane highway and begins to pick them up.

"Randy, wait for me!" A Datsun traveling East, swerves by the teenager, missing him by inches as the driver lays on the horn.

Moments later, Randy arrives at Neil Armstrong. "I'm here to pick up Amy Taylor. She's in Kindergarten." Randy tells the receptionist.

"Are you her legal guardian?" the young secretary asks.

"I'm her brother," Randy.

"Oh, yes, I remember you. Aren't you a senior this year?

"Please," Randy interrupts, "Can you get my sister. It's an emergency."

The young woman leaves to get Amy just as Brian enters the school. His breathing is heavy.

Moments later, the receptionist brings the child out. Amy's surprised to see her brothers as she runs to Randy, who picks her up and holds her close.

"Randy!" Amy says.

"I have to talk to my sister alone. Is it okay if we take her into that empty room over there," he asks the receptionist. "Sure. You can even close the door if you want."

Once in the room, Randy and Brian both get on their knees, with Amy in the middle.

"Amy," Randy begins in a halting voice, "You know Mommy went to heaven this spring. Well, today we found out that Daddy went to heaven too. So Mommy and Daddy will always be together. They'll always be happy and they'll never be sad."

The child remains motionless as she slowly puts two and two together.

"Daddy gone?" she whispers.

"Yes, Amy. Daddy's gone," Randy softly replies. The child's lower lip begins to quiver, and then she cries. Randy places his arms around her. Brian places his left arm around his brother and his right arm around his sister. All are weeping. When the three slowly emerge from the playroom, Randy quietly tells the receptionist, "There's been a death in the family. We've lost our father. Amy won't be here for a while."

"Oh, I'm so sorry. I understand," she replies with care. "Would you like to speak with her teacher or the principal? I know everyone will want to help any way they can."

"Thank you. Not right now. Maybe later. Thanks."

The receptionist watches the three leave with the child holding each brother's hand. Then she goes in to inform the principal.

In bed that evening Randy thinks: *Our father died, and I'm sick as a dog. Oh God, take me too.*

The next day, Iris and Randy are sitting in the office of Mr. DuPont. Brian is at home babysitting Amy. The funeral director takes out a pen and a pad of yellow business paper from his desk drawer.

"I am so sorry for your loss, but I'm here to help. Now there is a burial plot." "Yes sir, there's one next to my mother."

"Visitation will be tomorrow and Friday from three to five and from seven to nine. Will that be alright?" the funeral director asks. Randy nods.

"Now, have you thought about cremation?" Mr. DuPont asks. Iris answers *yes*.

Randy answers *no* at the same time. They look at each other.

"No, I don't want my father to be cremated," Randy says.

"I want my husband to be cremated," Iris replies coldly. "Look Iris, my father told my mother years ago that he never wanted to be cremated," Randy says, his voice rising. Mister DuPont feels uncomfortable, but realizes he's the referee.

"Mister Taylor, I don't mean to take sides, but under Illinois law, the widow is the executor of the estate. In essence, she makes the call." Randy sits fuming.

"Do what you want." Randy says as he storms out of the office and into the parking lot, lighting a cigarette.

On the way home, Randy and his stepmother argue.

"Look Iris, I've known my father a little longer than you have. Now I think if you really love him, you will respect his wishes."

"Don't play mind games with me. I am the widow. And what I say goes."

"You're not gonna bend at all, are you?" Randy says, more to himself than to Iris. After pulling into the garage, the two argue even when they get into the house. Amy has never heard two adults arguing. It moves her, and she begins to cry. Brian emerges from the bathroom as Randy picks her up and comforts her. Iris stands with her hands on her hips.

"This loss affects me too, but my word is law. What I say goes." She begins to walk upstairs then turns to look at the three.

"I've made my decision," she says as she continues on her way.

Brian looks at his brother. "What happened?"

"I'll tell you later," Randy replies as he comforts Amy.

After dinner, Brian does the dishes, Randy bathes Amy and Iris sits at the dining room table going over the funeral plans.

When Amy is put to bed, Randy reads her a story, tucks her in, and kisses her on the forehead.

"Now Amy," he says softly. "Stephi will baby sit you tomorrow. Iris, Brian and I have to go to a meeting. We won't be gone all day." The child clings to him.

"Don't leave me," she says.

"I'll never leave you honey," he replies. Randy holds her a while, then gently lays her down. He kisses her forehead again then quietly leaves as he closes the door, nearly all of the way. He quietly walks downstairs to the kitchen. He picks up a dishtowel and helps Brian. Iris emerges from the dining room.

"I'm going out for a while," she says.

"Where?" Randy asks. Iris looks at him indignantly. She picks up her purse, then leaves the house.

"Where do you think she's going?" Brian asks.

"To hell for all I care," Randy replies. The tension between the oldest sibling and his stepmother has been born.

In her Plymouth Duster, Iris can't comprehend that she's a widow at the age of twenty-eight and has three stepchildren to raise. She drives to a local bar.

"Do you know what she wants to do?" Randy asks.

"No," Brian replies.

"She wants Dad cremated."

"You've got to be kidding."

"No Brian, I wish I weren't. If she weren't a woman, I'd kick her ass!" The brothers walk downstairs to the family room, where they talk about the future, the funeral and what their father meant to them. Then Randy has an idea. Retrieving the phone book he looks up DuPont Funeral Home. Picking up the receiver, he dials the rotary phone. The owner picks up on the third ring.

"DuPont Funeral Home," he states.

"Hello Mr. DuPont. This is Randy Taylor."

"Good evening Mr. Taylor. How may I be of help?"

"Tomorrow's my father's visitation. It's very important that my brother and I pay our respects first. Is this alright?"

"Yes Mister Taylor. I can see to that," the owner says.

"We'll be over around two o'clock," Randy says.

"He'll be ready by then," the owner replies.

"Thank you Mister DuPont," Randy says.

"You're welcome Mister Taylor." They hang up their phones. The brothers talk for an hour. As Brian talks, he stops in mid sentence.

"Grandma and Grandpa Taylor are here."

"How do you know that?" Randy asks.

"I can hear their car," Brian replies. The brothers get up and walk to the door before the bell is rung. Brian opens the door and puts his finger to his lips.

"Amy's sleeping," he whispers. Each brother hugs and kisses the grandparents. Esther wipes her eyes with a handkerchief. Perry looks solemn.

"I'm so sorry for you children," Esther says. They walk down to the family room.

"I don't know if you heard yet," Randy says, "Iris wants Dad cremated."

"I'll have a talk with her," Perry says. "Would you like to stay here? You can sleep in our beds. Brian and I can sleep in the family room,"

"That's very kind of you honey, but we'll stay at The Matteson Motel," Esther says. Randy senses that his grandparents don't care for Iris either.

"Well, it's getting late. We must be going," Esther says. Hugs and kisses are exchanged, then the grandparents leave. Driving towards Sauk Trail, Perry passes a '72 Duster.

After lunch the next day, Randy takes Amy across the street where Stephie will babysit her. Arriving back at the house, he straightens his tie, while Brian gets dressed in his black suit.

When Brian is finished, Randy takes his keys from out of his pants pocket.

"Let's go little brother," Randy says.

"Shouldn't we wait for Iris?" Brian asks.

"What for?" Randy replies. The brothers walk out to the garage and get in the Buick. Randy buckles up and tells his brother to do likewise. He proceeds to start the engine. The V-8 turns over but doesn't start.

"C'mon bitch!" Randy states. The engine catches to life, but shakes.

"I'm gonna have to get a tune-up soon," he says. The Buick backs out slowly from the right side of the garage. Randy is frustrated. Backing any car out from this position is difficult due to the curved driveway.

When they're on Sauk Trail, Randy rolls down his window and tells his brother to do the same.

"That air-conditioner broke down the other day Brian, but I'll be damned if I get it fixed. Winter'll be here in six weeks." Brian reaches to turn on the radio; Randy catches his hand.

"I love music too little brother, but let's have a little respect for Dad, okay?"

"Sorry," Brian replies. After a moment of silence, Randy speaks. "Ya know Brian, today is so beautiful. The sun is shining, it's eighty-three degrees with a little wind—and we're going to see our dead father. If someone told me a year ago, our lives would be like this, I would've said, 'No way'."

"What's the meaning of all of this?" Brian asks.

"The meaning is this. Our parents are dead, and you, Amy and I are alive. We're gonna have to do our best to carry on," Randy says. Brian breaks another moment of silence.

"What about Iris?"

"Well, number one, she's gone against Dad's wish not to be cremated. Number two, she has shown her true colors, and number three, she's made my shit list," Randy says.

"I think she's gonna be tough to live with," Brian says.

"Maybe not," Randy replies softly. The 1970 Buick LeSabre pulls into the parking lot of DuPont Funeral Home in Matteson at 1:55pm.

CHAPTER SEVEN

The smell of flowers overwhelms the senses of the young men when they get inside. They're greeted by another funeral director who resembles Mister DuPont. A black sign with white lettering near a sitting room reads: Donald S. Taylor. A white arrow is beneath his name.

Francis DuPont Jr. escorts the brothers to an empty, well-lit chapel. Flowers line both walls. At the end of the chapel is a wooden casket, with a transparent white veil that hangs over a half coach lid. A tall pink lamp stands at each end of the casket. Donald's sons walk slowly. When they arrive, Brian's flood gates open. Randy places his arm around him. Donald Taylor lies in state, deep within the casket. His eyebrows are darker, his hairline is higher, and he has a wide lump on his neck that's been covered with a lot of make-up. He wears a dark brown suit, and his fingernails are manicured. To Randy, this is unusual. His father always bit his nails. Brian wipes his eyes then says:

"That doesn't look like dad."

"Well, that's a good thing," the older brother replies.

"How can that be a good thing?" Brian asks.

"Because we'll remember him in life, not in death," Randy says.

Forty minutes later after the arrival of both sets of grandparents, Iris and other family and friends begin to arrive. Great uncle, Adam Brady walks to the brothers and places his hands on their shoulders.

"Boys, I am so sorry for your loss. If there is anything I can do, please call me day or night—okay?" The boys nod, yet feel a bit uncomfortable. Uncle Adam is a distant relative who had a falling out with Donald years ago.

Many of the mourners are unknown to the brothers. Some are Donald's current and former students. At five o'clock, Linda Plant turns to her grandsons.

"Let's go get something to eat," she says.

"I'm not hungry. I'll stay here," Randy replies. The oldest sibling walks to the office, where Francis DuPont is about to leave for dinner.

"Mister DuPont, would you mind if I stay here? I'm not hungry," Randy says.

"That'll be no problem Mister Taylor. You stay as long as you like."

"Thank you sir."

People slowly disperse from the funeral home. Randy takes a seat in a cushioned chair in the sitting room. Soon, there is only the sound of traffic outside. Randy closes his eyes and lowers his head, *Lord Jesus, please help us to survive.* After a moment, he folds his arms and relaxes into the chair.

Five minutes later the door opens. Randy stands up and sees a beautiful woman with medium length wavy auburn hair, dark eyes, a dark blue dress that goes down to her middle shins and a business jacket to match. She's wearing black nylon stockings with black dress shoes and a white blouse.

"May I help you?"

"I'm here to see Professor Taylor," the young woman says.

"He's in chapel A."

"Thank you," she replies. The woman leaves. *Boy, is she easy on the eyes!* Randy thinks. Minutes later she returns as she extends her hand.

"My name is Darlene. Are you one of the funeral directors?"

"No, no I'm not. My name's Randy. I'm Professor Taylor's son."

"I'm sorry to meet you under this circumstance. Your dad was one of my favorite teachers. I wouldn't be where I am today if it weren't for him."

"That's kind of you to say that," Randy says. "I thank you for coming today." The couple shakes hands.

"God bless you Mister Taylor."

"Please. Call me Randy."

"God bless you Randy."

"God bless you too Darlene." The young woman leaves, as Randy catches the scent of her perfume. He also catches the sight of a diamond ring. *Forget it dude. She's married,* he thinks.

That evening, after dinner, Randy gives Amy a bath, reads her a story and tucks her into bed. Iris left the house earlier without telling her stepsons where she was going. Later, lying in their beds, the brothers talk of the visitation.

"Did you notice anything unusual about Iris?"

"No," Brian replies.

"She didn't cry."

The next day, following funeral services, Donald Taylor is cremated and buried in Tammy's plot. Iris has already found a buyer for the ground that was supposed to be Donald's final resting place. Randy doesn't eat anything at the mercy dinner. Iris is among the first to leave the dinner. When the young man gets home, Randy tells Brian to pick up Amy at Stephie's. "I'm staying here to have a word with Iris."

Randy finds Iris at the dining room table. He walks up to her and says, "Iris, I think it was rude of you to leave the dinner early."

"I had important paperwork to do."

"What paperwork?" he asks.

"That's none of your business," Iris says without looking at him.

Randy sits down next to her and says, "We want to get along with you, but you're making it very difficult. Now, I don't know what kind of an upbringing you had, but I assume it wasn't very good."

"My childhood is none of your concern," she says. Randy finds he's getting nowhere. He stands, pushes in his chair and starts to leave. He turns and says;

"And oh, by the way, from now on you'll park your car on the right side of the garage, not the left."

"I will not!" Iris snaps. Randy walks back and bends down.

"Iris, have you seen 'The Longest Yard' with Burt Reynolds?" She looks at her stepson with cold eyes.

"Well, there's a line in that movie that goes like this. 'To get along, you go along.'"

In the law office of Parker and Stone in the northern section of Richton Park, Iris, Randy and Brian sit in front of a large oak desk. Phillip Stone reads them the last will and testament of Donald Samuel Taylor. It states that Iris has been made executor of the will and that from Donald's one-hundred twenty-five thousand dollar insurance policy, forty thousand dollars will go to Iris. Sixty thousand dollars is to be set aside and divided equally between his three children for their education. Iris has the responsibility of overseeing the children's account until Randy reaches the age of twenty-one. (*That can't come soon enough*, thinks Randy.)

The mortgage on the house, along with any other outstanding debt is to be paid off with the remaining twenty-five thousand dollars from the insurance policy. Any money left over, which amounts to three thousand dollars, is to be used for Donald's funeral expenses. (Randy can't help but think about how much Iris gained by having Donald cremated and selling his burial plot.)

The will states that the three Taylor children and Iris all own the house equally and can live in it with a stipulation that the house cannot be sold until each one of the children has moved out permanently. At that time, if all four agree, the house and its' contents can be sold with the profit divided equally among them.

Iris has a cold expression on her face when the lawyer explains that she is responsible for all household expenses including food and clothing for the children until they reach the age of eighteen.

Autumn 1979 arrives. A small miracle has occurred. Iris makes an effort to get along with her stepchildren. Randy feels that his talk with her may have made a difference. The tension in the household has lessoned. Iris even offers small praises to Amy. Still, the bottom line is this. The Taylor children didn't come from her.

On a Sunday evening after supper, Brian clears the table as Amy helps him. Randy has gotten the dishwater ready.

"That's a good girl helping your brother Amy," Iris says. "I'm so proud of you." The child beams. Amy lets Iris bathe her as the child senses she may have a new mother. Randy walks upstairs to do his homework. Brian finishes the dishes.

After the bath, Iris reads her a story. When it's bedtime, Amy kisses her brothers then walks to her bedroom where she's tucked in by Iris. The light is turned off, and the door is closed halfway. Iris peers into the boys' bedroom.

"I'm going out," she says.

"Where?" Randy asks.

"I have to run a few errands," she replies.

"I'll leave the light on for ya," Randy says.

"Thanks," Iris says. Randy gets out his biology textbook.

"Running errands—on a Sunday night," he says to himself.

Two hours later, Brian closes his literature book and sits up from his bed.

"I'm turning in Randy."

"Me too little brother. These Mondays come awfully quick." The brothers change into their pajamas. Brian turns off the light switch on the wall, Randy turns off the lamp between their beds. Each bids the other a 'goodnight'. Randy's breathing slows instantly. The oldest sibling begins dreaming of a roller coaster that's slowly going up the track. This dream is triggered by the garage door opening. Randy is awakened by the sound of Iris's voice. "You took my lipstick after I praised you earlier!"

Randy jumps out of bed and runs to Amy's bedroom. The light is on and the child is sitting with her blanket to her chin looking frightened. Iris stands nearby with her hands on her hips.

"What's wrong?" Randy asks.

"She took my lipstick, the little thief. All of them have been missing and I found them in her room," Iris says angrily.

"Number one, there's no name calling in this family. Number two, that doesn't mean you can storm in her room late at night and scare the hell out her," Randy says. "You owe her an apology."

"I will not," Iris says, as she pushes past him to her own room.

Oh, I know what she's doing now, Randy thinks, *she's replacing all those stupid lipsticks into those precious little plastic make-up bags of hers. She keeps everything she owns in those dumb plastic bags. What a strange bird she is.*

Randy sits on the edge of Amy's bed and takes her in his arms. He speaks with gentle words.

"Amy honey, you can't take things that don't belong to you. Now, you never took mommy's lipstick. Why did you take Iris's?" Randy asks.

"I don't know," she replies softly.

"Promise me you won't do it again," Randy says.

"I promise."

The warm winds of September, turn into the cool breezes of October. Walking through the hallways between classes, Randy is surprised to discover that students and faculty that he doesn't know come up to him and offer their condolences. Their thoughtfulness means a lot to him.

After paying for his fifty-cent lunch, Randy picks up his tray and begins walking to a table. He sees his cross-country coach, Perry Bonham.

"Randy, why haven't you been at practice?" the coach asks.

"I'm not going out this year."

"Why not?" Bonham asks with great concern.

"Did you know my father died?" Randy asks.

"Yes, I'm so sorry," coach replies.

"My siblings need me, my GPA is slipping, and my stepmother and I aren't getting along."

"I see," Coach replies. "Randy, I support your decision, but at the same time we'll miss you. If there's anything you need, please let me know."

"Thanks coach." Several of his friends join him at the table including Douglas Elgin.

Being Wednesday, Randy works at Lakewood Bowl after school. The middle of the week is the busiest at the alley. Brian picks up Amy from Neil Armstrong Elementary. Randy left instructions for Iris on how to prepare the baked chicken.

Walking home after work at night, Randy discovers the front light is off. *Mom always left a light on for me,* he thinks. Once inside, Randy turns on the dining room light and takes out his monthly cross-country mileage sheet from one of the dining room drawers. As a freshman, coach Bonham gave everyone sheets to write their daily mileage down. Three years later, Randy's mileage sheet has now turned into a mini diary. Sitting on a chair, he takes out a pen.

Iris walks upstairs from the utility room to the foyer.

"I don't know why you write on that sheet of paper every night," she says.

"Does it bother you?" Randy asks without looking up. Iris walks upstairs loudly to her bedroom.

At the breakfast table the next morning, Saturday, Iris shows the brothers a list of chores, and who will do them and the manner of doing them. *You've got to be kidding!* Randy thinks.

"Iris, we've never done these chores this way. I think we'll stick to ours," Randy says.

"Look buster! I am the head of this household. What I say goes. You are not here to tell me, I am here to tell you!" Iris puts on her coat. She opens the door and turns to Randy.

"My way or the highway!" Iris says as she slams the door.

"I hope she doesn't make a habit of that," Brian says.

"She won't," Randy replies.

"She's mean," Amy says. When breakfast is over, Randy turns to his brother.

"Brian, do you have anything to do today?"

"No, not really."

"Do you mind babysitting Amy?"

"No I don't. You going anywhere?"

"I have to go to a meeting," Randy replies. A puzzled expression comes across Brian's face.

"When will you be back?" Amy asks.

"I'll be back in a few hours, okay sister?" The child holds up her arms. Randy picks her up.

"I love you Amy."

"Wuv you too Randy," the child replies.

"And you love Brian. Give Brian a kiss." Randy turns the child practically upside down as she kisses the middle sibling. Brian ruffles her hair, then Randy sets her down.

"I tell you what Amy. While Brian's doing the dishes, do you wanna play 'Daddy Gorilla'?" Randy asks. The child jumps up and down.

"Yes, I want to play!"

Twenty minutes later, Randy starts his LeSabre. He slowly pulls out of the garage. (Randy has to pull up several times to maneuver the Buick out of the curved driveway since he had to park it on the right side of the garage.)

Turning east onto Sauk Trail, Randy discovers his turn signal doesn't blink, although the light comes on. He will operate it manually, but only if someone is behind him. Randy turns right onto Cicero Avenue, heading toward Will County. He has a meeting with a 1978 Ford station wagon. Originally, he was going to tell Brian that he was making this short trip. Randy figured that Brian would want to go along and that would mean a baby sitter for Amy.

The Buick LeSabre runs smoothly now that Randy had it tuned up a week earlier. Deep down inside, he now feels that it still is his father's car. Randy looks in his rearview mirror. A '74 Chevy pick-up is behind. He operates the turn signal manually, as he lets the truck driver know he's making a left turn. Randy pulls into James Junkyard. He didn't question the Chicago Heights police officer as to why the Ford was towed to Will county, instead of keeping it in Cook.

Randy gets out, leaving his windows down. A warm front from the Gulf of Mexico embraces the mid west. Randy walks up the five stairs under an office sign and opens a wooden door that contains a small window. No one is behind the counter as Randy notices a restroom to the right. The door is closed. Taped to it is a playboy centerfold. Randy hears the flushing of a toilet, when a man of fifty walks out zipping his zipper.

"May I help you?" he asks.

"I'm looking for a 1978 yellow Ford station wagon that was brought in about two weeks ago," Randy says.

"Do you have any identification?"

Randy shows the man his driver's license. "It's my Dad's car."

"The man looks at his clipboard for a moment then says,

"Third row, forty yards on the right. Do you want me to take you to it? Seeing something like that can be a rough experience for a kid."

"No, if it's okay, I'd like to go alone. I just need to see it."

"I understand."

"Thank you," Randy says. The tall teenager begins to walk away.

Do you know you look like Rock Hudson?"

Randy turns to him, "I wish I had his money," he replies. "May I leave my Buick here?"

"Sure," the man says.

Randy begins walking. The wrecks of automobiles are just shadows of their former selves. *I bet each vehicle holds many tales,* Randy thinks. *It's amazing that all of these autos were once brand new.* Randy walks for what seems like ten minutes, then slowly his father's vehicle, comes into view. The young man puts a hand to his mouth. "Oh, my God," he whispers.

The front end is unrecognizable. The hood is bent like a lion's gum line sniffing the air. The driver's side tire is bent inward at a forty-five degree angle, and is flat. The windshield is shattered, at what looks like crooked spider webs. The driver's side door is askew. Randy walks closer as if in slow motion. The driver's side window is gone. Pieces of glass from the windshield litter the brown leather seats. The upper half of the steering wheel is bent. The brown dashboard is crooked and covered with dirt and dust. On the upholstery are what looks like dried tomato sauce stains—his father's blood.

Randy bows his head as a tear rolls down his cheek. *He didn't suffer. It was over in an instant.* Suddenly, Randy's sorrow turns to anger as he looks towards the sky and says in a strong voice. "This isn't fair God. I'm not even twenty and I've lost both of them. Why did they have to die? Can you tell me that, huh?" The young man retrieves his handkerchief from his back jean pocket, wipes his eyes, folds it, and places it back. He turns and walks. After three steps, Randy stops. Something out of the corner of his eye, catches his attention. Turning, he walks back. Randy bends down and looks at the map light on the ceiling of the car. Both lights have come on. Then, at the same time—they turn off. It's as if his parents are saying, "We're in heaven, we're alright and some day we'll be together again." A certain calm comes over him. Randy closes his eyes and prays. *Lord, always watch over my parents and their surviving children.* He remains motionless for several moments, then he turns and walks away. Randy doesn't look back.

When he's near the office, the owner steps out and opens a can of Falstaff.

"Wanna beer?" he asks.

"No thank you sir. I've gotta get back home," Randy replies.

"Say, I was wondering. You thinkin' about buying that Ford?" he asks.

"My father was killed in it," Randy says.

"Oh—I'm sorry for asking," James says. Randy gets in his rust-free, dull, light green Buick, fires the engine, and slowly turns around to Cicero Avenue. The dried corn stalks across the road are like the vehicles nearby. They're shadows of their former selves.

When Randy arrives back home, he discovers the garage is empty. He parks on the left side. Iris has gone shopping—for herself. As Randy steps inside, his siblings are there to greet him. He picks up Amy and gives her a kiss.

"You done with your meeting?" Brian asks.

"I'm here, aren't I little brother?" Randy replies. Amy wraps her arms around her brother's neck.

"Amy and I had lunch. Do you want me to fix you a sandwich Randy?" Brian asks.

"No thanks little brother. I'm gonna start cooking dinner, while Amy takes a nap."

"I don't want a nap!" she says in protest. Randy sets her down then squats to her level.

"Okay Amy, I'll make a deal with ya. You don't have to sleep, but I want you to rest—all right?" Randy asks. The child makes a face.

"Believe me Amy, when you're our ages, you'll want to take a nap!" Brian says.

"He's right sister. Now take my hand," Randy replies. The child reluctantly does, as she's led upstairs to her pink bedroom.

"Little children need a lot of rest, so they can grow," Randy says. Taking off her slippers and pants, Randy folds the latter and places it on a chair. The child gets in her bed, as Randy tucks her in.

"Just rest for a bit," he whispers. Randy kisses her then closes the blinds. He walks slowly out, as he closes the door most of the way.

"Randy, I'm gonna hang out at Lakewood Bowl," Brian says as he walks down the stairs.

"Be home by five," the oldest says. Turning on the radio at low volume, Randy finds WLS. A song from Supertramp plays as Randy takes out a package from the freezer. He fills one of the sinks with warm water, then takes out a knife from the drawer. Cutting the package, he removes the poultry, and places the frozen meat in the warm water. Randy washes his hands once more then takes out a bag of potatoes from the bottom part of the cupboard. The white sack is next to a twenty-five pound bag of sugar. Randy sets the bag of potatoes on a chair then retrieves a peeler, a peering knife and a cutting board. He fills a pot halfway with cold water. The joys of cooking and baking comes from his mother Tammy who always let him help her while he was growing up. Although Randy never knew he'd be using these skills so soon.

After peeling a number of potatoes, Randy wipes his hands on a clean hand towel nearby. He quietly walks upstairs and checks on his sister. Amy is out like a light. Walking back in the kitchen, Randy finishes the potatoes. He places a colander in the sink that's empty. Dumping the potatoes in the colander, he rinses them, and places them back in the pot. Filling it with cold water again, Randy sets the pot on the stove. Washing his hands, he then prepares the salad and then the green beans.

It is dark outside when Amy walks downstairs in the kitchen.

"I had a good rest," she says as she rubs an eye.

"Yes you did sister. Now go upstairs and put your pants and slippers on. Supper will be ready in twenty minutes," Randy says. Brian walks in the foyer as he takes off his coat.

"What's happening little brother?" Randy asks.

"I lost five bucks playing pool," Brian replies.

"Don't ever play for money little brother."

"Why not?"

"It could lead to a gambling addiction."

"It was only five bucks."

"Yeah, but that five bucks is in his wallet instead of yours. Always be careful with your money Brian," Randy says. "Let's sit down to eat." After Randy says grace, Brian asks a question.

"Should we wait for Iris?"

"No. I don't know when she's coming back."

After supper, Brian does the dishes while Randy gives Amy a bath. He helps her with her pajamas then the two walk downstairs to the family room. Amy picks out half a dozen books, then sits on her brother's lap.

"Amy, do you think you can read to me?" Randy asks. The child nods

"I'll help if you get stuck on a word." The child snuggles as she begins to read. Randy's rocking motion is gentle. When Brian is finished in the kitchen, he walks downstairs to the half bath and takes a shower.

Iris pulls into the driveway as she pushes the 'Genie' button that's attached to her visor. As the rectangular door lifts, so does her anger. She now has to park on the right side of the garage. Iris gets out and retrieves her shopping bags from the trunk.

Entering the foyer, she sets her bags down loudly. She walks downstairs, stomping her feet. Looking at her stepson she says, "You parked on the left side. That's my space," she snaps.

"And how was your day Iris?" Randy asks without looking at her.

"Don't get smart with me young man," she replies. Iris's eyes are as cold as a statue's.

"You shouldn't rock that child. You're going to spoil her."

"I'll be the judge of that, Iris," Randy replies. Amy curls closer to her brother. He doesn't realize, she's sucking her thumb. The stepmother begins to turn.

"And by the way Iris—I saved you a plate," Randy says.

"Did you finish the chores on the list?" she asks,

"No I didn't," Randy replies.

"You will obey my orders!" Iris snaps. Remember, my way or the highway." Iris walks upstairs to the foyer. Each step makes a 'thud'.

The next morning, Randy is awakened by the sound of drawers slamming, and cabinets banging. He gets out of bed and quickly walks downstairs to the kitchen.

"What's your problem?" Randy asks.

"I can't find the coffee filters."

"You can't look for them quietly?" he asks. The stepmother scowls.

"Look Iris, when Brian and I get up early, we're quiet for you. Now you can't be considerate?" Randy asks.

"Nuts to you," she replies.

"No, nuts to you Iris. From now on, you will be quiet for us when you get up early." Randy walks upstairs, shaking his head. Lying down again, he's unable to sleep. Fifteen minutes later, he gets up and dresses quietly. His clock radio reads 5:04am. Iris has cost him over an hour of his rest.

At the breakfast table with the family, Randy says grace and notices that his stepmother doesn't fold her hands. She's wearing a new light green dress and a pearl necklace.

"Lord, we are truly grateful for this food. May it nourish every cell we have. Amen." Randy begins serving the scrambled eggs, when Iris looks at the plastic pitcher. She stands and retrieves a ruler from the drawer. She places the ruler vertically against it.

"I made this orange juice the other day, and the level was on twelve. Now it's on five. You kids are drinking entirely too much of this," Iris says. Randy looks at his brother as if to say, *Is she for real?*

"Iris, I have something you can measure. And it's not the orange juice," says Randy. The brothers laugh. Amy, not getting the joke, laughs too. Indignant, Iris stands and leaves the room.

Several days later on Friday, ten inches of snow falls on northern Illinois. Schools aren't closed, but this doesn't surprise Randy. After dinner, he receives a phone call from his friend Dougie. Randy takes the call down in the family room. Brian begins to clear the table. Iris and Amy go upstairs. The friends discuss the science project they're working on. Randy loses track of time, but sees Iris leave the foyer with her coat on, as Brian walks by to take a shower. Five minutes later, Randy hangs up the phone and heads upstairs to retrieve his biology textbook. As he passes his sister's room, he hears her softly crying. Randy walks in as he sees Amy face down. With great concern he sits on the edge of her bed and gently turns her over.

"Amy honey, what's wrong?" Randy asks. The child wipes her eyes with her sleeve.

"Iris told me that when I grow up, I'll never get married."

"Oh Amy, that's not true. I don't know why she would say that. Iris hasn't known you for very long. I've known you all of your life. And do you know what else I know?" Amy looks straight at her brother.

"I know that pretty soon, you're gonna have so many boys after you, I'm gonna have to beat them off with a baseball bat." Amy laughs softly.

"Now sister, I'm gonna have a talk with Iris. And you listen to me. You know I'll never lie to you." The sister and brother embrace.

"I love you Randy."

"I love you too Amy."

"Hey Amy, you haven't had your bath, have you?"

"No," the child replies.

"Well, let me give you your bath, then you get your jammies on, and you can practice your reading."

Later, when Amy is put to bed, Randy retrieves his books from his bedroom. Brian sits at the desk.

"I'm almost done, Randy," he says.

"That's okay little brother. I'll do my homework in the family room." Randy quietly walks downstairs, sets his books and briefcase bag at the end of the sofa. Turning on the television at low volume, he sits down on the carpet in front of the sofa using the coffee table as his desk. Randy gets to work, beginning with geometry.

An hour later, his nicotine craving calls. Once in the utility room, Randy hears the garage door open. Moments later, Iris walks in and sets her shopping bags down.

"How ya doin'?" he asks as Iris sets her beer in the fridge. "I've got a question for you, Iris. Why did you tell Amy she'll never get married when she grows up?"

"I have my reasons," Iris replies coldly as she turns to walk away. Randy takes hold of her forearm.

"What are they?"

"Don't you ever grab me," she says coldly. Randy lets go forcefully.

"Straighten up, Iris, or else."

"Is that a threat?"

"Could be."

While Iris is in the shower, the brothers lie in their twin beds. A lamp is glowing on a small end table between them.

"I tried talking to Iris tonight, about telling Amy she'll never get married." Randy says.

"Wheredja get?"

"No where," Randy says. "Ya know, Iris is like a tiny pebble in your sock. You can walk, but your toe hurts." Brian rolls on his side, with his back to his brother. He adjusts his pillow and says, "Remove the pebble." But Randy doesn't hear.

"Goodnight little brother."

"Goodnight Randy."

CHAPTER EIGHT

The next evening after supper, Randy again saves Iris a plate. He does the dishes as Brian gives Amy her bath. Randy retrieves his briefcase along with several other books and folders and begins to work in the family room. His makeshift study area is growing on him. The low volume on the television is a way of blocking out most of the world.

Twenty-five minutes later, Amy runs down in her birthday suit, with Brian trailing with her pajamas.

"I ran from him!" she says laughing.

"Amy, get your pajamas on. I don't want you to catch cold," Randy says with mild authority. The child listens as Brian helps her.

"Read me a story Randy."

"Well sister, let Brian read to you tonight. I have a lot of homework, but I'll read to you tomorrow night—okay?" Randy asks. The child nods.

"Now give me a kiss."

"Sleep well Amy. I'll see you in the morning," Randy says. Brian and Amy walk the two flights of stairs to her bedroom. Randy focuses on his studies.

When Iris leaves work at Prairie State College, she drives to the nearest bar on Halsted Street. She doesn't get drunk but finds solace in the tavern. If she'd known she'd be a widow before the age of thirty, she never would have married Donald. At least if his death would have left her with enough money to really help her situation. *If Donald hadn't left so much to his children it would have made a big difference,* she thinks. Whenever she speaks to her friends at work about her stepchildren, she refers to them as 'the baggage.' Several hours later, she heads for Richton Park.

Randy crushes his cigarette in the ashtray as he stands at the counter in the utility room. Going back to his 'study area' he opens his American history textbook. Minutes later, he hears the garage door open. *Hope she's in a better mood tonight,* he thinks. Iris walks in the foyer and closes the door. Randy's surprised she didn't slam it. Iris walks downstairs.

"You didn't rake the leaves." Without looking at her Randy replies, "Leaves decompose." Iris then notices the television.

"You can't do homework with that TV on," she says harshly. Randy looks at her as if she doesn't know her name.

"I carry a three-point-zero grade point average. What does that tell you, Iris?" Iris walks to the half bathroom nearby. She closes the door and Randy decides to take a break. He stands and changes the channel. He sits on the carpet several yards away from the screen, with his arms behind him.

At the breakfast table the next morning, Randy fixes a pot of oatmeal, cuts slices of cantelope and toasts English muffins. Randy, Brian, and Amy sit down to breakfast but Iris is in her bedroom putting on pearls to go with her new dress.

"Lord, we are truly thankful for what we're about to receive. Amen."

Brian butters Amy's muffins while Randy serves the oatmeal. Iris walks downstairs, takes a cup from the cupboard, and pours herself coffee from the fresh brewed pot.

"Morning Iris. That dress looks nice. It must've cost a lot of money," Randy says.

"Don't worry about the cost," she replies coldly. The stepmother sits at the table, placing her napkin on her lap. She prepares her breakfast.

"You're not saying grace?" Randy asks.

"Don't need to." Moments later, Amy reaches for the sugar bowl, but knocks it over in the process. Iris explodes.

"You clumsy child, don't you know that sugar is expensive!" Anger rises in Randy, but he's mute. He gets up as Amy begins to cry. Randy walks to the side cupboard, opens it and picks up a twenty-five pound bag of sugar. Opening a drawer, he retrieves a pair of scissors. Cutting the top off, he slowly pours the sugar on the floor. Brian stifles a laugh. Iris stares, her eyes as cold as ice. When the last grain has fallen, Randy speaks in a gentle voice. "It's funny. Amy spills a little sugar and you bawl her out. I pour twenty-five pounds of sugar on the floor and you don't say a word. Iris, you need counseling—major counseling," Randy says. Iris stands and throws her napkin on the table.

"You kids are crazy," Iris says as she walks to the foyer closet. "Remember, I'm paying for everything so it's my way or the highway," she says. Iris leaves the house, slamming the door in the process.

"Amy, don't cry. Accidents happen. Now, you clean up your sugar and I'll clean up mine—okay?"

"Okay," Amy replies as she wipes away her tears.

"Randy, you got balls!" Brian says.

"I'm getting sick of that woman," Randy replies as he retrieves a dustpan and a hand broom from the kitchen closet.

After Randy bundles Amy for school, the two walk out to the Buick in the frigid air. Turning the ignition, the LeSabre has trouble starting when Randy says a prayer.

"Dear Jesus, please start this car, so I can get my sister to school." Turning the ignition once more, the engine comes to life.

"Praise the Lord!" he replies.

"Praise the Lord!" Amy says.

"Isn't God good Amy?" Randy asks.

"Yep. He sure is!" the child replies. Randy backs out from the left side of the garage and in seconds, the Buick's on Royal Drive.

After dinner the same evening, Randy fulfills his promise to Amy. After her bath, he reads to her and she reads to him.

"Your reading is improving a lot sister. Keep up the good work." Amy looks at him with a smile. Brian washes the dishes, sweeps the floor and mops it.

When the fifth story is completed, Randy notices his sister is not at all tired. Standing up from the edge of her bed, he begins to tuck her in. Amy is fidgety. Her brother speaks. "Now Amy, I've given you a bath, I sang songs, read you stories. Now, what's next?" The child thinks for a moment.

"Snacks," she says.

"No sister, sleep," Randy replies.

"But Randy I'm not tired!"

"Look Amy, you've got school tomorrow, it's after ten and you need your sleep so you can concentrate." The child makes a pouting face while folding her arms together. The oldest sibling is running out of choices.

"Okay, if I rub your back, then will you sleep?"

"I'll try," Amy says.

"No sister, there's no trying."

"Okay, I'll sleep," Amy says. Turning over on her stomach, the brother rubs her back lightly with his fingertips. Fifteen minutes later, Amy's eyes get heavy, as Randy's arm gets tired. When her eyes are completely closed, Randy slows his rubbing gradually and pulls up her blanket. Randy kisses her tenderly then quietly gets up. Randy walks to the bedroom where Brian is sitting at the desk. The room is dark except for the desk light.

"Man, getting her to sleep was a pain-in-the-ass!" Randy says.

"Her clock was wound wasn't it big brother? Maybe it's just a phase."

"Hope it's a short one." Randy lies on his bed with his hands behind his head.

"My book report isn't due until next week. I think I'll take the rest of the night off," Randy says more to himself.

"You should, between your school work, your job and taking care of Amy, you're wearing yourself out."

"Yeah, too bad Iris can't help me with her, but she's hardly ever here," Randy says.

"Ya know Brian, have you noticed that when she is here, she's such a bitch?" Randy asks.

"Avoid her," Brian says.

"How the hell can I avoid her? She lives under the same roof!" Randy says. A moment of silence comes between them, then Randy breaks it.

"Do you think of Mom and Dad?" he asks.

"All the time," Brian replies while keeping his nose in his textbook.

"God, I wish they were here!" Randy says. Another moment of silence comes between them. "Well little brother, I'm gonna take a shower and hit the sack. Man, I'm beat."

"This desk light won't bother you Randy?"

"Hell no," the oldest replies as he takes his pajama bottoms and t-shirt from under his pillow.

The hot stream of water messages Randy's neck, shoulders and back. He washes his body and his short black hair. The short hair representing a quality in Randy that Donald and Tammy had always liked. In spite of the popularity of long hair in 1979, Randy doesn't jump on the bandwagon for anything.

Following his shower, Randy turns out the lights in the family room but he leaves the outside and foyer lights on. He has a hunch Iris will be home soon. In the bedroom, he bids Brian a goodnight.

"Goodnight Randy. I won't be long."

Moments later Randy is asleep and dreaming of a swing on a hilltop. The grass is green, pink and purple wild flowers are blossoming near, as an orange Monarch butterfly flaps its wings in flight. A warm gentle breeze blows as the dreamer can almost feel it. The dreamer looks at the sun, but in reality it's the light coming from the ceiling. Randy hears two words.

"Brian, garbage!"

"Iris, what are you doing turning on the light?" Randy asks, his voice rising.

"Brian didn't take out the garbage and he's going to do it now!"

"Lay down Brian, you'll take the garbage out in the morning." His brother obeys as Iris gives him an icy look.

"Oh, if looks could kill, I'd be a dead man," Randy says sarcastically.

"You forget who's the head of this household."

"Well, if you're the head of this household," Randy asks as he gets out of bed and stands in front of his stepmother, "Then why aren't you ever here?"

"You kids will obey my orders whether I'm here or not." Iris says sternly. Over her shoulder Randy can see Amy coming from her bedroom.

"Oh this is good," Randy says as he walks past Iris bumping in to her. Taking hold of his sister's hand, he turns to his stepmother.

"It took me an hour to get this child to sleep. From now on Iris, when you come in late, you'll be as quiet as a mouse. And that's my order!"

The next evening, halfway through dinner, Randy's surprised when he hears the garage door open. Moments later, Iris walks in with one large shopping bag. Setting it down, she walks to the kitchen where Randy is sitting at the head of the table.

"Did you vacuum downstairs?" she asks him.

"No I didn't," Randy replies.

"Did you dust the furniture?" she asks again.

"I had to pick up Amy."

"Did you clean the downstairs bathroom?" Iris asks.

"Brian will do that this week-end while I'm at work." Randy says. Iris pauses then says; "I'm gonna take your plate away." The stepmother picks his plate up, but Randy thinks quickly. With his right palm, he slaps the bottom of the plate upward as the sphere and his remaining food fly in the air. Iris's eyes widen. Randy's unable to contain himself as he busts out laughing. His siblings join in.

"Did you think that was funny?" Iris roars. The stepmother retrieves her shopping bag and walks upstairs. Randy cleans up the mess as he says, "I couldn't pass that up!"

When the meal is finished, Randy turns to his brother.

"Brian, I want you to bathe Amy. I'll do the dishes."

"That'll be a nice change of pace," Brian replies. He takes Amy upstairs as Randy begins to clear the table. After the dishwater is prepared, Randy opens the refrigerator and picks up the plate on the top shelf. Removing the tin foil, he scrapes the food in the garbage. Minutes later, Iris walks in the kitchen. Opening the refrigerator, she looks for her dinner.

"Where's my plate?" she demands.

"I didn't save you one," Randy replies.

"And why not?"

"Because you picked mine up."

Iris slams the door of the fridge. Several items inside have fallen. Randy calmly walks to the sink with a grin on his face as Iris storms out of the house.

When the dishes are done, Randy walks upstairs. An idea has come to him. Upon entering his bedroom, he flips the switch on the wall near the doorway. Turning on the desk light, he picks up the chair and places it under the ceiling lamp. Standing on the chair, he reaches for the light bulb within the glass sphere. Randy unscrews each until the bulbs are off. Getting down, he replaces the chair. Flipping the wall switch downward he returns to the desk to begin his studies. Later, he reads to Amy and puts her to bed. Brian studies at the desk, while Randy takes a shower.

After both boys have been asleep for a while, Randy wakes up with a slight gasp and a cold sweat from the nightmare he's been having about Iris tormenting Amy to tears. Getting out of bed, he quickly but quietly walks to his sister's doorway, and turning on the hallway light, he looks in. Amy is fast asleep with her thumb in her mouth. Randy walks back and stops at his doorway. Taking two steps back, he checks in on Iris. She's lying in bed, as still as a corpse. Randy turns off the hallway light and goes back to his bedroom. Sleep doesn't come easily.

A warm front from the Gulf of Mexico brings above average temperatures to the mid-west. Halloween 1979 falls on a Wednesday. Randy purchases two outfits from Costumes Incorporated in Lincoln mall. He dresses as a clown, Amy dresses as a princess after school. Randy takes his sister trick-or-treating throughout Lakewood Estates. By 9 pm, the two are home. Iris is out and Brian is studying. Randy and Amy walk inside to the kitchen. Placing the two bags on the table, Randy dumps them both. Brian walks downstairs from their bedroom to the kitchen.

"Wow, look at all that candy!" he says.

"Do you want some?"

"Sure sis, I'll take these two. Thank you so much."

"That's nice of you to share, Amy." The child picks up a large chocolate bar and gives it to her oldest brother.

"Thank you sister. I'll have this with my lunch tomorrow. Are you gonna give one to Iris?" Randy asks.

"I'll give her this one," Amy says as she picks up the smallest.

"Now Amy, if you eat only a couple pieces of candy everyday, it'll last well into the new year and decade," Randy says.

"What's a decade?"

"A decade is ten years," Randy says as he takes a piece of paper and a pen from the drawer. He writes a diagram to show her: 1950-'59, 1960-'69, 1970-'79.

"We're in the last year of this decade, the nineteen seventies. In a couple of months, it'll be nineteen eighty; a brand new year and decade," Randy says.

"That's cool," Amy replies.

"Now sister, Brian is gonna give you a bath and read you some stories. I have to do my homework," Randy says then looks at Brian.

"Did you get any supper little brother?"

"Yeah, I had some leftovers."

"Did Iris come back from work?"

"She was in and out."

Randy sets the bags of candy in the dining room as Brian takes Amy upstairs. The oldest sibling takes off his makeup in the bathroom downstairs, then heads to his bedroom to hit the books.

An hour later, Amy runs in her brother's bedroom.

"Randy, rub my back."

"Amy I can't. I've got a lot of homework to do. Have Brian rub it," Randy says.

"He rubs too hard," Amy replies.

"Sister, if I rub your back all the time, you won't get to sleep on your own. And big girls fall asleep on their own—don't they?" Randy asks. Amy makes a sad face.

"I'm not a big girl yet," she says gloomily. Big brother gives in.

"Alright Amy, five minutes and no more," Randy says. *I'm such a damn softy*, he thinks as he walks Amy to her room. The child gets into bed.

"I have to tell Brian something, I'll be right back," Randy says. He walks downstairs to the foyer and looks to the family room. Brian is sitting on the floor watching television.

"Little brother, you done with your homework?"

"Yeah Randy, I did it when yuz were out trick-or-treating."

"Don't forget to take out the garbage."

"I won't."

Randy walks upstairs. He says prayers with Amy then rubs her back. Ten minutes later, he sits back down at the desk.

"Where was I?"

At 10:30pm, Brian turns the television off, but leaves the lamp on. Walking upstairs quietly, he enters the bedroom. Randy is winding down from his studies. Brian begins to change.

"I tell you what little brother," Randy says. "Don't ever take Mrs. Dulaney for American history if you can help it."

"Why's that?"

"'Cause she'll give you a shit load of homework every night. Man, I love history, but she's a complete nut case!" Randy says as he places his books in his briefcase.

"Another long day for the Taylor's. I'm gonna take a shower and go to bed," Randy says more to himself.

"Goodnight Randy."

"Good night little brother." He gets up from the desk and walks downstairs. He leaves the outside light on more as a habit than as a favor to his stepmother.

Randy enters the half bathroom and closes the door. Later, when it's opened, he's wearing his pajama bottoms, and a clean t-shirt. Entering the family room, Randy looks up to the foyer and can see the outside light has been turned off. *Iris is home,* he thinks. Turning the lamp off, Randy carefully makes his way upstairs to the foyer, and then another set of stairs to the dark hallway. A light can be seen through a crack in Iris's bedroom door. Walking quietly on the thick carpeting, Randy proceeds to his dark bedroom. He has stopped bidding his stepmother a goodnight. At his doorway, Randy stops. Taking several steps backwards he peers in the door crack. Iris is standing at his mother's chest of drawers; her back to the door. Something green is on top of the bureau. Randy squints—it looks like cash—lots of it. He quietly retires. He places his hands behind his head. *She can't make that much.*

At the breakfast table, Randy asks his sister, "Amy, do you want to say grace?" The child folds her hands with her brothers.

"God, thank you for this food. It's yummy!" The brothers laugh as Iris walks in the kitchen.

"Good morning Iris," Randy says as the stepmother prepares her coffee.

"Morning," she says flatly.

"It's Friday. Are you gonna join us for dinner?" Randy asks.

"I doubt it," she replies.

"So you're not joining us?"

Iris doesn't answer as she sips her coffee.

"Well?" Randy asks.

"I'm thinking," Iris says.

"I thought I smelled something burning." Brian says. Iris gives him a dirty look then slowly returns her gaze.

"I'll make it if I'm not busy."

"Where do you go after work?" Randy asks boldly.

"That's none of your business."

The rest of the breakfast is eaten mostly in silence then Iris says, "Brian, I need you to wash my car this week. Don't skip the bumpers like you did the last time."

Moments later she leaves without a word.

Randy turns to his brother, "Brian, I have to look for my science report. I want you to drive Amy to school."

"I only have a permit," Brian replies. Randy takes out a piece of plastic from his wallet and gives it to his brother.

"Now you have a license. Don't forget to give it back. And when you return, park the Buick in the driveway."

"And don't do any donuts!" Randy says as Brian laughs. Randy clears the table, washes the dishes, then looks for his science report. After five futile minutes he thinks. *Maybe I left it in my locker at school. What's wrong with me!*

The young man closes his briefcase, retrieves his jacket and scarf and walks downstairs. Brian greets him in the foyer and hands him his license.

The brothers get in the Buick. As Randy pulls in the Rich South parking lot he remembers something.

"Damn! I forgot my history book!"

"See ya Randy. I gotta go," Brian says. The middle sibling gets out with his books at his hip and heads for the entrance. Randy 'peels' out of the lot and drives the short distance to Lakewood Estates. Parking in the driveway, he quickly gets out. Unlocking the door, he wipes his boots then heads upstairs. Picking up his textbook from the desk, he turns and heads downstairs. Upon reaching the last step, he trips and falls and his textbook slides across the kitchen floor. Unhurt but angry, he gets up. Picking his book up, Randy notices the garbage is overflowing. *I may as well change it. I'm gonna be late anyway.* Randy sets his book on the table, takes off the lid and carefully lifts the bag from its white plastic compartment. He gently pushes the trash down as he ties the ends. Picking the bag up he walks to the foyer closet and pushes the button to open the garage door. A yard from the garbage can, the bag breaks as its contents spill onto the cement floor.

"Aw man! These garbage bags ain't worth shit!" Randy tosses the bag away, and walks into the kitchen. Opening the door under the sink, he takes out two bags and places one inside the other. Walking back in the garage, he begins to pick up the trash. Nearly finished, he picks up a piece of paper, and is about to place it in the new bag when the writing catches his eye. The young man looks closely and his mouth drops open when he sees what appears to be his signature.

It's his name, but the penmanship isn't quite right and only resembles his. Randy remembers the stack of money he saw in Iris's bedroom the previous night. He puts two and two together. Folding the paper, Randy places it in his pocket. He picks up the rest of the trash, ties the ends and places the bag in the metal garbage can.

Once in his car, Randy heads to the First National Bank of Richton Park. In the top drawer of Iris's bureau lies Randy's science paper. At the upper right corner is his signature.

CHAPTER **NINE**

Randy heads back to the house in a smoldering anger. He parks in the driveway and gets out. Unlocking the door, Randy walks to the dining room and turns on the light above the table. Growing up, Randy always knew were his parents kept the household bills. But until now, he never knew how much they were.

Randy lays the stack of envelopes on the dining room table and runs upstairs to get the calculator.

An hour later, Randy leans back in his chair and thinks, *money will be tight, but it's doable. I'm confident I can get on at Lakewood Bowl full time.* Randy pauses then says out loud, "Goodbye college—hello work." The young man stands and places the bills back in their envelopes. Placing the thick rubber band around them, he places the small bundle in its drawer.

It's almost eleven as Randy rushes into school. The bell rings and it is his lunchtime. Unzipping his cloth briefcase, Randy puts his books in his locker. He puts the briefcase sideways on the bottom and closes the narrow door. Walking to the cafeteria, Randy notices the dean of students, Mister Boyer walking towards him. *Just the man I didn't want to see,* Randy thinks.

"Mister Taylor, I need to see you in my office."

The two walk upstairs and enter a room near the main office. Mister Boyer closes his door.

"Have a seat young man," he says. Randy sits on one of the two cushioned chairs in front of the desk, placing his right ankle on his left knee.

"Where were you first, second and third periods?" Mr. Boyer asks.

"Well sir, I don't know if you're aware of this but my parents died this year. I stayed home this morning to do some paperwork."

"For the estate?" Mr. Boyer asks.

"Yes sir," he replies. Mister Boyer leans back in his leather chair and places his hands behind his neck.

"Mister Taylor, it's my job to punish students who are truant, but under the circumstances, I'll let you slide."

"Thank you Mister Boyer.

"You're a good student, Randy. Keep on the straight and narrow. You're almost there, you know. When I checked your records, I saw that you will have fulfilled all your requirements for graduation at the end of this semester. But, strictly speaking, you could leave school at the end of this semester and still receive a diploma."

"That's very interesting. Am I excused?" Randy asks.

At lunch, Randy sits at a table with his friend Dougie Elgin. The two are nearly finished with their meals.

"Dougie, when we're done, I need to talk to you outside in the smoking area," Randy says.

"Yeah, okay, I need a smoke anyway," he replies.

"Can I ask you something?" Randy asks.

"Sure," Dougie replies.

"How can you smoke and run cross-country?"

"Easy," Dougie says. "After I cough up the shit, I spit it out." Randy laughs as Dougie takes a baseball cap and places it tightly on his head.

"This cap brings me good luck. Coach Bohnam hasn't seen me in the smoking area. If he does, I'll either get suspended or kicked off the team, but what the hell, I'm addicted to the 'cancer sticks'. Let's go Randy." The two stand. Walking to the side of the cafeteria they place their trays on the slow moving black belt. Moments later, they're outside, but away from other students. A cool crispness is in the air. Randy lights his cigarette, as Dougie beats his new pack.

"There's Rhonda. Man, I'd fuck her brains out if she had any," Dougie says. Randy laughs and coughs at the same time.

"Dougie, you're real funny, especially when you're not trying to be." Dougie lights his cigarette as Randy gets serious.

"Dougie, I get where you're coming from about the smokes but you're not still messing around with weed and pills and acid and shit, are you?"

"No man. I'm done with that! That night—all that scary shit went down. If it hadn't been for you, Randy. I was going to jail, man! Or maybe even worse if those guys had got to me—I might be dead. And I might be dead anyway, 'cause if you hadn't covered my ass, my, Dad, Randy man—he would've killed me! You saved me, brother. You thought fast and you took care of me and I'll never forget you for that. I mean, you risked your own self to help me. I owe you, man. I really owe you! Big time.

"Do you remember what you said that next day?" Randy asks. Dougie exhales slowly.

"I said, "Randy, I owe you. Just like I just told you right now. And it stands—forever. Anything I can do to pay you back—*anything*—no questions asked—I am there my man. You can take that to the bank.

"Well my friend the time has arrived."

"What's going on? What do you need?"

"So—your family's in the funeral business and your Dad has a crematory—right?"

"Yeah. Where're we going with this?

Moving closer Randy says in a whisper, "I need you to dispose of a body."

"Whoa!" Dougie says, are you shitten' me? Seriously, are you shitten' me, Randy? Is this a joke?

"No joke, Dougie." as he moves closer to his friend.

"Who?" Dougie asks.

"No questions—remember?"

"That's right," Dougie replies. "But…I mean, Randy, what in the hell are we talking about—a dead body—for real? And you want it cremated?"

"Yes I do. And it will be for real in a little while and that's all I'm going to say to you—ever. The less you know the better for you. I want total protection for you. Now, first, I need a body bag."

Dougie flicks his ashes on the ground and doesn't look up.

"Are you with me, man? Dougie, are you with me? Can you get me a body bag?"

"I can bring you one on Monday," Dougie whispers and moves closer to Randy. "But man this is heavy stuff. I'm not sure…I just don't think I can do this!"

"You gotta get a hold of yourself. This isn't going to touch you, Dougie. No sweat. Honest. I would not ever do that to you. Now I'm gonna have to ask you for transportation. When the time comes. You understand?"

"You mean transporting the um…"

"Yea. The body."

"You mean one of our hearses? This is freaking me out!"

"No Doug. I'm talking about your car—the trunk."

"Oh, I couldn't use…"

"Look, the body can't be in *my* car. It might, you know leave evidence or something, you know?"

"Oh, those bags are sealed. There wouldn't be anything like that in your car."

"Look Doug, even so. I'm too close to the um…person. And I can't have my car seen when we dispose of it. That could do me in."

"Randy, what the hell! Oh, this is unbelievable. I'm freaking out! I don't think I can…"

"Look man. You go to that crematorium all the time, don't you? I mean in your own car. It's no big deal. You've told me you go there."

Dougie nods.

So when we pull up with our *delivery*, even if your car is spotted, no one would think it's odd or anything. Get it? Look, this is a bad person that has to be taken out…a *really* bad person who is hurting some innocent people—hurting them bad. And all you're doing is helping me a little—with disposal. That's all! You know I'd do it if it was you. Right?"

Dougie nods again. "I will bring the bag Monday. And make sure you bring something to stash it in. You can't walk around school with that. Oh hell, Randy, I know what kind of friend you have been to me and I know that I owe you."

"So you're in, my man? You'll help me with the other part? I can count on you?"

"Okay, Randy, I'm in."

The buzzer rings and students begin walking inside. Dougie drops his cigarette and squishes it with his boot.

"Randy buddy, I gotta go."

"See ya Dougie and thanks a lot." Randy says. "Monday. Don't forget."

"No problem," he replies as he walks swiftly to the glass double doors. *What the hell? What have I gotten myself into? What has Randy gotten into?*

Randy remains behind for a moment and takes one last puff. *This is all gonna work out.*

At Denny's restaurant on Route 30/Lincoln Highway that evening Amy can't decide what to have as she looks at a menu.

"Sister, you've got to make a choice. The waitress has been back three times," Randy says. The child points to a photo.

"Tuna cakes?" Randy asks.

"Yup, that's what I want!" she replies. The waitress arrives and writes down the orders. Brian chooses the fried chicken dinner—Randy the stuffed pork chops. The oldest sibling opens another sugar packet and pours it in his coffee.

"I love Fridays," Randy says. "No cooking for me, and no dishes for you little brother."

"Randy, I got a job!" Brian says.

"Where?" Randy asks.

"At Chernin's Shoes.

"That's great Brian, but make sure your hours aren't the same as mine. One of us has to be home for Amy. You know Iris never is."

"She was banging those cabinet doors in the kitchen again, and when she looks for a pan, she makes so much noise," Brian says.

"Well, I have a feeling she won't be doing that much longer."

"Randy, I have to go potty." "Brian, when our waitress comes back, tell her I need more coffee."

"You bet."

Randy and Amy walk to the doors of the restrooms. Randy bends down and whispers to his sister.

"Amy, you're getting to be a big girl. You go in the ladies room and do your business. I'll wait right here for you—okay?" Randy asks. The child nods.

"Don't forget to wash your hands!"

"I won't forget," Amy replies.

That evening to the surprise of all, Iris comes home early. But trouble begins almost the minute she gets in the door. Randy drinks a half a glass of water, then swishes the rest in his mouth and releases the rest into the sink, under the faucet.

"What did you just do?" Iris asks sternly.

"I spit out the water," Randy says.

"We don't spit in the sink," Iris says harshly.

"I didn't spit in the sink, I spat in the drain," Randy replies. Iris stares in anger.

"Gee, you're so pleasant, Dinah Shore would be jealous." Randy says. Iris stares a moment longer, then, like a gun on a battleship, slowly shifts her gaze to Brian.

"Brian, you didn't take the garbage out this morning and you didn't clean the downstairs bathroom."

"He had to study for two exams and he had a science project to work on," Randy says before Brian has a chance to answer.

"Who's talking to you anyway," Iris snaps.

"Well, I'm talking to you, Iris."

"Nuts to you, Randy!"

"Oh you say that all the time. Say something different." Randy counters, while Iris glares back at him.

"Amy begins to whimper and Randy places his arm around her as he looks at Iris. "Our mother never used harsh words."

"Well, I'm not your mother!" Iris shoots back.

"I know that Iris," Randy calls after Iris as she heads upstairs to the kitchen where she takes down a small iron skillet, and retrieves a carton of eggs from the refrigerator. Iris cracks three eggs in a bowl and scrambles them for her dinner. Randy takes his sister upstairs and helps her with her homework. She's proud of the little desk that Randy purchased for her a week earlier. Brian reads in his bed.

"I'm finished with my homework, Randy. Will you read to me?" Amy asks. The oldest sibling smiles.

"Only if you read to me!" Randy smiles. The two walk down to the family room. On the second story, Iris stomps down to the foyer and looks towards the family room just as Iris' voice booms, "Get upstairs and clean out the bath tub!"

"I'll clean out the bath tub after I put Amy to bed," Randy says Iris retreats to her room and slams the door.

After Amy says her prayers, Randy tucks her in and kisses her goodnight. He closes her door most of the way, and quietly walks downstairs to the kitchen. Iris has left Tammy's favorite skillet on the stove without washing it. Randy crosses paths with his stepmother in the foyer.

"Iris, you didn't clean the skillet that you used."

"Kitchen duties are your job."

Without a reply, Randy walks to the kitchen and cleans the skillet. After rinsing the pan, he places it on the stove, and turns the gas on high.

When the skillet is dried, Randy takes a potholder and places the skillet on the back burner to cool. Randy is upstairs cleaning the bathtub when he remembers that Iris was the last one to use it. Anger rises when a voice says: *Cool it big boy! Everything's gonna change real soon. You know that!*

Later, while having a cigarette and a beer in the utility room, he sees Iris with her coat on. She glances his way and says, "I'm going out. And by the way, you're too young to drink beer."

"That's okay, Iris, you're not my mother—so don't worry about it."

When Iris returns late that evening, Randy approaches her with a sheet of paper in his hand. "Do you know anything about these signatures?"

"No I don't," Iris says calmly.

"A lot of money is missing from the account that belongs to me and my siblings. Can you explain that?"

"I don't know what you're talking about," Iris says as she begins to walk away. Randy grabs her arm but she pulls away.

"You're a damn liar, I should call the cops on you." he says. Iris gives him a cold look.

"I'm executor of that account and I am to oversee it. It doesn't matter whether I sign your name or mine. I can do as I see fit. And Randy, if you ever touch me again, I'll call the police on *you*."

The next Saturday morning, Randy takes a small gift from the upper shelf in the closet. He's already dressed as the clock reads 8:03 am. Brian turns. Randy bends down over his bed.

"You awake little brother?"

"Yes I am," Brian says slowly and softly.

"Listen, I have to go to the Post Office to mail Aunt Molly her birthday gift. When Amy wakes, get her dressed and fix her breakfast—okay?"

"Uh-huh," Brian says slowly.

"I also have to work today at Lakewood Bowl. Do you work today?" Randy asks.

"Tomorrow," Brian says.

"That's good. I'm off tomorrow," Randy says. "See ya when I get back."

The garage door lifts and Randy discovers Iris's red Duster is a mere inch to the right of his Buick. *She had to get out on her passenger side.*

The Richton Park Post Office on Governors' Highway is only a mile and a half from Lakewood Estates. Randy pulls in the parking lot and gets out, holding aunt Molly's gift. Locking the door, he hurries to the building. The cold November winds blow fierce. The line is long. Randy gets in line, takes off his coat, and patiently waits his turn. When three customers are in front of him, Randy hears and sees a disgruntled clerk shaking his head.

"We can never keep good people here." Without knowing it, Randy's a good listener. An idea comes to him. When he steps up to the clerk's counter, Randy pays for the postage then asks a question.

"You accepting applications?"

"All the time," the clerk says.

"I'd like one please." The clerk hands him one then Randy walks to another counter and fills it out. When he's finished, the young man gets back in line but this time it is shorter. When the clerk's station becomes open, Randy walks up and hands him his application. The middle age man looks it over.

"Paul will be out to see you in five minutes. You can stand over there," the clerk says.

"Thank you sir," Randy replies. The young man steps to the window and waits. He knows that a job with the government pays well.

Eight minutes later, a young looking man with short brown hair, wearing a postal uniform, emerges from a side door holding Randy's application.

"Mister Taylor I'm Paul Micelli. Pleased to meet you." He extends his hand as Randy shakes it firmly.

"Nice to meet you, Mister Micelli."

"Oh, call me Paul. I feel so old when people call me Mister Micelli."

"Okay Paul," Randy says. The young man follows Paul to an office with windows on three sides. After closing the door, Paul instructs Randy to have a seat. The mailroom is near. Randy immediately discovers with the door closed, the office is virtually soundproof. Paul sits behind his desk and looks at Randy's application. The young man feels a little nervous.

"You're still in high school?" Paul asks.

"Yes sir, uh- I mean Paul," Randy replies. "But I graduate—or I mean, I will have enough credits to graduate so I'll be done with school next month and just pick-up my diploma in May." Paul's eyebrows rise.

"Of course, I will have to get verification of that. But that changes the whole ball game," Paul says, mainly to himself.

"Is that good or bad?" Randy asks.

"That's good. I need workers desperately."

"I've heard you're short handed," Randy says.

"That's right. I've had two people retire, and three others started their own businesses. When is your last day of school?" Paul asks.

"My last day is December 21st." Randy says. Paul picks up a pen and writes on Randy's application.

"If the school sends us everything we need, can you start right after Thanksgiving?"

"Part time," Randy replies. "But I can work full time on the 22nd."

"Full time after January 1st," Paul says. Randy looks confused.

"Here's why. You need to take a physical, and a Post Office test battery 470, which will be held next Saturday right here at 10am."

"What work will I do?" Randy asks.

"You'll start in the mailroom, sorting mail on a conveyor belt, and pulling out small packages and envelopes. It's easy but monotonous. And if you do well, you'll probably get promoted to clerk."

"Paul, what will my salary be?" Randy asks.

"We'll start you at ten dollars an hour." Randy's mouth drop opens.

"That's with forty hours a week, and no over time," Paul says.

"Will I get over time?" Randy asks.

"Here's how over time works. Every quarter or three months, you sign for overtime sheets. I'll ask if you want to stay for two hours, but if we're short handed, you can stay for longer. Also, family emergencies, sickness, vacations, all tie into overtime; but always remember to sign your overtime sheet or else I can't give you one minute of OT. Here, I'll write it down on this sheet of paper." Paul writes quickly and hands it to Randy.

"Now, I'll probably need you on the dock loading mailbags in the truck. How's your back?" Paul asks.

"I'm strong," Randy replies.

"You look strong. Has anyone ever told you, you look like Rock Hudson?" Paul asks.

"More than once," Randy replies.

"Well Randy, welcome aboard!" Paul shakes his hand and then says, "I'll see you the day after Thanksgiving."

"Thank you Paul." Randy stands and shakes his hand.

Upon entering the foyer, Randy takes off his boots and coat, and puts on his slippers. Amy runs to him from the kitchen as he picks her up and gives her a kiss.

"How's my little sister?" he asks.

"Fine Randy, but Brian's oatmeal stinks!"

"It does?" Randy asks as he places Amy down. The two walk in the kitchen.

"This oatmeal is watery," Brian says.

"Did you read the directions?"

"No."

"That's why it's watery." Randy takes out another pot and a measuring cup. He shows his brother the steps of preparing the concoction.

"Cooking's easy Brian. All you have to do is follow the directions," Randy says as the stepmother stomps down the stairs from her bedroom. Walking in the kitchen she pours her coffee without a 'hello' or a 'good morning'. She barks her orders.

"Brian, I want you to vacuum all of the rugs and clean the upstairs bathroom. Randy, I want you to sweep, mop, and wax the kitchen floor, and clean the downstairs bathroom." Randy looks at her in disgust and says, "Gee Iris, you're a member of this household. What are your chores?"

"Don't get smart with me young man. My way or the highway," Iris says indignantly. She opens the foyer closet and puts on her mink coat. When she opens the front door Randy says, "Are you cooking tonight Iris? I do believe it's your turn." The stepmother slams the door as Randy turns to his brother and says, "She gives me a headache from hell."

That evening, Randy assists Brian with dinner. Randy takes a break, and looks for Tammy's large cloth library bag. He finds it in the family room closet.

Monday dawns cold and blustery. Randy has kept his plan a secret, since his main focus is on Amy. Before first period, he tracks down his friend. Dougie Elgin is at his locker in the senior section. Randy walks up to him with the cloth bag folded under his arm.

"Hey Randy, I've got your item," he says as he picks up the rolled black body bag, concealed in a gym bag, from the bottom of his locker. Randy opens his cloth bag as if to say, 'trick-or-treat'. Dougie pays no attention to Randy's attempt at humor and quietly places it inside quickly and discreetly.

"My parents are in France, Randy," Doug says flatly. "All we have to worry about is Mister Higgins."

"Who's he?" Randy asks.

"He's our other director. He lives near the funeral home, but he's pretty much an airhead. When do you want me to pick *it* up?"

"Well, I don't know yet. You gonna be at your house tomorrow night?" Randy asks softly.

"Yeah, I have a paper to work on."

"Well Dougie, I'll keep you posted. Thank you so much," Randy says as he pats his friend on the shoulder, ending with a mock punch.

Dougie doesn't respond to Randy's light-hearted touch.

After second period, Brian walks to the junior section and finds a letter size envelope taped to his locker door. He opens it and reads:

BRIAN,

MEET ME IN THE SMOKING AREA

AFTER SECOND PERIOD.

--RANDY

Brian gathers his texts for his next class, shuts his locker and makes haste.

In the smoking area, Randy fires up a cigarette as a friend talks to him about the rock group Cheap Trick and hands him back his eight-track tape.

"I gotta get me one of those t-shirts man!" Randy sees Brian walk outside toward him.

"Scott, sorry but I have to talk with my brother a sec."

"Okay Randy dude. I'll see ya later."

"How's it goin' little brother?" Randy asks.

"What's up, Randy?"

"Yeah Brian. I wanna show you something." Randy takes out a sheet of paper from his inner jacket pocket, opens it and hands it to him.

"Why's your name on these papers? What are they?" Brian asks.

"It's my name but I never signed these things. Iris has practiced my penmanship."

"She forged my name on a number of checks. I went to the bank last Friday. Do you know how much is missing out of our inheritance money?

"How would I know?"

"Twenty-two thousand dollars!"

"Are you sure?"

"Here's the proof—in black and white."

"Randy, you oughta sue her so maybe we can get that money back."

"I think she's wearing most of it on her, but I've got a better idea," Randy says as he looks both ways. "Gonna take her out," he whispers.

Brian looks at his older brother as if he's just lost his mind. "That's not funny, Randy. Maybe we could just call the cops or that lawyer who read us Dad's will. You have the proof."

"I'm not kidding. Getting rid of her permanently is the only way we're ever gonna have any happiness. If we try to do it with the law, she's could outsmart us some way. And if she worms her way out of this—she'll make our lives hell. Worse than that, she'll make Amy's life hell. We can't take that chance."

"But what you're talking about is taking a bigger chance. You'll get caught."

"Not true, Brian. I know how to make it look like she just couldn't stand us any more and so she just took off."

"But how are we gonna survive? We're talking murder here! This is a bad idea."

"Look Brian, she has no love for any of us. She's stolen a chunk of our inheritance and, scariest of all, we can't trust her with Amy. The woman has got to go. Now, when you say 'how are we going to survive,' I'm glad you asked that little brother. Last Saturday I had an interview at the post office. I start part time after Thanksgiving. In January, I begin full time. And before Christmas break, I leave Rich South."

"You dropping out?" Brian asks with great concern.

"No little brother, I'm graduating. I'll have enough credits."

"How much are you gonna make?" Brian asks.

"With overtime, around twenty four thousand."

"Wow! That's a lot of money," Brian says.

"Don't get too excited little brother I'll be taking care of all the household expenses. And I'm probably going to have to help you and Amy with college money."

"What about you? Aren't you going to go to college? Mom and Dad wouldn't have liked that."

"Well they're not here anymore, are they?"

"How are you gonna do it?" Brian asks.

"Well, I'm going to make up a budget."

"No, Randy—I mean the other thing."

"Leave that up to me," Randy replies.

"When are you gonna do it?" Brian asks slowly.

"Probably tomorrow. Iris has Tuesdays off," Randy says calmly as the buzzer sounds.

"You better get to class little brother. I don't want you to be late."

Brian places his hand on his shoulder.

"I love you Randy, but I've got mixed feelings about this. I don't want you to get caught," he whispers. "We've lost Mom and Dad and we just can't lose you too."

"Nothing's going to happen to me." Randy says.

When the final class of the day is over, Randy runs into his brother in the hallway.

"Brian, you need to pick up Amy. I have to run an errand."

"Where are you going?"

"Just pick her up—okay?" Randy gets to his car and drives an hour to a hardware store he knows of in Naperville. There, he purchases a roll of duct tape. When he's finished, he walks to a nearby sports shop he'd been to with his grandfather and purchases an item that resembles a can of tennis balls. In it, is a green powder that hunters and taxidermists use to cover the stench of decaying flesh.

That evening after cooking dinner, helping Amy with her homework, giving her a bath, and putting her to bed, Randy is exhausted. *I'll wake up earlier and read my chemistry assignment,* Randy thinks. He takes a shower then goes to bed.

At 5:00 am, Randy's alarm goes off, but he resets it for six. When it goes off a second time, he curses himself for not getting up an hour earlier. And yet, he doesn't know that his decision not to get up earlier won't be in vain. After getting dressed, he takes his cloth briefcase in the kitchen. Randy makes a pot of coffee. While it's brewing, he takes his textbook out and begins reading.

Fifteen minutes later, Iris awakes to the aroma of the coffee. She walks down in her robe.

"The kitchen table isn't the place to do homework," she says.

"And how did you sleep Iris?" Randy asks. The stepmother gives him a cold look as she prepares her cup. After taking a sip she says, "This coffee is way to strong." Randy sets his pencil down and gives her a sarcastic smile.

"Well, if it's too strong, maybe you can prepare it next time." Iris dumps her coffee in the sink.

"Are you gonna get Amy dressed and fix breakfast?" Randy asks.

"That's your job."

"Everything's my job, isn't it Iris?" Randy asks, his voice rising slightly. The stepmother turns and walks upstairs. Randy follows as he gives her the finger when she enters the master bedroom. Opening Amy's door slowly Randy steps inside. He gently wakes up the child, then leads her to the bathroom to wipe her face.

"Did you sleep well sister?" Randy asks. The child nods.

"What do you want for breakfast, scrambled eggs or French toast?"

"French toast. Randy, I have to pee."

"Okay Amy, I'll be in the kitchen." Randy closes the door gently as he meets Brian in the hallway.

"Good morning little brother."

"Morning Randy."

"I want you to get Amy dressed. I'll be downstairs," Randy says. The brothers then hear a "SHHHHH!" from the master bedroom. Randy walks to the doorway.

"You okay Iris?" Randy asks.

"I'm trying to sleep," she says.

"Oh, I forgot. Today's your day off. I'm terribly sorry," Randy says. He walks downstairs behind his brother. Both enter the kitchen.

"I can't stand her," Brian says in a quiet voice.

"Hang in there little brother," Randy replies. Both hear the toilet flush.

"Get Amy dressed Brian. I'll fix breakfast."

At his locker after second period Randy thinks; *This is the first time all semester I haven't finished my chemistry assignment.* He gathers his texts and heads for class. Once inside, Randy takes his seat in the second row, then opens his textbook and notes. Mrs. Logan walks in with her books and folders to her bosom.

"Good morning everyone. My it's cold today."

"Morning Mrs. Logan," Randy says. The young man tries desperately to finish his reading assignment as his teacher takes roll. Before he knows it, roll call is finished. Randy feels a little apprehension.

"Now yesterday we discussed the properties of carbon and helium. Today we'll go over chapter eleven and discuss the properties of…" Before Mrs. Logan can finish, the electricity goes out. "Aaauughs" fill the classroom. Mrs. Logan pauses for an instant, not knowing what to do. Suddenly the fire alarm goes off.

Randy senses the excitement in the air as everyone makes their way carefully down the darkened hallway toward the stairway which is illuminated by a tall window. Nearing the stairway he hears a girl say. "Quit feeling my boob you creep!" Randy laughs along with others. At the bottom of the stairs he discovers the generator lights are on but they are providing only a dim light.

Once outside, teachers are directing students to a specific section of the parking lot as firetrucks race onto the Rich South campus. Soon the principal climbs on top of a car to address the students.

"We had a small electrical fire this morning—nothing too serious. But we must dismiss classes for the rest of the day."

A huge roar goes up from the students drowning out whatever else the principal is saying. Teachers are trying to quiet the students but many are already running for their cars. Randy sees Brian who calls out to him.

"I'm going with the guys to get a burger. You wanna come?"

"No, I've got some things to do. Then I'll pick up Amy."

"I won't be long, brother."

"Okay, Brian."

When Randy arrives at the house, Iris is sitting at the dining room table with a checkbook and some cash in front of her.

"What are you doing home?" she demands.

"The electricity went out at school," Randy replies.

Randy walks upstairs to his bedroom and opens his chest of drawers. He places one sock in his back pocket. He picks up the large cloth bag from his closet and quietly walks down to the kitchen. He sets the bag slowly on the floor. Walking into the living room, he shuts the thick drapes.

"What are you doing?" Iris snaps.

"Closing these drapes will keep the heat in and the draft out," Randy says.

"I don't feel a draft."

Without responding to her, Randy walks noiselessly into the kitchen and slowly lifts his right arm towards the iron skillet that's hanging on the wall. His hand begins to shake and his heart beats faster. Randy takes his left hand and places it over his right wrist to stop the shaking as he lifts the skillet quietly off its hook. An inner voice speaks. *C'mon, what are you waiting for?* The young man stands at the doorway to the dining room just a few steps from Iris who sits with her back to him. Almost immediately and without turning around, she begins to stand. The last thing Iris sees is a dark object out of the corner of her eye. The skillet strikes her head hard above her right temple. Randy hears her skull crack, as she falls face down on the living room carpet. She twitches twice and then is still. He stares at her for some time to be certain she doesn't move again. Then, setting the skillet down, he takes the sock from his back pocket and stuffs it in her mouth. He rushes to the kitchen, grabs the cloth bag and is back in the dining room in two long strides. Randy takes out the duct tape and the can of green powder. Holding the roll of duct tape in his hand, he loosens a piece of it and places it over her mouth. He wraps the roll around her head and face, securing it tightly over her nose and lips. He tears two more strips of tape from the roll, adding another strip to her nose and mouth. *Just for good measure*, he thinks. Placing her hands behind her back, above her buttocks, Randy wraps her wrists tightly. He wraps her ankles tightly then pulls out the body bag. He opens it and places it next to her. He easily rolls his stepmother into it.

Opening the 'tennis ball' can, Randy carefully sprinkles the powder on her then quickly zips the back closed. Checking to make certain that no powder is on the rug, he drags the body bag into the living room and pulls it behind the sofa. Just as he's checking to be sure the body bag isn't visible from behind the sofa, Brian bursts in the front door out of breath.

"Amy's—walking down the street," he pants. Randy places a hand to his head.

"Holy shit! I forgot she has a half a day," he says. The oldest sibling stands, taking out his wallet. He gives his brother a ten.

"Randy, did you...."

"Just go, Brian! Take Amy to Lakewood Bowl. Give me an hour Brian. At least one hour!"

"Oh, my God, Randy!" The young man looks as if he's going to be sick.

"Go, Brian! Please, listen to me, *please*!

Brian turns and rushes out the door.

Randy stares after him. But he's not thinking about Brian. He's decided that he has to move—the body from behind the sofa. In a moment, he's moved the sofa and is dragging the body bag down the stairs to the family room. (He doesn't allow himself to hear the sickening thud Iris's head is making on each step.) *You've got time*, he thinks. *You've got time to do this the right way. No mistakes!*

Once in the family room, Randy slides the wide door of the closet open, and begins removing items. When the closet is empty, Randy opens the door to the crawl space and turns on the light. He squats down to the end of the body bag and feels for Iris's armpits. He drags her to the entrance of the crawl space, and struggles to get her inside. The entrance is small, and Iris isn't. Randy gets on his hands and knees and enters the crawl space backwards. Again he places his hands under her armpits and slowly drags Iris toward him. Suddenly, Randy's hand lose their grip and he hits his head on one of the steel beams.

"Son-of-a-bitch!" he yells. His heart is racing as sweat pours off of him. From his crouching position, Randy is using muscles he's never used before. When the body bag is completely in the crawl space, Randy cautiously makes his way out.

After a moment of rest, he replaces the items he took out before. The moment he puts the last box in place, Randy runs up to the dining room. He's anxious to look at what Iris was working on at the dining room table. On a notepad, Randy sees that Iris has written, *cash $282*. Looking at the money scattered on the table, it looks about right to him. Then he picks up the checkbook and is stunned to see that it is the account that belongs to Brian, Amy, and him. Even though he knows Iris had been stealing from them, he's still shocked to see that she continued to do it even after he confronted her. He clears the table of the checkbook and cash and takes it upstairs with him as he goes into Iris's room, intent upon finding her checkbook. He drops everything on her dresser and suddenly remembers that he left the door to the storage closet wide open. Now he dashes back downstairs to the family room. The front door opens just as he is closing the closet door.

"Randy!" Amy says. The child runs to him and places her arms around his legs. He gives her several pats on the back.

"Hi sister. Did you have a nice day?" Randy asks.

"Yep! Only a half a day of school!"

"Now Amy, go back on the rug. You're tracking snow in," Randy says. Walking to the kitchen, he sees the skillet on the dining room table. Randy quickly retrieves a cloth napkin from a cabinet drawer and places it on the checkbook. He places the cash in his pocket, and picks up the skillet and puts it back in the kitchen. Tearing off a couple of paper towels, Randy steps to the foyer and squats down while wiping the floor. Amy looks at him.

"Randy, why are you sweating?" she asks.

"I've been doing push-ups," he replies.

"I can do push-ups too. Look at me Randy!" The child gets in a push-up position with her buttocks in the air and begins.

"That's very good sister." Randy claps and Brian follows suit. The child stands nearly out of breath. She walks to the kitchen to get a drink of water. Her brothers follow.

"Everything alright?" Brian asks.

"As planned," Randy replies under his breath.

"Do you want pizza for lunch Amy?"

"Yes. I love pizza!" she replies.

"That's good. I don't feel like cooking."

After lunch, Randy phones Dougie. His friend answers on the third ring.

"Elgin residence."

"Hey Dougie, this is Randy. How'ya doin'?"

"What's up?"

"Can you pick up that *item* this evening?" Randy asks.

"Yes I can, but it'll be after the visitation."

"What time will that be?" Randy asks.

"It's officially over at nine, but a few mourners will hang around till nine-fifteen or nine-thirty. Mister Higgins usually leaves around ten," Dougie says.

"Well, let's make it for ten-thirty. Is that okay?"

"It's fine."

"You haven't been here in a while. Do you remember where I live?' Randy asks.

"Royal Drive, fifth house on the left. The only curved driveway on the block," Dougie says.

"I'll be waiting for ya."

"Okay Randy, I'll see you about ten-thirty."

Randy hangs up the phone, hoping that all of the bases are covered. He realizes that he's taken some unnecessary steps but, he tells himself, they were only unnecessary because everything has gone so well. *At least that's the way it seems so far,* he thinks.

CHAPTER **TEN**

The evening meal is light. Vegetable soup and egg salad sandwiches. When the meal is finished, Randy gives Amy her bath as Brian cleans up the kitchen. The oldest reads to the youngest, then puts her to bed.

Randy does his homework. Later, he takes a break in the family room. Brian watches television after he finishes his homework. Twenty minutes later, Randy senses his brother's curiosity.

"Where is she?" Brian asks quietly.

"I took care of it, Brian—enough said. It's getting late. You better get to bed. I'll be upstairs in half an hour."

"Do you think I can sleep! Randy, you've got to tell me…"

"You are not involved in this and you are not going to *get* involved! If anything should go wrong—and it definitely won't go wrong—but if anything does go wrong, one of us has to be here for Amy. Don't you get that!"

"I just want to be careful—that's all. If there are ever any questions, you can honestly say you don't know a thing. Please just go to bed. Everything is going better than I even expected. Honest Brian. You'll see. I'll be up before eleven."

It's a lie. Randy says this so that Brian will get to sleep. *The less Brian knows, the better,* he thinks. *Just like Dougie.*

At ten o'clock, Randy quietly removes items from the family room closet. Opening the door of the crawl space Randy turns on the light switch and carefully removes the body bag halfway out.

At the Elgin Funeral Home, Dougie assists a woman mourner with her coat. Mister Higgins phoned in sick, so the younger Elgin is in charge of the visitation. Five mourners remain in the chapel. Dougie walks to the office in contemplation. He knows who he will be cremating tonight. His heart goes out to his friend. *Randy's mother was such a great woman. Randy deserves better than this. Too bad his stepmother treated him like dirt. I guess she had it coming so Randy just did what he had to do. That doesn't make him a...*Dougie hears the front door open as he leaves the office.

"Goodnight folks," he says.

"Goodnight young man," an elderly woman says. "Sorry we stayed late."

"No problem ma'am. That's why we're here," Dougie says. The teenager holds the door open, as the rest of the mourners leave. After the door closes, Dougie obeys his father's rule. And that is to wait ten minutes before turning off the lights (interior and exterior) and locking the doors.

Randy puts out his cigarette in the utility room. The ashtray is half full on one side, his pack and lighter on the other. The young man can smoke anywhere in the house now, but doesn't out of love and respect for his father.

It's almost quarter to eleven. He has already emptied the storage closet and dragged Iris's body out of the crawl space. Randy walks upstairs to the foyer and quietly paces in the dark. He peers outside. Across the street, the neighbors have their porch light on. Two minutes later, it turns off.

Randy is getting worried. The time is eleven ten and his friend hasn't shown up. He phones Elgin Funeral Home as a groggy Mister Higgins answers. Randy hangs up. *The phone line must connect to his house. Where the hell is Dougie? Did he get cold feet? No, Dougie wouldn't do that to me.*

After ten more minutes of pacing, Randy sees Dougie's car slowly backing into the driveway. Dougie gets out and shuts the door as quietly as he can. He walks up to the front door, where his friend opens it quietly.

"What are you doing big brother?" Amy stands at the top of the stairs, rubbing an eye.

"Just a minute," Randy says as he walks upstairs.

"Dougie and I have to move some furniture. Now, go back to bed, and I'll check on you later." Randy puts his sister to bed, tucks her in, and kisses her. He quietly walks back down.

"Down here," Randy says as he motions for Dougie to follow him to the family room.

Dougie notices that a closet has been emptied and its contents are neatly stacked just outside the closet door. "It's right here," Randy whispers as he walks into the closet and opens the crawl space door. "Let me get in here so I can lift from under the um—arms and maybe you can..."

"Actually, these body bags are plenty strong enough that you can just carry them by the four corners. You can even drag 'em if you have to. So just get in there and get a handle on your two corners, I'll grab mine, we lift and that's it."

"Well that's a whole hellavalot easier, my man."

Dougie's only response is to motion Randy to go ahead, grab the corners and lift.

Half-way up the stairs, Randy stumbles slightly, nearly causing Dougie to fall. "Sorry Dougie," he whispers, "I'm just kind of worn out from all this."

"Just put it down here so I can open your door. Then let me go out and open my trunk."

"Hey Doug, do you need some plastic or something for your trunk?"

"It's okay. I already took care of that. But these bags are really strong. Nothing gets out."

Randy notices that Dougie's car with the trunk lid up, is blocking any view of what the boys are putting into the trunk. And from the darkness of all their neighbor's houses, it isn't likely anyone is up anyway.

The body bag goes into the trunk easily and Dougie closes the lid quietly.

"Dougie, you know this means a lot to me. I mean, I know this isn't easy for you."

"No problem friend. You know I'm always on your side," Dougie says quietly. "I have been a little freaked about this but I know, man, that this was something you had to do. You had no choice. Right?"

"That's right. I didn't have a choice. It was the only way. You just don't know."

"I understand, Randy."

"There are no words. I mean thank you just isn't enough. So, will you be able to give me the um, you know, on Monday?" Randy whispers.

"Yep. It'll just be an ordinary box. Nothing special." Dougie explains.

Just to be safe, Dougie drives slowly out of the Taylor's driveway and onto Royal Drive and doesn't turn on his headlights until he pulls onto Sauk Trail.

"So long Iris," Randy whispers. "You can tell my parents why I took you out."

As he heads down the highway, Dougie thinks, *I still love the guy. But this is really still freaking me out.*

Saturday afternoon at Lakewood Bowl, Randy gives Joe his two-week notice.

"I hate to see you go, Randy. You're one of the best porters we've ever had."

"Thanks Joe," Randy replies.

Monday, early November 1979. After second period, Randy walks to his friend's locker with his cloth bag. Douglas is looking for a textbook.

"Hey Dougie!"

"Hi Randy. I've got your 'box'." Douglas hands to it to him and Randy places it quickly in his bag.

"I give you credit friend."

"How's that?" Randy asks.

Douglas lowers his voice to a whisper, "There's been a few people in my life that I wanted to take out. I just never had the balls. From what I've seen and heard about Iris, she wasn't in the same league as your mother."

Randy replies, ""I've asked God a thousand times why He took her. He hasn't answered yet."

"He will when He's ready. Well, I gotta go. Just one more thing."

"What's that?" Randy asks as Douglas continues to whisper.

"No more favors." I can get in deep shit over this. Please Randy. We're good, right?"

"I'll make damn sure nothing happens to you and yes, my man, we're good," Randy replies. Douglas closes his locker, as his friend pats his shoulder. *This went smoother than I thought,* Randy thinks as he walks to his locker steps away. Opening it, he sets his cloth bag on the bottom. Third period begins in one minute.

Randy parks on the left side of the garage next to Iris's Duster. He enters the foyer with his sister just as the phone rings. Wiping his boots, he walks in the kitchen and picks it up.

"This is Jack Gribble from Prairie State College. Is Iris there?"

"No she isn't," Randy replies coolly.

"She didn't come in to work today."

"Well, she left here at seven-thirty, her usual time," Randy replies.

"Would you tell her to give me a call when she gets in?"

"I will sir," Randy replies.

"Thank you. Good-bye." A realization overcomes the young man. *I'm gonna have to get rid of her car. In fact, I've got to get rid of everything Iris moved into our house.* Randy quickly places the box on the bottom shelf of the cabinet in the dining room. This area of the house is never used. "Amy, you watch Mister Roger's Neighborhood while I fix dinner—okay?"

"Yep!" she replies.

After dinner, while Brian is bathing Amy, Randy comes to a decision. He bounds up the stairs and goes into the room Iris occupied and takes $100.00 in small bills from the stack of money he placed on the dresser. He can hear Brian and Amy in the bathroom.

"Hey guys," he calls. "I have to go out for a couple of hours. Brian, help Amy with her school work. See that she gets to bed on time."

"Where are you going, Randy?"

"Yeah big brother, where are you going?" Amy repeats.

"I forgot about a meeting at school. I have to be there. I'll be home as soon as I can but I might be kind of late." Randy is out the door and in the garage before either Brian or Amy can comment further. Before getting into Iris's car he checks the trunk. Nothing there but the spare tire. The back seat is also clean and empty. From the glove compartment, he removes her car insurance information, registration and the manual for the Duster. He puts these in an empty grocery bag which he places on the front seat. Before backing out, he remembers to grab a screw driver and flash light from the tool box.

Soon Randy is driving north on the expressway, heading toward the big city of Chicago. He drives for some time before exiting onto the streets of Englewood—still well south of the glittering Loop. They call this the highest crime area of the city. *Let's hope so*, Randy thinks. He pulls into the first gas station he sees. He gets out of the car quickly, removes the license plate and puts it in the car. He has already made note of the location of the elevated station and is now cruising the side streets, looking for a legal spot to park the Duster without having to walk too far to the el. He finds a place in front of what looks like an abandoned apartment building. He gets out of the car, taking the grocery bag with him, and tucking the license plate under his jacket. He leaves the driver's side door unlocked. He walks quickly to the el station. He buys his ticket, runs up the stairs and hurries aboard a northbound train. He sits staring straight ahead, as if unaware of anyone else on the train. He's remembering overhearing a conversation some older guys were having at work. "It was the cops themselves told me that those cars stolen off the streets usually end up in chop shops within hours after they're taken. There's more money in that than in selling the car all in one piece."

Randy is picturing the Duster completely disassembled, lying in pieces on the floor of a dirty chop shop when he realizes his train has come to a stop in Highland Park. He runs down the platform stairs and spots an overflowing trash bin. He grabs some cans of soda and a couple of half-eaten slices of pizza from the bin and stuffs them into his grocery bag. Some soda spills out soaking the documents inside the bag. Around the corner, he finds another trash recepticle and tosses the dripping bag into it.

"Hey cabbie! Sir!"

"Where to, fella?"

"Can you take me to Richton Park?"

"Gonna be expensive."

"How much?"

"Forty, maybe fifty. Depends on traffic."

"I got enough. I need to get there," Randy explains as he gets into the cab. "I'm in school at the University and my Grandpa is real sick. I've got to get home tonight."

"Let's go then. You got an address for me?"

"Saint James Hospital on Chicago Road in Chicago Heights."

"That ain't Richton Park."

"But I want to go straight to the hospital tonight."

A little more than an hour later, the cab pulls up in front of the hospital. Randy gives the driver sixty dollars (forty-eight for the fare and the rest as a tip) and rushes through the hospital doors and heads straight for the nearest rest room. Ten minutes later, when he's certain the cab is gone, he leaves the hospital and begins running back to his house in Richton Park.

When he gets home, Amy is asleep and Brian is cleaning up in the kitchen.

"Where were you, Randy?"

"Look, I couldn't go into it in front of Amy. I got rid of Iris's car tonight."

"How?"

"I've gotta wash my hands before I do anything else." Once out of the bathroom, Randy tells Brian. "I just left it in a rough neighborhood. With any luck at all, that car will be in pieces by now."

"Randy, I need to know…"

"Wait, I want to tell you that I agree. There are some things you have to know about. First, I got a call from Iris' boss a while ago. He wanted to know why she didn't show up for work."

"I have to tell you how I did things and why and we have to figure out together what to tell other people. First of all, Amy."

The following afternoon when all three siblings are at home, Randy opens the conversation, "Now sister, you know Iris hasn't been here in a couple of days."

Amy nods.

"Well, we think she just left us. Isn't that right Brian?"

"Yeah, that's right." Brian responds.

"She was mean," Amy says.

"Yeah honey. She was mean because she didn't love us. And that's why Brian and I think she went away," Randy says. "You know that Brian and I love you. And we only want the best for you Amy," Randy says as he lifts the child onto his lap. The oldest wraps his arms around her. She looks up at him and says, "Will you read me a story now?" The brothers laugh. "Yes Amy, I'll read you a story and you read one to me!" The child gets off his lap and runs to her little bookshelf.

Later, after the child is asleep the brothers talk in their twin beds with their lamp on. Randy tells Brian about Dougie and the cremation. A stunned Brian does nothing but nod when Randy explains that the two of them have to dispose of the ashes in a safe place.

"Next, we have to get rid of everything Iris brought into this house—her clothes, jewelry, her personal papers—absolutely everything."

"Randy, do you think her boss will come looking for her?"

"I don't know but we can't take the chance. I'm even worried about Amy noticing that her stuff is still here. That's why we have to work fast. And as soon as we've cleared out the house, I have to call Iris's boss to tell him that it looks like she's left us permanently."

"Oh God, what are you going to say?"

"Little brother, in the near future, no matter what, there's gonna be people here asking questions. I figure that the less we say, the better. We just came home from school one day and Iris had taken everything and was gone. Period. And that's the story for everybody."

"No note or message or anything?"

"Nothing Brian. We say we keep waiting for a phone call but it never comes. Then we can say that we were kind of used to her not being here because she went out every chance she got."

"Like every night."

"That's right and she never wanted to do anything with us like have dinner or anything. And even when she was here, she was mostly up in her room."

"Wait! What are we going to do with all her stuff? And how are we going to fix it so that Amy doesn't notice?"

"I've been thinking and first we got to take Amy to stay at Grandma and Grandpa Taylors for the weekend."

"Do we tell them our story about Iris leaving us?"

"That's right. We say she just took off and we don't know what's happening. But we don't want them coming to the house until we get it cleared out. So we just say we're both working and busy all weekend and could they watch Amy."

"So what do we do with Iris's things?"

"We load up the car and take them over to Hammond and Gary one day and put them in charity boxes like the Salvation Army. Then we go up to Chicago, into the neighborhoods and do the same thing so that the stuff is scattered all over the place."

"Do you think it will work?"

"It should be fine. But we have to make sure we get rid of anything that might trace the stuff back to her. You know, clean out the pockets, purses and stuff. I was thinking that since she has so many brand new cloths, we have to make sure we cut off tags and maybe even some labels."

"That sounds okay to me. I think."

"If we do this right, we have nothing to worry about, brother. All of our bases are covered. The three of us are all gonna have great lives. We need to get some sleep now."

When Randy tells his Grandparents that Iris has left, they are anxious to help. At first, they want to come up and stay with them at their house. But Randy convinces them that Amy has her heart set on going to their house.

Next Randy phones Tammy's parents, Grandma and Grandpa Plant. They are outraged at what Iris has done but say they knew she would never last. They too want to come down to help out. But Randy explains that Amy is going to be with the Taylors for the weekend and he and Brian have to work. He promises they will all be together in Marrionette Park for Thanksgiving and insists that he has everything under control.

As soon as Randy and Brian return from dropping Amy off at the Taylors, he and Brian begin carefully packing up Iris' belongings in some old un-used boxes they found in the garage and storage closet. They have set a small box in the middle of the bedroom for anything they find that might tie the items to Iris. Randy has already placed her car registration and insurance papers in the box. They don't find much in any coat or clothing pockets.

When they get to the dresser, they first remove the contents of her purse, which was lying on top of the dresser. It comes as no surprise that Iris has everything in her purse inside plastic zipper make-up bags. Iris was apparently obsessed with plastic make-up bags. He remembers the night she was so upset with Amy taking her precious lipsticks. He saw her carefully placing them back into a series of clear plastic make-up bags. Why she kept her wallet and other things in such a bag is a mystery to him.

In the end, there is Iris's wallet, her driver's license, Social Security card, and some ID cards from her job at the college. Randy put them all back in the make-up bags, zip them and put everything in her purse. He also uses one of her clear, plastic zipper bags for the surprisingly few pieces of costume jewelry they have found.

"Am I nuts, or do you also remember Iris having a few pretty hot pieces of jewelry?" "You're right, brother. And where is her wedding ring? She didn't wear it after Dad died but you would think it would be in her dresser, unless…"

"Unless she sold a bunch of stuff. This is crazy, Brian and there is not one thing to show what she did with the money she inherited from Dad."

"What do you mean?"

"What I mean is, this checkbook on the dresser, which is for the account that was in *our* names. It is the only bank record that seems to exist. What in the hell did she do with the money she got from Dad?"

"Is there somewhere else we should be looking?"

"I can't imagine where."

With the house cleared of all of Iris's things, Randy and Brian head out early Saturday morning. They decide to go up into the city first to a large Salvation Army Center in the city on West 69th Street. The drop-off bins are nearly overflowing and they distribute some coats, shoes, sweaters and dresses between five different bins, tucking them in between the stacks of other drop-offs. Next they head to Joliet and finally end up at the center in Hammond. Before leaving Hammond, Randy tosses a non-descripted cardboard box into a trash can.

The boys have been careful to mix blue jeans and sweatshirts with Iris's well-tailored business suits, silk blouses and sweaters.

Their last stop before heading back to the house is the Rich South parking lot. It's nearly one in the morning when Randy parks in a far corner where large bushes darken the area so that the car is hidden. Randy has transferred the contents of the box containing Iris' ashes to an old paper bag. He collects the bag and Iris' purse.

"You're throwing that in the lagoon?"

"Yep, best place for it."

"Why didn't we just toss it in Lake Michigan?"

"Too much motion. I'd be afraid it would wash up on shore. This is safer."

"Okay, let's do it," Brian says as they unlock the car door."

"Stay here Brian."

"No, I'm coming with you!"

"You stay! Turn off the interior lights so no one sees me get out and keep watch to make sure there's no one around. I need you here."

After quietly slipping out of the car, Randy heads toward the deep, muddy lagoon near Stardom Field. He chose this sight because he knows for sure that no one ever bothers with the lagoon. Thick bushes and weeds have grown around it untouched for as long as he can remember and his dad once told him never to go near it because it was a lot deeper than it looked. He's not ever certain who owns the property. After struggling through the tangles of bushes and high weeds, he arrives at the water's edge and takes the purse, crammed with Iris' multitude of bulging plastic zipper bags. The weight feels just right as he takes it by the straps and swings it three times over his head before letting it arch into the water. It lands nearly in the middle of the lagoon and then sinks nicely into the blackness of it. When he returns to the car, Brian is standing just outside on the passenger side watching for him.

"It's done brother. Let's go home."

Sunday morning, before leaving to pick-up Amy at Grandma and Grandpa Taylor's in Kankakee, Randy slips a cardboard box under the driver's side seat.

"Last night when I said we were done, that wasn't quite true, Brian."

"Are you kidding me? I'm really beat after yesterday. What's left to do?"

"We're going to bid Iris—what's left of her anyway—a final goodbye."

"What? Oh, you mean—where do you have Iris, I mean, what's left? How are you gonna…"

"Don't worry about it, Brian. It'll be very smooth. I've got it all figured out."

As Randy heads toward the interstate, Brian turns on the radio and leans back closing his eyes. Some time later he awakens when Randy takes the exit to Manteno.

"We're getting off here?"

"Just for a brief and very informal ceremony out here in farm country—get it?"

"I get it, Randy."

Just a few miles away from the exit ramp, Randy heads down a two lane highway that stretches along massive farm fields. Once he's certain there is no traffic behind him and no houses in sight, he reaches for the box under the seat and hands it to Brian.

"Just open that one corner, brother and roll down your window. If you care to do the honors."

"I'd love to. Hand it over."

Randy slows a little as Brian rolls down his window.

"Iris, you used to say, 'My way or the highway.' Well, here's your highway!"

Once they arrive in Kankakee, they deposit the cardboard box in a dumpster in the back of a smelly pizza shop.

First thing Monday morning, Randy phones Mr. Gribble at Prairie State.

"When you called here last week, sir, I had just gotten home and hadn't gone upstairs or anything. But I have to tell you that when I walked past Iris' bedroom, it looked like all of her stuff that had been on the dresser and around the room—well it was gone. So I went in to have a better look and that's when I found that the closet was empty and so were all the drawers."

"Do you mean to say that Iris has moved out of your house?"

"It looks that way. Her car is gone. Everything of hers is gone. And hey, Mr. Gribble, I'm sorry I didn't call you sooner but I've been kinda busy."

"Oh, I can imagine, son. So was there a note or have you heard from her in any way?

"Nothing. Except for you, I can't even think of who to call who might know where she went. Do you think any of her friends— co-workers—I mean might have any idea?"

"I've talked with everyone I can think of and no one has any idea. They did say though, that Iris had seemed to be depressed— which is understandable. And, well, some suggested that—and remember these are just *suggestions* and not gossip—but they said they thought Iris had been spending a lot time in bars."

"Well, she was out a lot. And she didn't seem very happy."

"So who's with you kids?"

"I'm eighteen now and I'll be finished with high school at the end of this semester and I have a job lined up at the Post Office."

"But do you have any other family?"

"Oh yes, both sets of grandparents are nearby and they're helping us. Like I said, Mr. Gribble, we kind of got used to Iris hardly being around. My brother and I have been doing everything around here for—well, almost since my mom died."

"I know that, Randy and your Dad was proud of you boys for helping out so much."

"But, I don't know, maybe Iris just had to get away for a while and will be back. I just don't know. Who knows, we might just get a phone call from her."

"Well keep me posted and remember, if you kids need anything, don't hesitate to call me."

Thanksgiving 1979 is spent, as promised, with Grandma and Grandpa Plant in Marrionette Park. The Plants have invited the Taylor grandparents to share the holiday dinner with them.

Grandma and Grandpa Taylor are already at the Plant home when the children arrive. Randy can tell that the four have been discussing their situation. After the traditional dinner, Grandpa Plant opens the conversation that Randy has been anticipating.

"Well now, Randy, has there been any word from Iris?"

"No Grandpa. Nothing at all."

"You children just can't go on living alone like this," Grandma Taylor blurts out with tears in her eyes. "We want to help you."

"We know that," says Randy quietly. "We know that you all want to help. And we appreciate it. But we're doing just fine. Dad provided for us and as I've told you, I'll be starting my job at the post office next week—part-time at first, then full time after the first of the year. You're all welcome to check in on us any time and I promise, you'll see that we're doing just fine."

The Monday after Thanksgiving, Randy begins working part time in the mornings at the Richton Park Post Office. He knows he has to maintain a two-point-five grade point average. What he doesn't know is that his G.P.A. is slowly declining. Responsibilities that most seventeen year olds couldn't dream of have been placed on his shoulders. And yet the love he has for his siblings make it all worthwhile.

Among the duties he has to perform are sorting the mail and lifting the bags into the trucks. Randy is a strong young man— but he's not yet used to doing this kind of work.

Tuesday morning his back is tight. Mainly his lats, (the upper side back muscles) and traps, (the muscles between the neck and shoulders). Moving as if he's eighty, Randy prepares breakfast. He awakes Amy gently from her sleep, as Brian starts his day. The middle sibling has more energy now. He loves driving his sister to school. When this duty is done, he drives back, leaving the Buick in the driveway. Minutes later, the brothers are in the LeSabre as Randy slowly backs out onto Royal Drive.

"Do you like working in the Post Office?" Brian asks.

"It's a nice change of pace, but I'm sore as hell," Randy replies.

"You're lucky you don't have to go to school in the mornings," Brian says.

"Luck has nothing to do with it little brother. I planned ahead."

"How?' Brian asks.

"Back in May, I signed up for the B.O.S. work study program."

"What's B.O.S. stand for?' Brian asks.

"Beginning of the semester," Randy replies. "I was gonna use it for Lakewood Bowl, but then I got on at the Post Office. You can earn credits, just by working," Randy says.

"That's cool!" Brian says as the Buick pulls in the front lot near the cement steps.

"Look into it Brian and keep motivated," Randy says.

"Why do you say that?" Brian asks.

"Because successful people stay motivated. Now beat it! I have to get to work." The middle sibling gets out, shuts the door as Randy peels out of the parking lot, spinning gravel in the process.

Three inches of snow falls the following night. Among his chores since seventh grade was shoveling snow, but now Randy doesn't do it unless it absolutely needs it. Randy walks to his locker in the employee room, opens it and takes off his jacket. After sorting mail for two hours, he takes a short break. Randy pours himself a cup of coffee from the pot in the lunchroom.

"Has anyone ever told you, you look like Rock Hudson?" a voice asks.

"More than once," Randy replies. The co-worker extends his hand.

"My name's Shawn. Pleased to meet you."

"My name's Randy."

"Ya know, not only do you look like Rock Hudson, you look familiar—like we've met before." Randy examines his new co-worker and smiles.

"Cross-country meet last year at Rich East," he says. Shawn snaps his fingers.

"That's right! You passed me at the last part of the course. I slipped and fell on you at the end," Shawn says.

"I damn near died in the chute," Randy says. "The last half mile was pretty muddy."

"Yeah man, we had a lot of rain that week," Shawn says.

"Are you new also?" Randy asks.

"I started last June. Well Randy, I gotta get back to work. I'll see ya." Randy finishes his coffee then walks back to the mailroom. Pushing a cart of mailbags, he begins loading a truck.

Randy loves this new temporary routine, but there's a catch; he doesn't have time for lunch. Parking his Buick at Rich South, he quickly gets out and looks at his wristwatch.

Randy rushes to his chemistry class. He quietly walks in and takes his seat. Mrs. Logan gives him a stern look. She gives Randy his test as he mouths, 'Sorry I'm late'. The classroom is quiet as the student signs his name at the top.

At problem number eight, Randy's stomach begins growling like a tiger's. He places his left hand over his mid section, but to no avail. The growling continues. A girl starts to giggle, and another boy starts to laugh. Others follow suit. The teacher and the student make eye contact.

"I'm sorry Mrs. Logan. I didn't have time for lunch. Do you have a sandwich I can have?" Randy asks.

"No I don't," she says as the class roars.

"All right everyone, settle down," Mrs. Logan says. The laughter ceases as the tests are finished. The instructor stands and says; "Pass your test to the person in front of you." As Randy turns around, he's handed a small package of six peanut butter crackers.

"Thank you Misty," he says. *Man, she's got a rack that could feed Ethiopia!* Randy quickly opens the package so the sound will be camouflaged by the sound of the tests. He devours three of them. When the class period is over, Randy leaves in a hurry to the cafeteria. He finds it empty. He catches the attention of Miss Andrews—a kitchen worker. The middle age woman walks towards him.

"Miss Andrews, you're looking good today!" Randy says as he puts on the charm.

"Thank you Randy," she replies.

"Ma'am, I didn't have lunch. May I please have a sandwich?" The kitchen worker holds up a forefinger then leaves. In a quarter of a minute, she's back with a hamburger.

"It's cold," she says.

"I don't care. Thank you very much," Randy says. He eats quickly while walking to his locker. The bell for his last class is three minutes away.

When Brian opens the front door, the aroma from the kitchen ignites his hunger. Amy runs to him, as she throws her arms around his legs.

"Hi sister. Howya doin'?" he asks.

"Fine Brian," she replies.

"What's cooking, Randy?"

"Liver and onions little brother." Brian takes off his jacket and boots and places his slippers on. He walks in the kitchen with Amy.

"That's awesome!" Brian says.

"We haven't had it in a while. It was Dad's favorite." The doorbell rings as the oldest sibling can see the outline of a man wearing an official-looking hat—like a police officer— through the thin white curtain over the back of the front door.

"Take Amy downstairs," Randy instructs Brian.

"Hello officer," he says.

"Hello son, I'm Officer Krause. Are you Randy Taylor?"

"Yes, I'm Randy. How can I help you?"

"Can I come in?

"Sure Officer. I'm sorry, come right in"

The policeman steps in the foyer, taking off his hat.

"I'm looking for one Iris Johnson Taylor," the officer says.

"I haven't seen her," Randy replies, "I mean she seems to have moved out."

"Do you know where she could be?"

"Not the slightest," Randy says. The officer contemplates.

"How long has she been gone?" he asks.

"'Bout two weeks," Randy says.

"Do you know why she would leave?" he asks.

"No sir. After my Dad died, she was out a lot and it was like she would stay away for longer and longer periods of time. I think maybe without him, she didn't feel like she needed to be here. I don't know. We didn't talk all that much."

"And you say that you've had no phone calls or letters from her since she left?"

"Let's sit in the living room, sir. Come this way. No, we haven't had any messages from her at all." Randy sits on the couch and motions toward one of the armchairs. Officer Krause sits and takes out his notebook and begins to write.

"So, Randy, she's been gone two weeks."

Randy nods.

"Did she take her clothes and things with her?"

"She took everything. I mean everything that was hers."

"And she didn't' say anything to you when she was packing?"

"Oh no, she packed up while we were at school. So we came home, her car was gone, she was gone—nothing new there—but the big tip-off was that her room was empty. And that was it."

"She never mentioned moving anywhere or visiting someone or some place?"

"Nothing at all."

"So who's taking care of things here? I understand you have a younger brother and a sister who is quite young."

"I'm handling things. Just like always."

"There's no adult in the house?"

"I'm eighteen, sir. In fact, I'm working part-time at the post office and will have a full-time job there in January."

"You're finished with high school?"

"I will be in December. And my brother, Brian—he'll be turning seventeen soon so my sister is always with one of us and my Grandparents check in a lot. So everything here is fine."

"You aren't upset that Iris left you?"

"We hardly knew her. She and my dad were only married a short time and, like I said, once he was gone, she kind of lived her own life."

"Are you kids okay financially?"

"Yes. My dad left us some money. His insurance paid off the house. We're doing okay. And now I have this job, like I said, with the post office and my brother works, too."

"I see. You know Iris's boss at Prairie State College is very upset that she seems to have just disappeared—walked away from you kids and her job. Did Iris inherit any money from your Dad?"

"Yes, I think she got a pretty good settlement. Oh, and I did talk with Mr. Gribble at Prairie State. You can't blame him for being upset."

"I'll be checking with your father's lawyer regarding the will and all. In fact, son, have you been in touch with him to let him know that Iris is gone?"

"No, I guess I should, right?"

"Yes, you should."

"I'll be checking into some other things and will probably be back in touch with you soon. Thank you for talking with me. You kids let me know if there is anything we can do."

"Thank you, Officer Krause. We will do that but honestly, we're doing fine."

"I can see that and judging from that wonderful aroma coming from your kitchen—I suppose that I've been keeping you from your dinner—it's making me hungry."

"You're welcome to join us. I made liver and onions."

"Sounds great but my wife would be mad if I missed the one she's prepared."

When Brian hears the front door close, he and Amy come upstairs. "What did he want?" he asks.

"He wanted to know where Iris is," Randy says.

"What did you tell him?" Brian asks.

"I told him I didn't know. Let's have supper. Amy, let's eat. I'm starving!"

The following week is mid December. The decorated Christmas tree in the living room stands in front of the large window.

The holiday season had always been Randy's favorite time of year—until now. If it weren't for Amy, the artificial tree would remain in its box. With his parents gone, the season has taken on a somber tone.

At the end of his chemistry class, Mrs. Logan hands back the tests. A large red 'C-minus' is at the top of Randy's. *What the hell,* he thinks. *I'm otta here!*

"Well class, most of you did well. Our session is almost over. Have a wonderful Christmas break, and a great nineteen-eighty," Mrs. Logan says. The bell rings as students stand from their desks.

"Mister Taylor, I need a word with you," she says. Randy gathers his textbook and folder and walks to her desk as his classmates leave. He places his chemistry textbook on her desk.

"You won't be here next semester."

"No I won't," Randy replies.

"I wish you success and happiness Mister Taylor."

"Thank you Mrs. Logan. And I want you to know something," he says.

"What's that?" she asks.

"I want you to know that if you weren't married, I'd ask you out." His teacher gives him a smile.

"Well Mister Taylor, I'm very married."

"That's why I'm not gonna ask you out," Randy replies. Mrs. Logan busts out laughing.

"Good day Mister Taylor."

"Good day Mrs. Logan. It was a pleasure having you as my teacher." The young man leaves and makes his way to his locker.

He exchanges his chemistry book for his economics book, then hurries to his last class.

When his economics class is over, Randy turns the corner and heads to the main office. He opens the glass door and is greeted by the receptionist.

"May I help you?' she asks.

"I'm here to see Mister McGraw."

"This is in regards to?" she asks.

"My diploma. Today's my last day. My name is Randy Taylor."

"That's right Mister Taylor. I keep forgetting your name. I see so many students throughout the day." The receptionist picks up her phone and pushes the principal's button. Mister McGraw walks out in his usual gray suit a minute later. He shakes Randy's hand, as he gives him a paper stating that he has completed all of his credits for graduation.

"Congratulations Mister Taylor. By graduating early, you've accomplished what very few students have done in the history of Rich South. In some ways, I hate to see you leave," the principal says.

"Don't worry sir. I'm sure another student will enter this lovely institution and pull a bigger prank than I did." Randy says "Is Mister Jenkins here?"

"He's in a meeting at Prairie State College," Mister McGraw says.

"Good luck Mister Taylor

"Thank you sir." The receptionist stands and gives him a hug.

"Come and visit us anytime Mister Taylor," she says.

"Thank you ma'am," Randy says. Once downstairs, he opens his locker and begins to clean it out. For Randy, his feelings are bitter sweet. *I sure wish Mom and Dad were here for this day.* He thinks. Placing his folders, notebooks and math materials in his nylon/cloth briefcase, he zips it closed, then puts his scarf and letter jacket on. Looking at his empty locker he thinks, *I'll never open this door again.*

Snow is falling as Randy opens the glass door. He bids farewell to several classmates, among them, is Douglas Elgin. The others keep walking as Douglas stops.

"You coming in June for the graduation ceremony?" Douglas asks.

"I don't know. I might," Randy replies. Dougie's next question is quieter.

"Have you heard from the 'fuzz' yet?"

"I've had one cop come over to the house, but I played dumb with him. Everything's cool."

"Let's get together this spring and do some runnin'," Dougie says.

"That would be great! Gimme a call," Randy says as they embrace for an instant.

"Too bad you couldn't go out for cross-country this year."

"Well, I had three wonderful years. Take care my friend," Randy says.

Five year old Amy awakens early on Christmas morning 1979. She walks downstairs to the living room and spying the gifts under the tree, runs back upstairs to her brothers' room. "Randy, you awake?" she asks. "Randy, you awake?" she asks again as the oldest sibling stirs. The child moves to the edge of his bed and asks: "You awake Randy?" The brother opens his eyes.

"I am now," he replies.

"Santy Clause came last night!" Amy says. Randy slowly gets out of bed and places his robe and slippers on as the child runs downstairs. Randy makes his way to the living room. He picks up three gifts and hands them to his sister. She opens them eagerly. Brian walks downstairs in his robe and slippers, yawning and rubbing an eye.

"Merry Christmas," he says.

"Merry Christmas little brother," Randy says. The child opens her gifts and discovers two Barbie dolls, a dollhouse, and a pink and purple nightgown. She picks up two other gifts as Randy stops her.

"No sister, those are Brian's."

"Amy, that one is Grandma Plant's," Randy says. She sets that one down and looks bewildered.

"Sister, those are all of your gifts from Santa," the oldest sibling says. The child crosses her arms and pouts.

"Come here Amy," Randy says. The child walks over as he sets her sideways on his leg.

"Now listen honey. How many kings visited the baby Jesus?"

"Three," she says.

"And each king brought one gift. Now, how many gifts did the baby Jesus receive?" Randy asks. The child pauses then replies, "Three."

"Now, when Grandma's and Grandpa's Plant and Taylor come over, they're going to give you gifts. In total, you'll have more than three. Aren't you blessed?' Randy asks.

"Yeah," the child answers slow and reluctantly.

"Merry Christmas Amy!" Brian says as he opens his arms. The child gets off of Randy's lap and gives Brian a hug. Brian looks upwards. "Merry Christmas Mom and Dad," he says. The child mimics. "Merry Christmas Mommy and Daddy!"

"I've got a great idea!" Randy says. "Let's hold hands and sing 'Happy Birthday' to Jesus." After the song is sung, the child speaks.

"Randy, we need a birthday cake for Jesus!"

"Well sister, the stores are all closed. We'll get one tomorrow," Randy says. The child pouts.

"Now Amy, don't start. When Grandma and Grandpa Plant come over, they'll bring an apple pie," Randy says.

"But a pie isn't a cake," Amy says.

"Aw man! I forgot about the ham!" Randy quickly stands and walks to the kitchen. He preheats the oven then takes out the ham from the fridge. Opening a can of pineapples and a jar of cloves, he prepares the meat when Brian walks up to him.

"Thank you Randy," he says.

"What for?"

"For holding us together," Brian replies.

"It's my job. Why don't you open your present little brother?"

"I'll do it later with you and Amy."

"Get Amy dressed and then we'll open them."

It's almost noon when both sets of grandparents arrive with gifts, pies and covered dishes. Grandpa Taylor walks in carrying two bottles of wine. Everyone is festive during the exchange of gifts. Then the grandmothers and Randy retreat into the kitchen to get the holiday dinner on the table.

When grace is said, Grandpa Taylor remembers Donald and Tammy, "We thank you for this food Lord, for our beloved grandchildren and the love we have for our wonderful son, Donald and his beautiful wife, Tammy. They were a joy to all of our lives and how we miss them with all our hearts. Amen."

By the middle of the meal, both of the bottles are empty. The warmth of this holiday dinner is special to the oldest sibling Randy but without his parents, there is a void.

"So how do you like your new job Randy?"

"Pretty good Grandpa. It's physically demanding, but I don't mind. I begin full time next month."

"You're doing well grandson. I'm proud of you."

"Thank you Grandpa."

While Brian takes Amy downstairs to play one of her new games with her, the four grandparents take the opportunity to talk with Randy.

"Son," says Grandpa Taylor, "did you know that we have all been contacted by the police?"

"Grandma Plant called and told me just yesterday."

"Well, they only called the day before. It was us first then the Plants. And I'm proud to tell you that we all had the same thing to say—that because of you, you three are doing just fine."

"You know," says Grandma Plant, "they are only concerned about the welfare of you children."

"Now Mother, Randy isn't really a child anymore," says Grandpa Plant.

"I know that but you know what I mean Randy. And we all told them how grown up you are, how responsible and caring. They were very impressed."

"I guess there's been nothing from Iris," says Grandma Taylor. "What kind of a woman does that! And you know that your Grandfather talked with your Dad's lawyer."

"I'll explain that part," says Grandpa Taylor. "I phoned him as soon as I heard Iris had taken off—just to make sure, Randy, that everything was in order for you kids. And he says you already scheduled a meeting with him for after Christmas. I'm glad of that. But son, you should know that he learned that Iris took her inheritance all right. But she never deposited it in the bank or in any bank that he can find."

"What did she do with it, Grandpa?" Randy can't believe what he's hearing but it explains why he never found any of Iris's banking papers.

"Apparently, nobody knows. You see, the police have been checking around, trying to find out if she took her money with her or if she had a lot of debt but so far there is nothing."

It was clear to Randy that Grandpa Taylor and the other grandparents had discussed this among themselves because the other three were nodding their agreement as Grandpa spoke.

So that's why I couldn't find any checkbooks or any bank documents in Iris' name, thought Randy. *That's probably why she was using our money. But what did she do with the inheritance Dad left her?*

"Now here's the part we hate to tell you, Randy. The lawyer says it looks like Iris may have spent some of the money that was meant for you kids. I'm so sorry."

"I can't believe it! Why would she do that to us? Do you know how much?"

"Your lawyer is working with the bank to get a full accounting. But I can tell you she didn't get all of it. I'm so sorry, son."

"We'll be okay, Grandpa. I have a good job now and Brian is working and the house is paid off. It will be okay."

Christmas is over all too soon. Amy has received many gifts from both sets of grandparents. The brothers have mainly received gifts of money. After the grandparents leave, Randy gives Amy her bath. He reads to her then puts her to bed.

Later in their beds, the brothers talk. Randy fills Brian in on what their grandparents discussed with him.

"Of course we already knew Iris had stolen some of our money, even before Grandpa told me. But I wasn't sure about her having some kind of an account with her inheritance in it. "

"So you mean she never had an account with her own inheritance money in it?"

"I guess not. It's weird that there seems to be no evidence of the money Dad left her or what she did with it. In fact, there is nothing to really show us what she did with any of her money, except for all those damn clothes she bought. But that still doesn't add up to all the money that went through her hands. Maybe she owed a bunch to someone or—oh hell, I don't know. But that's all good—for me anyway."

"How is that good for you?"

"Look, Brian, if Iris had left a nice fat bank account behind— well, who takes off without taking all their money? That would look kind of funny. So it's working out for the best. It's good, brother. "

"Yeah, you're right, I guess. But it's still hard."

"What do you mean?"

"This Christmas was nice, but it wasn't the same without Mom and Dad," Brian says.

"We have to survive little brother. We have no choice."

CHAPTER **ELEVEN**

Jack Gribble sits at his desk at Prairie State College. For weeks now, his employee Iris Johnson Taylor hasn't shown up. He's called her house and talked with her stepson, he's talked to several of her friends, he's spoken with the police and he even located a cousin, with no success. No one seems to know where she could be. But no one he spoke with seems to have been all that close to Iris. No one really knows much about her personal life. He puts on his coat and walks out to his Plymouth and drives to the Chicago Heights Police Station. There, he fills out a missing person's report and gives it to detective Robert Morris.

"You know of course, Mr. Gribble, that with no indication of foul play, there isn't much we can do. An adult is free to drop out of sight any time he or, in this case, she wants to. And, given her odd financial dealings, maybe she had good reason to take off like she did."

"What do you mean by *odd financial dealings*?

"I'm not at liberty to go into detail since it doesn't involve her job or Prairie State but it does appear things were not quite right with her—let's say, spending habits. Of course, Mr. Gribble, if there's anything you can tell me that does involve her job or Prairie State?

"No, I don't believe there is anything here that involves Iris and any funds or spending. Nothing at all, except I did speak with a cousin of hers from Rockford. But that amounted to nothing since she didn't know much about Iris."

While hanging mailbags on December 27th, Randy's supervisor Paul Micelli walks up to him.

"Randy, I don't know if you've heard but Dave's having surgery soon. I need for you to start full time next week. Is that okay?"

"Yeah Paul, that's no problem!" Randy replies. The young man is elated. Since he first applied at the Richton Park Post Office, he's been itching to get on full time. Now, it's become a reality.

On the evening of December 31st, 1979, Randy lets Amy stay up until midnight. Making a tray of snacks, he serves them to his siblings as they watch television. As the ball slowly begins its descent in New York's Times Square, Amy looks at the screen as if she's seen snow for the very first time. Her eyes are wide, and her smile is broad. The countdown begins, as the siblings yell in unison. "TEN, NINE, EIGHT, SEVEN, SIX, FIVE, FOUR, THREE, TWO, ONE—HAPPY NEW YEAR!!" Four numbers light up; A one, nine, eight and a zero. The siblings embrace then Randy gives his sister her famous 'ride'. As with every ride in the past, her laughter is uncontrollable. Randy speaks as he sets her down. "Okay Amy, time for bed."

"I'm not tired," she says.

"Alright sister, you need a wind down period. Go get some of your books," Randy says. The child walks to her small case, and removes ten of them. Walking back to the sofa, she sees that her oldest brother's jaw has dropped.

"Amy, I'm not reading a library to you." This strikes her as funny as she laughs.

"Three books," Randy says.

"Four," she says.

"Okay four."

"Five," she says.

"Little sister, you're pushing the envelope. Four and no more," Randy says in a semi-strong voice. The child sits on his lap and snuggles against him. Randy opens a book, and then speaks to his brother.

"Brian, I want you to clean off the cocktail table."

"Do I have to?" he asks while lying on the carpet, watching television.

"You've got two choices. Do it now or before you go to bed."

The spring semester commences five days later. When Randy gets off work at 3pm, he punches out and walks to his Buick. Getting in, he turns the ignition. The engine doesn't turn over. Randy pulls the headlight switch out, and gets out of his LeSabre. He sees the headlights are barely on. *I should've replaced that battery back in September.* Randy gets in, pushes the button in, shuts the door and walks back inside. He calls the house on a pay phone. Brian picks up on the second ring.

"Taylor residence."

"Ay little brother, you're gonna have to get supper started."

"You working overtime?' Brian asks.

"No, my car won't start. I'm gonna have to get a new battery."

"What should I fix?" Brian asks.

"Just brown the ground beef that's in the fridge, and put a pot of cold water on the stove," Randy says.

"Why cold?" Brian asks.

"Because cold water is cleaner than hot. I should be back within the hour. See ya." Randy walks to a nearby auto parts store. Brian begins to prepare the meal, as Amy watches 'Mister Rogers Neighborhood'. Five minutes later, the doorbell rings. Brian wipes his hands, and answers the front door as Amy walks upstairs to the foyer. A tall bald man in an overcoat shows his badge.

"Hello, I'm detective Robert Morris. May I come in?"

"Yes sir," Brian says. The detective steps into the foyer and wipes his feet on the 'rub rug'.

"I'm looking for Iris Johnson Taylor," he says."

"Oh, sure. Would you like to sit down? We haven't seen her here since before Thanksgiving."

"She was mean," Amy says.

"Amy, don't interrupt when grownups are talking. Now go and watch TV quietly. Sorry detective—she's six."

"Do you know where Iris could've gone?" Morris asks.

"No I don't," Brian answers.

"Well son, have you heard from her at all—a phone call, perhaps, or a letter?"

"Nothing. She didn't even send a Christmas card."

"Well, that was mean. Do you know where she's from?" the detective asks.

"Not a clue. If my dad or Iris told us, I might not have been paying attention. I think she had an uncle from downstate but he died." Brian answers calmly. "She didn't talk much about herself and we never thought to ask my dad. Once he was gone, Iris was out a lot. We hardly saw her."

"Do you mind if I look around?" Morris asks.

"Well, my brother isn't home. It would be better if he was—but, if you're just looking around. I guess it's okay. Where do you want to start?"

Fifteen minutes later they were back in the living room. "So that's the whole house?"

"That's it—except for the garage. You want to see that?"

"No, that's ok Brian."

"Well son, thanks for the tour. I can see that your stepmother— well that she meant to be gone a long time."

"I guess, sir."

"Who's taking care of you kids?"

"My older brother and me," Brian answers

"I mean who is the adult taking care of you kids?"

"My brother is eighteen. He has a job and we're doing just fine. Plus we have our grandparents. They check in on us all the time."

"Okay—I'll be in touch. Thank you for your time."

"No problem detective," Brian replies.

Robert Morris gets in his sedan and drives back to the station in Chicago Heights. In his office, he does some research and makes several phone calls. He finds that Iris's parents are deceased and that she's an only child. She has no relatives in the south suburban Chicago area. He does locate that cousin in Rockford. But Shelia Johnson seems to know nothing of Iris's whereabouts and has had little recent contact with her. According to the Johnson woman, the two had been closer as younger girls but had kind of drifted apart. Closer to home, Detective Morris talks with both sets of grandparents. Even though he seems to have reached a dead end, leaving his office, he's unable to get Amy's words out of his head. "She was mean."

That night after they've put Amy to bed, Brian tells Randy about the visit from Detective Morris.

"I had to make a quick decision and I thought it would be worse if I made it look like we have something to hide."

"I understand, Brian. From what you've told me, you didn't say anything that they don't already know. And there isn't anything in the house for them to see that would make them suspicious. I think you did okay. In fact, you did better than okay."

"Thanks Randy." Brian says quietly as he remembers Amy's words—*she was mean*. He decides it's best not to worry Randy with something as trivial as that.

Randy receives his first paycheck from the United States Post Office, the first week of January, 1980. With it, he pays several bills, buys groceries, and even though there's still some inheritance money left, he puts away a little money for his siblings for college. With the money that's left over, he takes his parents 8 x 10 black and white wedding photo from the top of his chest of drawers and drives to Phil's Photography in Lincoln Mall. He has it blown up to an 11 x 17 inches and has it placed in an elegant gold frame. At home, he removes a painting of a woman in a white dress from the living room wall that Iris and brought home and hung, never noticing the signature on the bottom. He places the painting on the floor behind the oak cabinet in the dining room, ignoring the fact that a bit of the corner of the frame is sticking out.

Picking up the 'new' wedding photo, he places the back wire carefully on the nail above the sofa. Randy discovers that by closing one eye, he's able to focus on where the wire meets the nail. Stepping back, Randy sees it's a little crooked. He straightens the frame and steps back again.

"Perfect!" he says. *I'm not gonna say anything to Brian and Amy. I'll see if they notice it themselves.* Randy stares at the photo for a long while. He never realized that he looks more like his father than his mother.

"We miss you Mom and Dad," he says. Randy hears voices outside. He walks to the kitchen and begins to prepare hardboiled eggs for egg salad sandwiches. His siblings walk in the foyer, as he steps out of the kitchen.

"How'd ya do Amy?" Randy asks.

"I got a strike!" she replies.

"That's wonderful sister. You bowl better than Brian." Randy says. Brian and Amy take off their boots and hang up their coats. Slippers are put on, as they all walk in the kitchen.

"What's cookin'?" Brian asks.

"I'm gonna make egg salad sandwiches and chicken noodle soup," Randy replies.

"Brian, why don't you take Amy downstairs and play a game with her while I finish making lunch," Randy says. The middle and the youngest sibling walk downstairs. Ten minutes later, Amy runs in the kitchen.

"Randy, Brian's cheating!" the child says. The oldest emerges from the kitchen and looks down towards the family room.

"Brian, quit cheating."

"I'm not," he replies.

"Oh, just makin' up your own rules so you can win huh little brother?"

Brian laughs. Amy runs downstairs and with her little fists starts punching him. Brian laughs all the harder.

After lunch, Randy says, "Little brother, when you and Amy came back from bowling, did yuz notice anything?"

"No, notice what—where?

"Look in the living room," Randy says. Brian gets up as the youngest follows.

"That's cool!" Brian says.

"That's Mommy and Daddy!" Amy proclaims. Randy picks her up.

"Yes sister. You're right," he says.

"I miss Mommy and Daddy," the child says sadly as she places her head on her brother's shoulder.

"We all do sister. But Mommy and Daddy are watching from heaven. They can see everything we do," Randy says.

"They can see Brian cheating!" she says.

"Yes they can. They can see Brian cheating."

Icicles are dripping from the gutters. The mounds of snow in Cook County Illinois are now mere patches. Warm winds from the Gulf of Mexico are warming the Midwest. And with one month left of school, Brian is itching to have his own room. Lying in their beds late one night, he turns to his brother as he's adjusting his pillow.

"Are you gonna move into Mom and Dad's bedroom Randy?" he asks.

"We'll, since we seem to have passed the police questions and the detective inspection—" Randy says as he pauses for a moment. "Yeah Brian. It's probably been long enough, I think. I'll move into their bedroom this week-end."

The middle sibling clenches his right fist and moves his arm towards him in victory. "Yes!"

"Goodnight little brother."

That weekend, Randy calls the Salvation Army in nearby Park Forest to donate the queen size bed. His father had purchased it right before the wedding, and now Randy can't even think of sleeping in it. When everything is loaded onto the truck, Randy gives each man a tip. He then dismantles his bed and takes it to his parent's bedroom. He places the frame against the wall, facing the windows. As he stands contemplating, Randy realizes his parent's bed was in the same spot. Randy wheels the bed frame against another wall, so that his bed will face the closets, parallel to the windows. When the box spring and mattress is added, he's astounded at how much room he has. He walks to the adjacent bedroom, and slowly moves his chest of drawers. The tiny wheels on the bottom squeak in protest. Randy picks up the phone on his mother's nightstand and phones the Salvation Army. He asks if they have a desk. The clerk says they do and it has a matching chair. According to what he is told, the dimensions of the desk will be perfect.

"How much?" Randy asks.

"Thirty-five dollars." He can afford this but is also a bargain hunter due to the fact that he's had to grow up fast.

"I have twenty-seven in cash," Randy replies. "Will you take it?"

"Yes we will sir," she says.

"Okay, I'll be here for a while. Randy cleans the right closet that had belonged to Iris. He doesn't touch the left closet, still containing most of his father's clothes. The delivery is made, while Brian and Amy are bowling. Randy instructs the men to place the desk and the chair in the corner of the room. When this is done, he quickly tests the chair by sitting in it. The chair is old but comfortable.

Instead of giving them tips in cash, Randy hands each of them a gift certificate to Cal's cornbeef restaurant on Sauk Trail.

"Thanks buddy," one says. "This is one of my favorite joints!"

The front door opens and Brian and Amy are back. Taking off their coats and changing their footwear, they go upstairs. Brian is overjoyed at his 'larger' dwelling.

"I got two strikes Randy!" Amy exclaims.

"That's wonderful sister. Now, why don't you go downstairs and watch television while I cook dinner."

"Your bedroom looks so big Randy," Brian says.

"Yes it does, but it's kind of weird that I'm in here. I still think of it as Mom and Dad's room."

"Randy, graduation is coming up soon. You going?"

"No I won't."

"You might regret it years down the road," Brian says.

"Pleeeaase!" says Amy.

"What day is it on?" Randy asks.

"Saturday, June ninth," Brian replies.

"I have to work that Saturday," Randy says.

"At seven-thirty in the evening?" Brian asks. The oldest pauses then says:

"Okay little brother, you've twisted my arm." Brian and Amy clap.

"It's no big deal," Randy says.

"Yes it is! You don't graduate from high school every year—do you?"

"I'll get the invitations out tomorrow," Randy says.

That evening after Amy is put to bed, the brother's watch the ten o'clock news. Part of the broadcast features the explosion of the Mount Saint Helens volcano in Washington State.

"Lord have mercy. Look at all of that smoke, Brian! I'm glad we don't live there." Brian bids his brother a goodnight. Randy remains in the family room and watches the 'Tonight Show' with Johnny Carson. Later, he has a smoke in the utility room. Upon retiring, Randy walks to his former bedroom then realizes he has a new one.

Randy attends the one and only rehearsal in the school gymnasium, while Brian watches Amy. It's been five months since he's seen his classmates, and the reunion is uplifting. Randy crosses paths with his friend Barbi in the hallway near the gym. She gives him a kiss on the cheek and shows him her engagement ring.

"That's beautiful Barbi! Who's the lucky guy?" Randy asks.

"Jeff Powers. He's an insurance salesman. He was gonna marry some woman named Iris, but he changed his mind. He's going to marry me!"

"Lucky him," Randy says.

"I've never been so happy in all of my life!" Barbi says.

"Just make sure you don't go swimming with that on. You'll sink to the bottom of the pool," Randy says with a smile. Barbi playfully punches him in the stomach then sees her girlfriend in the distance.

"Oh, there's Carol. I'll see you at graduation Randy." Barbi gives him a quick hug, then runs off. Moments later, Douglas walks up. The two embrace.

"Howya doin' Randy?" Dougie asks.

"Just working and taking care of my brother and sister," he replies.

"Man, I can't believe this moment has arrived. Remember when we were dipshit freshman?" Dougie asks.

"Now we're dipshit seniors," Randy replies.

"Well, I guess I don't have to ask what you're doing after graduation. How's work Randy?"

"It was hard back in January but now I'm used to it. What are you gonna do Dougie?" Randy asks as he lights a cigarette.

"I've been accepted at Illinois State University on a two year track scholarship!"

"Why just two years?" Randy asks.

"Here's the 'game plan'. I'm going to do two years of college, one year of mortuary school and one year of apprenticeship and then I will become a full-fledged funeral director with my dad!"

"That's wonderful Dougie. I'm proud of ya! You know, in the three years I ran cross-country I only beat you once." Randy says.

"I was hung over," Dougie states. A stern voice comes out of nowhere.

"Mister Taylor, do you see that 'no smoking' sign?" The voice belongs to Mrs. Harrison.

"I forgot how to read," Randy says.

The graduation ceremony begins at seven-thirty in the gymnasium. Both sets of grandparents are in the audience, along with Brian and Amy. The seniors are standing in the hallway outside the gym in alphabetical order. The guys wear red gowns and caps, the girls wear dark blue gowns, and the dignitaries wear white. Randy likes his tassel with a golden eight/zero at the top.

The music begins as the seniors begin their slow walk into the gymnasium. Once seated, the class valedictorian, Peggy Schaffer steps up to the podium and begins her address. Randy likes his position. He's seated near the double doors and has a good view of the commencement. Halfway into her speech, Randy sees one of his classmates get up and leave. *If he's gonna get sick, I can't blame him.* When Peggy's speech is over, everyone applauds. The choir sings, "America the Beautiful."

The next stage is the introduction of the principal Mister McGraw by one of the dignitaries. Randy yells, "Way to go, Quick Draw!" His classmates nearby laugh. When the applause ceases, the principal makes his speech and the diplomas are handed out by the dean of students, Mr. Boyer. The dean shakes the guys' hands and kisses each girl on her cheek. As he hands Sara Kingston her diploma, she leans backward while giving him the finger. Randy and others roar with laughter. He's still laughing when he gets in line and feels a tap on his shoulder from his classmate George Teeman. Randy turns.

"Sara made my day," George whispers.

"She made my whole damn year!" Taylor whispers back. When it's Randy's turn, Mister Boyer hands him a duplicate diploma and shakes his hand.

"You're not gonna kiss me are you Mister Boyer?" Randy asks. The dean makes a slight scowl which turns into a smile. Randy walks off stage. The ceremony proceeds. After the last diploma is handed out, several more songs are sung then Mister McGraw gives a final speech. The ceremony is over. During rehearsal, the seniors were instructed not to throw their caps in the air. The order has fallen on deaf ears. Randy takes off his tassel, and throws his cap in the air along with three hundred others. The graduates file out of the gymnasium to a long row of tables that contain refreshments. Many graduates hug each other. Randy does the same with his friends and several of his teachers. A number of girls are shedding tears, but Randy himself doesn't feel sad. His new life began the previous January.

"Randy!" Amy exclaims. The child runs to her brother as he picks her up, she hands him a flower.

"This is for me?" Thank you sister!" Randy says. Brian and both sets of grandparents emerge from the gym. Randy sets his sister down and hugs them all.

"Well little brother. You know what to look forward to next year," Randy says.

"Aren't you glad you came?" Brian asks.

"I sure am!" Randy says.

"I got the picture!" Brian says.

"What picture?" Randy asks.

"Of all the caps in the air."

"I can't wait to see it."

"We're all going to Tivoli's restaurant," Grandma Plant says.

A young woman in a two-piece bikini is standing at a tall chest of drawers in a large bedroom. Cash is on top of the bureau. The woman has her back turned. The viewer holds a small cast iron skillet in his right hand. He walks slowly, like a lion stalking his prey. As the viewer gets closer, his arm is raised and the skillet strikes the woman in the back of her head. The woman falls on the carpet. Iris turns and raises her upper torso. Bringing her knees to her bosom, she locks her hands in front of her shins, tilts her head and gives a big smile. She talks slowly, but continues to smile. "Randy—you're such an asshole." The oldest sibling awakens, giving off a slight gasp. He turns on his lamp and is for a moment disoriented. *Where's Brian? No—wait, I'm in my parent's room.* Randy's chest is wet from sweat. Taking his t-shirt off, he wipes his chest with it, and places it in his clothes hamper. Taking a clean t-shirt from his drawers, he puts it on. Randy checks on his sister who's sleeping soundly. He then walks downstairs, the soft glow from the bottom portion of a lamp lighting his way. Randy walks in the utility room, turns on the light switch and lights a cigarette.

Brian gets up and walks to the bathroom down the hall. When he's finished, he walks back, then peers into Randy's room. The lamp is on, but the bed is empty. Brian quietly walks downstairs to the utility room. His brother puffs on a cigarette. He squints as he looks in.

"You okay Randy?" he whispers.

"I just had a bad dream. I wanna talk to you little brother. I'm beginning to regret what I did."

"Wait, hold on. Let me tell you something. Last week, my classmate Wendy Kimble presented a report on verbal abuse. In it, she said the effects of verbal abuse can last well into adulthood. Now there's a little girl upstairs whose life you saved." Brian says.

"I know what you're saying but…"

"Hell Randy, come to think of it, if you hadn't taken her out—I would have. She stole from us. We couldn't trust her around Amy. Like Amy said, she was mean, just plain mean. You did the only thing you could have done. You've got to understand that."

Brian works part time in this summer of 1980. When he's not at Chernin's Shoes, he takes turns with his brother, taking Amy to the Lakewood pool, near Neil Armstrong Elementary. On this hot and humid Saturday in July, Brian is at the shoe store—bored out of his mind. Business has recently been slower than a snail.

At four o'clock Brian punches out along with his co-worker. Carl drives him to Lakewood Bowl, where the two shoot pool. Halfway into their second game, Carl has an epiphany.

"Oh no, I forgot to pick up my grandma at the mall! You don't mind walkin' home do ya Brian?" Carl asks.

"No, it's cool," Brian replies.

"See ya at work." Carl leaves quickly. Brian finishes the game, then decides to go home. He places the balls in the black square plastic rack, then returns them to the counter/control center. He pays Joe.

"How does Randy like his new job?"

"He likes it a lot," Brian replies.

"Tell him I said 'hello,' son. I miss him around here."

"I will. Take care Joe."

Brian leaves the coolness of the bowling alley, into the heat of the outdoors. *I haven't heard 'son' in a long time,* he thinks. As he nears the house, Brian sees that the garage door is down. Then he spots a wonderful sight in the driveway—a 1975 Chevrolet Monte Carlo that shines like a diamond. He quickens his pace. The car is light blue, a two-door, with a dark blue landau top.

The windows are rolled down. Brian sets his arms on the driver's door, but quickly pulls them back. "OUCH!" he says, not realizing the metal is hot from the stifling temps. Brian places his hands on his knees and checks out the blue cloth interior. The automobile smells brand new.

"And what company do we have?" Brian asks out loud. He admires the car for several minutes more then walks in the house. Amy runs up from the family room, as Randy hangs up the phone in the kitchen.

"Whose car is that, big brother?" Brian asks.

"Mine! I traded the Buick in. That LeSabre kept nickel and dimin' me because of that high mileage it had," Randy says.

"Can we go for a ride?" Brian asks.

"Sure. We'll eat dinner out too. I don't feel like cooking," the oldest says. Amy gets excited as Randy locks up the house. When they get to the Chevy, the child can't decide whether to sit in the backseat or the front.

"C'mon Amy, make up your mind," Randy says. The child sits in the back, behind the driver's seat. The brothers get in, with Brian sitting 'shotgun'. As Randy is about to close his door, his intuition kicks in. Turning around, he sees his sister's leg is out. Randy sets it in with his left hand and closes the door with his right.

"Amy, I almost closed the door on you. Keep your leg in the car!" He turns the ignition. This engine is quieter.

"Where didja get this?" Brian asks, as the backup lights come on.

"My co-worker's grandfather passed away a couple of months ago. She saw me putting a new battery in the Buick, and she could tell I wasn't too happy with that old car. Her grandmother gave me a deal I couldn't refuse. They own Anderson's Auto's in

Crete-Monee," Randy says. "This car has ac—which I'm turning on—rear window defogger, cruise control, AM/FM stereo radio, tilt steering wheel, and only seventy-six hundred miles. I had to dip a little into my part of the inheritance, but I'm working six days a week now, and next year I should be getting a raise." Randy turns left onto Cicero Avenue. "My payments are only a hundred and twenty a month, after my down payment."

"Brian makes me change into dry clothes at the pool locker room," Amy says.

"Can you blame him sister?" The driver rolls up his window, as Brian does the same.

"Leave your window open a crack."

"What difference does it make?" Brian asks.

"Because the outside air, will draw in more of the cool air. It makes the air-conditioner run more efficiently."

"That's cool!" Brian says. "No pun intended." The Chevy passes Vollmer Road, an area where there are no buildings and houses.

"Now check this out little brother. This car will shit 'n' git!" Randy floors the gas pedal, as all three feel pressure from their seats. The speedometer needle goes up to eighty-five.

"You swore," Amy says.

"Big brothers are allowed to swear," Randy says.

"Nice pickup, Randy."

The car slows down to sixty.

"I won't drive like that all of the time, I just wanted to show you the power of this three-fifty V-8."

"Can I turn on the radio?" Brian asks.

"Sure, little brother. Any station you want," Randy replies. Brian pushes the buttons until he finds WLS. A song by Sniff 'n' Tears blares from the speakers.

"I love this!" Brian exclaims. "What's the name of it?"

"*Driver's Seat.* They're singing about me, little brother."

The Monte Carlo makes its way to an A&W Root beer establishment in northern Country Club Hills.

"Is this where they bring the food out to you?" Brian asks.

"Yeah, but we'll be eating our supper inside," Randy replies. The Chevy pulls up to the parking block, as the siblings get out and walk into the restaurant.

Once the three are back outside in the parking lot, Randy asks, "Brian, do you have your driver's permit with you?"

"Right in my wallet," he replies. Randy hands him his keys.

"Are you serious?" he asks. His brother nods.

"Randy, you're alright!" Brian says as he opens the driver's door. Getting in, the middle sibling adjusts his seat and mirrors. Using Randy's phrase, 'Look before you leap' rule, Brian looks behind him before he backs out. The Chevrolet smoothly pulls out of the parking lot.

"This car is boss!" Brian says.

"I thought I was the only one who uses that phrase," Randy says.

"This car is boss," Amy says. The oldest turns around to the youngest.

"You like my new car, sister?" The child nods with a smile.

"You know we can never eat or drink in here—right Amy?"

"I want a car Randy," Brian says.

"Well little brother. Number one, you only have a permit. Number two, you should wait until you graduate."

"Why?' Brian asks.

"Because your part of the inheritance is drawing interest. Besides, you don't have problems with transportation right now. I drive you everywhere." The Monte Carlo heads south to Richton Park. So much talk about cars makes Randy think about the Duster he abandoned on that dark street in Chicago. *All this time has passed*, he thinks, *and, thank you, God, not one word about Iris's car. It musta been snatched up by some gang or someone who took it to a chop shop. I'll bet that's what happened. No sweat.*

The next Saturday, the oldest sibling gets off work at 1pm. Brian has taken Amy to the Lakewood pool. Earlier in the morning, Randy retrieved his pamphlet, 'The Rite of Penance' and placed it on the front seat of his car. His mother was Catholic his father Protestant. On the day of their wedding, Donald and Tammy had gotten married in the Cook County courthouse. It was Tammy's decision to send her boys to Catholic institutions until high school.

After punching out, Randy takes off his uniformed short sleeve shirt, while leaving his t-shirt on. He doesn't mind working Saturdays, since the shift is only five hours long. Stepping outside in the heat, Randy walks to his Chevy. He gets in and starts the engine, cracks open each window, turns on the ac, folds his shirt setting it on the passenger seat, puts on his sunglasses, and pulls out of the parking lot.

Randy attended Saint Emeric Elementary and Junior High in Country Club Hills from the fifth to the eighth grade. Since graduating in 1976, he has not been back—until now. Traffic is light as the young man makes his journey. Randy has chosen his alma mater for the fact he doesn't want to be recognized.

Father Eric Hughes left Saint Emeric the same year that Randy graduated. Mrs. Miller, the school's secretary has retired.

As he turns onto the school's street, Randy goes back in time. As a fifth grader, his family was living in Country Club Hills. Ten year old Randy would take a bus from the bus stop down the street. One evening, a snow storm had blown into the 'Land of Lincoln'. As the bus turned right and was nearing the school, Randy had freaked out a bit. To him, it looked like the roof of the school was gone. The boy realized there was snow on it. The snow on the roof of the school matched with the sky.

The Monte Carlo pulls into the parking lot. Randy sees several cars and a sign near the entrance, which reads:

RESERVED FOR FR. TERRY COFFMAN

Randy pulls in with the trunk of his car facing the double doors. He kills the engine and places the 'trans' in park. He sits for a moment. He feels as if he has stepped back in time. The young man gets out and locks his door. He slowly walks to the school. The first thing he notices is that the old building still smells the same—like an old building . Straight ahead are the classrooms, to the right are several offices, (including the principal's), to the left is the church. Randy walks into the sanctuary. He can almost see himself as a child, wearing his alter boy garb helping the priest with the bread and the wine.

Several people are standing near the confession booth. Randy enters a pew, kneels and silently prays. When the last person enters the booth, Randy leaves the pew and walks to the front of the sanctuary, his heart racing. He takes out the Penance pamphlet. After several minutes, a woman walks out and enters a pew to pray. Randy slowly walks in. He hears a small door open as the priest welcomes him in a soft voice. The young man speaks: "In the name of the Father, and of the Son, and of the Holy Spirit.

Amen." Randy listens to a text of Scripture about His mercy, and the calling of men to conversion. The young man begins.

"Father forgive me. It's been four years since my last confession. Here are my sins. I've lied to my parents, I've shop lifted, I've experimented with drugs, I've used the Lord's name in vain, and I've, uh—I've—taken away a life." The priest is silent. Randy reads from his pamphlet. "Father of mercy, like the prodigal son I return to you and say: 'I have sinned against you and am no longer worthy to be called your son.' Christ Jesus, Savior of the world, I pray with the repentant thief to whom you promised Paradise: 'Lord, remember me in your Kingdom.' Holy Spirit, fountain of love, I call on you with trust: 'Purify my heart, and help me to walk as a child of light.'" Randy closes his pamphlet in silence.

"My son," the priest finally begins what will be a long interrogation. Randy answers each question truthfully as he weeps silently. When Father asks him if he would be willing to turn himself in, Randy clears his throat and wipes his tears.

"I cannot possibly do that, Father," he says in a strong voice. "I have to take care of my siblings. I will not leave them. I *can't* leave them. No matter what."

"Can you tell me honestly whether any innocent person has been accused of committing the sin—the crime—that you committed?"

"No sir, no one."

"Do you understand, son, that absolution is given only if you are truly sorry for your very serious offense and that you never commit such a sin again or allow anyone else to be punished for your sin?"

"I understand, Father and I promise…" Randy's voice is again choked with emotion. "I promise that I will never, ever do…that terrible thing or let anyone else pay for my actions."

"Your penance my son, will be thirty Hail Mary's and forty Our Father's. Now bow your head in prayer." Randy obeys as he reads along as the priest speaks.

"God, the Father of mercies, through the death and resurrection of His son has reconciled the world to himself and sent the Holy Spirit among us for the forgiveness of sins; through the ministry of the church, may God give you pardon and peace, and I absolve you from your sins in the name of the Father, and of the Son, and of the Holy Spirit."

"Amen," Randy says.

"Give thanks to the Lord, for He is good," the priest says.

"His mercy endures forever," Randy reads.

"You're dismissed my son. Go and sin no more. "

"Thank you Father." Randy makes the sign of the cross then steps out of the booth. Walking quickly to the rear of the church, he turns toward the sanctuary, genuflects, makes the sign of the cross and proceeds out the door. Getting in his car, he drives away.

Randy chooses the parking lot of Garofalo's grocery on 183rd street, to do his penance.

A month later, Randy throws a party for Amy's seventh birthday. Both sets of grandparents attend as well as Amy's friends. Later, while taking a cigarette break in the utility room, Brian walks in to get a couple more bottles of soda from the refrigerator.

"Amy's really enjoying her party, uh little brother?" Randy asks.

"Yes she is. But, it's not the same without Mom and Dad."

"We have to do our best, don't we," Randy says.

The start of the 1981-82 school year, Brian's a senior, and Amy's in second grade. Randy's used to his five and a half day workweek and is no longer sore from his duties. The realization of not attending college, bothers him but little. He knows he must take care of his loved ones.

After punching out on a Friday, Randy is excited. *I have tomorrow off. I don't have to be back until Monday!!* He bids several co-workers to have a nice weekend then walks outside. Seeing a woman struggle with several boxes, Randy hurries to help her as two of them fall on the pavement.

"Let me help you," he says. The postal worker picks them up as their eyes meet.

"You look familiar," Randy says. "Where have I seen you before?"

"At the funeral home," she replies.

"You're Darlene."

"And you're Randy. We know each other's names!" they say in unison. Both laugh.

"I'll carry these boxes inside," Randy says.

"That's very kind of you," Darlene says. The two talk as Randy holds the door for her and notices there isn't a ring on her finger. He sets the two boxes on the counter next to the other one.

"Well, it was nice seeing you again Darlene," he says. A clerk is open as Darlene holds up a finger.

"Wait Randy. I want to talk to you some more," she says. When she is finished paying for the postage, Darlene walks with Randy outside.

"Do you want to get together sometime?" she asks.

"You're not married?" Randy asks.

"I was until five months ago. I'm real busy with work, but how about mid September?' Darlene asks.

"That'd be great. Let me give you my phone number," Randy says. Walking to the passenger side of his Chevy, he opens the door and gets out a pencil and a piece of paper from the glove compartment.

"Wow, nice car." Darlene says.

"Thank you. I got it two weeks ago." They exchange phone numbers.

"I'll call you in three weeks?" Randy says more than asks.

"That'd be fine," Darlene says with a smile. The two shake hands then depart.

That evening after supper, Amy excuses herself to go to the bathroom. Randy reads the paper as Brian finishes his dessert.

"Randy, can I talk to you about something?" he asks.

"Sure little brother," he replies.

"Well, there's this girl at work that I really like and—"

"Cut it off," Randy interrupts him.

"I wasn't finished with what I was going to say," Brian says angrily.

"Look little brother. My friend Matt told me this quote one day. 'Don't get your meat, where you make your bread.'"

"What does that mean?" Brian asks.

"It means don't mix business with pleasure," Randy says.

"I really like her!"

"Look little brother. I'm only trying to save you heartache, and possibly your job." Brian storms out of the kitchen, as Randy sets his paper down. Looking up he says, "Yeah Mom and Dad, I can't get to him either."

CHAPTER TWELVE

Randy and Darlene's first date is at the end of September at Bob Evans in Matteson. Darlene tells him that she's a graduate of Hillcrest High School.

"My brother and I would've gone there if we'd stayed in Country Club Hills," Randy says.

"Maybe we would've met there." Darlene says.

"Is that where you met your ex-husband?" Randy asks.

"Yeah, that's where I met him," Darlene says gloomily.

"I'm sorry. You don't have to talk about him if you don't want to." The waitress comes by and takes their orders.

When they're finished eating, Randy asks her if she would like to see where he lives and she accepts the offer. Driving south on Cicero Avenue, flashing lights appear in Randy's rearview mirror. He curses in his mind then pulls onto the shoulder as his heart beats wildly. The police cruiser drives by.

"He's not after me," Randy says calmly. Darlene smiles—not knowing the true meaning of his words. He turns right onto Sauk Trail. Randy slows as he drives by his alma mater.

"That's Rich South High," he says. Darlene is startled.

"So that's where it is. I've heard about your school, I just never knew where it was," she says. Randy pulls into Lakewood Estates, and then right onto Royal Drive. He shows Darlene the home.

"What a beautiful house!" Darlene says.

"Yeah, my parents had good taste," Randy replies.

"It's so sad and shocking that they both died so young."

"I guess God wanted them to be with Him. We'll see them again. My siblings are at Lakewood Bowl. Would you like to meet them?" Randy asks.

"I'd love to!" she replies. The elder Taylor drives the short distance to Lakewood. Getting out, they walk inside to the control center. Randy introduces Darlene to Joe.

"Nice to meet you young lady," he says.

"Where's my brother and sister?" Randy asks.

"They're on lane twenty-seven," Joe says. Randy thanks him and the two walk down the concourse. Amy notices them. She runs to her brother, as he picks her up.

"Sister, how'ya doin'?" Randy asks. "Amy this is Darlene." The child turns her head as she wraps her little arms around her brother's neck.

"Oh she's shy. It's okay sister. Darlene doesn't bite." They walk to lane twenty-seven when Randy sets his sister down. He introduces Darlene to his brother.

"Nice to meet you," Brian says.

"Likewise," Darlene replies as they shake hands.

"Shall we join them in a match," Randy suggests.

"I'm not very good," Darlene says.

"Neither am I. What size shoe do you wear?"

Later, when Randy is driving back to Bob Evans, to Darlene's 1972 Mustang, she comments on his siblings.

"I like your brother, and your sister's adorable!"

"Yeah, she's a little live wire," Randy says. He pulls up to her white Ford.

"I had a good time, Randy. Thank you for the lunch, bowling and letting me meet your family." Darlene extends her hand and gives him a smile that says, "Next time I'll kiss ya!"

"You're welcome," Randy replies as he embraces her. She doesn't resist.

"You wanna call me in a few weeks?" Randy asks.

"Sure," Darlene replies. "Take care." The young woman gets out. Randy's intoxicated by her perfume, her demeanor and her curves. Making sure her car starts, the two wave to each other. Randy drives away in a state of bliss. When he gets home, he asks Amy what she thought of Darlene.

"I like her," his sister replies. "She looks like Mommy."

"Do you really think so?" Randy asks.

"Yep."

By October, President Carter and Governor Reagan have debated. The brothers have switched roles for a while. Brian cooks the dinners and Randy does the dishes.

On this Wednesday evening, Brian and Amy are in the family room rough housing, while Randy cleans up the kitchen. He has removed his work shirt and is wearing only a t-shirt and his work pants. Randy turns the radio on above the fridge when he hears a thud and then, "Oh my God," from Brian as Amy bursts into hysterics. Running downstairs, Randy sees blood covering

Amy's forehead and running down her face. He races upstairs, gets a clean dishcloth and applies pressure to the wound.

"What happened?" he asks.

"She tripped and hit her head on the end table," Brian says.

"Jesus, Mary and Joseph! We're going to the hospital." Randy says as he leads his sister upstairs. Amy's hysterical, but Randy keeps his cool. Fortunately, he hadn't closed the garage door yet. He opens the passenger door as his siblings get in. Randy runs to the driver's side, gets in, and fires the engine. He peels out of the garage onto Royal Drive. The rear tires smoke upon hitting the petal to the metal.

"Keep pressure on her forehead Brian!" he demands. The folded dishcloth is sixty percent red, as Amy continues crying. She begins to cling to the driver.

"No sister, stay with Brian. I have to drive. You're gonna be okay, honey. You hang in there," he reassures. Two things are in Randy's favor. It's after rush hour, and he's beating all of the yellow lights. Upon the fifth one, he hears a horn to his left. A collision has just been avoided.

A mile from Saint James Hospital in Chicago Heights, there are lights he can't beat—the flashing lights of a police cruiser in his rearview mirror. The Monte Carlo doesn't slow down. "He'll get over it," Randy says to himself. Near the emergency entrance, Randy instructs his sister.

"Hold the dishcloth on your forehead Amy. Press real hard." She obeys while crying. The Chevy grinds to a halt, as Randy opens his door.

"Stay in the car!" an officer shouts. Ignoring him, Randy gets out and runs around to the passenger side while shouting to the officer, "My sister is bleeding! She needs a doctor!" Brian opens his door and hands Amy to Randy. The officer is now close enough to see the bleeding child.

"What happened here?" he shouts.

As the sliding doors open, Randy, once again ignoring the office, bellows. "I need a doctor—now!"

A nurse moves from behind the counter and points. "This room sir."

Randy places his sister on the examining table as the nurse covers her with a clean towel and begins to examine the injury.

"How did this happen?" she asks the boys.

The officer, standing in the doorway, listens intently as Brian explains how Amy fell into the table at home.

While the nurse cleans the wound and puts a temporary compress on it, she asks an aid to notify one of the doctors to come into the examining room. When the doctor arrives, he introduces himself as Doctor Snyder and instructs the nurse to get the necessary items in order to stitch the wound.

"Hold her hands son," the doctor says as he examines the wound.

"Amy, you've got to be still. The doctors need to fix you, but you're making it hard for them," Randy says. The child obeys, but continues crying.

"Be brave honey. Be brave sweetheart!" Randy says.

"I want my mommy!" Amy says between sobs.

"She's here in spirit and so is Daddy. But your big brothers are right here and we'll take good care of you."

"Are you her legal guardian?" the doctor asks as he glances over at Randy. "Just how old are you?"

"Yes, I'm her brother and her guardian and I'm eighteen. Our parents are dead and my younger brother and I take care of our sister."

"You'll have to show us your ID and give your insurance information at the desk, son."

When the doctor finishes, he tells Randy that he has to bring Amy to see their regular physician within three days. "Make sure she doesn't scratch her stitches," Doctor Snider says. "And watch her to make sure she doesn't get nauseated over the next twenty-four hours."

Randy thanks the doctor and the nurse. The child sits up as she wipes her eyes.

"Amy, tell them thank you," Randy says. A muffled 'thank you' comes from the child's lips. The nurse squats down, so she's eye to eye with her patient.

"You were such a brave little girl, I'm going to give you a surprise. Would you like that?" she asks with a smile. Amy nods.

"Okay honey. I'll be right back," the nurse leaves. Moments later, she comes back with the biggest sucker Randy has ever seen.

"Good Lord! It'll take five weeks to finish that!" he says.

"Here you go sweetie," the nurse says as she hands it to her.

"Whaddya say Amy?" Randy asks.

"Thank you miss nurse," the child says. Nurse Janis gives the child a hug. Amy then looks at her brother's blood stained t-shirt and says, "Randy, you spilled coffee on you."

"Yeah Amy, I'm a messy drinker!"

Once Randy takes care of the insurance paperwork and shows his ID, he takes Amy by the hand and goes into the waiting room to look for Brian. He finds him standing with the police officer, looking impatient and a little freightened.

"Randy, Officer Burke wants to talk to you."

"Now your brother explained what happened to your sister and he told me about your parents and all. But you should not have been speeding."

"I was afraid for my sister and I had to get her medical help fast. I couldn't stop for you."

"I had no way of knowing you had an emergency but if you had stopped I would have helped you get to the ER even faster. You just can't take matters into your own hands. I could arrest you for what you did."

The thought of being arrested is terrifying and Randy uses all his will power not to show his fear.

"I didn't know I was breaking the law. I was just trying to help my sister. Officer Burke, she's my responsibility. She and Brian depend on me."

"Look, I'm not going to arrest you or even give you a ticket. But I want you to understand that regardless of your special circumstances, taking care of your siblings and all, you still have to obey the law. Being so young and having legal custody of your sister and your brother—you have to be a model citizen. Any slip-ups and…" Officer Burke lowers his voice so that Amy won't hear—"this little girl could be taken away from you. You understand?"

"Yes, sir I do."

"No slip-ups, young man. Now get this little girl home."

"Thank you officer. I appreciate it," Randy says. The oldest gives Brian his keys.

"You want me to drive?" he asks.

"I'm a little shook up right now."

That evening as Randy tucks Amy in bed, he speaks tenderly to her.

"Now little sister, you mustn't pick or scratch your stitches. You promise?' he asks.

"I promise," she says. "Randy, I miss Mommy and Daddy."

"I know, honey. We all miss them, but we have to stay strong, don't we?" Randy asks.

His cigarette is halfway finished as Randy stands at the counter in the utility room, drinking a beer, thinking about all that could have gone wrong. *The main thing is that Amy is okay. But that cop. Could Amy be taken from us? No, I'd never let that happen! Oh God, am I going to have heart failure every time I get near a cop?*

Seeing his brother, Brian walks in, "You did good Randy."

"No, you did good little brother. Man, we acted fast!"

"I thought that cop was gonna cause us some problems," Brian says. "Do you think they could really take Amy away?"

"No, Brian—not a chance. We'd have to do something terrible for that to happen. Going a little over the speed limit wouldn't do it. He should've known it was an emergency when we got to the hospital. What did he think we were doin'? Out fuckin' joy riding or somethin'?" Randy asks as Brian busts out laughing. Randy places his finger to his lips.

"Amy's sleeping little brother," he whispers.

"Randy, you can be so funny at times."

The next weekend, Randy makes Amy do something that he's never made her do before—write 'thank you' notes. Donald and Tammy always made their sons do it. As a boy, he despised it. He can still hear his mother's words: "Randy, if someone takes the time to buy you a gift, you should take the time to write them a 'thank you' note." Now, the firstborn understands. Amy was given the gift of life.

At the kitchen sink, Brian washes the dinner dishes, as his siblings sit at the table. Amy has a pen in her little hand, as Randy gives her the first card.

"You're gonna thank the two doctors and the nurse. Here are their names."

As October turns into November of 1980, the weather gets colder, but the relationship between Randy and Darlene gets hotter. Their second date is at Poppin' Fresh Pies on Cicero Avenue near Lincoln Mall. They talk of many things. Randy's parents are brought up in the conversation.

"Were you closer to your mother or your father?" she asks. Randy pauses.

"I never thought about that before. I guess I was a little closer to my dad. He used to make me laugh."

"How?" Darlene asks.

"Well, when we had Sugar—she was our German Shepard; sometimes on a Saturday morning, he would stand at our doorway and cup his hand to his mouth. Then he would say, 'It's eight o'clock. Time to clean up the dog shit, dog shit, dog shit!'" The two laugh.

"Did your father remarry?" Randy's pulse beats faster.

"He did, but my stepmother left a year ago."

"That's too bad. You've all been through a lot. I was thinking—" Darlene is interrupted, as a waitress walks to them.

"Would you like more coffee?"

After dinner, Darlene drives the short distance to the three interconnected movie theaters near Lincoln Mall. There, the couple see 'Urban Cowboy' with John Travolta and Debra Winger. While watching the movie, they hold hands. After the show, it's dark outside. Darlene leaves with her coat unbuttoned. She drives Randy home in her Mustang. Darlene is driving because Brian is hanging out with his friends while Grandma Plant babysits. He used Randy's car to take Amy to Marionette Park.

Near the house, Randy notices the garage door is down and the porch light is off. He instructs Darlene to pull in the driveway. She does, as she kills her headlights and places her transmission in 'park'.

"I had a wonderful time Randy."

"Me too Darlene. Now I bet you're thinking , *I wonder if he'll kiss me!* She smiles and replies, "Yes, I'm thinking that." The couple wraps their arms around each other as their lips meet. This time Randy's heart beats faster for a different reason. Darlene's mouth is warm, moist and full. Through her perfume, Randy can make out a whiff of her natural scent. After a short while, he slowly places his hand on her left breast. Darlene breaks the kiss and leans forward.

"Randy, you're moving too fast. Let's go slow—okay?"

"I'll respect your decision. I'll call you tomorrow?'

"If I'm not in, leave a message."

"Have a safe trip home. Call me when you get in." He kisses her goodnight then exits. Brian is standing in the foyer as Randy walks in the house.

"I heard her pulling in."

"We were talking little brother," Randy replies.

"Talking with your hands?" Brian asks as Randy smiles and gives him the finger. Brian gives his brother a playful punch in the stomach.

"You like her Randy?" Brian asks.

"I'm crazy about her."

A week before Thanksgiving, Randy tells his sister she'll have to get her stitches out.

"I don't want to go big brother. I'm scared," the child says.

"Look sister, you don't want to look like Frankenstein, do ya? Now, the pain won't be as bad this time," Randy says as a look comes across Amy's face as if she's about to cry.

"Listen honey, I'll make a deal with ya. You be a brave girl again, and when we leave the hospital, I'll take you to any restaurant you want," Randy says. The child's eyes brighten.

"Any restaurant?" she asks.

"Any," Randy replies. The child contemplates.

"Mister Benny's," Amy says. Randy's mouth drops open as his eyebrows come together in amusement.

"Mister Benny's on Cicero Avenue?" he asks. The child nods as Randy places his palms to his temples.

"I'll have to sell my car to go there!" he says as Amy laughs.

"Okay sister, I'll take you there."

After the procedure, nurse Janis looks at Randy. "The scar can be covered up with a little make-up."

"Can I wear lipstick too?' Amy asks with a smile.

"You're not wearing lipstick until you're eighteen," Randy says. Her smile vanishes.

"Why?"

"Because I said so!"

"She's growing up quick," the nurse says.

"Is there any way to slow her down?" Randy replies.

The months pass and June of 1981 arrives. Both sets of grandparents arrive along with Darlene and other relatives. Brian's graduation ceremony is held in the gym. This year, all of the seniors wear black gowns and caps, with a red, white, and blue tassel. Randy is impressed with the color scheme. Just before "Pomp and Circumstance" begins, Randy leans towards his sister and whispers. "In ten years you'll be doing this Amy."

After graduation, a reception is held for Brian at Jardine's New/Old Place in Tinley Park.

Earlier that spring, Brian applied to a number of colleges. Randy tells his brother that if he remains in state, his tuition will be cheaper. The siblings visit the campuses of Illinois State in Bloomington-Normal, University of Chicago, Eureka College in Eureka Illinois, and, at Brian's insistence, Notre Dame in South Bend Indiana.

Randy uses his vacation time for the West Virginia trip. He phones their Uncle Herb and Aunt Molly to make arrangements, and get directions. Two days later, Randy packs his car. All are excited, especially Amy.

"How long will it take to get to West Virginia?' Brian asks.

"I don't know little brother. I predict five tankfuls. I haven't been to the 'Mountain State' since I was little," Randy says. Dawn is breaking. Red and purple-gray cloud patches envelope the sky.

Randy makes sure he has enough money; cash along with his checkbook. He places two gallons of water in the trunk.

"Amy, we're almost ready. I want you to go potty."

"But I don't have to," she says.

"Well sister, try—okay?" The child walks back in the house.

"That goes for you too Brian. Once I get on the interstate, I'm not stoppin' for a while."

Ten minutes later, Randy locks the house and gets in. He had filled the tank the previous night. The Chevy backs out slowly, as the driver pushes the button on his visor. The garage door begins its noisy descent.

"Amy, why don't you go in the back and lie down. That pillow's for you."

"I'm not tired Randy, I'm too excited!"

"Let me know if you change your mind. We won't stop for breakfast for about two hours."

When they get on Interstate 80, Randy sets his cruise control by pushing in a button at the top of a lever that looks like a turn signal, then releasing that and his foot off the accelerator at the same time. The radio dial is tuned to WLS-FM/American Top Forty. All three get into a song by Sheena Easton.

Later, Randy points something out to Brian. "Check this out little brother. We're well into Indiana, and the needle on the fuel gauge hasn't budged!"

After a hearty breakfast at a truck stop, Randy tops off the tank, and writes down the cost and the gallons. While Brian handles the driving, Amy takes a nap in the back seat as Randy rests his head on a folded towel against the window.

A downpour begins near Columbus. Randy and Amy awaken at the same time.

"Howya doin' little brother?" Randy asks.

"Pretty good. I've had to slow down a bit on account of this storm," he says.

"Did you sleep well Amy?' the oldest asks.

"Yep!" she answers as she stretches and yawns.

The rest of the journey consists of three more stops. Amy's aware she's in West Virginia for a short while, when she sees the 'Welcome to Pennsylvania" sign.

"How can we be in Pennsylvania already? I thought West Virginia is a big state!" she inquires. Randy turns around. "We just drove through the northern panhandle. That part of the state isn't very wide." Randy takes a pen and a piece of paper from the glove compartment and draws a rough outline of the Mountain State. He shows it to her.

As the Monte Carlo nears the Mason Dixon line, he disengages the cruise control. Getting off at exit 155, Brian cautiously listens to his brother. Turning left, the siblings see nothing but green hills. "These mountains are so beautiful," Amy says. Slowly, a large light blue two-lane bridge comes into their view. Brian crosses it then pulls into an old white gas station on the right. Brian parks the car, as everyone gets out. After using the restrooms, Randy phones his uncle from a pay phone.

Uncle Herb greets his niece and nephews. Randy follows him to their house where Aunt Molly is waiting.

"My, you children are getting big!" She hugs all of them. The aroma of stuffed chicken reaches them from the kitchen. Brian and Amy are shown their rooms. Aunt Molly tells Randy he can sleep in the rec room. He doesn't mind. The sofa's quite comfortable.

After breakfast the next day, Uncle Herb drives the family downtown. He parks on High Street near a restaurant called The Dining Room. Everyone steps out into the July heat.

"Now, I'm going to show all of you the University, but first we're going to see it by way of the PRT," Herb says.

"What's a PRT?" Randy asks.

"It stands for 'Personnel Rapid Transit'. It's a transportation system that connects both campuses.

"I drove under one of the tracks yesterday near that arena," Randy says.

"That's the coliseum." Herb says. At the Walnut PRT station near the courthouse, everyone walks up the stairs. Herb places in one quarter then says, "Push the 'medical' button." Each one takes turns pushing the small metal revolving bar. Amy gets excited as one of the PRT cars pulls around.

"The train's coming!" she exclaims. Everyone laughs.

"My little brother will be going to class in style," Randy says. As the sliding door opens, Amy begins to walk toward it.

"No honey, we have to get in here. We have to let those invisible people get off," Aunt Molly says. The door closes, as the car moves several yards. The door opens again and everyone boards. The door closes, then the car moves by way of an electronic rail. Herb points out the sights.

"This is the Monongahela River to your left. Those three buildings up there are a part of Woodburn Circle, which I'll show later on. Next to Woodburn Circle is the old Mountaineer Field. I'll show all of you the new one momentarily." The car accelerates. "What's the top speed Uncle Herb?" Randy asks.

"Around thirty-five miles-per-hour." Moments later, Herb points out that Beechurst Avenue turns into Monongalia Boulevard. "Now as soon as we cross over Mon Boulevard, we're entering the Evansdale campus. The other campus is called the Downtown. Over there is the Coliseum."

"It looks like a space ship!" Amy says.

"That's right honey. Right now we're passing the Engineering PRT. Those four buildings there are called Towers." *I could never live here,* Randy thinks.

"And coming into view is our new Mountaineer Field."

"It looks like it's in the middle of nowhere," Randy says.

"That's because it used to be a golf course. That grayish white building to our left is University Hospital." When the car stops at the Medical PRT station, the doors open as Amy begins to walk out.

"No honey, we stay on," Herb says. The child returns to her seat. The car makes a small circle, then heads back. At the Beechurst PRT station, everyone gets off.

"Ya'll don't mind climbing a set of stairs, do you?" Herb asks.

"No we don't. It'll be good exercise," Randy says. At the top of the outdoor stairs, he's breathing a little hard, as Randy takes out a cigarette and lights it.

"You know, Brian, you could save a lot of money if you lived with me and your Aunt Molly. We'd love to have you. I mean if you decide to come here for school."

"Well, to tell the truth, I have decided to come to West Virginia University. My friend Dennis and I are both coming here." He looks at Randy who is stunned by Brian's announcement. "And I really appreciate your offer, Uncle Herb and Aunt Molly but I'm gonna reside at Towers. My friend Dennis and I are gonna be roommates."

"Uh—Uncle Herb. I'm gonna talk with Brian for a minute. Will you excuse us please?" Randy asks. The oldest sibling pulls his younger brother to the side and whispers strongly.

"Listen little brother. It's your decision where you go to school and I can understand why you want to go here. But if you stay with Uncle Herb and Aunt Molly, you won't have to pay for housing, and all of your meals will be taken care of."

"But Randy, I *want* to live in a dorm and Dennis is gonna be my roommate."

"Yeah, you already said that. Brian, I'm just trying to save you money, at least for the first year. Since you've decided to go to an out of state school, you're gonna need to watch your pennies or your gonna blow through your share of the inheritance." Randy says. The two walk back to the waiting family. "Ya know Brian, sometimes I just don't understand your thinkin."

"Uncle Herb, thank you for your offer, but maybe next year," Brian says. The party walks down the street. Herb shows them Saint John's church and Newman Hall. After a short walk, Uncle Herb points out The Book Exchange and The Discount Den. As they continue down High Street—the main street of downtown Morgantown—they arrive back at the eatery called *The Dining Room*. The first thing Randy notices about it is the color scheme; yellow walls with a dark brown lunch counter and booths of the same hue on the other side. Round stools are fixed to the floor in front of the counter and a reddish brown wall to wall thick carpeting covers the floor. The aroma of cooked onions permeates the air.

After lunch, Herb drives everyone to Towers dorms on the Evansdale campus. Brian is in awe. Upon entering Brooke Tower, the seventeen year old already feels like he's a student. The welcome area is open and large. The party walks to the counter straight ahead under a sign that reads: WELCOME TO WEST VIRGINIA UNIVERSITY. A tour guide shows them the grounds. Brian is intrigued that all four Towers—Brooke, Lyon, Bennett and Braxton are connected. One can go to each building without going outside. Little Amy loves the cafeteria.

Once back at the welcome counter, Brian pays his academic deposit.

"Your housing packet will be mailed within a week," the woman at the counter says.

"Thank you ma'am," says Brian beaming.

The next day, Uncle Herb takes everyone to see the Pittsburgh Pirates play the Cincinnati Reds at Three Rivers Stadium.

Back home again in Illinois, Randy's new position of clerk requires that he works two Saturdays each month. Randy is not scheduled to work the first Saturday in July and since Brian is working at Chernin's Shoes, Randy and Amy have just finished breakfast and are planning the day when the phone rings. Randy picks it up and finds Paul on the other end.

"Randy, Nathan went home sick. Can you come in this morning?"

"Sure Paul," Randy says.

"Thanks 'T-Man'! Get here as soon as possible."

"Come on sister, let's go."

"Where are we going?" Amy asks.

"I'm going to work, and you're going to a babysitter," Randy says.

"Stephi's on vacation," the child says.

"Are you sure?" Randy asks.

"Positive."

"Well, let's check anyway." Randy takes his sister's hand and crosses the street. Ringing the doorbell twice, there is no answer.

"See, I told you so," Amy says. Walking to another neighbor's house, Randy finds they too are not home.

"Am I going to work with you?" Amy asks excitedly.

"Yes you are. I'll be right back," Randy says as he rushes into the house. Grabbing several coloring books and a box of crayons from Amy's bookcase, Randy darts upstairs but trips in the process. He curses, gets up, gathers everything, steps outside, and locks the front door. Getting in his Chevy, he sets the items on the seat between his sister and him.

"I can't believe I'm going to work with you! Goody goody gumdrops!!" she says.

"Well sister, I'm not taking you to play with you. You're gonna sit, color, and be a good girl—right?" The child nods.

Once inside, Randy explains, "You can sit at any of these tables and color." He reaches in his pocket for coins. "Here's some change if you want something to eat or drink. The vending machines are there, and the bathrooms are down the hall." Randy gives her a kiss. "I have to go. I'll see ya." He hurries to punch in.

Thirty-five minutes later, a middle aged heavyset woman walks in the break room. She purchases a grape soda from a vending machine.

"What's your name, honey?" she asks.

"Amy."

"My name's Shirley. Please to meetja."

"Nice to meet you ma'am," Amy says.

"Oh please. Call me Shirley. Does your daddy work here?"

"No, my daddy's dead. My brother Randy works here."

"Oh, Randy's your brother! I like working with your brother."

"He's silly," Amy says with a smile.

"Why's he silly, honey?' Shirley asks.

"'Cause he makes me laugh," the child says as Shirley looks over her shoulder.

"That picture is pretty."

"Would you like to color one?" Amy asks.

"No thank you honey, I have to get back to work," the woman says.

"Nice meeting you Shirley," Amy says.

"You too, honey."

CHAPTER THIRTEEN

At twelve-thirty pm, Randy continues sorting mail. He can't help overhear Shirley nearby talking to another co-worker. "I have my grandfather's car since he died but Dan and I have our own vehicles. I don't know whether to keep it or sell it." Randy's eyebrows raise. He knows Brian is itching to have his own car. For the past three months Randy has been letting him drive to work, with the oldest riding 'shotgun'. He's getting tired of this. Randy walks to his co-worker.

"Shirley, I couldn't help but overhear you. My brother's in need of a car. Do you wanna sell it to him?" Randy asks.

"Sure Randy. Any relative of yours is a friend of mine."

"What kind of car is it?" Randy asks.

"A 1973 Chevy Nova, only nine thousand miles on it. Do you want to look at it after work?"

"Sure," Randy replies.

"You can follow me home."

Twenty minutes later, Randy follows Shirley to her home in Steger, roughly twelve miles from the Post Office. A two-car garage attaches to a ranch house. Attached to the garage is a carport. In the open sided shelter is a car covered with a tannish auto cover. Randy parks next to Shirley on her driveway. "Nice place Shirley," Randy says.

"Your house is pretty," Amy says.

"Well, I thank both of yuz. My husband and I have lived here since 1963. Randy, will you help me remove this cover?"

"Sure," he says with a smile. The cover is removed from the bottom portion of the front bumper to reveal a shiny candy-apple colored Nova.

"Wow, that's sharp!" Randy says.

"That's pretty," says Amy.

"My grandfather said that it's been only rained on twice."

"It looks like it's never been rained on at all," Randy replies.

"How much are you asking Shirley?" Randy asks.

"Eleven hundred," she replies.

"I think Brian can afford that."

"Randy, I'm hungry," the child says.

"We'll be leaving soon sister."

"I want you all to have dinner with us!" Shirley says.

"Are you certain? I mean, I have to pick up my brother. Randy asks.

"I made a huge pan of stuffed peppers—there's more than enough for everybody. I insist."

"Thank you kindly. I'll go and get Brian. Come on Sis."

"She can stay here with me. You pick up your brother and Amy and I will get things ready." Shirley and the child exchange smiles.

"Shirley, you're very kind." "And when yuz come back, you both can meet my husband. You remember how to get here?'

"Yes I do," Randy says. He gets in his Chevy and drives to Chernin's Shoes in Matteson. The excitement he had when he purchased his Monte Carlo is building again; although not for him, but for his brother.

As Randy pulls into the plaza, Brian is already waiting outside. Randy pulls up to the curb as his sibling gets in.

"Good news little brother. I won't have to drive you to work anymore."

"Why?'

"Because I've just seen a car that's perfect for you."

"You have?" an excited Brian replies.

"Yep. And I'm taking you to see it right now." The Monte Carlo makes its way to Steger. When Randy gets to Shirley's, he parks parallel to the house, not knowing if her husband came home from work. The two get out as the front door opens. A big man with white short hair emerges. He extends his large hand and smiles.

"Hello boys. My name's Bob." The young men shake his hand while introducing themselves.

"I'll show you the car." He and Randy smile, Brian doesn't.

"It rolled off the assembly line eight years ago. Let me show ya what it has." Bob says. Brian's mood is neutral, Randy is puzzled by this.

"How much is it sir?' Brian asks.

"Oh, you can call me Bob. It's eleven hundred, but since you're the brother of one of Shirley's favorite co-workers, she's instructed me to take off another two hundred dollars." Still, Brian isn't phased.

"Uh Bob, I'm gonna talk with my brother. Can you give us a minute please?"

"Sure, go right ahead," Bob says. Randy takes his brother to the sidewalk.

"Brian, for nine hundred dollars, this car's a steal. Now what's the problem?" Randy asks as his brother looks down.

"It's a four-door," Brian says glumly.

"Well who the hell cares!" Randy whispers.

"Listen little brother, do you know what a four-door means?"

"It means you'll be paying less auto insurance than I will for my car. A four-door is considered a family car, so what if it isn't considered cool. Driver's of a family car are considered to be a less risk." Brian perks up. Randy continues. "It also means it'll be easy to pack before you go to college. Trust me, getting things in and out of my back seat is a real pain-in-the-ass! Now if I didn't have my car, I'd buy this one." Randy says as Brian contemplates.

"Okay big brother, you've convinced me."

"I'll buy it sir—I mean Bob," Brian says.

"Let's go for a test drive!" Bob says.

After supper, Shirley and Brian agree on a three hundred dollar down payment.

"I left my checkbook at home," Brian says.

"I'll write a check, and you can pay me back little brother." Shirley gets a pen and a pad of paper and writes a receipt. She tears the paper from its pad and hands it to Brian, as Randy finishes writing a check. With the exchanges, it's official.

When they get home, Brian checks the mail and discovers his housing packet from West Virginia University has arrived. Among the items are a campus guidebook and a housing contract. Brian completes this at his desk, while Randy gives Amy her bath. Brian also phones his friend Dennis. They agree on Brooke Hall at Towers dorms. Brian also completes a roommate matched survey. Brian puts his and Dennis's name on the application, signs his contract and writes a housing deposit payment check of seventy-five dollars.

Once Brian pays off his Nova and obtains auto insurance, Randy drives him to Steger, while Amy holds a plate of homemade cookies covered with tin foil.

"Well little brother, I guess this is the last time I drive you anywhere."

"Unless I break down," Brian replies.

"If you pull preventive maintenance on a regular basis, chances are, you'll never breakdown," Randy replies. Pulling near the curb in front of the house, the siblings can see that the Nova is backed in the driveway. Brian gets out and tells his sister to give him the plate.

"I want to give it to Shirley," the child says.

"I'll let ya sis but I don't want you to drop the plate as you're getting out."

At the front door, Randy rings the bell. Shirley opens the door and Amy hands her the plate.

"We baked these for you," she says.

"Why thank you sweetie," Shirley says. Bob walks from the kitchen and greets them.

"Would yuz like to stay for lunch?' Shirley asks.

"No thank you," Randy says. "We just had lunch."

"We're going swimming!" Amy says.

"That's wonderful honey," Shirley says. Bob hands Brian the two keys. "This one's for the doors and trunk, and this one's for the ignition. Congratulations on your first car Brian! Take care of it," Bob says with a smile.

"I will. Thank you both for the great deal." Brian says. As they walk to the Chevy, Bob shows Brian where the emergency brake is, since their driveway is at a slight angle.

"Follow me to the house Brian?" Randy asks.

"I'm gonna cruise around a bit," he replies.

"Brian, when you get to the house, park on the right side of the garage."

"Aw Randy, I wanna park on the left." he says sarcastically.

"Don't mess with me little brother," Randy says as Brian laughs. The two vehicles leave in the scorching heat. Later, Randy shows Brian all of the fluid levels in the engine. He gives him an extra tire pressure gauge as well.

The next Saturday at the breakfast table, Amy asks her brother a question. "Randy, can I have a tea party?"

"Sister, I don't know anything about tea parties."

"It's when my girlfriends come over, and you serve us tea and cookies," Amy says.

"That's it?" Randy asks.

"You have to get dressed up," the child states.

"Sure sister. I'll throw a tea party for ya. I think mom's teapot is in the oak cabinet. Excuse me a minute Amy." Randy gets up from the kitchen table, and walks to the dining room. Squatting down between the oval table and the cabinet, he opens the doors. Looking intently, he doesn't find it. Standing and turning around, he analyzes the table. Removing several chairs, he goes to the end of the table, and pulls it out. Amy hears him as she enters the dining room.

"What are you doing big brother?" she asks.

"I'm making the table longer. Amy, should we send out invitations?" he asks.

"I think so," she replies.

"Invitations it is. If we're gonna do this, we may as well do it right. Now, where does mom keep that leaf?" he asks more to himself.

"What's a leaf?" Amy asks.

"A leaf is a part of a table that goes in the middle. You see where I pulled the table out? Well now there's a space in the middle. We can't have that, can we?"

Randy walks to the end of the oak cabinet and looks between the wall and the back of the bureau. As he's doing this, his right foot bumps Iris's golden picture frame. "It's probably on the other side," he says.

Randy walks to the other end of the bureau and looks carefully.

"I found it!" he says. The child gets excited. Randy removes the leaf from its place and carefully picks it up. He sets it slowly in the middle of the table. Lining the holes up, Randy walks to the end, and gently closes the table.

"Now sister, we need more chairs. Will you help me get them from the utility room?"

"You betcha!" she replies. The two begin to walk downstairs.

"I have to go potty."

"While you're going potty, I'm gonna have a cigarette." Randy walks to the end of the counter, retrieves a stogie, and fires it up.

"Did you wash your hands?" Randy asks.

"Yes," the child replies.

"I didn't hear any running water." The child puckers her lips in her mouth. She knows she's been caught lying. She turns around and re-enters the bathroom, as Randy takes a puff. After she's done, Randy places his cigarette in his ashtray. He lifts two folded chairs from against the wall and hands them to her.

"Are these too heavy for ya?" he asks.

"Nope," Amy replies. The chairs are placed on the sides of the table. Randy counts.

"Little sister, we have ten chairs. That means ten girls including you. How many invitations do we send out?" he asks. The child pauses.

"Don't strain yourself," Randy says.

"Ten," she replies.

"Let's fill out your invitations tonight. Now, since I can't find Mommy's tea set, I'm going to have to buy one. Let's go to Lincoln Mall." The child begins jumping up and down. "I need a new dress too big brother!"

"Don't you have some in your closet?" he asks.

"They don't fit me," Amy replies.

A week later, girls in their dresses, begin arriving at the house. Randy wears a dark suit with white gloves. *I feel like a damn butler.* Amy motions with her little finger and whispers, "Randy, you're supposed to wear a tuxedo."

"Amy, as 'Geraldine' says, 'What you see, is what you get!'" he whispers.

"Who's Geraldine?" she asks.

"You don't watch *The Flip Wilson Show*. I'll tell you later." When the girls are all seated, Randy makes an announcement. "I'd like to welcome you all to Amy's tea party. My name is Randy and I'll be your host. On the table, we have trays of cookies and snacks. To the upper right of each plate is your teacup. I will serve the tea, but be careful, it is hot." Randy walks in the kitchen and lifts the elegant teapot from the kitchen table. He begins serving.

Fifteen minutes later, a Nova pulls in the driveway. Brian gets out and walks in the foyer. Seeing the girls at the dining room table, he stifles a laugh. Randy walks up to him and speaks strong yet quietly.

"Little brother, you're gonna have to make yourself scarce."

"But Randy, I just got off of work. I've got things I have to do."

"Those things can wait Brian. Now do this for Amy—okay?" Randy asks. Brian makes a face then leaves. Randy returns to the table. "That's Amy's other brother Brian. He has a case of the giggles." The girls laugh.

Middle of August, 1981. The day Brian leaves for college has arrived. The oldest sibling is nervous, although he doesn't show it. Randy helps him pack his Nova, and remembers several things he may have overlooked.

"Brian, do you have two gallons of water?"

"Yeah."

"Your checkbook?"

"Yeah."

"Don't be blowing all of your money. Do you have your lamp?" Randy asks.

"Yes Randy, I have that."

"Directions. Do you have your directions?"

"Yeah."

"Uncle Herb and Aunt Molly's address and phone number?"

"Yep. I've got that."

The oldest contemplates for a minute. "I'll be right back," Randy says as he walks back in the house. Moments later, he's back as he hands Brian a bar of soap.

"What's this for?" Brian asks.

"Because you stink real bad." Randy says as he and Amy laugh.

"Only kidding little brother. You're gonna use that bar of soap, if you brake down."

"What do ya mean?" Brian asks. Randy retrieves a piece of paper from his pocket and unfolds it. "You're gonna get in your back seat, and write these two words on your rear windshield." Randy hands him the paper. Brian sees them backwards but realizes that from the outside they will read—*CALL COPS.*

"A kind truck driver will get on his 'cb' and contact a state trooper," the oldest says.

"Randy, you think of everything."

"I have to," he replies.

"Are you going to pick up Dennis?' Randy asks.

"I offered, but he wants to take his Charger. His car is boss!"

"So is yours. You want breakfast Brian?"

"Naw, I better get going. I'll eat breakfast near Indianapolis," Brian says.

"Well, this is it," Randy says. The brothers embrace hard.

"Be careful Brian. Give your heart to your books." The embrace is broken, when Brian squats down. He hugs his sister and gives her a kiss.

"You be good sister," he says.

"I'm gonna miss you Brian," Amy says, her voice crackin'.

"I'll be back for Thanksgiving," he replies.

"That's a long ways away."

"Well Amy, you keep busy, and before you know it, it'll be turkey time." Brian stands, holds up his arms waist high with palms open and says, "I'm off to college!" "Write to us little brother," Randy says then he walks up to him.

"Brian, one last thing before you go. My biology teacher told me once that if you're always a step ahead, you'll never fall behind."

"Thanks Randy, I'll keep that in mind."

"Write us."

"I will."

"Goodbye Brian. I love you," Amy says.

"Love you too sister." The Chevy backs out onto Royal Drive as Randy and Amy walk to the curb. Brian slowly drives away, waving until he is out of sight.

Well Amy, it's just you and me now.

"Let's get some breakfast sister."

The next two months pass quickly. By mid October, snow flurries arrive in Cook County. It's been two days since Randy has gone through the mail because of overtime at the Post Office. On overtime days Randy sends Amy to Stephi's house across the street. When Randy gets off work, he picks up Amy and thanks Stephi for watching her. Randy slips her cash by shaking her hand. The two siblings go out to eat, since Randy's too tired to cook.

After helping Amy with her homework, giving her a bath, and putting her to bed, Randy has a little time for himself. Retrieving a can of beer from the utility room fridge, he opens it then lights a cigarette. With the exception of the television on in the family room, the house is still and quiet. It had been just two years since his parents died. It had been a different world then.

Randy smokes his cigarette down to the filter then snubs it out in his ashtray. He takes a large swig of beer then walks to the family room. He sits in the Lazy-Boy chair and sets his beer on a coaster. Going through the mail, he comes across a white business envelope with West Virginia University as the return address.

"You've got to be kidding me!" he says aloud. Randy walks to his bedroom and gets his address book. Walking quietly back to the family room, he dials Brian's number on the white rotary phone. Brian picks up on the second ring.

"Hey little brother. How'ya doin'?"

"Doing okay. How are you and Amy getting along?"

"We're getting along alright. You know yourself, she can be a handful at times. Say Brian, have you received your mid-term grades?" Randy asks.

"Well, I-uh-I got it, but then I lost it." Unbeknownst to Brian, Randy gets a copy of his mid-term reports since he's the executor of the estate.

"That's okay little brother. I have a copy of it in my hand. Now what's this bullshit? One C, two D's and an F! You've been going to a lot of parties haven't you?' Randy asks.

"A couple," Brian says.

"It's more than a couple. Now little brother, you better get with the program! This first taste of freedom is going to your head. Now you haven't written Amy in five weeks."

"I don't know what to write," Brian says.

"You can write about all the parties you're going to and all of the classes that you're not!"

Brian laughs.

"It's not funny Brian. Now you better get your grades up. Don't make me come to Martinsburg and kick your ass!"

"It's Morgantown," Brian replies.

"Wherever. You can do better than this little brother. Now I'm not saying you can't go to any parties. I am saying, you can't go to parties all of the time. I've told you before, there's a balance to life. Now the next time I see your grades, the lowest one I wanna see is a C plus—understand?"

"Yeah," Brian replies.

"Today's October 19th. Wish Mom and Dad a happy anniversary. Take care, love ya, bye." Randy hangs the phone up forcefully, then immediately regretting it on account of Amy sleeping. He quietly walks up the stairs and turns on the living room light. He gazes at his parents wedding photograph.

"Mom and dad, I'm doing my best—happy anniversary."

On a Friday in mid November, Randy picks up Amy from school after work. The child gets in, and begins coughing after she closes the door.

"You don't sound too good little sister," Randy says.

"I don't feel very good," she replies. He places his hand on her forehead.

"You're running a temperature. I'll check it as soon as we get home." Minutes later, the garage door noisily descends, as the two siblings take off their coats and boots in the foyer. Randy instructs Amy to have a seat at the kitchen table. Darting upstairs, he retrieves the thermometer from the medicine cabinet. He walks down, while shaking the device.

"Open wide, sis." She obeys as he gently places the thermometer under her tongue. Randy looks at his watch. Taking out the thermometer, he looks at it closely.

"One hundred one degrees. Go upstairs, change into your jammies and go to bed. I'll get the vaporizer ready. It sounds like your sinuses are clogged."

"What will the vaporizer do?" she asks.

"A vaporizer will put moisture in the air, so you can breath better. Now, I just have to remember where mom kept it." The child walks upstairs as Randy begins looking for the vaporizer. The first place he thinks of is the closet in the family room. Walking downstairs, he opens the door and begins searching. He doesn't find the vaporizer but he does find several television trays. Randy puts one together and places it in Amy's bedroom near her window. The child places her hand over mouth as she coughs. *She doesn't sound very good at all,* Randy thinks. Walking in his bedroom, he looks in his mother's former closet. It isn't there. *The utility room, I bet it's there.* Randy walks down the two flights and opens the cabinets above the counter. He searches in vain. Closing the cabinets, he opens the bottom one. Bingo! Randy takes the box out with a picture of the vaporizer on it, and places it on the counter.

Upstairs, he fills the vaporizer with water, takes it to Amy's room, plugs it in and waits for it to sputter to life. Randy sits on the edge of Amy's bed.

"I'm going to heat you chicken noodle soup," he says softly.

"I'm not hungry," Amy replies weakly. Randy pauses.

"Will you eat just half a bowl?" he asks.

"Oh, all right" the child says reluctantly. Randy walks downstairs as the phone rings. Darlene is on the other line, but he doesn't talk to her long. Randy prepares the soup, then walks downstairs to retrieve another television tray. Putting it together, he brings it upstairs and sets it on the side of Amy's bed. The oldest knows the procedure from his own childhood.

Later, Randy is pouring the soup in a bowl, when the phone rings. Grandma Plant is on the other end.

"How are things going Randy?" she asks.

"Work is going fine grandma, but Amy's sick."

"Oh, bless her heart. I'm coming down this evening."

"Grandma, that would be wonderful. The front door will be open. I'm fixing Amy some chicken noodle soup."

"You're a fine man Randy."

"Thanks Grandma. Don't forget, I'll have the door unlocked for you."

"Okay son. See you in a bit."

Carrying the bowl of hot soup, Randy carefully walks upstairs and places it on the TV tray. "Okay, sister, just take small sips. Remember it's hot. But it will help you feel better."

Randy rushes downstairs to unlock the front door and runs back up to Amy's room to see how she's doing with her soup.

"Half a bowl finished," she says, "I can't eat no more. I'm so cold."

"You did good sister. Let me get you another blanket." Randy gets a blanket from her closet. He places it on her bed, and tucks in the length of her body.

"Is that better sister?" he asks.

She nods.

"You rest Amy. I'll check in on you later—okay?"

"Okay," she replies softly. Randy leaves quietly while closing her door halfway.

In the kitchen he fixes himself a sandwich and prepares himself a can of vegetable soup with crackers. After eating and cleaning up the kitchen, Randy takes Amy's temperature again. It has risen to one hundred and three degrees.

"Sister, I'm gonna have to take you to the hospital," Randy says. The child cries softly. He sits on the edge of her bed.

"Amy, listen honey. Your temperature is very high. You have the chills, and the doctors know more about your sickness than I do. I'll put your clothes on over your jammies since you have the chills."

Tests show that Amy has a bacterial infection that is going to require large doses of antibiotics and, after several hours in the emergency room, she is admitted to the hospital. Once she's settled in her room in the pediatric ward, Amy turns to her big brother.

"Raaandy, am I going to die?"

"Sister," he says gently, "You're going to be fine," he whispers. "Now you get some sleep and by tomorrow you're going to feel much better."

A staff doctor comes into the room to meet Amy and tells Randy that a nurse will be in immediately with the first doses of antibiotic. As he walks from the room, an announcement comes on the public address system asking that all visitors must leave for the night.

Hearing this, a terrified Amy pleads, "Don't leave me, Randy! I don't want to stay here without you. I'm so scared!"

"Wait, just a minute, honey," he says then walks to the doorway and talks quietly with the doctor.

"Doctor, please let me stay with her tonight."

"I'm not sure I can do that. Your sister will get good care here and we do have rules."

"Look sir, I'm not trying to ask for special favors but my mom and dad both died a couple of years ago and except for me, Amy's all alone. She's been through a lot and I'm all she has. She'll be so terrified if I have to leave. What do you say?

"You take care of her yourself?"

"Now that my younger brother has gone off to college—it's just me."

"How old are you?"

"I'm nineteen, I have a full time job with the post office and, doctor, please—I just can't leave my little sister here alone tonight when she's so sick."

"I'll tell the nurse to bring you a blanket."

"And a pillow if you can," Randy replies as he walks back and slides the big arm chair next to her bed, "I'm staying here tonight!" Amy gives him a big smile.

The next morning, a nurse takes the child's temperature as Randy calls his supervisor.

"Take all the time you need 'T-Man'. Give my love to Amy."

"Thanks Paul. I really appreciate your kindness and understanding." As Randy hangs up the phone, the nurse speaks.

"Good news Mister Taylor. Her temperature is down to 99.3 and she's getting her appetite back. She ate nearly all of her breakfast."

"Great! Now she can eat me out of house and home again. Amy, I have to go back to the house for just a little while. I'll be back later—okay?"

Amy is enjoying watching cartoons on television, but she pauses to give Randy a hug and a kiss. "I'll be okay, Randy. I feel better, it's day time, and you will be back in just a little, little, little while—right?"

"Back in a flash, little sister."

Lying in the chair all night, Randy was able to get just a few hours of sleep. His back and right hip is sore. He's looking forward to napping in his own bed. Pulling into the garage, he kills the engine and looks up. "Thank you Jesus."

Randy unlocks the front door, not realizing that it wasn't locked to begin with. Once upstairs, he takes off his clothes, tosses them on the floor and falls into bed. He's instantly asleep.

Several hours later Randy is awakened by someone who is both ringing the doorbell, pounding on the door and calling his name. He races downstairs and opens the door, "Come in Grandpa."

As his grandfather enters the house, Randy can see that something is wrong.

"Grandpa, are you okay?"

His grandfather turns and puts both of his hands on Randy's shoulders, tears streaming down his face. It's your grandmother. She's gone, Randy," as he dissolves into tears.

"What are you talking about! Oh no, Grandma was coming over but we left for the hospital and I never thought to phone her. Oh Grandpa! What have I done! Is this my fault?"

The old man wipes his eyes with his handkerchief.

"No Randy, it wasn't because of anything you did. They said it was a heart attack. It was so fast."

"But I was talking to her last night. She sounded fine." Randy is too stunned to think.

"She told me she was going to your house because Amy was sick. I told her I should go with her but she said it wasn't necessary. You know how stubborn she can be." I was laying on the couch, watching the game when I heard her looking for her purse in the kitchen. Then there was a crash and then nothing. When I went in, she was on the floor. She was gone—just that fast. I called for help but there was nothing—just nothing they could do."

"Grandpa, please sit down." *This can't be happening again*, Randy thinks.

"I tried to phone you—all night, I tried but no answer. Now I realize you were at the hospital with Amy. How is she, son?"

"She's doing better. She should be released soon." But it's as if someone else is talking because Randy is far away, trying to make sense of yet another loss.

Two days later, Amy's released from the hospital with a three-day bed rest. Funeral arrangements have been made for Grandma Plant. Brian arrives home for Thanksgiving break.

Stephi babysits Amy while the funeral takes place. And the Taylor siblings once again begin the process of dealing with loss.

Brian's first year at West Virginia University is a modest success. He finishes with a 2.5 grade point average and is glad to be home for the summer. To celebrate, he purchases a debut album. The band's name is Asia. Amy likes it so much, she insists that she have her own copy.

Amy's invited to her first sleepover at a friend's house in nearby Frankfurt. This summer of 1982 is especially hot. The bills at the house go up, but so does Randy's salary. By a stroke of luck, three of his co-workers have retired, and two others have started their own businesses. Randy's duties are now a combination of working in the mailroom and as a clerk up front.

At the end of his lunch break, he gets a phone call. It's Amy.

"Hi Randy!"

"Hi sister. How was your sleepover?"

"It was great! We stayed up late, playing games, eating treats and singing songs. My friend Barbara has woods nearby. We're gonna go on a hike!"

"You be careful sister. Do you want me to pick you up or is Barbara's mother going to drive you home?"

"She's going to drive me home."

"Okay Amy, I have to get back to work. Love you."

"Love you too Randy."

That evening while Brian takes his shower, Randy and Amy sit in the family room.

"How was your hike?" the oldest asks.

"It was great! We saw grasshoppers, butterflies, frogs, dragonflies, deer, and two dogs stuck together. I hope they weren't fighting," Amy says. Randy laughs.

"Oh sister, they'll be alright. They were just playing," he says.

"We helped Mrs. Webster bake a cake. Can we bake a cake Randy?' she asks.

"Sure sister. It shouldn't take long. I think we have everything we need."

"The first thing we need to do is wash our hands. Next we take out all of our ingredients." Randy takes out a yellow cake mix from the cabinet and hands it to his sister.

"Read the back Amy."

"Three eggs, half cup of oil, one cup of water…"

"Slow down sis."

"What pan do we need?" Randy asks as the child looks closely.

"It says nine ex thirteen," she replies.

"That means nine by thirteen inches."

Once the cake has been in the oven for a while, Randy shows her the 'toothpick' test. "If there's any cake on the toothpick, that means it isn't done. Always place the toothpick in the middle of the cake." Randy takes out cooling racks, and places the pan on them and the two wash the utensils, and straighten up the kitchen.

Later, while Randy is tucking Amy into bed she asks, "Why are boys and girls different?"

"Because God made them that way. Now go to sleep Amy. Brian will take you to your swimming lessons tomorrow." Randy kisses her goodnight, then closes her door most of the way. He walks downstairs to the utility room to have a cigarette.

The next day before punching out for lunch, Shirley walks up to Randy.

"I'm going to Cal's. Do you want a sandwich?"

"Sure. Get me a Reuben please," Randy says as he takes out his wallet.

"That's okay. You buy next time," Shirley says. "Uh Shirley, when you get back, I need to talk to you."

At a corner table in the break room, Randy thanks his friend for lunch.

"No problem. What do you want to talk about?"

"Well, lately Amy's been curious about boys and girls."

"You know what that means?" Shirley asks. "It means you should have the 'talk'."

"She's so young," Randy replies. "I should wait a while."

"How old is she?"

"Almost nine."

"How old were you when you learned about 'the birds and the bees'?" Shirley asks.

"I guess I was about ten," Randy says slowly.

"There you go Mister Taylor!"

"I shouldn't have to do this. This is my mother's job!" Shirley places her hand on his shoulder as if to give him maternal reassurance.

"Randy, you're going to be fine. I'll bet it'll be easier than you think."

"I hope so."

After work, Randy phones for a pizza before he leaves the Post Office. When dinner is over, he turns to Brian.

"Do you want a piece of cake little brother?"

"Randy, you know I don't like cake."

"But we made it!" Amy says.

"Okay sister, I'll have a little piece." Brian takes out a regular kitchen knife, and slices a thin piece. He 'wolfs' it quickly. "Not too bad," he says.

"Gee Brian, you ate that so fast, are you sure you tasted it?" Randy asks. Brian scowls. "Yes, I tasted all of it." he takes out his keys. "I'm gonna go to Dennis's house. I think his sister likes me."

Once Brian leaves, Randy tells Amy, "Little sister, how about we talk about how babies are made?"

The next Saturday after work, Randy drives Amy to Kankakee. She'll be spending a week with Grandma and Grandpa Taylor. The oldest isn't complaining. He's looking forward to spending some time with Darlene.

After arriving back from Kankakee, Randy drives to Darlene's house in Olympia Fields. Their relationship is blossoming. Recently, they've all been going to church together on Sundays. Randy stops at a florist and purchases a bouquet of flowers.

"I'm here baby." he calls. Darlene emerges from the kitchen. They greet one another with a kiss then he hands her the bouquet.

"Thank you Randy. I'll put these in a vase, while you peel potatoes," she says.

"You're kitchen smells great! What's cookin'?" Randy asks.

"I've got a ham in the oven. I know you like pineapples, so I put extras on it. Would you like some wine?" she asks.

"That'd be great." Randy answers as he washes his hands.

"How are Amy and Brian?' Darlene asks.

"The former is in Kankakee, the latter—God only knows where he is."

"He lives with you. You should see him all of the time."

"Well babe, I don't. When I'm working, he's at Lakewood Pool with Amy and when he's working, I'm at the pool with Amy. Brian spends a lot of time at his friend Dennis's house. He has a huge crush on his sister. I'm surprised they're not dating. Ya know, ever since he got his Nova and started college, I see very little of him. He also loves to eat out, which leaves Amy and me alone at the dinner table."

"I guess he's not your little brother anymore."

"Oh hon, he'll always be my little brother. He just loves his independence. I've told him to watch his inheritance, but he doesn't listen to me. Other than that, he's pretty smart."

At the small dinner table, the couple sits across from each other and holds hands. Randy says the blessing. "Lord, thank you for this food we're about to eat. Thank you for our family and friends, and thank you for sending this wonderful woman into my life. Amen." Darlene smiles.

"Randy, that was so sweet!" Randy leans over and kisses her passionately. "Your food's getting cold."

"That's because you're making me hot!" Randy replies.

"Sit-down," she playfully commands. Randy obeys as he digs in.

"This meal's fantastic. You sure are a wonderful cook." Randy says.

"You did the potatoes," Darlene says.

"Aw, anyone can do potatoes," Randy replies.

"I'll do the dishes," Randy says. "You go and sit on the sofa."

"I can help you," Darlene says.

"No hon. You did the cooking. I insist. Sit and watch the 'James Bond' of broadcasting.

"Who's he?" she asks.

"Peter Jennings," Randy replies.

Thirty minutes later, Randy hangs up the towel on the oven handle. He walks into the living room when Darlene says, "My feet are so sore." Randy sits on the floor in front of her, as he gently takes off her black dress shoes. He begins to massage a foot. Darlene turns off the television by way of the remote. With her head leaning back, she relaxes.

"I love my job, but when I have to do these presentations, I'm on my feet all day."

"Oh, that feels so good. There's magic in your hands!" Randy messages her heel, Achilles tendon, and then the lower and upper calf muscle.

"That's not my foot. You're being naughty," she says with a smile. Randy explains, in exaggerated lip motions. "Your calf is attached to your leg. Your leg is attached to your foot. So therefore, your calf is attached to your foot!"

"No it's not. You're trying to get fresh with me!" Darlene says.

"Yes I am!" Randy replies as they laugh. He proceeds to rub her other foot.

"Did you know Darlene, there are twenty-six bones in the human foot?" he asks.

"I didn't know that," she replies.

"And one bone here," Randy says as he places her foot between his legs.

"You bad boy!" Darlene says as she playfully kicks him in the face. Both laugh as Randy continues to message one foot, and then the other.

"I bought a hammock the other day. Let's go try it out."

They walk out to the backyard where a large white hammock is tied between two maple trees. Other trees are near. Around the perimeter of the yard, are tall thick bushes. Privacy is guaranteed. They snuggle, cherishing each other's warmth and scent. In sync, each rubs the other's forehead and hair. A warm summer breeze blows, bringing with it the scent of lilacs. The hammock swings gently.

"I like your tall bushes. The seclusion's great."

"There's poison ivy at the base," Darlene replies.

"I'll get rid of it the next time I come."

"How?" she asks.

"I'll purchase a squirt bottle at the hardware store, and I'll fill it with extra strength bleach. Then, I'll squirt the bleach on the leaves. The poison ivy will choke and die."

"I never knew you could kill it that way," Darlene says.

"I could set fire to the ivy, but then your bushes would burn."

"Don't do that," Darlene replies. Silence comes between them until Randy breaks it.

"Darlene—I love you," he whispers. She doesn't respond.

"You don't feel the same?' Randy asks.

"I've been hurt," she says.

"I'm not gonna hurt you," he replies. Darlene snuggles tighter.

"I know." They fall asleep but are awakened when rain begins falling. Getting up, they walk quickly to the back door.

"I have to work tomorrow," Darlene says.

"I have to cut the grass if it stops raining. Brian's never around to do it." They kiss, then Randy starts to leave. Opening the front door, Darlene stands with her arms crossed.

"Randy," she says. He turns.

"I love you."

"I love you too," he replies. "I'll call you." He runs to his Chevy. As soon as he gets to his Monte Carlo, the heavens open.

CHAPTER **FOURTEEN**

By August of 1982, Brian begins his sophomore year at West Virginia University. He and Dennis rent an apartment off campus in a sector called South Park.

Amy begins the third grade at Neil Armstrong Elementary. At the dinner table one evening, the child picks at her Brussels sprouts.

"Eat your veggies sister," Randy says.

"I hate Brussels sprouts," she replies.

"This isn't a restaurant Amy. You'll eat what is served to you," Randy says. The child makes a face, then proceeds to eat one.

"You want to grow up to be a successful woman—don't ya?" Randy asks. She nods "Well, successful women eat Brussels sprouts!" After several bites, Amy asks a question.

"Randy, what's a smtwtfs?" A puzzled look comes across his face.

"What do you mean?" he asks.

"When I walked in my new classroom today, I saw August on a board, and below that is the word smtwtfs. Randy's smile turns into a laugh.

"What's so funny?" Amy asks.

"Oh sister! We share the same silliness. That's not a word. Those letters represent one day of the week." Randy takes a pad of paper and a pen from a drawer and writes;

Sunday, Monday, Tuesday, Wednesday, Thursday, Friday, Saturday. He shows it to her then pats her head with the pad playfully. "When you finish your Brussels sprouts, I have a surprise for you."

"What is it?" she asks.

"Finish your plate," Randy says.

"Don't eat fast Amy, or you'll choke. I don't want to take you to Saint James again," he says. The child finishes her dinner.

"Last week was your birthday. Did you have a good time at your party?" Randy asks.

"Yep! I sure did!" she replies.

"Well, there was a gift I wanted to give you, but the store ran out of them. Yesterday, they received a new shipment. So on my lunch break, I bought you one." Randy stands and turns her chair to face him.

"Now, you hold out your hands and close your eyes." She complies. Walking to the kitchen doorway, he turns.

"No peeking Amy!"

"I'm not Randy. I'm not peeking!" she says.

"I'm messin' with ya sister." The oldest brother walks upstairs to his bedroom, then walks right back in the kitchen. He places the item in the palms of her hands.

"Open your eyes." Amy does as she finds a pink gift-wrapped square with a white bow ribbon and bow. She's excited.

"I think I know what this is!" she says as she unwraps it. The gift is Michael Jackson's new long playing album.

"Check that out sister. A 'thrillernois' in Illinois!" he says.

"Aw, thank you Randy!" Amy says as she sets the album on the table and gives him a hug.

"Can I play it now?" she asks.

"Play one side before your homework, play the other side after."

The school year ends, and the summer of 1983 begins. Randy is surprised and proud that Brian made the Dean's list. "It's better than my shit list, ay little brother?" he kids.

Toward the end of June, Randy discovers something that puzzles him. The hinges on the screen door facing the backyard, keep coming loose. On this sweltering Sunday afternoon, Darlene's in the kitchen cooking dinner. Brian's with his girlfriend, Randy's inspecting the screen door and Amy's in the backyard playing with an orange ribbon that's attached to a straight wooden stick. Swinging the stick, the ribbon moves gracefully.

"Hey sister, go in the shed and get me a 'Phillips'." Randy says.

"A Phillips?" she asks.

"Yeah, it's got four points on it," he replies. Moments later, Randy turns around. He places a hand on his forehead as he says, "Jesus, Mary and Joseph!" There, Amy stands with a pitchfork!

"No sister, that isn't it." Randy leads her to the shed, where he opens a toolbox. He retrieves a Phillips screwdriver from the top compartment and shows her the 'points' on the end. He walks to the screen door and tightens the screws on the hinges.

As the summer days go by, both lawns at the house on Royal Drive get thicker and taller. Randy's irritated with Brian. He hates that he has to keep after him about cutting the grass, cleaning his room, and completing his chores. When Brian gets in from a late night date, Randy lays down the law. He's smoking a cigarette in the utility room, when Brian walks in to retrieve his clothes from the dryer.

"Little brother, you need to cut the lawns, do your chores, and keep your room clean, or I'm going to start charging you rent."

"You can't do that!" Brian says in protest.

"I can and I will," Randy replies sternly. "Who's the executor of the estate?"

"You are," Brian replies.

"Bingo. Now, I'm working six days a week, and raising Amy. You can at least earn your keep around here."

"Well Randy, I've limited my parties and I study my ass off. But you can't relate to that—can you?" Brian asks sarcastically. Randy sets his cigarette in the ashtray, takes his hands and grabs Brian's shirt while shoving him against the wall. Through clench teeth he says, "Listen here you son-of-a-bitch. I gave up college so that you and Amy can go. Now let me mention something that you can't relate to. I graduated from Rich South a semester early. Or did you forget about that? Now, you're gonna do what I tell ya, or you're gonna get the hell out of here!" Randy shoves Brian's chest while releasing his hands. He leaves the utility room. The ashes of his cigarette are long.

The next morning as Amy slowly gets dressed, Brian makes his bed, then walks down to the kitchen where Randy's making French toast at the stove.

"I'm sorry I got smart with you last night," Brian says.

"I'm sorry I was rough," Randy replies. The brothers hug, then playfully spar.

"See that Amy has some French toast when she comes down, Brian. I have to go out for a while."

"No problem, brother."

Soon after, Randy gets in his Chevy and goes of to run errands.

When Amy finally comes down for breakfast, she whines because she wants to go to the pool and thought they would be leaving right after breakfast.

"Sister, I have to mow the lawns, and then I'll take you to the pool."

"I don't want to wait for you. I'll just go by myself then," she says.

"Randy won't like that," Brian replies.

"He'll understand," the child says.

"Oh, he'll understand alright. You'll wait until I'm finished and then I'll take you."

"I don't have to listen to you," she says.

"And why not?" Brian asks.

"Because you're never here—so there!" Amy shouts as she storms off to her room, without having breakfast.

Brian waits until after the morning dew is burnt off. He mows the front lawn first for the simple fact that it's smaller. After raking, and bagging the grass, he has a quick lunch break, drinks a soda, tops off the lawnmower, then proceeds with the larger back lawn.

He guesses that Amy is still in her room pouting and will come down for lunch when she's hungry.

The skies turn cloudy and then dark. Halfway finished, it begins raining. Brian kills the lawnmower, then quickly puts it in the garage.

Funny Amy hasn't come down for lunch. No breakfast and now no lunch. I better check on her, he thinks. But when he goes upstairs to her room, the door is open and Amy isn't in there. The rain begins to pound harder as he runs through the house looking for his sister. Suddenly he races back up to her room. When he doesn't find her swim bag in its' usual place, he quickly grabs two clean towels from the bathroom and he gets in his Nova. He drives fast to Lakewood Pool. When he arrives, people are running to their cars. Lightening slashes the sky, thunder is booming and Amy is nowhere to be found. Mild panic sets in. *If she went to the pool on her own, she may have headed home by herself,* he thinks. Driving slowly through Lakewood Estates, Brian searches left and right. Ten minutes later, he sees a group of girls playing in someone's ditch. Pulling up to them, he opens the passenger door.

"Amy, get in here!" Brian's voice is just as strong as Randy's.

"I've been looking all over for you! You know that you're not allowed to come home on your own. You should've stayed at the house and waited for me in the first place. So now you're in a lot of trouble."

"I don't have to listen to you," Amy says.

"You've said that before, but I bet I can change your mind." Brian turns around and heads to the house. As he pulls in the garage, Amy opens the door before he comes to a complete stop. *She's not gonna push my buttons,* Brian thinks. As Amy heads upstairs to her bedroom and changes into dry clothes. Brian walks to the kitchen and pours himself a glass of milk. Randy walks upstairs from the half bath, combing his hair after taking a shower.

"I need to talk to you," Brian says as Randy walks in the kitchen.

Later, when Amy comes down from her bedroom, she crosses paths with her oldest brother. He points to the kitchen.

"Sit down Amy, I need to talk to you." The child obeys.

"Brian tells me you went to the pool by yourself today. Is that true?" Randy asks as Amy's head is hung low.

"Amy, you can be kidnapped just like that," Randy states as he snaps his finger. "A vehicle can pull up to you, and a man can throw you in. It can happen within seconds! When I'm not here, you have to listen to Brian. I know he's not here as often as I am, but he's your big brother too. Now you're grounded for a week. No swimming, no record playing, no watching television. You can read, and you can do puzzles. When Brian finishes mowing the back lawn, you will rake the grass in piles and put it in garbage bags. After meals, you will do the dishes. Is that understood? Have I made myself clear?" Randy asks as Amy nods.

"Enough said." Randy stands and leaves the kitchen.

It rains for the next two days. Randy plans a bar-b-que the following Sunday and has invited Grandma and Grandpa Taylor, Grandpa Plant, Darlene, Brian's girlfriend Natalie, and Shirley and her husband Bob.

The sun shines on this Sabbath. After church, Randy takes the grill out of the shed and rolls it to the patio and gets the bag of charcoals. Brian starts the lawnmower as Amy stands nearby with a rake. Randy empties the bag in the grill, then places the charcoal in a pile. Walking in the garage, he picks up a can that's in a corner. Shaking it, Randy discovers that it's empty. He hears his brother mowing.

"Oh Lord, he didn't do it. Tell me he didn't do it!" Randy walks around the house, carrying the can to the backyard. Randy motions his hand in front of his neck, indicating to kill the engine. Brian turns the button off, as the mower quiets. He walks towards his brother. Randy holds the can up to his waist.

"Brian, what does this read?" he asks.

"Gasoline," he replies. Randy turns the can over.

"Now what does it read?" Brian's eyes widen as his mouth opens.

"Lighter fluid," he says.

"You put the lighter fluid in the lawn mower! "I can't believe I did that!" Brian says.

"I can. I can believe it. Now go to the hardware store and get more lighter fluid so that I can light the charcoal.

"Can I go too?" Amy asks.

"It's his car," Randy replies.

"Can I go with you Brian?" she asks.

"Sure sis. C'mon."

By the fall of 1983, Amy's girlfriends get cockier—and so does Amy. On a hot Saturday morning in September, Randy tells his sister to clean her room.

"I don't want to. It's Saturday. Saturday's supposed to be a fun day." she replies.

"Okay sister, we'll do this right," Randy says as he takes out a quarter.

"I'll flick this in the air, and you call it. Heads I win, tails you lose, fair enough?" Amy nods. Randy flicks the coin high in the air, as Amy calls 'heads'. He catches it with his right hand, then slaps it down hard on his left. Removing his hand, the profile of George Washington appears.

"Go clean your room." The girl slowly walks upstairs.

"I always lose," she says. Her brother whispers, "Yes you do."

Randy is concerned about Brian. A year earlier Brian had made the Dean's list. Now, as he looks at the letter from WVU, Randy sees one 'C', and three 'D's. *Brian's partying is going in cycles.* Randy hates to write letters, but figures it will be more powerful.

March 18th, 1984

Dear Brian,

I've looked at your mid-term grades for this semester. I'm very disappointed and I'm afraid for you. Your college career is winding down. At the rate you're going, you'll be fluncking out just when you should be looking forward to graduation. Don't look back twenty-five years down the road and say, "I wish I've done better." Because at the present time, you can do much better.

Last year you made the Dean's list. I was so proud of you. Now what the hell happened? Just because you did great one semester, doesn't mean you can slack off. Professional athletes have to give one-hundred percent—and this is in practice. Why do you think the late great Roberto Clemente was so awesome? Well, he played baseball year round. He was also a man of intense focus. And that's what you must have Brian. You're in the homestretch. You must focus on the finish line.

You'll probably get this letter when you and Natalie come back from Florida. Hope you had a good time, but leave your partying down there.

Love, Randy

P.S. call me when you get back.

The next day, on his lunch break, Randy drives to Eagle grocery store down the road. He purchases soap, shampoo, toilet paper, toothpaste and one other item. *Gonna have to buy this sooner or later. May as well be sooner.*

On a Monday morning in April, Randy drops Amy off at Neil Armstrong Elementary. She's wearing jeans, tennis shoes, a baseball t-shirt, and her brown hair is long, straight and down to her shoulders.

"Have a nice day sister."

"You too Randy."

At the Post Office six hours later, a truck is late. Paul walks up to Randy.

"You don't mind staying a while longer do you 'T-Man'?"

"No I don't Paul, but let me call Neil Armstrong Elementary. I'm gonna be late picking up my sister." Randy phones the school and leaves a message with the receptionist. Then he punches out for his break.

Randy gets one hour overtime. After punching out for the day, he quickly walks to his car. Driving to Amy's school, he's just above the speed limit. As he turns into the parking lot, Randy's eyebrows come together as his mouth drops open. Amy's standing near the curb. She's sporting black nylon stockings, black shoes, a black mini skirt, two tank tops—one black the other gray. She's wearing heavy mascara, and her hair is bunned up. The girl opens the passenger door and gets in.

"Halloween's a little early this year!" Randy says. "You're not dressing that way."

"But Randy, all of my girlfriends are!"

"Amy, if your girlfriends jumped into Lake Michigan in January, would you do it?"

His sister simply stares back at him.

"Look, it's my job to take care of you. I pay for everything. I keep the house going. I try to give you everything that you need. I protect you. Therefore, I make the rules. When you're on your own, you can wear anything you want. As long as you're, my responsibility, you will dress modestly. You will not dress like a 'lady of the evening'."

"What's that?" she asks.

"A whore," Randy replies. He pulls into the garage. Brother and sister get out and walk in the house. Darting upstairs Amy yells, "You never let me do anything!" then stomps into her bedroom and slams the door. Randy walks upstairs and gently knocks. "Sister, I wouldn't make a habit of that," he says coldly. Taking a deep breath, the oldest sibling walks down to the kitchen to cook dinner.

After Randy helps Amy with her homework, they watch a little television as he drinks a beer. Nine o'clock is the girl's bedtime. They walk upstairs. Amy gets in bed, as Randy begins to tuck her in.

"You don't have to do that if you don't want to," she says flatly. A puzzled expression comes across his face.

"I always tuck you in," Randy replies.

"I know, but you don't have to if you don't want to." Amy turns her back on her brother and falls silent. Randy pauses, then walks from the bed. Turning the light off, he closes the door part way. In the utility room, he smokes a cigarette and thinks. His sister is changing before his very eyes.

Darlene and Randy are walking along a beach. The perfect couple. She, with her long dark hair and hour glass figure in a two-piece bathing suit. He, with his broad shoulders, developed pectorals and flat abs in his swimming trunks. The couple begins to run lightly. After a while, Darlene runs a little faster, breaking away from her lover. Randy adores her, inside and out. He takes in the scene. Her hair blowing in the wind, her buttocks jiggling, her breasts bouncing. When she is twenty yards ahead of him, she stops, turns around, and putting her hands on her face—screams.

Randy awakes not to Darlene's screams, but to Amy's.

"Holy shit!" Randy says, as he throws off his covers. He runs to her bedroom and turns on the light. Her bed is empty. Randy realizes her screams are coming from the bathroom across the hallway. He turns the knob—it's locked.

"Amy, what's wrong?" Randy asks.

"I'm bleeding!" she replies. Randy rushes to get the box of feminine napkins. He runs back and knocks on the door.

"Open up Amy, I'm not gonna come in. I need to give you this box." Randy hears an unlocking, as the door opens by inches and Amy reaches for the box.

"Take a shower, then read the directions. We'll talk when you're finished." The door closes, then Randy hears the water from the shower. He walks down the hall.

Fifteen minutes later, Amy slowly emerges in her pink bathrobe with her hair wet. Randy stands in the doorway of his bedroom.

"You all right?" he asks. Amy nods

"I was scared," she says.

"You scared the hell out of me too."

"Do you have any questions sister?" he asks as she pauses.

"Why do I feel dirty?" Amy asks.

"Oh sister. Don't feel dirty. All girls go through this. You're becoming a woman now. It's God's plan. And God's plans are never dirty. Now go dry your hair. You shouldn't go to bed with a wet head."

As Randy is going over the bills one evening a week later, he sits at his desk and shakes his head. *Brian's away at college, and these utility bills keep going up!* He soon finds the reason. Amy's been taking longer showers, she flushes the toilet often, and she never turns the lights off.

The day being Saturday, Randy drives to Gee Lumber on Crawford Avenue and purchases two solid bricks and an item called a 'governor'. He drives back to the house and places one brick in each water tank. Next, he installs the governor that's attached to the water heater in the utility room. Randy then writes a sign for Amy and places it in the downstairs bathroom, in the corner of the mirror.

Unless you go #2, flush the toilet every <u>other</u> time. –Randy.

The girl walks in the house after bowling. Walking downstairs to the family room, she's elated.

"I got a turkey today!" she exclaims.

"When are you going to cook it?' Randy asks.

"No silly. I got three strikes in a row!" she says.

"Oh—that turkey, very good sister. I've never done that before," Randy says. "Now Amy, I've got a question for you. Since Brian's away at college, wouldn't it make sense that our household bills would be getting lower?" Randy asks. Amy nods.

"That would make sense little sister. But in reality—they're getting higher! And I found out why. You never turn the lights off when you leave a room, you flush the toilet many times, and you take long showers. You've got to start turning off the lights. Read my sign in the corner of the mirror." Amy complies.

"What does that mean?" she asks.

"That means when you pee, you don't flush the toilet. The next time you pee, you do flush. Now when I take a shower, it only takes me about ten minutes. Starting today, when you take a shower, the hot water will turn off after ten minutes."

"How does that work?" Amy asks.

"Never mind how it works. Our bills have to get lower so I can put more money into your college fund. You do want to go to college—don't you?" Randy asks.

"Yep." she replies.

"Okay, let's go upstairs and have lunch."

Randy doesn't tell Amy that since Brian has been in college, he realizes that their inheritance may not be enough to cover both his brother and sister going to college.

As 1984 turns into 1985, Amy has identity issues. She wants teen-ager privileges. She wants to be treated as an adult, although she's caught in the middle, between adulthood and childhood. Amy wants a later curfew, but her brother refuses.

"All my friends stay out late on the week-ends," she says.

"All of your friends don't live here," Randy says. "Your sleep is more important." The girl stomps upstairs and slams her bedroom door. He was forced to grow up quickly. And now he serves not only as a big brother but a father figure as well.

As Amy's growing pains intensify, the frequency of her door slamming increases. Randy is at his wit's end. Driving his sister to school one morning, he gets an idea. After dropping her off, he drives back home.

Randy's shift goes smoothly. He's well rested, all of the trucks arrive on time, he receives a bonus check from his supervisor Paul, and Shirley treats him to lunch. He feels especially strong this day.

When he picks up Amy from school, she shows Randy her spelling test.

"I got an A."

"That's very good sister. I'm proud of you," Randy replies.

When they get home, she heads upstairs, but her mood quickly changes. Hurrying down into the kitchen she asks Randy, "Where's my door?"

"I took it down," he replies.

"Why?" Amy demands.

"I got tired of you slamming it."

"I hate you, Randy!"

"You'll change your mind," her brother replies.

"No I won't. I won't change my mind." Amy storms to her room as Randy quietly follows.

"Look sister, I don't slam doors. When Brian's here, he doesn't slam doors. Now why should you?" Randy asks as Amy sits on the edge of her bed with her arms folded.

"Now when you act like a young lady, instead of a spoiled brat, I will replace your door. It's up to you Amy, the ball's in your court," Randy says. The girl cries. Randy's heartstrings are pulled. He sits next to her and takes her in his arms.

"I don't like punishing you, but you can't act like a maniac every time you get mad."

"I miss Mommy and Daddy,"

"We all miss them Amy. Growing up is tough. I know—I've done it before." The girl breaks from his embrace.

"Control your temper—okay?"

In this spring of 1985, it's 'May showers that bring June flowers'. In the break room at the Post Office, the electricity flickers off and on. Shirley and Randy eat their lunches with other co-workers nearby. All hear the rain on the roof.

"My daughter's birthday is coming up. She wants the album, 'The Turn of a Friendly Card' by The Alan Parson's Project, but I can't seem to find it anywhere," Shirley says.

"If you have a stereo at your house, I'll loan you my album and you can record it, then give the cassette tape to your daughter."

"That's a wonderful idea Randy."

"I'll bring it tomorrow," he says.

"I'm off tomorrow, I'm going to Saint Charles to see my mother," Shirley says.

"Why don't you have Bob stop by for it tonight."

"I will and since Bob will be there, do you think he could borrow your lawnmower? Ours is in the shop."

"Yeah, that'll be no problem," Randy replies.

"If it keeps raining like this Amy, we'll be floating home," Randy says. The girl laughs. As the car nears the house, Randy pushes a button on his visor. The garage door lifts. Parked on the right side, is a Chevrolet Nova.

"Brian's home!" they say in sync. As they get out, Amy runs in the house. Brian emerges from the kitchen and Amy throws herself into his arms.

"Hi'ya doin' Amy?' he asks. Randy walks in the foyer and embraces him.

"How's my little brother? When did you get in?"

"About an hour ago. Gee, Amy is getting tall." Brian says. The siblings seat themselves at the kitchen table. Outside, the rain ceases.

"You didn't attend your graduation ceremony?" Randy inquires.

"It was for the medical school and the law school. Undergrads don't have there ceremony until next week. But it's okay big brother. Our department had a wonderful reception in the Mountain Lair."

Just then, a pickup truck pulls in the driveway. The doorbell rings and Randy gets up to answer it. It's Shirley's husband, Bob. "Come in the kitchen and have Chinese with us. I ordered too much food," Randy says.

"Oh, I might have a taste. Do you have any coffee?" Bob asks.

"I'll make some," Randy replies. The doorbell rings again as Brian answers it. It's Stephi from across the street.

"Hello Brian, is Amy here?' she asks. The girl runs to her.

"We're having a birthday party for Kelly. Would you like to come?" Stephi asks.

"Randy, can I go?" she inquires.

"Sure. Go party your butt off," he replies. Amy thanks him as Randy prepares Bob's plate. The older gentleman thanks him as the aroma of fresh brewed coffee fills the kitchen.

"I'll look for that album before I forget," Randy says. Bob turns to Brian as Randy leaves.

"How's the Nova holding up?" he asks.

"Great Bob! I was reluctant to buy it, on account of it being a four door, but I'm glad I did." The two make small talk. Later, Brian says, "I'm gonna take a long hot shower then go to bed. See ya Bob. Enjoy your meal."

"I found it." Randy says as he returns to the kitchen. "I need to put my albums in alphabetical order." Randy hands the record to Bob then pours him a cup of coffee.

"Shirley likes this new wave stuff, but I'll stick to my country," Bob says.

"How do you like your coffee?" Randy asks.

"Just like my women—hot and black!" Bob replies. Randy laughs as he carefully places Bob's cup near his plate.

"Thank you son. Shirley left two hours ago. I was gonna get a sandwich at Cal's on the way back, but I guess this timings perfect."

Suddenly, both hear cursing from downstairs.

"Oops! I forgot to tell Brian about that governor," Randy says as both laugh.

"I installed one when my oldest daughter was in high school," Bob says.

Randy continues. "I was going over my bills last week Bob, and my water bill went through the roof! And then it dawned on me. Amy's been taking hour-long showers. I said, 'That's enough of that man!' I bought a governor the next day."

After Bob's finished he thanks Randy. The men go outside to the garage, and load the lawnmower onto the bed of the truck.

"When I bring it back, it'll be topped off," Bob says.

"Just don't put lighter fluid in, the way Brian did," Randy says as Bob laughs.

"He did that?" he asks.

"Yep! He thought it was gasoline. And I'll be damned—it worked." The men bid each other a farewell as Brian comes upstairs from the family room with a towel around his waist.

"Man, that water turned ice cold!" he says.

"I forgot to tell you Brian, I installed a governor," Randy says.

"What's that?" he asks.

"That's a device that turns off the hot water after ten minutes. Our lovable sister was taking hour-long showers. I tell you what. Go upstairs and take a bath. The governor only works for the shower."

"Sounds good to me."

After he cleans up the kitchen, Randy vacuums the dining room. He's careful not to bump the painting that sticks out a bit from behind the cabinet. No matter how hard Randy tries, he doesn't succeed.

Amy receives "Born in the U.S.A." by Bruce Springsteen for her twelfth birthday. Brian begins teaching math at Hillcrest High School, twelve miles away. Amy enters the seventh grade and begins babysitting for the Henderson's down the street.

On this Saturday evening, Darlene's over watching a movie with Randy. Brian's on a date with Natalie, and Amy's babysitting the Henderson's son Phil. Randy and Darlene pick up Amy after eleven and when they get back to the house, the girl shows off her earnings.

"That's wonderful Amy, your first money. Now let me show you something." Randy darts up the stairs to the cabinet in the dining room where the bills are kept. In no time, he's back. Placing three white business envelopes on the cocktail table, they read: Give-Save-Spend.

"Amy, every time you earn money, you need to put a third in each envelope. If you want to get your car in four years, place a little more in the 'Save' envelope." As my friend Dwayne Ramsey says, 'Everything is owned by God. We just manage it for Him.'"

"How much is a third?" she asks. Randy retrieves a pen and a pad of paper. He writes down her total amount, then divides that number by .33 by placing the decimal point two digits to the right, Randy shows her long division.

"I've already had long division."

"Sorry, Amy I forgot," Randy says. The girl turns to Darlene.

"I can do a somersault, watch me!" She performs the movement as Darlene claps. The oldest sibling scowls.

"Amy, it's after midnight. You shouldn't be doing somersaults when it's time for bed." Randy says.

The spring of 1987 brings an early thaw and an early anticipation among many girls at Neil Armstrong Elementary School who are looking forward to moving on to high school in the fall. Amy's friends are raving about the movie, "Some Kind of Wonderful." And now Amy's begging Randy to take her to see it.

"Well little sister. You've been doing your chores, your grades are good, you obey the sign in the downstairs bathroom, you turn off the lights when you're through, and I don't have to work this Saturday—yeah, I'll take you." The girl gives him a hug.

At the Cinema Theaters near Lincoln mall, Amy and Randy wait in line. She sees some of her friends and waves. Then she looks at her brother, and motions with her finger. Randy bends down as Amy whispers. "My girlfriend Sherry likes you." Randy whispers back. "Tell Sherry I'm too old for her, plus I have a girlfriend." The line moves faster then Randy pays for the tickets.

At this stage of her life, Amy notices boys but isn't crazy about them. She has no concept what a 'love triangle' is until she sees "Some Kind of Wonderful." In an emotional scene Keith, played by Eric Stoltz runs after Watts, played by Mary Stuart Masterson. The image is very powerful to the twelve year old as Amy begins to cry softly. Randy places his large arm around her small shoulder.

"It's only a movie," he whispers. As the credits begin to roll, Randy stands.

"No big brother, I have to read them," Amy says.

Housework isn't at the top of Randy's list, but he makes an honest effort to do his share. He learned from his mother to always vacuum first and then dust. Randy has two vacuum cleaners. One for the bedrooms and another for the family, living and dining rooms. Being a creature of habit, he does each in order respectfully.

When he's nearly finished with the dining room, Randy vacuums around the oak cabinet, near the entrance to the kitchen. He bumps the golden frame that's between the wall and the back of the cabinet. The thought of placing the golden frame painting completely behind the oak cabinet doesn't occur to him.

June of 1987, Amy Taylor graduates from Neil Armstrong Elementary in the upper fifth of her class. As one of her gifts, Randy takes her to Marriott's Great America amusement park in Gurnee Illinois, just north of Chicago. The party also includes Darlene, Brian and his girlfriend, Natalie.

The summer passes quickly and Amy's freshman year at Rich South is coming up soon. Orientation is held in mid August and she goes on a tour of the school, has lunch in the cafeteria, and listens to several speeches.

"How was your orientation Amy?" Brian asks.

"It was neat. I'm so excited about going to high school! I even met my principal," she says with a smile.

"What do you think of 'Quick Draw'?" Randy asks.

"I think he's a nice man. His voice is strong, yet comfortable to listen to. Why do you call him 'Quick Draw'?" Amy asks.

"Because he's a hunter," Randy replies.

Randy drops Amy off at Rich South High on her first day of school. Before opening her door, she turns to her brother.

"I'm kind of nervous," she says.

"Little sister, you'll be alright. Before you know it, this'll be routine. I'll pick you up right here after work. If it rains, wait in the cafeteria. You can see Sauk Trail from there." Randy gives her a hug, a kiss and ruffles her hair.

"Break a leg kid!" Amy opens the door and gets out. As Randy pulls away, he looks in his rearview mirror. His sister walks up the stairs quickly—a good sign.

After her last class, Amy does her homework and reads in the library. She can walk home now that Randy has given her a key, but for now she feels more secure knowing that he is picking her up. A blue Monte Carlo pulls in front of the school, as Amy stands with her books to her budding bosom. She gets in with a smile.

"I take it you had a good day?" Randy inquires.

"It was easier than I thought, but I keep forgetting the combination to my locker."

"You'll remember it sister. I had the same problem my first day of high school. Just write it on a notebook or something for now."

"Randy, I've been invited to a Halloween party tomorrow night. Can I go?" Amy asks.

"I don't know—*can* ya?"

"May I go?' she asks.

"Who's having the party?" Randy asks.

"My friend, Michelle. You've met her—Michelle Johnson. It's at her house and it starts at seven."

"Will there boys be there? Where does Michelle live?"

"The other side of Lakewood, right near that red, white and blue fire hydrant. Yes, Randy there will be boys."

"Will her parents be at home and what time does it end?' Randy asks.

"It ends at ten and her mom and dad will definitely be home and, before you ask, yes, you can call them to make sure."

"You can bet that I will call."

At the Halloween party, Amy meets Stan, who's also a freshman. They hit it off immediately and are comfortable with each other.

As the weeks go by, Amy talks of Stan a lot. While washing the dishes, Randy says, "Sounds like he's your boyfriend."

"He's not my boyfriend, he's just a friend," Amy replies.

"Then why are you blushing?" Randy asks with a smile. Amy covers her face with the dishtowel as she says, "I'm not blushing!" They laugh.

It's the spring of 1988 and Amy decides to audition for a role in the class play. She's thrilled when she gets the part. In the evenings after her homework is finished, she studies her lines and learns her cues.

On opening night in the east cafetorium, the performance is greeted by a full house. Grandma and Grandpa Taylor, Grandpa Plant, Randy and Darlene, Brian and Natalie and Randy's friends, Shirley and her husband Bob are all there to see Amy. In Act two scene two, Amy walks onto the stage and begins to deliver her lines. Halfway through, Randy places his hands over his eyes. He knows that she's skipped several lines, causing a fellow actor to miss a cue. Randy can see that for the rest of the performance, Amy never regains her confidence. When the play is over, the audience gives a standing ovation. Darlene leans to Randy and whispers, "I have to go to work early tomorrow. Call me the day after." As Amy emerges with her fellow students, she looks less than thrilled. Randy gives her a hug and a kiss. Her grandparents do the same while giving her a half a dozen roses. Brian and Natalie also extend their congratulations, then leave to prepare food at the house. As Amy gets in Randy's car, she bursts into tears.

"I can't believe I messed up!"

"Listen Amy, even the greatest actors and actresses of the world have blown their lines."

"But I worked so hard," she says.

"I know you did Amy, but look at it this way. There are hundreds of students that wouldn't have the courage to even make an attempt. Now, you can't do better than your best. Even though you flubbed your lines, I'm still proud of you! It takes a lot of courage to get up on that stage," Randy says.

"I feel so stupid," Amy says.

"Let me tell you a story," Randy says as he slowly backs out of the parking lot. "Many years ago, there was this boy who blew his lines in a play. Too embarrassed to go home to face his family, he sat down on a curb nearby and put his head in his hands. Moments later, this girl comes walking by. Feeling sorry, she sits next to him. She comforts him and encourages him. Now check this out," Randy says as he speaks slowly now. "That boy was Dad, and that girl was…"

"Mom!" Amy says. She wipes her eyes as a smile comes across her face. "I never knew that. What a beautiful story," she says.

As Randy turns into the driveway he says, "You know, you had a pretty good part for a first-timer. How many lines did you have?"

"Nineteen," she says.

"Dad had two!" Randy replies. Both enter the house laughing.

After Easter vacation, Randy pulls in front of Rich South.

"You don't have to pick me up today Randy, my girlfriend will drive me home."

"Your girlfriend has a car?" he asks.

"She's a junior," Amy replies.

"Who is this junior? What's her name?"

"It's Jenny Branch. You know, she's Shirley and Bob's niece."

"Oh, sure I remember her. Shirley tells me she's a great girl."

The siblings hug.

"Have a good day sister. Keep your chin up."

"Thanks Randy. Bye." She leaves then walks upstairs inside to the freshman lockers near the east cafetorium. The day flies.

Later, Randy punches out, then drives to Eagle supermarket nearby. At home after putting the groceries away, he takes a moment to relax. Sitting in the living room, he gazes at his parents wedding portrait above the sofa. *What would my life be like if you were still here? I can only imagine.* Randy closes his eyes. "I'm gonna cook dinner now. I wish you both were here to enjoy it," he says aloud.

Amy gets out of her friend's car with a Kleenex in her hand.

"How was school sister?" Randy asks from the kitchen. Amy muffles an "Alright." From the sound of her voice, Randy can tell she's been crying. He walks into the foyer as she hangs up her coat.

"What's wrong?" he asks.

"Stan broke up with me."

Randy opens his arms as his sister goes to his embrace.

"I loved him," Amy replies.

"I know you did, now listen. God has another boy all picked out. Repeat after me, 'A broken heart still beats.'"

"A broken heart still beats," Amy replies.

"Say it three more times," Randy instructs. His sister complies.

"There, do you feel better?' he asks.

"No I don't," she replies.

"Sister, you're going to be fine. Let me tell you something else you don't know." He breaks the embrace. "When I was your age, I fell madly in love with this girl. We dated for a while, then she left me for another boy. Like you, I was devastated. Well, now she's in prison for murder."

"Who did she kill?" Amy asks.

"Her husband."

Amy breaks into laughter.

"Amy, I'm cooking your favorite. Stuffed green peppers with mashed potatoes." A little smile forms on her face.

October, 1989. Amy is a junior. She's coaxed by her girlfriend, Nancy to join her in trying out for the cheerleading squad.

"I won't make it," she says.

"Oh come on Amy. You've got the face and the build of a cheerleader." Nancy says.

"Do you think so?'

"I know so! Tryouts are next Tuesday at three in the gym. Mrs. Ingram is the coach.

Reluctantly, Amy tries out for the cheerleading squad—and makes it. Slowly, her confidence grows. She learns the moves and the routines quickly and almost effortlessly.

The first basketball game is at home against Tinley Park. During Rich South's first time out, a basketball player catches Amy's eye. To her, he looks like a tall Paul McCartney. The girl is smitten. At halftime, the cheerleaders perform flawlessly. In the stands are Randy and Darlene, Brian and Natalie. Randy nudges Brian's arm.

"Look little brother, Mrs. Logan and 'Quick Draw' are here!"

"That's unusual Randy. I've never seen them at a basketball game. And certainly not together. You don't think they're involved do you?'

"Number one, they're both married to different spouses. Number two, they're cousins."

"How do you know that?" Brian inquires.

"Because I know everything," Randy says.

Both teams rack up points. In the end, The Rich South Stars triumph over the Tinley Park Titans 74 to 71.

The next day Amy and Nancy are eating lunch in the east cafetorium when Nancy suddenly looks startled.

"Oh shit, I forgot to see my guidance counselor. Sorry Amy. I have to run honey." Nancy gets up and leaves as a tall boy walks over with his tray.

"Okay if I sit here?"

"Sure," Amy replies as her heart quickens. It's the basketball player. The boy extends his hand.

"My name's David Nelson." The girl shakes his hand.

"My name's Amy Taylor. Nice to meet you."

"You're a cheerleader," David says.

"And you're a basketball player," Amy replies.

"Well, I try to be. That game against Tinley Park was close. I didn't think we we're gonna pull it out. Remember we were down fourteen points at halftime? Our next opponent is Rich Central. We're really gonna have to have our act together."

The two talk and hit it off. When David's finished he says, "Well, I gotta go. History class is waitin'. You wanna have lunch together tomorrow?' David asks.

"Yes I do, but my girlfriend Nancy will be here. Is that alright?' Amy asks.

"Sure, that's ok," David replies. He stands and picks up his tray.

"Well Amy, I'll see ya tomorrow."

"Okay David," she replies. The junior finishes her lunch, unaware that she's smiling.

Randy's hours have changed and he's in the kitchen snapping peas when Amy walks in. She's singing to herself as she hangs up her coat.

"I think my sister had a good day," Randy says. Amy walks in the kitchen and hugs her brother.

"Your sister had a great day!"

"What happened, didja hit the lotto?" Randy asks.

"No something better. I met a boy!" she says.

"See, see sister. Wasn't I right? God did have another boy all picked out. What's his name?"

"His name's David and he's on the basketball team."

"And to think you weren't gonna try out for cheerleading," Randy says as he playfully flicks her ear.

"Cut it out." she says with a smile as she backs away.

"When am I gonna meet him?' Randy asks.

"Can he come over for Sunday dinner?" Amy asks.

"Sure. By all means." Randy says.

"But not this Sunday," Amy says. He has to help his father move some furniture."

Brian arrives ten minutes after his siblings begin eating. The aroma of stuffed pork chops intensifies his hunger.

"Is it hard to make these, Randy?" Brian asks.

"No it isn't. Just get your pork chops pre-cut at the meat department before you leave the store."

The fall semester of 1989, Amy takes a driver's course the school offers. Now with her permit, Amy begins nagging her brother to take her driving.

After she does the dishes, Randy gives her his keys. Amy's so excited, she opens the front door.

"Wait sister. What are you forgetting?" Randy asks.

"Oops. My coat!" she replies. Randy mutters a playful 'pitiful' as she opens the closet door.

"Before you put it in reverse sister, I have to tell you something. Brian's car is not here. But we're going to pretend that it is. Start the car. Now put your foot on the brake, put the transmission in reverse, and slowly pull straight out." The girl obeys. When the front bumper is at the garage entrance, Randy speaks.

"Now turn the wheel sharply to the left." The girl complies.

"This Chevy has a long hood Amy. If you turn too soon, you're gonna hit his car. We'll both be angry and you'll be out of some money." Amy looks both ways before backing out onto Royal Drive.

"And speaking of money, how much have you saved?"

"Four hundred dollars," she replies. Randy rubs his salt and peppered stubble face.

"There's not many used cars out there for eight hundred bucks. You're gonna have to do better than that. Maybe you can ease off on your record buying."

"But Randy, I love music." Amy says.

"I love music too sister, but I've got a car and you don't. Life's about making choices isn't it? Turn right after you make a complete stop at that sign and we'll just stay in Lakewood Estates."

"I want to go on Sauk Trail."

"We'll go in due time," he says.

"Aw Randy, please." she whines.

"Amy, if you moan and groan, I won't let you drive my car at all."

"Well then, I'll just drive Brian's!" she says. Randy busts out laughing as he looks at her.

"You think Brian will let you drive his car?" he asks.

"No he won't," Amy replies.

"Well sister, why are you talking? Why are the words leaving your mouth?"

After forty minutes, Amy pulls into the left side of the garage.

"You did good Amy. Practice will raise you confidence."

CHAPTER **FIFTEEN**

The first Sunday in November of 1989, bitter cold descends upon the Chicago region. At 4:30 in the afternoon a brown '73 Delta eighty-eight pulls in the driveway. A bumper sticker reads, "Parents Rule." A tall young man wearing a letter jacket gets out. The doorbell rings as Amy answers it. She greets her boyfriend with a hug. Then she turns to her siblings.

"David, I want you to meet my brothers. This is Randy and Brian. Amy points to her boyfriend.

"This is David." Each brother shakes hands with him. Amy feels giddy.

"Dinner won't be ready for twenty minutes. Would you like something to drink?' Randy asks.

"A pop please," David says.

"I'll get him one," Amy says as she darts downstairs to the utility room.

"You can come in and sit at the kitchen table. I'm almost done cooking," Randy says. "We've seen you play David. You're pretty good," Brian says as Randy prepares the salad.

"We lost to Rich Central big time," David says.

"Don't get discouraged. The season's still young," Randy replies. Amy walks in the kitchen and sets David's beverage in front of him. He thanks her.

"Where's my pop?" Brian asks.

"You didn't say you wanted one," Amy replies. She darts downstairs again. Randy gets an idea as he winks at his brother.

"Who do you play next?" Brian asks.

"Kankakee Eastridge," David replies.

"I hear they're pretty good."

Amy walks upstairs to the kitchen and gives Brian his soda.

"Amy, that's not fair. Where's my pop?" Randy asks. The girl throws her hands up in the air and utters a playful "AAUUGH!" The brothers laugh as David chuckles.

"We like teasing her, don't we Brian?"

Grace is said, then dinner is served. The menu consists of a roast, glazed carrots, boiled potatoes, salad, and French bread with butter. The phone rings as Brian stands to answer it.

"Randy, I'll take this downstairs." Five minutes later, Amy excuses herself to go to the bathroom. Randy sits at the head of the table, his elbows on the tablecloth, his hands together. David is sitting next to him. The oldest sibling speaks softly to the young man.

"David, I know you like Amy. And she really likes you. But I expect you to respect the fact that Amy is a nice girl who still has college ahead of her. So, if you'll pardon the expression—keep it in your pants. You got it?"

"Yes sir," David says.

"Don't call me sir. Call me Randy."

"Yes Randy," David says. Brian walks upstairs to the kitchen with Amy behind in seconds.

"I forgot to call Natalie," Brian says.

"David, we have chocolate-peanut butter pie for dessert. Would you like a piece?"

"Yes sir, uh- I mean, Randy."

"This pie's store bought, but it tastes homemade," Brian says. Randy takes the pie out of the fridge and cuts everyone a big slice.

When David gets ready to leave, he thanks Randy for the meal and shakes hand with both brothers. Randy retrieves his lettered jacket from the closet.

"Big brother, please get mine too. I wanna walk David to his car," Amy says. The two walk outside in the frigid air. At his parent's car, they hug each other.

"I like your brothers," David says.

"Randy's strict, but with Brian, I can get away with murder," Amy says as she tightens her coat. David gets in then rolls down the window.

"I hope this isn't too soon to say this, but—I love you," Amy says.

"What took so long?" David asks. The girl playfully hits his shoulder.

"Come here," he says. David kisses her lips as Amy's hair falls down as if to hide the passion.

"I'll see ya at school tomorrow," he says.

"Where else will I be?" she asks. He starts the engine, and slowly backs out. Amy waves as he blows her a kiss.

That evening, Randy takes out the vacuum cleaner from the foyer closet. Lifting it slightly several times, he thinks, *It doesn't take long for this bag to fill up.* Taking the package from the top shelf of the closet, Randy retrieves a new one. Turning the vacuum cleaner over, he unzips the back, when a flashback commences. He sees himself zipping a black body bag. Randy stands and places a hand over his eyes. Brian walks up from the family room.

"You alright Randy?" he asks.

"Yeah Brian, I have just a little headache. I'll be okay," he replies. Randy carefully changes the bag. Dust floats in a sunray that emits between the curtains. Zipping the back, he carefully places the old bag in the garbage. Randy proceeds to vacuum the living and dining rooms. When he's nearly finished with the latter, he bumps the golden frame that sticks out from behind the oak cabinet.

Brian lets Amy drive his car but once. He corrects her every mistake, which in turn angers the sixteen year old. As she pulls in the garage she says, "Randy's strict, but he has more patience than you when it comes to my driving. I'm never gonna drive your car again."

"I know, Amy. I know you won't drive my car again," Brian says. The girl storms into the foyer as Randy walks out from the kitchen.

"Amy, what's wrong?" he asks.

"Brian criticized my driving the whole time. He didn't give me any compliments for anything!" The middle sibling walks in the foyer.

"Little brother, what's the problem?" Randy asks.

"She can't drive worth a damn," he says.

"She's learning Brian. Have patience. I remember when you were learning how to drive. Turning the ignition when the engine was running." Amy begins to laugh.

"Did I do that?" he asks.

"Don't play dumb with me Brian. You know damn well you did that." I can name other things too," Randy says.

As the spring of 1990 arrives, Amy's junior/varsity cheerleading squad wins first place in the cheerleading competition of Cook County. Amy gets her driver's license in April after she pays her auto insurance. She's completely thrilled. That same weekend, she approaches her brother on a Saturday afternoon in the utility room.

"Randy, may I talk to you?" she asks, hiding her nervousness.

"Yeah sister, what's up?' he asks as he takes a drag from his cigarette.

"David's parent's car is in the shop, and he wants to take me out to dinner and see a movie. Would you—let me use your car?" she asks innocently. Randy exhales away from her slowly.

"Well—Darlene's coming here soon to listen to some records. What time is the movie?' he asks.

"Nine o'clock."

"Near Lincoln mall?" Randy asks as Amy nods.

"It'll be about two hours long. You'll have to take David home. Where does he live again?"

"Matteson," Amy replies.

"Okay, roughly fifteen minutes to take him home. You'll be coming back around eleven thirty—yeah, you can take my car." Amy gives him a huge hug, then softly claps her hands. Randy holds up a 'peace' sign.

"Two conditions—one, you be home at twelve midnight and not a minute later, and second, you come back with a full tank of gas. Now follow me, I want to show you something." She follows her brother out to the garage. Randy opens his door and sits behind the wheel. Taking his right index finger, he points right at the fuel gauge.

"What does this word say?"

"Unleaded," Amy replies.

"You're going to put unleaded gas in the tank—not leaded. Lead gasoline will ruin the engine." The two walk back in the house as Amy uses the phone in the kitchen. Randy walks to his bedroom to retrieve the extra set of keys when he hears his sister.

"David, he said yes! Isn't that wonderful?" The girl screams with happiness.

"Why am I starting to regret this?" Randy asks himself out loud. Finding the extra set, he walks downstairs. Amy puts her coat on as this April is chilly. Randy walks to the foyer, holding up the spare set.

"Amy, a car is not a toy. If I see or find out you've been treating my car like a toy, I will take away your license. Do you understand?' he asks.

"Yes, I understand," she says. He gives her his keys. Amy hugs him and says 'thank you'.

"You and David have a nice time."

"We will. Thank you again Randy." He walks outside after her, and stands on the tiny porch with his hands in his pockets as Amy walks in the garage.

"Wear your seat belt," he says.

"I will," Amy replies. She gets in and closes the door. Moments pass as she adjusts the seat and the mirrors. The engine starts as the white back up lights come on. Amy slowly pulls out of the garage, then turns as the front end meets the entrance. Randy waves. The girl looks both ways before backing onto the street. On Royal Drive, she waves then slowly drives away.

Now I know how Mom and Dad felt, when I first drove their car.

A white '72 Mustang turns onto Royal Drive from Sauk Trail. The driver notices the blue Monte Carlo coming towards her.

"Now, where's he going?" Darlene asks as she slows while rolling down her window.

"Where are you going honey?" Darlene asks.

"My boyfriend and I are going to dinner and to a movie. Randy's letting me use his car!" Amy says with a big smile.

"Well, you be careful," Darlene says.

"I will." Both go their way. Darlene parks her Mustang in front of the house, parallel to the sidewalk. She gets out, walks to the door, and rings the doorbell. Randy greets her with a hug and a kiss.

"Darlene, the next time just walk in."

"I just spoke with Amy. Are you nervous she's driving your car?" Darlene asks.

"Very," Randy replies.

"Then why are you letting her?"

"Number one, David's folks car is in the shop. Number two, at one time, my parents let me use theirs." Randy fixes Darlene a drink and prepares her a sandwich. Even though the couple are under thirty, they enjoy evenings at home.

Randy takes out a number of record albums and they listen to A-HA, The Police, Fleetwood Mac, Asia, and Van Halen. At

11:35pm, the two are snuggled on the couch listening to an Alan Parson's Project LP when they hear the garage door open.

"Our wonder girl's back," Randy says.

"How was your evening?' Randy asks.

"It was wonderful!" Amy says.

"What movie did yuz see?" Darlene asks.

"'Children of a Lesser God'" Amy replies.

"I thought that came out four years ago in '86" Randy says.

"It did. David wanted to see it, and it was showing near the mall. Oh, David filled your tank," Amy says.

"Tell him I said 'thanks'."

"He loves your car."

"Tell him I love my car too," Randy says as he extends his arm, palm up.

"I don't want to shake your hand," Amy replies.

"My keys." Randy says. "My sister's getting to be a smart aleck." Amy laughs as she hands them to him.

"I'm going to take a bath and go to bed. Thanks again Randy."

Moments later Darlene says, "I have to work tomorrow."

"On a Sunday?" Randy asks.

"I have a couple coming in from Ohio. They want to see a house in Crete-Monee." Darlene slowly stands up then places her arms around Randy. She kisses him.

"I've enjoyed this evening," she says.

"Me too. Changing those records was great exercise!" he says sarcastically. The couple holds hands then walk upstairs. Randy helps her with her coat, then walks Darlene to her car.

"It's pretty chilly for April."

"It is, but you've kept me warm tonight." Darlene replies. The couple kiss passionately. Darlene gets in her Ford. Rolling down her window she says,

"Give me a call. I love you."

"Love you too," Randy says.

The next weekend Randy does the vacuuming. Once again, he bumps the frame with the upright. *I've got to get rid of this painting. I bump into it all of the time.* Turning off the upright, he puts it away in the foyer closet. Retrieving the frame, Randy blows the dust from the top. He studies the artwork for a moment. A young beautiful woman wearing a white, high-neck dress. She sits on a huge rock, reading a letter. A waterfall is nearby. Her chestnut brown hair is worn up in a bun. Red and yellow flowers are near her feet. A partial rainbow is in the sky. Randy takes the painting out to his car and places it on the floor in front of the backseat. He doesn't notice the tiny signature and date on the bottom left hand corner—*Frederick Johnson* 1918.

Randy's in good spirits because it's Saturday and he has the day off. The temperature has warmed to the mid 60's, with only a few white clouds in the sky. Getting in his car, he drives to the Salvation Army on Sauk Trail in Park Forest. Harvey Smith, a truck driver, has just finished loading three small tables, a dozen chairs, and ten boxes of books. His destination is Rockford, roughly an hour and a half west of Chicago. A blue Monte Carlo pulls in the parking lot as Harvey slides the rear door down. Getting out, Randy retrieves the painting from behind his seat.

"Hey, Buddy!" Randy calls. The truck driver turns.

"Do you work here?" Randy inquires.

"Yeah," Harvey says.

"I'd like to donate this."

"Gee, it's really beautiful. Thank you sir," Harvey says.

In the Thrift store, Captain Gerald Heller finishes showing a new employee how to work the cash register. As he walks outside, Heller rubs his forehead, hoping to relieve a headache that has been bothering him when he notices his truck driver.

"There ya are, Captain, what should I do with this painting?" Harvey asks.

"Put it in there," he says, gesturing by pointing with his thumb over his shoulder. By pointing, Captain Heller meant that Harvey should put the painting in the store. But because he was gesturing in the direction of the truck, Harvey thought Captain Heller wanted him to put the painting in the truck along with the other items going to Rockford.

Amy borrows Randy's car two more times in April and in May. The first time she is punctual, the second time she isn't. Randy crushes his cigarette when he hears the garage door.

"Sister, there's no reason to be late. You have a watch on, and there's a clock on my instrument panel. Punctuality is so important. Now I don't talk for my health, I'm healthy enough," Randy says as he turns to cough in his fist. Amy stifles a smile.

"Let this be a warning to you. The next time you're late, you're grounded and it will be the last time you borrow my car." Amy walks upstairs feeling a bit ashamed.

It's spring and excitement fills the student body at Rich South High. David Nelson is out of state for the weekend, visiting his grandparents and Amy is left with no plans when she gets a call from her best friend.

"Hey my cheerleading sister! Let's do something this weekend!"

"What do you wanna do?"

"I'm game for a movie," Nancy replies.

"I've seen many with David."

"Well, let's just cruise around. We'll think of something."

"Okay Nans, when will you pick me up?' Amy asks.

"I can't use my folks car Amy, they're going out of town,"

"I'll ask Randy if I can use his.

"Give me a call Amy." Randy's at his desk, paying the bills, and adjusting the budget when Amy approaches.

"Randy, may I use your car tonight?"

"Reason?"

"My girlfriend Nancy and I want to go to a movie near the mall," Amy says. Without looking up, Randy replies, "Darlene's taking me to her parents house for dinner. You can use it as long as you remember the rules."

"Thanks big brother," she says. "I'll remember. I promise."

"Let me change out of my uniform and I'll give you the keys." Amy leaves as Randy closes the door. He told her part of the truth. Randy needs to change, but he also doesn't want his sister to know where he keeps the extra set of keys. Opening his top drawer, he lifts his folded t-shirts and retrieves his spare set.

After riding aimlessly for half an hour, Nancy has an idea.

"Let's go to I.S.U." Nancy says.

"Too far," Amy replies.

"We'll make it back. It'll be so much fun!"

When Darlene pulls into the curved driveway, the clock on her instrument panel reads, 2:30am. The porch light is off, and the garage door is down.

"I had a great time tonight."

"Me too. I think your parents are beginning to like me," he says.

"Oh Randy, they've always liked you." The couple embrace and kiss passionately. A minute later, lips are parted, as Randy slowly unbuttons her blouse. She looks around.

"Darlene, no one's gonna see us."

"Alright," Darlene whispers. Randy carefully lifts each cup, exposing her voluptuous white breasts. He tenderly messages them. Darlene tilts her head back, and closes her eyes while she strokes the back of his head. Her breathing deepens. Randy knows the answer, but asks anyway.

"Does this feel good?" he whispers.

"Yes—it—does!" Darlene replies. He messages her left breast, and begins kissing her right one, especially around and under the nipple. Darlene moans softly. The porch light is turned on.

"Oh shit!" Randy says. "Little sister, is worried about her big brother." Darlene quickly adjusts her bra and buttons her blouse.

"Have to work tomorrow. Call me tomorrow night." They kiss.

"Love you."

"Love you too."

As Randy walks in the foyer he is surprised to be greeted by his brother.

"Amy hasn't come home yet," Brian says.

"Aw man! She hasn't even called?" Randy asks.

"Not a word. I would have called Nancy's parents but I don't know their names or even where they live."

"Oh, God, I don't know either. Something told me, this would eventually happen. It's so late, I'm gonna have to call the cops," Randy says.

"Do you think calling the police could cause us any trouble? Brian asks.

"I don't think—oh, I don't know. But I'm worried about Amy." Just then they hear the garage door open.

"Brian, you can go to bed. I'll handle this."

"No. I'm her big brother too."

Amy walks in.

"Where the hell have you been?" Randy asks.

"It's not my fault, Randy, I had a flat tire," Amy pleads.

"Gimme my keys, Amy."

She hands them to him and he walks directly into the garage. Brian looks at Amy and whispers, "He's furious!"

When Randy comes back in, he's is even more upset.

"Amy, there's two-hundred and twenty miles added to my odometer, the fuel tank reads a quarter full, and my spare tire is in the trunk. Now, I'm gonna ask you again. Where have you been?" Randy asks.

"Nancy and I went to a party—at Illinois State." Randy's mouth drops open.

"I didn't say you could go there. You told me you were going to see a movie. You lied!

"No, Randy, we just decided at the last minute and I didn't know how to reach you and Nancy thought we'd make it back on time."

"You had no business going that far without my permission. You know better than that. You're grounded for a month and you can forget about my car permanently!

"But Randy! This isn't fair!"

"It's a good thing Nancy's not our sister. I'd ground her ass too!"

Amy runs up to her room in tears.

The next two days Amy doesn't speak to Randy, more out of shame than anger. She knew she made the wrong choice. On the third day, the siblings have just finished their supper. Randy looks at his brother.

"Brian, I'll do the dishes tonight. I need to talk to Amy." He excuses himself.

"I have to call Natalie, then grade papers," he says. Randy sighs, then looks at his sister.

"The other night, I was worried sick. You didn't even call Brian to say that you'd be late. I didn't know if you'd gotten in a wreck, or if you were kidnapped, or if you were murdered. Amy, you're always gonna have rules to obey.

"Please don't make me worry like that ever again. If you're going to be late—call me. Believe it or not, there are phones everywhere."

"I'm really sorry, Randy. I know I was wrong. I'm so sorry."

"Just please never do that again, Amy."

"I promise. Listen, I'm going to take a bath. Later, will you help me with my homework?"

"You know I will," he replies as he gives her a hug.

The next day, it's the brother's turn to talk. Randy suspects that there's something wrong with Brian. He's been agitated for the past several days and he seems to be distracted.

"What's wrong, brother?" he asks. Brian hangs his head low.

"Natalie and I have broken up," he says somberly.

"Why? You two were really good together."

"She's—well she's pregnant with someone else's baby." "I can't believe this, Brian. Are you sure?"

"I'm positive. She admitted it!"

"You must be hurt beyond belief," Randy says.

"Oh, I'm hurt alright. I'm also mad as hell. I wanna kill the fucker!"

"No brother, you don't want to do that. Mom used to say, 'Everything happens for a reason.' I tell you what Brian. Let's bow our heads and pray—okay?"

"Dear Lord, we pray to You, to give Brian strength during this most difficult time. He's full of hurt and anger. Please help him to control his emotions. And please help him find a woman who will really love him. Brian has been through an awful lot these past few years. He's a good man, Father. Help him to continue to be a good man. In Jesus name we pray. Amen." Brian looks at his brother with tears in his eyes.

"Randy, I don't know what I'd do without you. Thank you for praying for me." The brothers embrace.

May is prom time. Randy adjusts his camera as he stands on the driveway. David is wearing a dark blue tuxedo and Amy is wearing a long pleaded ivory dress with sparkles. The couple stands in front of a large evergreen tree as a backdrop, their arms are around each other.

"Okay smile!"

"Let me take a few more." Randy shoots several more exposures then sets his camera down. Walking over, he places his left hand on David's shoulder and his right hand on Amy's.

"You two are such a beautiful couple," he says.

"Aw Randy, that's so sweet!" Amy says as she gives him a hug. When the embrace is broken, he looks at David with open arms.

"Give me a hug David, I don't bite," Randy says as Amy laughs. The front screen door opens as Brian emerges.

"Randy, you got a phone call."

Late May, 1991. Rockford, Illinois. Sheila Ann Johnson is a middle class working woman who loves shopping at second-hand stores and thrift shops. Her favorite—the Salvation Army Thrift store on Charles Street. On this day, Sheila carefully goes through the clothes rack before making a choice. Finding a pink and purple blouse, she holds it across her torso. She concludes it will fit. The price is two dollars. She carries the blouse on its hanger while examining several sets of dishes. Next, she makes her way slowly to the book section. Tilting her head sideways, she reads the titles but nothing seems to interest her. Straightening her neck, she heads to an art section in a corner of the store. The prints and frames are in a fixed metal crate. Sheila looks at the first, then gently moves it forward. The second is an abstract—a form of art, she really doesn't care for. The third is a mass of blotches. As she quickly moves this forward, the next one takes her by surprise. This painting shows a woman wearing a white high neck dress. She sits near a waterfall, reading a letter. Red and orange flowers are near her feet, with a partial rainbow in the sky. Sheila sets her bag down and picks up the painting. In the bottom left hand corner is her great grandfather's signature and date. *Frederick Johnson* 1918. It's being sold for twenty-five dollars.

"No, Iris would never give this away." she says softly to herself. Sheila walks quickly to the young woman at the cash register.

"Pardon me miss. How long has this painting been here?" Sheila asks.

"I don't know ma'am. I just started working. Although I can look up the invoice," she says.

"Please do," Sheila says. The cashier holds up an index finger.

"I'll be right back," she says as she walks to the file room. Minutes later, she returns holding an index card.

"This painting came in along with some tables, chairs and a number of boxes of books, ten months ago," the employee says.

"From where?" Sheila asks. The employee looks closely.

"From Park Forest—the Salvation Army in Park Forest." the girl replies.

"Do you know if that's anywhere near Richton Park?"

"Oh yes, it's right next to Richton Park, practically the same community. I grew up not far from there and…"

"I'll take it." Sheila says handing the cashier two twenties.

"You're buying the painting?"

"Yes, and could I please use your phone?" Sheila asks. The girl picks up the receiver and hands it to Sheila.

Early June, 1991, sixteen year old Benjamin Elgin, puts on his jock strap, shorts, a t-shirt, socks and running shoes. He stretches in the family room. His brother Douglas is a funeral director with their father at Elgin Funeral Home.

THE SURVIVING SIBLINGS

"Benji, don't you want any lunch?" his mother asks as she walks in the family room.

"No thanks Mom. I had a pretty large breakfast several hours ago. I'm gonna take a long run."

"I read somewhere that running everyday is bad for you," she says.

"Well, I guess that's good because I haven't run in three days, Mom."

"What's the best thing about running?"

"I'd say watching my shadow."

Mrs. Elgin laughs as her son kisses her on his way to the kitchen to drink a quick glass of water.

"See ya, Mom!"

"Have a good run, honey."

Rebecca Thomas loves her new Cadillac. She has driven it up from Springfield to visit some friends in Hammond, Indiana and is now heading west to see her mother in Frankfurt. On the interstate she had set the cruise control. Now on Sauk Trail near Rich South High, she drives manually, and feels a little gutsy. She floors the gas petal as she passes a runner.

That woman in the Caddie is driving like her ass is on fire, Benjamin thinks, just as he hears a loud BANG. The Cadillac has blown a tire and is swerving like a fish. It goes off the road and into the lagoon in front of Stardom Field. The front end sinks quickly. Benjamin runs his fastest.

As Benjamin dives into the lagoon, Rebecca, realizes that she cannot open the car door and pounds on the window in panic. The interior is filling fast as Benjamin reaches the car and tries to open the door. Soon the water pressure in the car is equal to the pressure outside of the vehicle. The driver is completely submerged when Benjamin finally forces the car door open and pulls her out and to the surface.

"Are you alright ma'am?" he asks. She nods and both fall to the ground gasping. Just then, Benjamin hears a truck approaching. Getting up, he runs through the grass and weeds to Sauk Trail. Waving his arms, the driver slows. Benjamin runs to the driver's door.

"Mister, a woman's car is in the lagoon!"

"Is the woman in the car?' he asks.

"No sir. I pulled her out. Please go to Lakewood Bowl and call the cops," Benjamin says.

"I'll do better than that." The driver gets on his 'cb' or citizens band radio and is connected to the police department. An ambulance, a fire truck and a tow truck are quickly dispatched.

Within minutes, a Richton Park police officer is directing traffic around the scene. Paramedics wrap the soaked and stunned Rebecca in a blanket as they check her for injuries. A diver assists the tow truck driver, connecting the chain to the Cadillac's frame. Another officer walks over to Benjamin.

"Here's a blanket for you, son."

"Thank you, sir. But I'm fine."

"You did good. You did good, young man. Do you know who this woman is?

"What do you mean sir?" Benjamin asks.

"I mean—you saved the Governor's wife," the officer replies.

Benjamin's mouth drops open. "Wow, she's the wife of..." is all he can say.

"Now, I'll need to ask you some questions. Let's start with your name, son."

After the officer is finished with Ben, the young man goes over to Rebecca.

"I just found out who you are, ma'am," Ben says.

"Please call me Rebecca. Thank you for saving my life! I really thought I was going to die," she tells him as she shivers and pulls the blanket around her. "I can never thank you enough for what you did. You were so brave. What is your name?"

"I'm Ben Elgin."

"Ben, I want you and your whole family to come to the Governor's mansion in Springfield to have dinner with us. "Please," she says to the police officer, "will you give me Ben's phone number."

As the chain between the Cadillac and the tow truck tightens, the sedan is slowly removed from the lagoon. The authorities find an item attached to the front bumper—it's a muddy, vine-covered purse.

Days later, early in the morning, Sheila Johnson drives to the police station in Richton Park. She sits in the office of Lieutenant Wilson, sipping a cup of coffee. The painting is on his desk as he takes down the information Sheila gives him about the painting and why her cousin, Iris would never have left it behind.

"I just have a bad feeling about what happed to my cousin, Lieutenant."

"Looking over the notes from your police interview shortly after your cousin disappeared, you didn't seem to feel that way."

"Well, I've been thinking. I mean after all this time has passed. I can't believe that not one person has heard from her—*ever*—to this day! Do you know of anyone who has heard from her?" Sheila asks.

"No, we have no record of anyone."

"And I was told that she took everything with her."

"That's the way it appeared."

"I know that Iris is or was, well let's say—different and kind of cold. But something isn't right. And I've been thinking about how she told me that she and her stepson—the oldest one— never got along. At the time I thought, oh, stepparents and step children usually don't ever…"

By noon, Lieutenant Wilson, the chief of police and a homicide detective have gathered in the chief's office. They have studied the painting, reviewed the interview with Sheila, and have now moved on to another matter concerning the Iris Taylor case.

"It's definite," says the detective, "That purse has been in the water a long, long time. They knew right away it didn't belong to the governor's wife. And it was that heavy plastic make-up bag that helped preserve the driver's license. It is definitely Iris Taylor's license, her credit cards, a brush, a small make-up kit, couple of lipsticks, sunglasses and six hundred dollars in cash. We have to drag or possibly even drain that old lagoon to see if there's anything else in all that muck."

Later that afternoon, Amy has her picture taken in her gold cap and gown. Her grandparents, Sheila and Bob, Randy and Darlene, Brian, neighbor Stephi and other friends and relatives gather around her. Her tassel is red, white and blue, with a gold '91 on top.

The party gets in several vehicles and heads for Rich South High. This year, graduation ceremonies are being held outside. The day can't be more perfect. The temps are in the low eighties without a cloud in the sky.

Commencement begins at 7 pm sharp. When all are seated, Mister McGraw the principal makes his speech.

"Greetings dignitaries, friends, relatives, alumni and seniors. Four years may seem like a long time, especially when one is a freshman …"

After Mister McGraw finishes, the choir sings the national anthem. The valedictorian makes his speech. Amy sits near the stage. She has been selected by the graduating committee to sing her own composition, "Tomorrow is a Thought Away." When she is introduced, she is greeted by a thunderous applause as she steps up to the microphone. When all is quiet, a pianist plays the introduction. Amy sings on key in her soprano voice. Darlene sits next to Randy. He leans over to her and, nearly overcome with emotion and says, "I remember when my mother brought her home from the hospital."

Mister McGraw is re-introduced. He makes a short speech then begins handing out the diplomas in alphabetical order. As Amy accepts hers, she shakes the principal's hand as Randy takes a photo nearby. As the ceremony concludes, the graduates throw their caps in the air. The Rich South High School graduating class of 1991 has officially graduated. A band plays standard and the graduates hug each other in celebration, as their family members crowd around. When he finally reaches Amy, Randy hugs her the hardest of all as he whispers, "I wish Mom and Dad were here today." The youngest sibling whispers back, "They're here in spirit." Amy kisses his cheek. The embrace is broken.

"I'm so proud of you sister," Randy says.

"I'm proud of you too big brother," she replies.

"Why?" he asks. Amy chokes back tears then says, "For holding us together!"

A voice is near. "Amy?" her boyfriend asks.

"He wants me," she says.

"Go get him," Randy replies. Moments later, Amy grabs David's hand as she runs to her brother.

"Randy quick, take our photo. The sun's a perfect sphere!" The oldest sibling adjusts his 35 millimeter camera, focuses the lens and takes seven exposures. The sun is behind Amy and David.

"I can't wait to see them!" she says. David's uncle Charlie speaks in a strong voice nearby.

"C'mon Davy, it's time to party!" David looks at his girlfriend. "Can you come?" he asks. Amy looks at Randy. "May I go?" she asks.

"Be home at midnight, not a minute later," Randy says. Amy hugs him and Darlene then leaves with David. Darlene wraps her arm around Randy's arm as they slowly walk away.

"This was an excellent graduation!" she says.

"It was perfect. I think this is the first time Rich South has held a graduation outdoors." He stops, and kisses Darlene while giving her a huge hug.

"Honey, I love you."

"I love you too," Darlene replies.

"Excuse me darling, I'm going to run to the restroom before we leave." Randy kisses her then departs. Minutes later, two Richton Park police cruisers turn in off of Sauk Trail. Their sirens mute, their lights flashing.

WA